Lesson One . . .

BJ introduced Lee Anne. "And now Dr. Harrison will begin Introductory Healing Arts."

Lee Anne put her fists on her hips. "Let me ask a couple questions, just to get a feel for what you do now." The Hippoi, like students everywhere, tensed in expectation of the questions. "If you had a friend who had a persistent, unexplained hoof lameness, what would you do for her?"

Selena smiled with relief at the easy question. "Speak to the Carron, and leave her to die."

Lee Anne looked at her blankly and finally nodded. "Okay. We'll talk more about that. Now, what if you see a friend rolling on the grass, in pain, what would you do—"

Hemera scratched her red hair in confusion. "I would ask him what was wrong. Wouldn't you?"

"Right, right. You can ask what's bothering him," Lee Anne said. "He says, 'My belly hurts. It hurts a lot.' What do you do?"

Hemera said simply, "I would speak to the Carron and leave him to die." The others nodded approval.

Lee Anne muttered to BJ, "I can see the first-aid quiz ain't gonna be multiple choice."

S0-AWC-931

Ace Books by Nick O'Donohoe

THE MAGIC AND THE HEALING
UNDER THE HEALING SIGN

UNDER THE HEALING SIGN

NICK O'DONOHOE

ACE BOOKS, NEW YORK

This book is an Ace original edition,
and has never been previously published.

UNDER THE HEALING SIGN

An Ace Book / published by arrangement with
the author

PRINTING HISTORY
Ace edition / March 1995

ISBN: 0-441-00180-7

ACE®
Ace Books are published by The Berkley Publishing Group,
200 Madison Avenue, New York, NY 10016.
ACE and the "A" design are trademarks
belonging to Charter Communications, Inc.

PRINTED IN THE UNITED STATES OF AMERICA

10 9 8 7 6 5 4 3 2 1

UNDER
· T · H · E ·
HEALING
SIGN

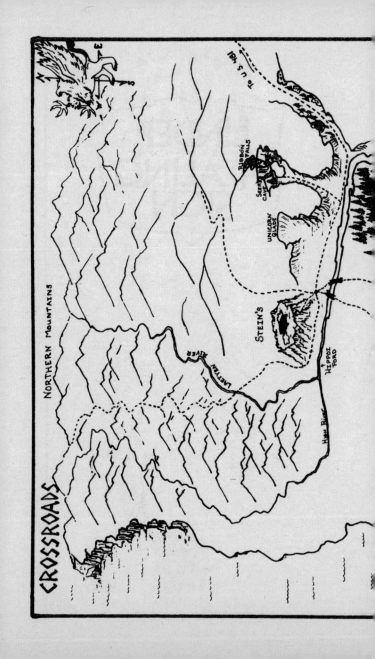

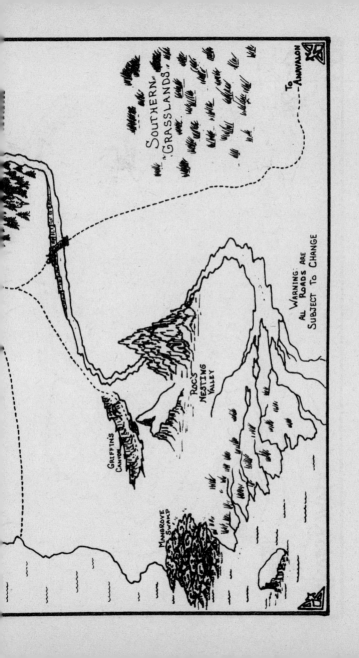

Being admitted to the profession of veterinary medicine, I solemnly swear to use my scientific knowledge and skills for the benefit of society through the protection of animal health, the relief of animal suffering, the conservation of livestock resources, the promotion of public health, and the advancement of medical knowledge.

I will practice my profession conscientiously, with dignity, and in keeping with the principles of veterinary medical ethics. I accept as a lifelong obligation the continual improvement of my professional knowledge and competence.

—**The Veterinarian's Oath**

PART

·1·

O·N·E

THE FIRST LAW of small towns is that you will unexpectedly meet someone who knows you wherever you go. When you have something to hide, you meet the most inquisitive person you know.

BJ was rolling her cart down the aisle at Kroger's and looking curiously at the woman on the cover of the *Time* magazine she had picked up, when someone said sonorously, "Daydreaming in class, Miss Vaughan?"

BJ winced. When you graduate, you hope to leave your classroom embarrassments behind. In vet school, BJ often stared into space, following trains of thought determinedly to wherever they led. She had been teased unmercifully about it by the lab techs.

The woman talking to her was dressed far better than she had been in classes, but her clothing was so predictable that BJ barely noticed the change.

The wool jacket was stylish, but too loud; the matching skirt was perfectly tailored, but too short. The add-a-bead necklace had three more beads on it than BJ remembered.

The perfume was overly sweet, but had a bite to it. BJ smiled politely and said, "It's good to see you, Stacey."

It wasn't. Stacey Robie had a God-given ability to say the wrong thing.

At a shower for a second wedding, Stacey had blurted to the bride after four drinks, "I bet it's easier, knowing you can bug out if it sucks."

3

When a friend announced that he was gay, Stacey had said, "Great. I'm sure other men will like you better than women do."

To a male friend who introduced his new girlfriend, Stacey had said seriously, "You know, I think it's really neat how they always have red hair and they're all the same size. You'll meet the right one yet."

BJ hadn't realized how much Stacey liked her until, at a keg party just before graduation, Stacey had said tearfully (and drunkenly), "I'll miss you. You're so sweet."

"You're sweet, too," BJ had replied, startled.

Stacey sniffled loudly and miserably. "No, I'm not. I'm a bitch."

BJ had always simply assumed that Stacey was stupid.

Stacey looked BJ up and down. "That's a nice skirt. Did you get it at a craft fair? It's pretty irregular."

BJ spread the folds. "I made it myself."

Stacey laughed. " 'Made' it? There's only one seam."

"Made it," BJ repeated firmly. "I sheared the sheep, carded the wool, spun the thread, and wove the cloth." It had taken a month. "One of my clients helped me." She smoothed it with pride. "It's from one of my first patients."

"Wow. Kind of an odd doctor-patient relationship," Stacey said vaguely. She poked at BJ's full shopping cart. "Judging from the skirt, I'd have expected more organic foods and green leafies. And here you are buying almost nothing but pasta, rice, and canned goods." She looked up. "But look at all the weight you've lost. Twenty pounds. Maybe even thirty."

This was unkind. BJ had survived on junk food, like most vet students who had no time to cook, and had always been on the edge of overweight.

She said only, "I think I look better."

"You look terrific. Muscles in your arms and a skinny waist, and you've lost about a third of your butt. How'd it happen?"

"I hike." BJ lifted her skirt slightly to show how battered her leather boots were. "I practice in the hills."

"You haven't gone mountain woman on us, have you? I thought Lee Anne Harrison was the only hillbilly in our class."

BJ laughed. "I miss Lee Anne. We had a good time."

In fact, she had also come to town to mail four letters: one to Lee Anne Harrison in Raleigh-Durham, one to Annie Taylor in Chad, one to Dave Wilson at Cornell, and one to her brother Peter in Chicago.

"A good time? I always thought, after that mess in Small Animal rotation, that you'd never show your face there again."

BJ, in the midst of a breakdown and the onset of a congenital illness, had failed a senior year rotation.

"I get back there quite a lot," she said easily. "Mostly to use the library and to ask questions of people. I dropped by today, in fact, and saw Sugar Dobbs. I get back here nearly once a month."

"And see Sugar? I can't blame you there," Stacey said slyly. "Hey, I'll never tell."

BJ frowned. "I dropped off my shower present. Elaine Dobbs is five months pregnant now."

"Oh. Well, scratch Sugar, then. Or I guess you'd better not. What about where you work? Do you have a fella?"

"Not exactly." But BJ was blushing, and hating herself for it.

"Ah-HA! C'mon, tell the dirt."

"He's not exactly a fella, just someone I'm seeing."

"Good for you." Stacey punched BJ's arm. "I always said if you fixed yourself up a little you'd do just fine. It beats chasing some of the dregs we knew in Vet school. Remember Dave Wilson? I wonder where he is now. Drunk, I suppose."

"Cornell, doing his doctorate. He calmed down a lot last spring."

"That's right, you and he were in a rotation together, weren't you? The one that truck burned up on—"

"I heard later that it was arson," BJ interrupted. "Did they ever catch whoever did it?"

"If they did, nobody told me. Say, what was that rotation for, anyway? Sugar Dobbs taught it, but he'd already had all of you in Large Animal rotation—"

"It was a skills refresher," BJ said, avoiding Stacey's eyes. "It helped me a lot. Really, it isn't all that different from my practice now."

"Well, then it can't be much use to people with normal practices. Or Dave. Have you heard from him at all? I guess that's a rude question," Stacey finished thoughtfully. "He never calls girls, afterward."

BJ said gravely, "I'm sorry that you found that out." Stacey looked stunned, but BJ continued, "Where are you practicing?"

"Norfolk." She said "Nofuhk" with studied carelessness. "In a three-vet practice just outside the base. You know," she said as seriously as if she were imparting a recent revelation, "there's nothing like a good location for a practice. You wouldn't believe how much business we do. All companion animals, and we refer all our emergencies. 'Send that there cat down the road,' " she said, in an exaggerated parody of a Western Virginia accent.

Several shoppers, Kendrick residents who had probably lived in Western Virginia all their lives and had similar accents, stared at her.

BJ, mortified, finished for Stacey, "So you like your practice?"

"Like it?" She laughed. "I pinch myself sometimes. Four months out, and making thirty-seven grand. Kurzie—Dr. Kurzweiler says he'll negotiate a buy-in a few years from now." She finished politely, "How about you? Where did you say you were again?"

"Up in the hills, out beyond the Jefferson National Forest. The people are wonderful there."

Stacey frowned. "That's a poverty pocket. How can you make any money up there?"

"In some ways the practice is worth its weight in gold."

"Unbelievable. How much does your boss pay you?"

BJ smiled. "I have my own practice."

It was worth it to see Stacey's face drop.

"I live in the same building I practice from," BJ admitted. "It doesn't make much profit, but I'm learning a lot." She laughed. "I still have no idea how to set different prices for cases."

Stacey grimaced. "I get it. You're another charity queen like Annie Taylor. At least you didn't go off to Africa; what, does she have some sick thing for parasites and dysentery?"

BJ was silently impressed. In two minutes, Stacey had casually trashed all of BJ's closest friends from school.

Without a pause, Stacey added, "I suppose that beats DeeDee Parris. I can't believe she found a job somewhere; was she really a drug addict?"

BJ looked around before answering. "They tested her and found morphine in her blood," she said carefully. "They found syringes and vials from the vet school in her apartment, along with other things she had stolen."

"That's right. She tried to tell wild stories about talking animals and werewolves, real La-La Land stuff. I remember now; she'd stolen other stuff from the vet school. Stealing to pay for drugs, right?"

"No. The drugs were stolen, too, remember? I think she stole because she couldn't help it, or because she didn't care that it was wrong." BJ paused, then added, "Stacey, I really think we shouldn't talk about her. I'd advise you not to, really."

Stacey looked puzzled. "Sure, if it bothers you. You always were nicer than I was . . ." She made another leap of subjects. "So, how are your skills? Did that remedial rotation do any good?"

"It saved my life," BJ said truthfully.

"Good. God knows I've needed my skills. Know what happened just this last month?"

BJ sighed. Stacey had the rapt expression BJ had seen on fishermen who couldn't help retelling a great catch story.

"It was a Monday night at five-fifteen, so I was ready to go home and get something clean on, and in came this awful woman and her cat, a rangy old tom that had been doing nothing in the litter box but squat and scream. I said, okey-dokey, a nice little FUS case."

FUS was Feline Urinary Syndrome, the kind of urinary blockage common to tom cats, and often quickly fatal.

"So I dropped him onto the table and felt his bladder. Holy shit, it was the size of a tennis ball, and nearly as round. Way too full. So I passed a catheter up into it, and I got out a hell of a lot of bloody urine, looked like tomato juice—"

An elderly man buying tomato soup scowled at them and put the soup back. "I've seen it," BJ muttered.

"Okay, so Tuesday morning I talk to the owner, tell her what a perineal urethrostomy is, and she says, go ahead. Time to de-boy the cat." Stacey was locked into her own story, the way a baseball fan might quote statistics. "I knock him out, castrate him, cut him, do the P.U.—totally routine, and I'm done."

A college student, male, winced. BJ said hastily, "Why don't we talk while I finish shopping?" and rolled her cart forward rapidly.

Stacey was undeterred. "Anyway, so I get him into post-op, and we're monitoring him. The suture looked fine, the incision wasn't red or swollen, but the cat's gum color was awful, and he wasn't eating or drinking at all."

BJ nodded and pulled the cart quickly past a knot of people buying ground beef. They weren't likely to enjoy surgical details. "Did you go back in?"

"Not yet." Stacey was enjoying the retelling. "But by the third day, I'm frantic. You should have seen me. Here he was, a perfectly normal cat, except he's got to be bleeding out somewhere. I finally said to my tech, I said, 'Holy shit, what the Christ is happening to this goddamn cat?' "

A small boy stared up at her admiringly. BJ said hastily, "Let's go to the deli counter," and pushed ahead.

"So I thought, Did I miss a bleeder? But I was sure I'd gotten all of them. So I read up, and thought about it, and you know what I figured out?"

BJ picked up a round of salami, unsliced. "You decided the bleeding was from the penile muscles," she said calmly and so quietly that no one else heard. "They retracted when you transected them and bled into the retroperitoneal space. You transfused the cat and saved the day. Good thinking."

Stacey's face fell. "Well, yeah." She brightened. "Everybody makes the same dumb-ass mistake, right? So tell me, how about your practice—any tough cases?" Stacey looked sympathetic. "I remember how clumsy you were last spring; I thought something was wrong with you or you were on drugs."

BJ remembered vividly how clumsy she had been, and how frightened it had made her. "I'm a little better." She considered. "Well, I had to reassemble a cat's femur."

"Wow." Stacey looked completely blank. "Like a hit by car?"

"No, a hit by rock. It fell off a cliff. It's a large animal, about the size of a bobcat. Local wild species."

"Jesus." But Stacey recovered her poise. "And you didn't refer that? That's kind of irresponsible, isn't it?"

"There was no way to move the patient. We'd had a lot of rain."

Stacey tsk-tsked at her. "Serves you right for working in the boonies with the hicks and hillbillies." The woman weighing sliced cheese sucked in her breath sharply. "So the patient went belly-up?"

"Oh, no. I monitored it for three days, around the clock." The cat had slept next to her bed; BJ had slept very little and had checked it almost every hour. "To be honest, I did have to go back in once, but it all worked out. The cat's doing fine."

Stacey shrugged. "Well, some of them live no matter what you do. Sugar Dobbs used to say that in class." She did a bad impression of Sugar's Western accent. "So, honey, any other tough cases?"

BJ considered. "None to speak of."

Stacey nodded. "A nice, comfy, dull practice. Some days, when I'm tired, I want one of those."

Her eyes went wide in mock-remembrance. "Oh, that's my other news: My parents have said they'd help me buy a practice. I said, 'Let me see if Kurzie makes a good offer first.' And they're buying me a brand new four by four truck just in case I need it, even though I told them I don't." She raised her hands in mock resignation, let them fall. "So," she said, "how are your folks?"

The loss was too fresh for BJ not to react. "They're both dead," she said quietly.

Stacey's mouth was a little round O. "Oh God, that's right. Your mother killed herself last spring. Oh God, I'm so sorry. I didn't mean anything. I feel terrible."

"That's all right."

"No, I just feel awful." And Stacey clearly did; she had tears in her eyes.

"Stace, forget it."

"I can't." She stamped her foot like a small child. "I hate when I do this, and I always do it." She wiped her eyes furtively, then checked her watch. "Oh God, I better hustle off; I'm meeting Ken for dinner."

She did not invite BJ, and BJ did not mind. "Do you two have jobs near each other?"

"Not too far apart," she said easily. "Six hours by road. He's in Philadelphia. We keep the highways hot, every other weekend or so."

BJ noted that Stacey was no longer wearing an engagement ring. "Say hello for me. I didn't get a chance to tell you; you're looking great."

Stacey dimpled. "I'll give him a kiss for you. And thanks." She hesitated, then said, "I don't know how to put it, but you're looking really amazing. Kind of earth mother and otherworld. I didn't know you could look like that." She patted BJ's arm. "Take care. And keep looking around; I'm sure you'll find somebody for yourself." She added encouragingly, "After all, there's so much less competition out in the hills."

She flitted off. BJ, mouth hanging open, watched her leave, then smiled. You had to be amused by Stacey; your only other option was to throttle her and stow the body in the frozen foods display.

BJ caught her own reflection in one of the glass freezer doors, stared at it, and smiled wryly. The dark hair was longer, but had sun color in it even in the fall. Her eyes were still dark, but calm instead of sad. "Earth mother and otherworld . . ." Was feeling peaceful so rare?

BJ paid up, in fresh tens, and rolled the cart out to her truck, a secondhand field truck with the Western Vee seal painted over on the doors.

Stefan was slouched in the driver's seat, knees up against the wheel, reading.

He was wearing loose-fitting blue jeans, an affected gray fedora, which he loved, and a Western Vee U T-shirt which he was terribly proud of. Over the shirt he had a battered cotton sport coat from the thrift shop.

He was reading a biology text as avidly as BJ used to read suspense novels. Occasionally his lips moved on a difficult word, and he made a note in the margin.

He hopped out hastily when she tapped the window. "I will help to load—" He still had a noticeable Greek accent, though college in Western Virginia might change that.

They opened the largest cabinet in the back, shoved aside the tanks of isoflurane and halothane, and loaded in groceries.

"Did you buy almost everything you might need?"

"I think so." Unless she got a difficult case, she might not come back to town for a month. "Do you need to stop by the dorm for anything?"

He looked hurt. "Of course not. I brought my books for the weekend, and paper and pens—" He grinned at her. "And cat treats, of course."

She shut the cabinet, double-checking the latch. "Then let's go."

Stefan charged back around the left side of the truck.

"I'll drive," he said eagerly. "Can I? You are a better map reader."

"And that's important. Sure." BJ took the copy of *Time* up front with her, curious to see how the world had changed.

She took her mail, wrapped with a thick rubber band, off the dash and shoved it under the passenger seat.

Stefan pulled three wooden blocks out from under the driver's seat; they each had a cutout in the shape of a large sheep's hoof.

He popped one onto the brake pedal, one onto the clutch pedal, and one onto the accelerator, testing that each was firm.

Then he slipped his shoes off, padding and all, and put his hooves on the clutch and the brake.

As they pulled out of the parking lot, he put on the radio loudly. Stefan loved the idea of having music any time you wanted it. WVUT screamed in their ears, something about having a breakdown and liking it a lot.

BJ turned it down a little. "Do you mind?"

"Not at all." He smiled at her and recited, " 'A good driver pays attention to the road, not to the radio.' I will be a good driver."

She kissed his cheek. "You are a good driver. And a good fella, except you're not exactly a fella."

"Please, what is a fella?"

"Nothing. Just slang." She reached under his hat and scratched around his horns the way he liked.

Stefan grinned and turned onto the 481 bypass; they rolled into the late afternoon shadows.

T·W·O

TWILIGHT IN WESTERN Virginia comes early to the valleys, tantalizingly late to the hilltops. Stefan and BJ rode west of Kendrick, to the edge of the Jefferson National Forest, and made a sharp left turn down a barely visible gravel road.

BJ watched, smiling, at Stefan's concentration, his tongue poking between his lips, as the truck wove down the road alongside a mountain stream which grew louder with each curve. They crossed it three times, and at each crossing the surrounding trees, pines and cedars, seemed to grow taller and older as the shadows deepened.

At the third crossing, BJ pulled a leather-bound book from her backpack. She barely glanced at the gold-embossed title: *The Book of Strangeways*. Stefan glanced at it and shuddered.

"You tell me when I must turn, right?" As he grew more anxious, his accent grew more pronounced.

"I promise."

"Did you ever not wonder," Stefan said, "who made the book in the first place?"

BJ considered. "I thought that it always existed," she said finally. "Like Crossroads itself. After all the book can't be destroyed."

"But Crossroads can be."

"It won't be," she said firmly. "And I promise we'll get back to it again."

Stefan relaxed and drove. He slammed on the brakes once and pointed eagerly to a raccoon; he correctly identified a yellow-shafted flicker in bobbing flight, flashing the white tuft and yellow side feathers of its tail. The road descended toward the edge of the Jefferson National Forest, and a three-way fork in the road.

BJ sighed and opened the book to the Virginia road map. This part would never feel easy and normal.

As confident as she had sounded to Stefan, she hated traveling by using *The Book of Strangeways*; all she could think of was what would happen if they skidded off the road.

The van would almost certainly roll, in these hills, tumbling through the second-growth timber, down to some resting place against the trees. Probably, laden down with gas cans, white gas, and flammables, it would turn into a fireball within seconds of something dripping to the engine block or the exhaust.

And when it was all over, someone—some *thing*, if they had been on the Strangeways—would find the wreck and reach gingerly between the bodies to pull out an unscorched, undamaged *Book of Strangeways*.

"Left here," she said. "And right—no, *left* again; they've changed it."

The road fork was new, the map in the book apparently old, but the new fork showed clearly. Stefan swung quickly to the left, and they continued their descent beside a now-roaring stream.

The truck body rumbled as the gravel shifted to chunks of rock, then cobblestone. Most of the road forks and twists were bright, with the lightness of freshly turned stone with pick marks still on it. The trees grew taller and darker, virgin timber that dwarfed the straggly dogwoods and mountain laurel clinging to the rocks beside them. The stream along the road turned to alternating falls and pools.

The stone slab which made up the final bridge was a welcome landmark by now. Immediately below it a falls roared, and the stream flowed half underneath the tangled roots of virgin cedar and pine, and BJ knew that they were no longer in Virginia or America.

Ahead, in the woods, something screamed. From a side road something bellowed as if in answer. BJ double-checked *The Book of Strangeways* to be sure of the turns.

Stefan pointed ahead. "See."

BJ looked. A flock of blackbirds were chasing an owl, diving at it repeatedly. The owl beat its wings slowly, almost clumsily, as they chased it through the woods. BJ had seen owls driven by smaller birds before.

The blackbirds turned abruptly and drove the owl low along the road, edging towards a left-hand fork which seemed to parallel the stream.

Stefan shouted, "No!" and pulled toward the left, honking the horn and waving out the window.

Ahead of them, the owl hesitated, its body and wings grown suddenly blurry, and backflapped frantically; then it was quickly jerked down and sideways.

Dimly, shimmering around the edges of the lane, they could see a towering gray man-thing with the head of a turtle, its beak snapping up and down on the still struggling owl.

"Don't pull too close," BJ said sharply. She felt sick. Stefan veered to the right, but looked over his shoulder once more. BJ glanced out the side window; the ravine was sheer, the lower road gone.

Subdued, Stefan said, "We see that thing every time. I think that it lives its whole life at a Strangeways, waiting for that to happen."

"Like an ogre," BJ said, "waiting in the road for a traveler." She added, suddenly thoughtful, "I wonder if that's why so many of our fairy tales take place on journeys and roads."

Stefan said dubiously, "Professor Wythe says it's because roads are"—he carefully aped his professor's educated Southern inflections—"external symbols of internal exploration."

BJ was intrigued. "Which class is that?"

"Myth and Legend 2200. It is a sophomore course," he added proudly, "but I tested out of the per—prequi—"

"What was the prerequisite?"

"Greek mythology."

BJ laughed and ruffled the hair around his horns again. "Of course you did."

Stefan laughed, too. "But now I don't know anything again. It's all different, never story and always symbol. I even asked Dr. Wythe what 'fauns' meant."

"Stefan, you didn't." BJ was shocked and amused.

"It was all right. I kept my hat on."

"Well, be careful." BJ's curiosity won. "What did Dr. Wythe say?"

Stefan looked straight ahead at the road. "He said that fauns were 'symbols of a sexual impulse aware of itself but contained by innocence.' He said, 'The innocence renders the sexuality acceptable, and may even heighten it for some.'" This time Stefan's imitation of his professor's diction sounded strained.

In silence, BJ pointed which way to turn. Finally she said naturally, "And how are your other classes?"

Stefan said gloomily, "I may fail freshman English."

"No."

"Yes." He nodded vigorously, dark curls bobbing under the fedora. "I write hard, I think well—BJ, I never wrote before. I make letters, and spell words, but it is not *writing*." He sighed loudly. Stefan was very bright, and found it hard to be bad at things.

BJ put a hand on his shoulder, then pulled it back to steady *The Book of Strangeways*. "Left, then left here. What do you think your problem is?"

He considered. "She writes notes on my paper, but not long ones. I think it's something she does not like about my planning, about the way I put things together."

"Tell Stein and the Griffin," she said firmly. "No one knows more about order than a griffin, and he's very well educated." She added, a trifle grimly, "And no one plans better than Stein."

Stefan grunted, spinning the wheel clockwise as they made the final turn to the right. They followed the road across the cliff face, above a bend in a river half a mile wide.

BJ stared down at it, fascinated. She couldn't help herself. The Potomac and Virginia's New River had the same effect on her. One summer morning she had driven to this cliff and watched as the mist boiled downward in the valley, gradually revealing the river below.

"Welcome to Crossroads," Stefan said softly. He was happy to be home. He hitched his trouser legs up, relishing the now-rare feel of air against his woolly legs.

BJ shook herself. "This English course—Stefan, I know you're bright enough."

He said nothing, but looked pleased.

"The key is to plan ahead, as though the term is a battle campaign or a goal. What does she want you to learn? What is the toughest assignment?"

"The research paper," he said promptly. "Twelve pages, double-spaced, on a topic assigned at midterm—"

"Fine." BJ vaguely remembered her own freshman English courses; the research paper would have been easier if it hadn't been so dull. "Ask for a topic. Pick one you like that you think the teacher will like; that makes your work easy." She considered. "Mrs. Sobell, at the university library, can help you learn to do research."

He looked at her in confusion, then smiled. "The short little woman who came to Crossroads? She keeps the university copy of *The Book of Strangeways*."

"She prefers that you say 'small person,' " BJ corrected. "And she hides the book as well as keeps it."

"Good." He frowned. "I think she should hide it very well, that is what I think."

"Me, too," BJ said, but added thoughtfully, "Did you ever wonder, though, what would happen if all copies of *The Book of Strangeways* were hidden forever?"

He smiled at her. "Then you would not come back and forth, Dr. BJ. And Crossroads would not have a vet."

"Or I'd be trapped in Crossroads." She smiled at him. "And you'd be trapped in a world with old movies. How's life outside classes?"

He grinned at her. "I saw on the library—I rented the tape, and took it there—a movie called *The Gay Divorcée*. Fred Astaire—"

"I was wondering when you'd see him."

"His feet," Stefan said wonderingly. "He has the big, flat human feet that are so stupid and clumsy, like yourself—"

"Thanks."

"Oh, but no, I mean, mine are better to dance on." He added seriously, "And your feet are really lovely, BJ, I didn't mean—"

"Never mind. So you liked him?"

"I danced for three hours after. My roommate, he said he would shoot me if I didn't stop."

She laughed. "Poor Willy. Does he know what you are, yet?"

Stefan shrugged. "I think maybe he wonders. He does not ask. He is good. I will tell him, if he asks."

BJ considered cautioning him, then decided to leave it alone. "How's dorm life otherwise?"

"All right. There are too many of us, but that is college." He looked sideways at her, suddenly worried. "BJ, can I ask about something?"

She sighed. "Always." Stefan had a great many questions about life in Virginia.

"The first week, in the Paulson Hall, we had seminar—we had a seminar," he said more carefully. "It was about drug use. People told what they know, to warn the other ones who might not never have seen a drug."

BJ braced herself and said, "And what did you say?"

"Nothing." He slumped in the driver's seat, clearly ashamed. "BJ, I did not want them to know. But if what I had happen, what was done to my body, could help them, then I should tell them—"

"No." BJ's vehemence cut across the sound of the wheels on rock, of the motor hum. "A woman gave you morphine without telling you what it was. Your physiology made you addicted almost immediately. Neither of those things can happen to them."

"The drugs came from your world." He said it without accusation. "But you say I don't need to tell them, for their good?"

"Stefan, you couldn't help them. Your own problem was different. And there are other drug dealers, but the approach wouldn't be the same. She told you she'd make you smarter—"

"And I was stupid, so it worked." He half-closed his eyes, staring bitterly ahead as the cliff wall to their right flickered by, reddening foliage deepening the sunset colors.

"You were naive. She knew it; that's all."

He nodded. "And where is DeeDee Parris? Is she in prison?"

BJ had dreaded Stefan's asking about this, but he had to know. "No. She did community service, and she managed to get a job. She even graduated."

"It can happen." Stefan's cynicism astonished BJ, who had no sense of what drug addiction can do to one's feelings about the weakness of integrity. "If you push at people, if you frighten people, if you tell them what they want, they won't fight you. Listening to what you don't want to hear is harder."

During the ensuing silence, BJ double-checked the map automatically as the cliff receded from the right side of the road, and a sloping plain to the river, rich in grasses and flowers, grew and spread.

BJ said finally, "So you liked Fred Astaire?"

"Of course. He was magic. I wish I could take dance classes." The ache in his voice was solid, as permanent as someone saying, I wish I were taller. He glanced at her face and said quickly, "I know, BJ. My legs, my hooves—"

"I know it still hurts." She stared out the side window at the retreating cliffs. "We all want something we can't have, Stefan. Something we will never have. All of us."

She shook herself, then said lightly, "You know the road from here. Now I can check my mail."

She laid the bundle from her post box on top of *The Book of Strangeways*, and flipped the rubber band off it and onto the floor of the truck. (Stefan glanced at the return addresses interestedly as she sorted the junk mail.)

This year's AVMA conference was in Las Vegas. BJ read the program description and shook her head, laughing. "I don't think so." Beneath it was an envelope with a packet for pharmaceuticals; BJ slit the envelope, read the cover letter, and carefully wrote "Save" on the outside.

She lifted the envelope; underneath was a postcard with the word GREETINGS in large, headline-font letters. Stefan read the first line and said excitedly, "New York the City!"

It was a black-and-white photo of a chalk outline on asphalt. The asphalt was darker in a spot near the chest.

Stefan glanced at it and laughed. "They draw on the streets?"

"Sometimes." BJ turned the card over. The message was block printed. "YOU DID A LOT FOR ME MY SENIOR YEAR. I WILL NEVER FORGET. I PROMISE I WILL PAY YOU BACK."

BJ stared at it, barely noticing the two D's intertwined, like a brand, just below the "Welcome to New York" caption at the top of the message space.

Stefan said, "That is nice. You must have done someone a favor. It's good when someone remembers."

"Some people always remember." She slid it under her papers. "How are your other classes?" She tapped at the biology text. "Surely you're doing well in this."

He nodded so vigorously, his hat flew up and down. "I have not missed an answer yet on the tests. I love it. I want to know it all. Please, I have another question."

BJ smiled. "I might not know the answer."

"Oh, but you've taken the course, to become a veterinarian; you must know. Please, what is a Batesian mimic?"

"A what?" She flipped through the index of the biology book. "Oh. A Batesian mimic. It's named for the biologist who figured out that some harmless species imitate the looks or the behavior of some dangerous species."

He looked sideways at her with the polite, blank look of someone who wasn't understanding a word.

"Okay. Did you see the monarch butterflies, flying south this afternoon?"

"You know I did." He had talked about it excitedly, describing how he had leapt after them in the softball field behind his dormitory. BJ had silently thanked God that Stefan's prosthetic shoes had stayed on, and had explained about butterfly migration.

"Well, there's a butterfly called the viceroy that looks like the monarch, only smaller. And because the monarch tastes terrible, nothing wants to risk eating the viceroy. The mimicry protects the viceroy as well as if it actually tasted terrible."

He considered. "It is like Stein or the Griffin," he said finally, "because they do not act like what they are. Or like the games in Stein's tavern, which seem like just games, and do not seem to hurt anyone. Or like the Wyr, when they look human. They seem less dangerous than they are, even when they seem dangerous."

"Batesian mimicry in reverse," BJ said. "We all pretend to be something normal and harmless, when we're not."

He turned to her, startled. " 'We'?"

"When I'm in Kendrick, I pretend to be just a vet somewhere normal. I hide part of myself."

"You hide part of yourself a lot, Dr. BJ. That is why you surprise people with ideas."

BJ said hastily, "I just think about things. And I hide my work in Crossroads for a different reason, to save it from my own world." She added thoughtfully, "And it isn't the reverse of Batesian mimicry, really. One species mimics another to save individuals; we each pretend to be something else to save Crossroads."

Stefan pointed to his right. "And there is why," he said eagerly.

In the sloping meadow above them, below the cliffs, were a herd (no, a *serenity*) of unicorns, grazing quietly and moving steadily to the west. They were close-knit for defense, as usual. BJ stared eagerly for the one whose horn she had mended; the golden ring would have told her instantly. They were too far away. She craned her neck to watch them, feeling proprietary and sentimental; the unicorn was her first case in Crossroads.

"They are wonderful," Stefan said happily. "They are why you love Crossroads."

"Oh, I don't know." She patted him again. They were doing a lot of touching, these days. After a moment, she pulled her hand back, and they didn't speak again.

They rounded the last bend and, over the crest of the hill, they saw a whitewashed stone cottage with quarter-pane windows, stone-chimney, and thatch roof—one of many, occupied and unoccupied, in the rounded hills of northwestern Crossroads. "Home," BJ said easily, and turned quickly to look over her shoulder.

It was too late to see the copper flash as the bends of the Laetyen River took the sunset. The first time she had seen it, peering from the unglassed window of the barely furnished cottage, she had been lonelier than she had been in her entire life, even when her mother had died. She had stared down at the huge river in the alien landscape and thought: Whatever happens to me here, I must deal with by myself.

The western sky was a rose-colored band; the truck bumping upward as rapidly as the light was fading. A tiny stream, out of the spring from which BJ took water for drinking and for her practice, rippled beside the two lanes which the truck rumbled up.

Stefan pulled sideways in front of the freshly repaired but apparently ageless cottage, and shut off the engine. "Home," he said uncertainly, and set the parking brake.

An enormous white kitten-shaped cat, nearly four feet long, bounded stiff-legged toward the truck, mewing.

"Daphni!" Stefan leapt out and hugged her. "How is your hip? Don't sniff my pockets, naughty flowerbinder; you will have your treat."

The flowerbinder rubbed against him, purring desperately with a sound nearly as loud as a lawn mower.

He removed a plastic bag with a carefully wrapped catfish fillet in it. "Here we are, pretty girl. Do you want it? Mmmm?" Daphni sat crookedly on her hind legs, mewing, and snatched at the fish without clawing Stefan's hands. In the months that BJ had known him, no animal had ever hurt Stefan.

Stefan laughed and let go of the fish. "She looks well," he said almost jealously.

"She misses you," BJ said in almost the same tone, and added, "I wish her hip were better."

"She is perfect." Stefan stroked her ears. "You saved her life, Dr. BJ."

BJ's sign creaked in the gentle evening breeze. She and a friend named Melina had carved a plank in the shape of a four-legged animal, and had wrapped a cloth bandage around one leg: the Healing Sign. BJ had insisted on carving half of it herself, knowing all the while that Melina could have done better alone.

BJ began unloading, leaving Stefan to play with Daphni until he collected himself. Predictably, he sprang forward with guilty energy and did as much work as she had, in half the time. They unloaded the truck cabinets rapidly, using the last of the light.

Stefan closed the doors of the empty truck and stared down the hill into Crossroads. "Now I will go ask B'Cu how my flock is."

B'Cu, a shepherd who spoke mainly Bantu and who had lost his own flock to predators, had gladly taken the responsibility of caring for Stefan's sheep. The question of Stefan's graduation and return had not been discussed by either of them.

Stefan grimaced. "I also go to be tutored." His accent was coming back.

"Is that so bad?"

"It's terrible," he said frankly. "Stein and the Griffin, they both know so much, and they ask so many questions. And they remember the questions from week to week, and check to see if I have their answers."

"Be sure and tell them about English. I think they can both help you."

"I will." Stefan looked down the road toward the central crossroads and Stein's; the inn was not visible in the haze of evening. "It will be late," he said awkwardly. "Stein said I may stay at the inn."

"Ah."

He looked without enthusiasm at the books in the front of the truck, but didn't pick them up. "It is an easy walk."

BJ knew what he wanted. "Stefan?"

The look of frantic appeal in his face made him impossible to tease.

"You'd better take the truck to Stein's. Be sure to give Chris the lemons; he needs them—"

"For *dolmades*, the stuffed grape leaves. I know." Stefan licked his lips, then kissed hers, but restrainedly. "I love you, Dr. Beej. Care for yourself."

He threw open the truck door, leapt with an easy, twisting bound onto the seat, and started the engine as the door swung shut. He checked the mirror, fastened his seat belt, and put his fedora back on. The hat had been BJ's idea and gift; it was vital that Stefan always put it on when leaving Crossroads for school.

BJ stroked Daphni and watched the truck until it disappeared around a turn. "We," she said to herself slightly breathlessly, "have a problem."

Daphni squeaked at being held too tight. BJ shook herself and began carrying groceries inside.

She dropped the last load beside the stove, a glass-doored, cast-iron monstrosity that she and Stefan had hauled over from Virginia and set up one blazing August day when it had seemed superfluous. The stovepipe hole, chiseled painstakingly through the stone-and-mortar chimney and sealed around with concrete, was a point of pride for BJ.

To its right was a wood box; a wicker basket of shavings, tinder, and kindling was perched on it.

She cleaned the ashes from the grate, then put new tinder and kindling in and lit it. Behind the glass door, the flames danced quickly up as the hot air rose. BJ waited, then laid logs around the small fire and closed the door again.

She picked up the half-gallon cast-iron teakettle that served for practice hot water; a dozen brisk strokes at the sink pump, brought in with the sink from a Blue Ridge Mountain farm, filled it. She set it on top of the stove.

She lit the hurricane lamp, carefully checking the flame to make sure that it didn't soot the glass chimney, then carried it and a notebook outside.

It was dark but clear, and the stars were amazing. BJ, who had spent most of her life in suburban Virginia, had gaped at the brightness of stars in the Appalachian Mountains; here in the foothills of Crossroads, the starlight was practically piercing. She listened, but heard few animal calls. Most of the animals in Crossroads, for their own motives, tried very hard not to attract attention.

She walked outside to a small wooden bench and sat. She checked the simple double circle of stones in front of her, then sat on the bench, carefully checking to make sure she was directly over the scratch mark. As the moon rose, she noted the time and fullness, sketching in her notebook the line made by moon and stones. On her next trip to town she would leave copies of the sketches for Dr. Estevan Protera, a physics professor who had asked, through Sugar, for BJ to make the observations.

Just before she went in, a shadow passed across the moon, obscuring it completely. A moment later she heard a scream, far off, and the wind came up. She shivered and hurried into her cottage.

The room was warm, the kettle boiling. Daphni mewed sleepily but did not move from under the wooden table. BJ made tea quickly, setting the kettle aside so it wouldn't boil dry.

Before settling in for the night, she checked her "office," the left half of the cottage, for morning. A clean lab coat, fresh from the washing kettle in the back shed, hung on the hook; her stethoscope, penlight, and thermometer were already in the pocket. The steel table was rolled into the corner; BJ frowned at it. She knew how many lives had been saved by disinfected surfaces, and how vital it was (even in Crossroads) to have a cleanable steel table and not a wood one that soaked up blood and fluids, but it had been expensive, and difficult to move, and it looked terrible in her home. She resolved, for the hundredth time, to get a nice tablecloth to cover it at night.

The spray bottle of 10 per cent bleach was full; the rag basket on the wall beside it held clean, bleached rags. The disposal hamper beneath it was empty.

In the corner, nicely shrouded, were EKG equipment and a portable X-ray machine for field work, which Sugar Dobbs had helped her modify with a soldering gun; both ran off the portable generator which she kept in the shed outside the window.

In the other corner was a hand-hewn wooden cabinet containing patient cards.

The addresses were descriptive and exotic: "by the cave near Ribbon Falls off the Kendrick road paralleling High River" was fairly short as locations went.

Descriptions of the patients were even more extended.

On top of the cabinet was a bulky three-ring binder. She opened it, turning to the carefully lettered title page: Lao's *Guide to the Unbiological Species: An Addendum*, by BJ Vaughan, D.V.M. The table of contents, done on lines penciled in with a ruler and then erased, took up half a page and stopped abruptly after "Vertebra displacement in centaurs."

She laid the binder down regretfully; she had nothing to add today.

She put a wool shawl over her shoulders, picked up a book, and began where she had left off:

"I went to the woods because I wished to live deliberately,
to front only the essential facts of life, and see if I could not
learn from what it had to teach, and not, when I came to die,
discover that I had not lived."

Walden, inside an English class, had seemed alien and inapplicable; here, living simply and in miraculous remission from an inevitably terminal disease, it seemed one of the most important and wonderful books of any world. She read slowly and carefully.

Daphni curled against and on her feet, at first purring thunderously and finally falling asleep, breathing regularly with a slight respiratory whisper that BJ had already examined her for a hundred times. BJ smiled, remembering how Lee Anne, when BJ had told her where she was going, had said, "Won't you miss television?"

Someone knocked at the door, loudly. BJ rose, rearranging her shawl so that it covered her right hand. From a drawer in the table she took a catchlet—a small sword with a wide crosspiece that hooked up at either end—and she draped the shawl over it. She moved the table candle so that it would be behind her, leaving her hands difficult to see. Her time in Crossroads had taught her a great deal.

She unbarred the door and stood well to one side after tugging it open. Hearing the sudden skitter of animal feet in the grass near the door, she dropped back, half-crouched, letting the table lamp illuminate the outdoors.

Two round-eared, flat-nosed puppies with big feet skidded to a stop in the doorway and peered at her attentively. A third, smaller puppy bumped into them and climbed almost on top of them; they snarled and it backed away instantly.

They were gray-furred and silver-eyed, with small upright tails, and BJ was in love.

"Come here," she said, dropping to her knees. "No, c'mon." When she stretched out her arms, they backed away from her, their ears tucked back. She tossed the shawl aside, catchlet hidden under it, and tried again, clucking at them.

Daphni, waking, hissed. BJ waved a hand at her. "Be quiet." Affronted, the flowerbinder leapt onto the bed and, in the absence of vegetation to hide in, pulled the covers over the cat's head.

Gradually the pups' ears came forward, and they crept toward her. It was probably the odd silhouette in the shawl that had spooked them. "That's it. Okay, okay . . ." She finally touched one; it sniffed at her eagerly, wrinkled its nose, and backed off again. "Aww. Don't I smell right?"

She heard a footstep and looked up in embarrassment. Of course someone was there; the puppies hadn't knocked for themselves.

The woman had dark hair and dark eyes, as BJ herself did. Perhaps that was why the puppies had been willing to come forward at all; BJ wasn't sure how well wolf pups could see.

Looking more closely, BJ noticed the woman's prominent cheekbones and slightly slanted eyes; she looked Eurasian. She was wearing a homespun white shift with black homespun breeches. BJ had the feeling they had met before.

The woman said quickly, "Are they well?" Her face was marked with pain and care; it looked like a French painting of peasant life in the nineteenth century, but her teeth were straight and beautifully white.

"I can't tell without looking at them more closely. I don't mean to be rude, but can this wait until morning? Normal office hours are sunup to sundown." In a land with no clocks, those were the most sensible hours BJ had found.

"They will not wait."

"All right." Even in Crossroads, client eccentricities were a standard part of practice. "I'll look at them tonight. Are these your pups, then?"

"No." The woman said it proudly, almost arrogantly, and with a chill BJ knew why she looked odd.

But she was inside, and BJ was now out of reach of the catchlet as the woman grabbed her shoulder and said distinctly, pointing to the pups, "My children."

T·H·R·E·E

THE WOLF PUPS sniffed around the room with interest, the smallest trotting a slight distance from the other two.

BJ, still on her knees, looked from side to side warily. She didn't have a weapon within reach, and the woman was between her and the door. In human form, the Wyr were less formidable than as wolves, and the transformation was painful enough and took long enough to leave them vulnerable.

But the woman might not be alone. BJ had a long scar on her arm from an encounter with the Wyr; they often tormented and teased victims before killing them. Daphni's hip injury was probably caused by the Wyr having driven her off a cliff.

BJ stayed still. The woman said flatly, "You fear me."

"I have fought your people before." But BJ thought that the woman knew.

The woman looked down, unsmiling, at BJ on the floor. Finally she pointed to the pups. "You must look."

When she spoke, BJ saw her teeth: perfect, white and regular, brighter than BJ's were after a trip to the dentist. She remembered, shivering, why a grown woman's teeth would look so new.

The wolf pups, her children, bounded through the cottage sniffing the furniture and the covered veterinary equipment. The metal table fascinated them; in spite of BJ's scrubbing, it probably retained the scent of a great many patients.

BJ stood slowly. It would not do to look hasty or frightened. "You can't bring them back tomorrow?"

The woman shook her head violently back and forth. BJ was reminded against her will of a dog shaking a toy. The woman repeated. "Look at them. Now."

Then she said something extraordinary, for one of the Wyr: "Please."

"All right."

The woman turned and said sharply, "Katya. Grigor. Horvat."

The larger two rocketed over and wrestled unconcernedly, nipping at each other and yelping. The woman said again, "Horvat!" The third, darker and smaller, trotted over to stand between the Wyr woman's legs and look up at BJ curiously.

BJ knelt cautiously; the third pup stayed put. "Hi, fella," she said softly, and held out a hand, ready to pull it back if the pup bit.

The pup sniffed at her hand, then licked it tentatively, then took her fingers in his needle-sharp teeth and tugged her hand back and forth. His play was much weaker than the others'.

"Are they from the same litter?"

The woman nodded. "They are all."

The way she said "all" made BJ look up. "This is your entire litter? Your children?" BJ was hazy on wolf litters, but three seemed a low number. Unless—

"Was it your first litter—Excuse me. Were these your first children?"

"No. Eight others. Dead now."

BJ decided not to ask. "Did you have this last set as a wolf, or a human?"

"As Wyr," she said defiantly, and added, "But with fur."

BJ looked into the woman's ashamed but defensive face. "Human women have one baby at a time, sometimes two, rarely three or more."

"Wyr have five. Sometimes six." Her eyes dropped.

BJ hated needing to know. "Did you have more?"

The Wyr woman's fingers worked and tightened over each other restlessly. "Yes. Three dead."

BJ let out a long, slow breath. Her brief stay in Crossroads had taught her that teratology and Abnormal Repro were largely useless here; the land itself healed most fetal problems. "What was the—what were they like?"

"Too small." And in the woman's haunted voice, BJ could almost see them: What veterinarians and Agricultural Science people called "unthrifty animals," as though the pups were to blame for spending their own mass. They never had enough flesh to live.

After a moment, BJ nodded. "What did you do?"

"Dug a hole." Only the Wyr woman's twisting, working fingers betrayed her feeling.

"I'm sorry," BJ said gently, but the woman looked back with arrogant indifference. The Wyr did not apologize, nor did they seek sympathy. "Do you need an exam as well? If you changed to a wolf—to your other form, perhaps I could tell you why you had difficulty carrying—"

"No!" It came out a sharp bark. "No. I know why. I was—ill." She looked deeply ashamed.

"You—" And BJ remembered her. "You're Gredya."

"Yes." And Gredya nodded, eyes downcast and mourning, apparently sorry to be herself.

BJ looked longingly at her shawl, under which the catchlet lay, out of reach by the door.

She had seen Gredya twice. Once was in a circle of human Wyr kicking a flowerbinder; Gredya had begun metamorphosing into a wolf, and BJ had threatened to kill her while she was help-less.

The other occasion involved a battle with Morgan, who had addicted several of the Wyr to control the animals she could never tame, one of the species who could lead Morgan into Crossroads with an army. Gredya and her kin, in wolf form, had nearly killed BJ and the other vet students who were defending a copy of *The Book of Strangeways* against Morgan.

Now BJ could picture clearly the end of that battle: Gredya's human skin shiny with the sweat of metamorphosis, her mouth wide open as she howled on the news that there was no morphine for her withdrawal-racked body.

Gredya hesitated, fought with herself, and finally said, "The woman Morgan—"

"Is gone." BJ added, honestly, "I think she survived. She may try to come back."

"She must never."

Gredya's cheeks were even more gaunt than usual. The strain of transformation kept all Wyr thin; Gredya looked pinched, and her eyes had lost the cold, calm assurance of the Wyr, taking instead a wretched, unquiet look.

In her wolf form, first as a morphine addict and then under-going withdrawal from it, Gredya had carried and delivered a damaged litter.

Horvat pawed at Gredya's feet and looked up anxiously.

She stooped and picked him up, grunting. He snuggled against her chest. She lay her head against his and, in a gesture that looked remarkably natural, licked his muzzle.

BJ reached out and ruffled Horvat's fur. The pup cringed away from her and into Gredya.

She said to BJ, "I should kill him. The pack says." Gredya looked defensively into BJ's eyes. "I will not."

BJ had a sudden chilling thought. "Will the father wish to come see Horvat?"

"No." Gredya looked BJ directly in the eyes. "He is dead. Vlatmir. By your friend."

The scene, chaotic though it was, was still clear in BJ's memory: an oversize adult wolf, driving Annie back against the wall of Stein's, poising to rip her throat out. Annie, tossed a knife by Stein, plunging it into the wolf seconds before she would have died. One of BJ's best friends had killed Gredya's lover.

"And you came to me," BJ said finally.

Gredya looked away. "I had to. I have no one."

BJ took a deep breath and said, "I'll start with one of the bigger ones." She was trying to apply what she knew about dogs to wolves who weren't really wolves; any approximation of a normal pup for a benchmark would help.

Gredya nodded and said sharply, "Katya!" and pointed. One of the large pups scurried over to BJ. Horvat, peering between Gredya's feet, watched anxiously.

BJ did the same exam on all three, first quickly on Katya and her larger brother, Grigor. When those two were done, Gredya said, sounding gentle for the first time, "Now Horvat."

Horvat lay on the floor, pretending not to hear.

"Horvat?"

He still didn't move.

"Shy patient," BJ said easily, and scooped him forward, tugging his scruff and nearly lifting his scrambling feet off the stone floor. She held him down and began the final examination.

First she took his temperature rectally—she still had little idea what a normal temperature was on a werewolf, but the thermometer also demonstrated that the anus was developed. Her professor in Small Animal Medicine, whose knowledge she respected without respecting the man, had recommended taking temperatures to check for atrezia ani. BJ thought it wouldn't be necessary to check in pups this young, but decided she'd rather be absolutely sure; if the digestive tract were sealed, the animal would die.

She pulled the thermometer out and checked the reading, then wiped the instrument and set it aside. Now she palpated Horvat's rear legs and hips. She twisted each leg carefully in its socket. No hip displasia, but—"His hind legs splay out a little to the right and the left. Is that normal in your puppies?"

Gredya frowned. "You tell me."

BJ winced. One of her vet school instructors, a rail-skinny ex-basketball player who lived in his beat-up Lakers T-shirt, had constantly snapped, "You tell me" to tentative questions at rounds.

She lifted each leg, pumped it as though she were making Horvat do aerobics, then set it down. "It's probably just normal variation, an individual quirk. Watch him to see if he has any trouble getting up or lying down."

Moving on, she prodded Horvat's skinny belly, trying to elicit a yelp, then sighed and gave up. With the Wyr, it was impossible to tell whether they were healthy or merely stoic. She felt carefully around his navel—and got it.

"Umbilical hernia," she said with relief, pleased to have found something. Being watched by a werewolf was amazingly like doing rounds in vet school.

"What is?" Gredya knelt, peering anxiously, and BJ was ashamed for feeling complacent about something that made her client so desperate.

She rolled Horvat on his side. "The Ultimate Outie. See this button of flesh? That should be on the inside of the dog—Oh, God, I'm sorry; it should be on your child's inside—anyway, it's been forced out. All I have to do is bloop it back in, for now."

"Bloop." Gredya eyed her suspiciously.

"A technical term meaning reinsertion of umbilical material digitally." BJ pressed with her finger. Horvat squeaked, more out of surprise than pain, as his umbilicus popped back into his body. "I'll want to double-check that, later. Sometime down the road it may need surgery."

Gredya nodded, clearly impressed. BJ wished it were always that easy to win over a client.

The rest of the exam went well. She probed Horvat's skull for fontanels, the soft spots that indicated a failure to form and match properly on the part of the skull plates. The plates overlapped beautifully, probably because Horvat would one day need to transform himself into a human child.

She looked in his mouth, half expecting to see a cleft palate, and she checked his bite pattern by coaxing him to play with a sheet from one of her notebooks. His jaw seemed a trace overshot, but nothing severe enough to worry about.

The other pups, curious, came back and nuzzled BJ. She patted them cautiously, eyeing Gredya. Weren't wolves fairly protective of their young?

All BJ said was, "He'll be fine. Some things I should look at, and I wouldn't be surprised if he always stayed smaller than the others. Will the pack help you raise him, if you explain?"

Gredya didn't quite laugh at BJ. "The pack? Not now. They fight. All fight."

"Can't your leader—"

"No leader." Gredya shrugged, a ripple that ran down her back like an animal shaking off water. "So they fight."

"Dominance battles." BJ had seen one such battle on a nature show, and had seen still photographs of male wolves with scars around their eyes, across their muzzles, even on their throats. And for now, at least, the Wyr had no alpha wolf, and would fight until they settled on one. At least the Wyr, transforming themselves back and forth from human, wouldn't scar.

Gredya pointed down to where Horvat lay trembling under BJ's hands. "You keep him."

BJ's jaw dropped. "You mean, raise him? Care for—No, I couldn't. God, I *couldn't*." This was no wolf pup; Gredya was giving away her child.

"You will," Gredya said, adding bluntly, "or he dies. Please. I need."

Horvat whimpered, looking back and forth. From her short contact with the Wyr, BJ could imagine what would happen to a fearful pup, and how quickly it would be done.

"It's all right." She stroked his back, amazed at how silky the fur was. "You're just perfect, aren't you? Yes, you are." To Gredya she said, "I'll take care of him. I promise."

He struggled away from her and bounded back to Gredya, whimpering. Katya and Grigor, taking a cue from Horvat, nosed hopefully around Gredya's feet, shoving him aside.

"They are hungry," she said finally.

"I can feed Horvat milk, fortified," BJ said thoughtfully. "But the other two should keep their regular diet." She grabbed Horvat by the scruff, pulling him away from his mother.

She saw Gredya's face, and let go. "One more time won't hurt him."

Gredya nodded, stepping out of her clothes unself-consciously.

One more time hurt her. Those perfect white teeth crackled as they fell from her jaw, and the whites of her eyes blossomed red as the blood vessels ruptured. Her fingers fell off, but she

managed to shove the pups aside while she ate each finger—
conserving mass, BJ reminded herself, but felt sick watching.
Gredya shrieked, then howled as her jaw extended forward. Large
flat masses moved under her scalp at the back; BJ tried to watch
clinically, but was horrified to realize that the masses were skull
plates, overlapping as Gredya's brain case altered.

The pups, oblivious to their mother's pain, clamored at her
quivering body and dove for it as she righted herself shakily.
They barely waited until the transformation was complete to dive
for her nipples.

A few moments later, the puppies were nursing happily, Horvat
deferentially nudging his way behind Katya and Grigor. BJ,
cleaning the bloody remains of transformation from her floor,
wondered what kind of desperation could drive a mother wolf to
surrender her child, and how dangerous the resentment could be.

Horvat insisted on sleeping in the bed with her. She couldn't tell
whether it was affection, loneliness, or some kind of dominance
struggle with Daphni. All she could tell was that Daphni was
hissing, Horvat was growling, and no one seemed to be getting
any sleep.

Finally she picked Horvat up and set him firmly on the floor.
"Tough luck. Go to sleep."

Horvat sniffed resentfully, but appeared to accept her decision.
He curled up by the bed and dozed off almost immediately, his
rapid, regular breathing punctuating the steadiness of the night
breeze.

The breeze outside picked up.

Horvat caught it before BJ did; his ears, still round and lopped
over, tried to prick up, and he whimpered.

BJ was confused for a moment, then moved quickly to the
window. Horvat got in her way, growling.

She stepped over him and barred the shutter, pulling the curtains tight in front of it. She was concerned only about light
leaking out; the shutter, in this instance, would be no protection at all.

The shutter rattled, and the wooden eaves over the cottage
groaned. From outside she heard the frightened milling of sheep;
someone's flock, broken free of the cote, was huddled under her
eaves. Daphni squeaked and dove under the bed.

BJ tiptoed toward the door, hoping to see out the peephole.

Horvat edged in front of her, then stood at the door, legs slightly
spread, pug nose pointed. He curled his lip up, and a scruffy ridge

of fur rose along his back as he brought his tail up, curved, in challenge.

Tree limbs on the hillside around them creaked and snapped. The sheep bleated in panic.

BJ stepped forward once more; Horvat nipped lightly at her leg and hopped between her and the door again, in combat stance. He growled more loudly at the approaching menace.

In spite of her worry, BJ was charmed.

"No, honey." She scooped him up by the scruff; he snarled and struggled.

By now the rafters were groaning, and dust and chaff falling. The door creaked. BJ drew back against the wall, and, remembering stories a Midwestern friend had told her about tornadoes, tugged one-handed at the kitchen table, holding Horvat in the other, until she and the wolf pup were under the table in the far corner.

The wind became as loud as a freight train, a steady roar. Horvat quit struggling and growling; he snuggled tight against her, whimpering.

She arched her body over him and waited, filled with a sudden panicky vision of the roof being torn off, and a single eye, wider than the table and completely pitiless, peering into the hut before inserting a massive talon.

There was a screaming bleat outside, then another. Something scraped against the stone wall of the cottage. The wind dropped off abruptly.

BJ let go of Horvat; he ran around the room, sniffing at the debris. BJ felt around the floor shakily until she found the matches, then struck one and looked around by its light, which flickered in the dying breeze.

The room was covered with dirt and dried grass, sifted down through the roof boards. A day's thatching work would plug the cracks again, and two days' painting restore the inside. The air was filled with dust.

BJ quietly thanked God that Crossroads cured allergies as well as other problems. She lit the candle in the glass hurricane chimney and gathered up her bedclothes to take outside.

Horvat sneezed several times and scratched at the door. "All right," BJ said, unbarring it. "But stay by me."

He bounded out. "No. Heel," she commanded, and added as though she were sincere, "Guard me, Horvat."

His stubby tail wagged, and he pulled back beside her, looking alertly to the left and right as she shook out the bedclothes. It was cold enough that she wrapped the comforter around her like a shawl after shaking the dust out. She hung the other blankets on a bare tree limb, beat them quickly, and left them for the light breeze to shake out.

When she walked, Horvat kept pace with her, barely a foot from her side the entire time except once, when she was inspecting the damage to the outside of the cottage. He bounded over and sniffed interestedly at a dark stain next to a fresh scratch, white in the moonlight, where something had scraped vertically up the cottage wall.

He turned away from the stain to look at her, wagging his tail hopefully.

She swallowed. "Sorry, honey. There's none left for you."

He bounded back to her side, accepting. BJ glanced at the sky, but there was nothing even in the distance.

She picked Horvat up. "Do you know what the Great are? Do you know the bargain the people of Crossroads made with them, before I ever came to live here? They protect us, and we never harm them or their children. They come as they please and eat as they please; do you know what that means, every night?"

He whined and licked her nose. She laughed and kissed his, and he struggled to be set down.

She went back indoors and remade her bed when the dust settled. Horvat snuggled against her, and this time even Daphni let him sleep in peace.

F·O·U·R

BJ HAD NOT even one second of thinking that the night before had been a dream. She was jolted awake by Horvat nipping playfully at the sleeping Daphni and Daphni taking one swift, accurate swipe at Horvat's nose.

Horvat, yelping, fled across BJ's supine body; Daphni, limping, pursued. BJ flung an arm up to protect her face and grunted as a cat the size of a German shepherd pounded across her chest.

BJ let Daphni out.

"Dawn," she said weakly, the wind still knocked out of her. "I overslept."

She added water to the tea kettle, pulled a robe on quickly as the chill hit her, tossed kindling and larger sticks of wood on the embers in the stove, then stumbled back to the door and opened it. Daphni ran in and reclaimed the bed, as cats always have and will.

Horvat dashed out quickly and squatted in the grass. "House training" is a loose term, but at least he had gone outside.

"Good boy," she said sleepily in his direction, and tiptoed out, chivying him back inside before he could scamper off. She closed the door, opened it and hurried inside to get her notebook (and her slippers), ran out again, down to the circle of stones and made a hasty mark of the sun's position with a guilty note that she had missed actual sunrise by a few minutes, then stumbled back to the house to try and wake up normally.

There was a client waiting for her, standing patiently under the Healing Sign. The sign creaked slightly in the morning breeze as the client ducked his head bashfully and smiled, showing almost six inches of fangs from one side of his head to the other. He quickly closed his lips and looked apologetic.

The Meat People looked like short, squat humans except for their nearly ear-to-ear-mouths full of pointed teeth, no molars at all. They were largely silent, perhaps because articulating was so difficult for them—perhaps, also, so as not to scare those they communicated with. They nodded politely, they gestured, and they tried to smile carefully with their mouths shut. Really, if you could forget about the teeth, they were quite nice.

This one had carried a fawn from wherever it had been hurt. BJ's own breath caught in her throat as she heard the deer's bubbly, labored breathing. Its coat was losing the white dappling of infancy, but now it was dappled with red.

"Let me examine the fawn, Mister—"

"Dohnrr." His teeth, sharper than pencil points and as long, showed as he spoke. He closed his mouth quickly and looked apologetic.

"Donr." She smiled back at him, though the Meat People made her nervous. She held out her hands. Dohnrr held the fawn up.

A predator had been at it last night. Considering that the Great had been through, BJ was inclined to count the fawn lucky, if it could heal. She began the exam.

It didn't require much. One sinus cavity was exposed and bloody—that was painful, but stitchable. One eye was lost, possibly to a fang, considering the long groove below it through the cheek. The lower jaw was broken and hanging, with a clear bite mark where it had been seized and tugged. The neck was ripped in several places, but not deeply enough to sever the jugular.

A single bite had exposed the trachea, where a jagged, dark hole showed. The rasp of air through it explained how the poor animal was still breathing.

BJ had no need to look further. "I'm sorry. I can't help the fawn. I really can't. Even if I could make it live for a while, it's too maimed to have a life in the wild. It should really be killed."

She added, "You could eat it."

A tear trickling down his cheek, Dohnrr nodded glumly. He stroked the fawn's trembling head, then held it up to her again with less hope and mimed an injection.

"I could," she said. "But the T-61, the fluid I put in its body, would mean that you shouldn't eat it afterward. Can you kill it quickly and without pain?"

Dohnrr hesitated, then pointed with one clawed finger to the fawn's neck and looked at BJ questioningly.

"Yes." BJ had been thinking more in terms of a mercy bolt, the small spring-loaded bolt made expressly for punching into large animal's skulls. She had not thought of bringing one to Crossroads, but wondered what she could rig up. "I can sever the spine, right there"—she guided Dohnrr's muscular little hand—"between the fifth and sixth vertebrae. The fawn would die quickly. Let me see what I have that's sharp enough to do the job—"

The little man's upper lip drew back in a rictus that exposed inch-long, razor-sharp teeth. His head flashed down and across the fawn's neck, his cheek brushing BJ's hand before she could move. His tears were damp on her knuckles.

He straightened as the fawn shuddered once and lay still, a deep perpendicular slash across its neck. The fawn's head sagged against its breast at an extreme angle. Dohnrr hugged it as a child would a doll, eyes shut with grief. His teeth and lips were stained red.

He opened his eyes and stuck a clawed hand out to BJ. "Thnghrr," he said through his bloody teeth.

BJ took his hand shakily. "You're very welcome."

Dohnrr reached behind himself and swung forward a freshly killed and dressed ring-necked pheasant, its neck broken. Probably it had wandered in from Virginia. The Meat People would pay for services in gold if pressed, but considered it impolite; they preferred to pay in something made with their own hands. BJ thanked him, and he carried the fawn away tenderly.

She took the pheasant inside, pumped water over it, and set it aside to eat later, all the while thinking of the mangled fawn. "Predators," she said disgustedly, then patted Horvat and Daphni while she sipped her tea, wondering how best to cook a pheasant.

Sipping, she considered the problem of keeping Horvat. He had been good enough about relieving himself outdoors; how easily could he be trained? "Horvat?" she said. His round ears tried to prick up. "Are you smart?"

Horvat looked at her alertly, small tail wagging. He seemed eager to learn.

"Horvat," she said slowly, "walk across the room and halfway back, then stay there."

He trotted quickly across the kitchen, sniffed interestedly at the pantry, remembered her request and walked halfway back, lost interest and got in a life-or-death battle with the braid rug.

BJ foolishly tried to pull the rug away from him before she caught herself. "Horvat, let go. Bad wolf. Horvat, behave."

She took a deep breath and bellowed, "NO!" Horvat froze, dropping on his backside on the wood floor and staring, stricken, up at her. Finally he edged over, almost on his belly, and licked one of her feet.

"No, it's all right," she found herself saying. "It's okay. You just shouldn't do that . . . It's all right. I love you," she added, and realized that she very soon would.

Horvat looked up hopefully, then cocked his head, grinned up at her, and leapt, tugging her bathrobe pull open. She grabbed for it, stepping back. He snatched the slipper off her upraised right foot.

"Horvat!" Hopping, she chased him around the kitchen. He shook his head from side to side, tossing the slipper in his mouth and tearing at it.

For a dizzying moment she thought of saying, Do you know, I saw one of your relatives do that to a brown man barely two feet high?

Horvat dropped the slipper and squeaked repeatedly at the door. It took BJ a moment to recognize it as a bark.

She snatched up the slipper and hopped outside, listening to the gallop of hooves on the hill behind the house.

"Great," she panted to herself. "What a wonderful way to greet a queen."

Galloping downhill toward them was what looked like a woman on a horse. Closer up, it was clearly a woman *and* a horse, one of the Hippoi—centaurs. She galloped beautifully with her Arab hindquarters, holding her olive-skinned human body as erect as a horsewoman in the ring for dressage.

A colt and boy, legs flailing to keep up, rocketed along behind her. He was half out of control on the hill, laughing with delight.

As the centaur woman came closer, BJ could plainly see a homespun jacket over her statuesque human body. The plume of breath from her mouth and nose was larger than a human's, partly from the mass of body she breathed for and partly from her own high body temperature.

She raised an arm ceremonially as she stopped, and the excited boy/colt behind her stopped as well. He looked ahead nervously at BJ and sidled behind his mother's body.

BJ, robe tied and slipper back on, bowed ceremonially, "I greet you, Carron."

"I greet you, Doctor," the centaur said back. Then she smiled and said wistfully, "Do you know, even after all these months, I see my Nesyos when someone calls me Carron? Please, let me greet you better."

She bent down, arms open, and BJ leapt forward willingly. "Hello, Polyta."

Polyta swept her up and off the ground in strong arms and kissed her on both cheeks. "Oh, BJ, always it is so good to see you! Every time I think of you, I think of my sweet Sugarly alive and just born."

"That was Lee Anne," BJ said embarrassedly. "And of course Sugar—Dr. Dobbs." Which was where "Sugar-Lee" had come from.

Polyta shook her head violently, dark curls shaking to either side of her huge, dark eyes. "It was you as well. Otherwise, he would have died." She set BJ down.

BJ turned and smiled. "Hello, Sugarly."

The four-month-old centaur looked to be a twelve-year-old boy, growing at a colt's rate from his initial size. He put a finger in his mouth while he stared at BJ, then ran off behind a corner of her cottage.

Polyta said easily, "Oh, he is impossible. He sulks because his favorite grandmother was too hurt to walk, and now we have left her to die."

Sugarly peeked around the corner resentfully, then disappeared again.

After a moment BJ said, as casually as she could, "At the ford, in the river?"

Polyta looked offended. "Oh no. I know that is traditional, and Nesyos would have said that is how it should be, but no. I left Medéa with food and drink, on the spot where she broke her leg. I even left wine. And then I sent word to the Great, to come get her. They were in the air last night."

BJ refrained from glancing at her cottage wall. "I know."

"Then you know that maybe her life will even save a life." She finished earnestly, "Remember, the Carron is the Chooser of the Dead, not the maker of them."

If one of the Hippoi were injured, or ill, or simply incapable of staying with the others on their endless march through Crossroads, then the lagging centaur was left for predators. It was the way of herd animals through the ages, even the way of some nomadic humans. BJ, terminally ill herself but granted a reprieve by her physical contact with Crossroads, found the Hippoi's customs unconscionably hard.

"On saving lives—" BJ said slowly.

"You have thought about what I said?" Polyta's face betrayed her eagerness.

"Quite a bit. I talked about the class you wanted, then thought about the class you needed."

Polyta looked down earnestly at BJ. "I have seen so many bad births. So many deaths. You said once that there were classes in giving birth; such a class, if it can help at all, is so badly needed."

BJ nodded. "I agree. I think it's wonderful that you would do this." She gestured to Sugarly, who ducked his head back around the building resentfully. "It's not the traditional role of a Carron, is it?"

Polyta smiled ruefully. "The Carron does what is needed. I wish it were not needed."

BJ leaned forward, tipping her head backward and up until her neck hurt. "Then let me teach something more extensive. Let me teach prenatal care, and diet monitoring, and the importance of exams and checkups." She took a deep breath. "Please let me teach first aid, and ways to prevent lameness, and ways to help the sick get well quickly."

She looked into Polyta's compassionate but unanswering face. "I know it goes against what the Hippoi do. I know you're supposed to let the sick die. I want to help the barely sick from ever getting that sick. That's all.

"It's called preventive medicine," BJ finished desperately, knowing that the term would mean nothing to Polyta.

Polyta looked dazed. "Choosing death by preventing it? This has never happened."

"Why can't it?"

"Let me tell you." Polyta leaned forward after looking to see that Sugarly wasn't listening. "We move a great deal now, to keep a diet. We scatter seeds, let things grow, and return to harvest them."

BJ nodded. Stein had once told her it was "one of the stages between hunting-and-gathering and true agriculture." The Griffin, though he himself was a carnivore, had sniffed and called it "farming for species with low attention spans."

Polyta went on. "What if there were more of us, and we had to move even more? What if there were never enough food, and I watched all our children starve? Has that ever happened to groups of animals, Doctor?"

BJ answered unwillingly, but honestly. "In my world it happens all the time. Sometimes it causes overgrazing; sometimes it destroys a prey species and then the predator starves, or sometimes it just destroys the environment—the land it happens in." She added dryly, "Some people think it's happening to humans now, and about time, too."

Polyta smiled slightly. "You sound like your Dr. Sugar Dobbs just now. Please say hello to him for me."

"He speaks highly of you," BJ said. Sugar Dobbs was happily married, but how could an ex-rodeo rider not think highly of a female centaur?

Polyta shook herself, her long tangle of dark hair rippling in time with her horse tail. "But back to our discussion. When Nesyos was Carron, and we slept side-by-side, often he would fret about such things. I know he seemed stern to you, but he was very lonely and worried for us all. 'What will I do, Polyta,' he would say, 'if someday there are too many of us, and I must choose healthy ones to die? What if I have a child, and can't bear for it to hate me as I hated my father, for choosing to let Hippoi die?' "

BJ had seen Nesyos recommend that his own unborn child be sawed apart in the womb, to save Polyta's life. "He made such decisions bravely," she said carefully.

"I must, too," Polyta said. "I feel it more, now that Sugarly is born."

They stood together in the sun, not speaking. Sugarly, bored, came around the corner of the cottage and peered in the windows.

Finally Polyta said, "Can you understand that I will still tell my people what they must never do, even if you teach them how to do it?"

"Of course."

"All right." Polyta said it with relief. "Begin teaching us as soon as you can."

"I'll need to consult with Lee Anne. She's better at—" BJ nearly said "horses." "Well, she's much better with the Hippoi."

"How soon will you know?" Polyta, once committed, was anxious to start. "How will you tell her?"

"I mailed a letter—" Polyta looked confused; BJ amended: "I sent a message to Lee Anne yesterday, giving her an outline of what I was looking for and asking for help."

Polyta laughed. "You are the same BJ. You think faster than others."

BJ had no answer to that; fortunately, she didn't need one. Sugarly was pointing in the cottage door and laughing, dancing back and forth on his tiny hooves.

Polyta trotted over and mussed his hair. "What is it, pretty little one? Does the doctor have something funny?" she asked—

And froze.

BJ ran over quickly and saw Horvat, shaking his head from side to side and bracing his paws against the floor, growling furiously. He had the half-torn bird from Dohnrr in his teeth.

"That was my lunch," BJ said, then added, delightedly, "He's learning to hunt! He's killing it and guarding it!"

"How good for him," Polyta said neutrally. "And you are caring for him now?"

"For a while." BJ didn't understand the change in Polyta's tone.

"Of course. You care for many species." Polyta glanced down at Sugarly. "The grandmother Medéa, the one I said was lame? That was the Wyr's doing." She put a hand on BJ's shoulder, with all the strength of the Hippoi, and BJ was as planted in place as if a tree had fallen on her. "They wanted to tear her throat out. Always with the not-tame hooved animals, the Wyr tear the throat and the face." Her throat tightened as she spoke, the veins standing out clearly.

Sugarly, nervous at the serious talk, sidled up against his mother's free side. Polyta put her arm around his shoulders. "But she didn't let them, did she? She kicked, and thrust, and drove them off. But one of those she kicked stayed and bit at her leg—an act of self-defense, I know it—and tore the strong part, the string for the muscle, I don't know—"

"Tendon." BJ felt sick. "It ripped her tendon out. Smart animal."

Polyta nodded. "Very smart of it. If she gets away, then we abandon her, and soon or late the Wyr eat anyway." She looked into the far distance, as though she could see the aging Hippoi, crippled in the grass. "So she limped over to me, and asked what to do, and I sent word to the Great. We stayed with her as long as we dared, and would not give her to the Wyr."

She squeezed BJ's shoulder harder, her horse tail swinging back and forth. "Keep this animal away from my people, BJ. They would kill it—"

"Him. Horvat." She could feel her ears turning red; she was angry with Polyta.

"They would kill Horvat, no matter how good he was now." Polyta let go of BJ's shoulder and stroked her straight black hair the way she had done with Sugarly. "You called your teaching preventive medicine. Killing that little one would be preventive, might save as many lives as your classes would."

BJ said levelly, "I kill ticks and fleas and heartworms, not larger predators. It's an odd distinction, but one I'll stand by."

Polyta said only, "Very well." She turned to go, and BJ's heart ached.

She wheeled and came back. "I forgot to tell you: Your friends Rudy and Bambi are getting married."

"I was sure." Rudy and Bambi's species was half-deer and half-human; their people lived in the rough terrain to the northwest of Crossroads. BJ had met them at Stein's several times, when she had been a vet student in Crossroads.

"They will marry at Stein's, at the new Stein's, at midmorning of the second full moon this fall. Rudy asked me to tell you, and asked me to tell the other students. Can you get word to them?"

"I promise." BJ was as relieved to be still speaking to Polyta as she was happy at the coming wedding.

"Good. Rudy and Bambi want you and Annie and Lee Anne to join the bridesmaids. They warned that you will need to run a lot. They want Dave to be something Rudy calls 'best man.' Does that make sense?"

"Oh yes." BJ smiled, picturing Dave Wilson's face when he heard. He would want a disgustingly rowdy bachelor party, but at least he would understand the honor of serving as best friend for someone of another species.

Polyta smiled in an embarrassed way and tossed her head, hair rippling again. "I don't understand, but I'm glad it pleases you. Goodbye, BJ." She bent and kissed BJ's forehead, as much a blessing as a farewell. "Sugarly!"

They trotted away, Polyta shying wide of BJ's doorway. BJ went back inside; for no reason, she picked up the struggling Horvat and hugged him, then patted Daphni, half from guilt. She didn't let Horvat outside until she was sure Polyta was gone.

Lunch was uneventful, except for edgy sparring for snacks between Daphni and Horvat. So far, Daphni held the upper hand with age and claws; at some point soon, energy and the normal growth of the Wyr would give Horvat an edge.

BJ was rinsing the lunch dishes when the knock came: an authoritative one-two-three rap which sounded like a resident advisor checking a smoke-filled dorm room. Only three knocks, and they still sounded foreign here. BJ opened the door, catchlet in her hidden right hand. This time she would be ready.

She stared in front of her, completely unprepared, at a woman who stared back unflinchingly.

She was wearing a denim miniskirt, reddish-brown stockings, and a faded T-shirt displaying a pig with wraparound sunglasses and a Mohawk haircut. Below it, almost unreadable, was the motto "High on the Hog: Church Hill Barbecue." Over the T-shirt she wore a denim vest with hand-sewn roses, a pentagram, and an absolutely beautiful orange and gold embroidered dragon. Dangling from each ear was a silver filigree skull, Mexican judging by the design, and in a second hole in her left ear there hung a silver star.

The woman's hair was a bright, nearly crimson red. It looked artificially colored, but BJ dismissed that notion; anyone dressed in this kind of outfit would never settle for a mere red dye.

It bothered BJ that the strangest thing she had seen in Crossroads was probably a resident of Richmond, Virginia.

The woman stared back at her determinedly. She pulled her hair back with one hand, caught herself and folded both hands in front of her like a soloist, cleared her throat, and said firmly, "Are you a witch?"

BJ set the catchlet in her right hand on the windowsill near the door. She did not move out of reach of it. "Why would I be a witch?"

The woman gestured at the sign overhead. "You're an animal healer; I know that. You cure animals by magic?"

BJ considered. "No. Mostly with medicine, and I've always assumed that the rest was luck."

"Then what," the red-haired woman said, pointing like a trial lawyer on the home stretch, "are your fairy rings for?"

BJ stared, confused, at the rings of rocks she had laid out according to the directions in Dr. Protera's letter. "Certainly not for fairies," she said finally.

"Do they focus Ley lines, perhaps? Do they magnify normal energies?"

"As far as I know, they don't. They're laid out to provide coordinates for astronomy."

The woman frowned. "That's always been a theory about Stonehenge. I didn't believe it then, either."

BJ said crisply, "Well, I can't speak for Stonehenge, because I didn't build it. But I laid out these rocks myself, and I can show you their use."

But she made no effort to get her notes. This woman was annoying her.

The red-haired woman scratched her head. "You sound like someone from my world. Someone from Virginia, in fact. What's your name?"

"BJ Vaughan," she replied, but didn't offer her hand; it was within reach of the catchlet. "Yours?"

"Fiona Bannon." She said it modestly, but with a trace of expectation, as though she expected it to be famous some day.

"Fiona . . ." It did remind BJ of something important. "Are you someone I should know?"

"You might." Fiona looked desperately hopeful. Clearly, being known was something she wanted terribly.

Obligingly, BJ worked at it. "I went to school in Virginia; from your shirt, I'm guessing that you did too."

"Western Vee." Fiona made a sketchy bow. "I'm a non-tech major in a very tech-y world. I'm a graduate student now." She said it the way someone in a romance might announce being a knight or a squire.

BJ said suddenly, "You wrote 'Toward a Science of Magic.' "

"You read it?" Fiona was surprised but, BJ noticed, by no means diffident. "Where?"

"The Western Vee library, in the stacks." BJ had seen it there when she was trying to learn everything she could about Crossroads. "Why, is it published somewhere?"

Fiona's embarrassed annoyance made BJ aware of her mistake. "Of course not. Nothing about Crossroads can be, yet." She looked eager again. "Tell me, did you agree with it?"

Not "did you like it?"

BJ said carefully, "I thought the main idea was striking."

Fiona frowned. "You're saying politely that you don't believe in a science of magic. But you're in a science; doesn't that influence you?"

"Medicine is practice more than science. Medicine is what works." She added more honestly, "Sometimes it's what you hope works."

"And sometimes you don't know why it works."

"A teacher of mine said 'Doctors don't think, they know.' " BJ said it in Sugar's drawl. "It was the only lie he told in class. I think he wanted us to know, as often as possible." BJ knew that she wanted to know more about Fiona. "Can you come in for tea?"

Fiona smiled, and looked pretty and fun. "Do you have decaf?"

"So," BJ said as she put on the kettle, "how long have you been living in Crossroads?"

Fiona looked puzzled only a moment. "Of course. You saw that I walked here. I've only been here a couple weeks since the start of Fall term at Western Vee—"

While BJ made tea, Fiona chatted about the things she missed in Virginia: computer bulletin boards, mosh pits at concerts, FM radio at two in the morning. BJ listened, surprised at how the same feelings pulled at her. As an undergraduate and graduate student at Western Vee, she had been less than a day's drive from home. She had never studied abroad, had never even been out of the country for more than two weeks at a time. Until she came to Crossroads, she had never learned what it felt like to be far away from home.

Fiona munched on the scones BJ presented (day-old, but fairly good). "So, can you practice all by yourself here, without a support staff?"

"I have to." BJ was new enough to feel self-conscious about dependence, but in Crossroads even white lies were dangerous. "I go back and look things up whenever I can. If the weather's all right, I take my bad cases there."

"Sure. Still . . ." Fiona crossed and uncrossed her legs, rocking in the straight-back chair. "You're what my work is all about. Empowerment and self-reliance."

BJ blushed. "I wouldn't go that far . . ."

Fiona thumped her cup down. "Of course you wouldn't. That's your whole problem, and the kind of weakness I want to eliminate."

Before BJ even had time to be insulted, Fiona went on, waving her arms. "Empowerment is internal. It comes from feeling validated, feeling that the structure of society supports your goals and dreams. If people don't have that, they don't have anything. Do you know what magic is?"

BJ opened her mouth, then paused. "Maybe not."

"It's power for the powerless, that's what. It's money for the poor, food for the hungry, safety for the insecure, for everybody who lives on the edge and gets no support from society. You know how people think that magicians are really evil, when nobody thinks how badly even good people need magic?" Fiona's eyes were shining. "You know what magic is really like? It's like crime. You only turn to it when nothing else works." Fiona folded her arms and waited for BJ's reaction.

BJ needed to wait a while; it was a strange idea to digest. Finally she said thoughtfully, "But people avoid turning to crime because it's dangerous. Is that a problem with magic?"

Fiona shook her head vigorously, setting the skull earrings spinning. "Not a problem." The twin skulls rocked, grinning at BJ.

"Not a problem. Okay." Something else struck BJ. "But if anyone disenfranchised went looking for magic, why haven't more people found it by now?"

"If I were really flaky," Fiona said solemnly, and BJ looked aside quickly, "I'd say that people who found magic no longer needed the mainstream, and hid from it, and that's why we don't normally hear of them. The traditional answer is that everybody who ever looked for magic failed to find it because it doesn't exist. By now it's the only answer anyone even thinks of."

"And you're looking for a totally new answer."

"Kind of." Fiona looked out the window thoughtfully. "Do you know where all the roads in Crossroads lead?"

"Nobody does." BJ said, then amended, "That I know of."

"Right. They're in *The Book of Strangeways*." Fiona proudly showed photocopies from her backpack. "It's in the Western Vee library, and it's definitely not governed by normal physics. It updates itself. You know about *The Book of Strangeways*, right? Otherwise you wouldn't be here."

BJ nodded, but thought to herself that Fiona was way too trusting of strangers.

"So you know that on the Strangeways, at the meeting points of Crossroads and other places, the rules are different." She shifted gears abruptly. "Do you know the Monument Avenue neighborhood of Richmond?"

"Some." BJ had seen the avenue, with its parade of equestrian statues and town houses with fan lights over the door.

"There's this really great restaurant near there, art gallery and redneck bar all in one, that serves Mexican and German food and drink. You can buy margaritas and Dos Equis, or Beck's beer and Old Milwaukee, and you can have an enchilada with nachos and sauerbraten and knockwurst. You know what they named it? The Texas-Wisconsin Border. Like it's a roadhouse cafe on the border of Texas and Wisconsin." She stopped and folded her arms again, waiting for BJ's conclusion.

BJ was getting used to her. "And that makes you think . . ."

"That we've always understood about the Strangeways and invisible borders, but we don't remember that we know." She added as though it were less important, "Plus it makes me wonder what we should be taking out of Crossroads, that would mix with our own lives, that we haven't found yet."

BJ considered what Fiona said, trying to figure out what she could safely confide. Did Fiona already know about the immunity to viral diseases and the complete absence of degenerative disease in Crossroads? And what possible department at Western Vee could Fiona be working in? "So, what department are you in?" she asked.

Fiona's pale skin reddened. "English. I wanted Physics, but you know . . ."

BJ didn't, but let it pass. "Is this an independent study?"

"Ostensibly I'm on leave, researching books on magic and demonology."

That stopped BJ dead. Graduate work in medicine and the sciences was fairly rigid, and certainly rigorous; independent studies in BJ's field were nearly nonexistent. "You mean, books like *The Necronomicon*?"

Fiona said seriously, "It wasn't ever real, you know."

"I assumed."

Fiona went on. "No, mostly they're a lot of dull stuff. *The Book of the Damned*, *The Booke of Secrets*, *The Satanist Bible*—I don't mean to make fun of anyone's religion, but that was written in the sixties by someone who didn't want to do much research. And older books, like the *Malleus Maleficarum*, and the *Discoverie of Witchcrafte*." She frowned. "It's a good thing my Latin's all right, or I'd be lost. Not that medieval Latin is much good in itself."

BJ dazedly reminded herself that just because someone seemed scattered, it didn't mean she was stupid. "And did you really read all those?"

"And more. You'll have to come over and see my library; I brought a number of them with me to my cottage. Plus I've got more on diskette, on my laptop; I found a whole bunch more through Internet, on computer databases; did you know that there's a Wiccan database?"

"I had no idea," BJ said sincerely.

"Oh yes. And several Satanist organizations, and a number of black and white magic cabals . . . I traded E-mail with a Voudou group from Cap-Haïtien, but you can't learn much that way; most magic is never committed to paper—hardly ever to print." Fiona, whose hair had fallen over her forehead as she sipped her tea, peered out from under it solemnly. "Really. It's pretty disheartening."

"Didn't you learn anything about real magic from books?" When Fiona looked offended, BJ added, "I mean, something that worked in the physical world?"

Fiona nodded seriously. "Just one thing. It's more than I've even seen confirmed before. Watch." She waved her hands in a circle, reminding BJ of people who practice T'ai Chi. Then, stopping abruptly, she said, "This is going to take about ten minutes; is that okay?"

"Sure." BJ poured water from the still-warm kettle into the dishpan. "I'll start these, if it doesn't distract you."

"Hey, go ahead." Fiona resumed waving her arms. From time to time she muttered in a low voice. "*Vale, daimonai, liht gewyrcan* . . ." BJ listened without really paying attention; nothing Fiona said in the chant made sense. A fairly small amount of what Fiona said made sense, period, but BJ was learning to tell the difference.

Fiona finished, "Θχ *!*" and folded her arms, waiting. BJ, putting away a plate, stumbled and dropped it. The fragments skittered across the floor to all corners of the room. She pulled her arms to her sides reflexively, afraid to move, thinking only of how clumsy she had become before Crossroads healed her, and how Huntington's chorea had nearly claimed her brain and nervous system.

Fiona dived forward, scraping up fragments. "Gosh, I'm sorry. I couldn't warn you without stopping the spell."

"Did you do that?" Despite all that she had seen in Crossroads, BJ found this extremely hard to believe.

Fiona nodded. "And it works every time, exactly the same. Are you all right?"

"And that's from Earth?"

"That's from England after the Crusades; I don't know where it came to England from. Some of the words are Latin, some are Arabic, I think, and some I don't know at all. Why do you say 'from Earth'? Are you sure this isn't Earth, in some weird way?"

BJ blinked. Fiona was disorienting. BJ had the uncomfortably foreign and fortunately rare feeling that she was speaking with someone brighter than she was.

"It's like Earth," she said finally. "The constellations are similar. The periods of the moon are similar."

"Ahh," Fiona said, and looked frustrated. "I should have thought of that."

"You can't think of everything. Anyhow, now that you mention it, it's a lot like Earth. It's just the spectacular differences that threw me."

"Even here," Fiona said, "difference is suspect."

"Here," BJ said gently, "even similarity should be suspect."

Fiona looked confused, but defiant. "Can't you just look at things and tell what's odd? It's only in a few of the animals and at the turning points of roads that this place is strange. . . . That's how the Stumbling Curse was created, I think; it's a bunch of cultures focused into one phrase with one goal. You know, I think I can learn everything I need about magic at the edges of the Strangeways. I'll bet that's the place to try everything I've learned."

BJ bit her lip. "That's a really terrible idea," she said bluntly. "The edges change all the time. The roads change, the turns change, and you could end up somewhere no one you've read about ever dreamed of living."

"Doesn't that fascinate you?"

"It scares me," BJ said frankly. "I'd be happier for you if it scared you."

"Oh." Fiona looked politely blank, like someone talking to a favorite aunt who is forty years out of date. "So, how have you liked living out here? Don't you miss music?"

"I sing a little," BJ said. Her voice, generally clear though not trained, had surprised her as the summer went on.

Fiona shook her head sadly. "I sing. It's not the same."

"No, but it was new to me. I never sang before."

Fiona shook her head, dismissing the whole concept of self-made music. "Listen, I've loved talking to you, and I'd love to do more. I need to get my cottage in order, my books are only half unpacked, but I wish we could talk more. . . ."

"Would you like to have dinner with me, at Stein's?" BJ would happily have made dinner for Fiona; she had already found that company, when one lived alone, was welcome. However, at Stein's she would have a world of examples to point out, and perhaps she could save Fiona from making dangerous mistakes.

Fiona brightened. "I haven't been there yet. Of course I know of it."

"I've wanted to go." BJ, thinking about it, realized that she had not been to Stein's without Stefan for nearly a month.

"Then meet me there tonight. I have some business there . . . Listen, I know I'll sound strange, maybe even a bit stodgy to you—"

"Oh, no," Fiona assured her, and clearly it was true.

"—but on the way into Stein's you'll meet a nasty parrot who will tell you the rules of the place. Please pay attention, OK? When you're in Crossroads, rules can be vital."

"When you're anywhere," Fiona said, "rules are worth challenging." She turned and smiled in the doorway and was gone.

BJ picked up the remaining tea dishes, half expecting them to break in her hand, and stared out the empty doorway. "Was I that young last year?" she said shakily to herself. "Was I ever like that?"

She realized as she did the dishes that there were two answers to that question, both worrisome:

No, she had never been that smart.

And, even when she had thought herself terminally ill, she had never been that reckless. If she had been, she would almost surely be dead now.

F·I·V·E

BJ TRUDGED SLOWLY up the hill to Stein's. Even after half a year's familiarity, the view was wonderful.

Stein's was set in a wide valley, on a single hill which dominated a five-way crossroads. A sign at the crossroads pointed up to a rocky circle.

Stein's was a compact wooden building with thick walls. It had an upper room where Stein himself slept, and its windows were angled so that it had no blind spots where someone could approach unseen. It was centered in a circle of rocks, with one pond above it and one immediately below, the top one fed by an artesian well. BJ knew from experience, and from a day's brief combat, that the inn depended on water power from the upper pond and held some surprises for unwary invaders.

BJ ascended the hill easily, walking the road that left her in plain view from Stein's. At the top of the hill, Stefan had left her van parked near the door. BJ had a fleeting memory of the Western Vee veterinary van, burning in front of the inn. She patted the fender of her own van and went in.

The original Stein's had burned to the ground, but the entrance was the same as it had been before: a bolt-studded, cross-beamed door on a narrow wooden entryway commanded by slits for archers or sword-wielders. The design was from Japanese fortresses. The outer door was closed, a fair indication even in cold weather that Stein's itself was closed. BJ tugged on the door until it creaked open slowly.

Just inside the door stood a parrot perch and, facing it, a tray of biscuits. The perch was empty.

A calm voice with a trace of a Polish accent called from beyond the entryway, "He's off somewhere doing something unspeakable. Just be grateful and come in."

BJ shoved the inner door open. It was heavy and required both hands. If she had been entering with a weapon, she would have been at a serious disadvantage.

The air was rich with garlic, onion, and rosemary. Across the room and not far from the roasting hearth, a slender, elderly man with lively eyes nodded slightly at her entrance. A monstrous, badly scarred animal with the body of a lion and the wings, head, and talons of an eagle bowed gracefully and respectfully to her. Between them, and entirely surrounded by open books, Stefan stopped taking notes and raised a hand to her; he looked as many people look when they see sunrise.

A female faun, bare to the waist but with a thick cotton apron on, bounded over to her. "BJ."

"Hi, Melina." BJ greeted the faun, kissing her on the cheek. After a few embarrassing weeks, BJ had finally told Melina that she did not like kissing on the lips, even the Christian kiss of sisterhood.

Between Melina's small, perfectly round breasts hung a beautiful hammered bronze Coptic cross, a gift sent from Annie in Chad, by way of BJ. Melina hardly ever took it off; it was the only Christian symbol that BJ had seen in Crossroads.

BJ looked around at the familiar faces from Crossroads and beyond, to where an extremely old Mediterranean and an African Pygmy were cooking together and arguing: Chris and B'Cu, the oddest culinary team on any world. No one spoke to her, and Chris and B'Cu did not stop glaring at each other; clearly there was some tension just now. BJ pretended to ignore it and smiled at Stein. "How's the new ale?" she asked brightly.

Stein scowled. "Who knows? I haven't been allowed to try it."

"What?"

He gestured angrily toward Chris. "His Holiness the Patriarch of the Greek Orthodox Church there, he says that we should brew for two weeks longer than we used to. He says that's why it always tasted bitter the first week."

"Why don't you just open it anyway?"

Stein looked at her tiredly. "I don't know. When you have a patient who bites, why don't you just pet it anyway?"

BJ winced. Chris, a Greek immigrant to Kendrick, was BJ's

greatest triumph, and her worst mistake. He had run a restaurant in Kendrick with his son. Lost and confused, a victim of Alzheimer's, Chris had been brought into Crossroads at BJ's suggestion, ostensibly to manage the cooking while Stein's was rebuilt. Mostly it had been to let Crossroads restore Chris's health and mental faculties. Chris had owned and managed two restaurants in his lifetime; if he had any hope of recovery, it lay in the therapy of working in a restaurant in Crossroads while his mind shook off the degenerative effects of Alzheimer's and healed.

Chris had arrived at a charred ruin surrounded by freshly cut lumber. There were tarps and sleeping areas for the volunteers. Among the workmen, he had seen fauns, centaurs, and a terrifying monster who spoke civilly and introduced himself as the Griffin. The Griffin was convalescing under one of the tarps and helping oversee construction. For a week, Chris had been frightened and silent, moving quietly out of the way while people ate and worked.

After a week, he began cooking over an outdoor fire. The food was simple but delicious, spiced with wild-growing parsley and onions. Stein, delighted, provided more herbs and, on request, mutton, beef, and even fish.

Chris had requested help building a flat grill. Others helped him; soon, he was directing them. They obeyed, obligingly at first, then patiently, finally resignedly.

Chris demanded better cuts of meat, fresher parsley, stronger rosemary. He was up at dawn, checking the lamb and cattle carcasses and frowning at Stein, Melina, and B'Cu.

BJ was first aware of the tensions at the inn when Stein sidled up to her and said conversationally, "So, this Chris had a wife. Tell me, how do you think she died?"

BJ could sympathize. Chris had never worked in a restaurant he had not owned and run absolutely. Stein was ostensibly an innkeeper; principally he was a military commander, and, for the first time in his adult life, he had been outflanked.

She turned to the worktable in the cooking area. "Chris. B'Cu."

B'Cu, a Pygmy who had fled Africa and arrived in Crossroads, glanced at her and smiled, then turned back to helping Chris. The moment he looked back at Chris, he scowled.

The elderly man, in a cotton shirt and baggy pants that probably were new in 1945, held his hands out, palms up, and smiled at BJ. "Beej. How's doctor?"

"Fine, Chris." He was waiting for more. "Really fine."

Now he looked serious. "How's my Stan, my Constantine. OK?"

"He's absolutely fine." She fished in her pocket. "I brought a letter."

He grabbed it away, barely remembering to mutter "Thanks." B'Cu rolled his eyes and moved aside to let Chris work while he read.

They were roasting lamb on a vertical spit which Chris had bullied Stein into installing. The spit turned slowly on a secondary belt which Chris had insisted be connected to the rebuilt water wheel. Chris, still reading, stuck a long, sharp knife against the outer edge of the turning roast, effortlessly peeling off narrow strips of the most-cooked meat into a drip pan.

B'Cu, who believed in seeing his (well, Stefan's) lambs and sheep from womb to pot, was helping. B'Cu stretched on tiptoe, pared meat off the spit which they had removed to the counter, and laboriously chopped slices of it.

Chris snatched the knife from B'Cu and demonstrated the proper way to slice and chop, with the knuckle of the guide finger bent against the knife blade and the finger itself curled out of harm's way. B'Cu snatched the knife back angrily, but did it Chris's way thereafter.

A huge pot bubbled on the fire. B'Cu, frowning at it, said something in clicks and strange vowels to Chris, shaking his head.

Pocketing the letter, Chris gestured at the drying herbs hanging by the fireplace: dill, rosemary, mint. Clearly, this was not the first time they had been through this argument.

B'Cu shook his head and stepped away from the pot.

Chris dropped the ladle and roared at B'Cu, "*Vrazo!*"

B'Cu scowled back stubbornly.

BJ whispered to Melina, " '*Vrazo*'?"

"It means, 'I boil.' He's making soup."

"Does it also mean 'I'm angry'?"

B'Cu snapped a single phrase back. Melina shrugged before BJ could ask.

"And that means 'hyena.' It's an insult." They turned to Stein, who added tiredly, "He says it a lot."

B'Cu tore his apron off and ran lightly out the rear door. Chris shouted after him, and gestured to Melina and to the grill. She sighed, but smiled at him and trotted over.

After a few minutes, she was singing in a soft, clear voice, a song Chris had taught her about missing his homeland:

"Ah, sweet *patrida*, when shall I see you again?"

He relaxed, leaned over and kissed her cheek, and began singing with her.

BJ turned her attention back to the tutoring session. Stefan, perspiring freely, looked like a martial arts student under trial. He was scribbling in a battered spiral notebook as the Griffin and Stein questioned him closely about the class he was failing.

"Do you understand," the Griffin asked, "what this supposed fount of knowledge thinks she wants of you?"

Stefan shook his head miserably.

"Then know her better." The Griffin spoke kindly, but stared Stefan in the eye unrelentingly. "If you graduate from this school, then you may be the first person in the history of Crossroads to become a veterinarian." He lifted a deprecatory talon towards BJ. "The efforts of Dr. Vaughan notwithstanding, you cannot imagine what that might mean to us."

Stefan nodded. "And it is what I want. But first I must pass this research paper course."

"That will be no problem." Stein, a tactician who had spent next to no years in classrooms, shrugged off Stefan's worry. "Think of it as combat." Unconsciously, Stein shifted his feet for balance. "To receive a good grade, find and exploit weaknesses, right?"

BJ said feebly, "I thought the point of study was learning something." Stein and the Griffin each shot her a look, and she shut up.

Stein folded his arms. "Now. This writing teacher: What does she like?"

Stefan screwed up his forehead, and finally said, "Nearly every class, she says that no one knows any history any more."

"A traditionalist." The Griffin nodded. "A formidable opponent."

"But now we know her weakness, right?" Stein pointed a finger at the Griffin. "Find a subject she's heard of but doesn't know much about, research it in the library, and teach her that, in one tiny area, you know more history than she does."

"She wants good research," Stefan said reasonably.

"Research," the Griffin interjected, "is focused and organized history."

Stefan looked puzzled. "History is everything. Please, how can I organize history?"

"No one knows, but everyone is certain," the Griffin said dryly. "Is your professor liberal, or conservative?"

"For Virginia? Liberal, I think. She does not like to talk about kings or presidents."

"Perfectly valid, and her approach will teach you a lot. Write an essay focusing on some group of minorities in history."

"Minorities? The small groups?" Stefan was genuinely puzzled. "But history is written by the people in power. How will this teach me of history?"

"With excellent perspective. Minorities spend most of their lives recovering from history."

"Recovering from history," Stein said thoughtfully, and shook his head quickly. "Nobody does." He withdrew into himself. Stein was the only survivor of his family, who had taken part in the Warsaw Ghetto uprising against the Germans during World War II. No one he had even met in his childhood had survived.

To cover an uncomfortable silence, BJ interjected, "Morgan's a minority, and she's important to Crossroads history."

"Morgan is not a minority," the Griffin corrected. "She is an individual. Minorities have group characteristics. Morgan has red hair, slender fingers, long muscular legs, and a greater love for the texture and moisture of blood than any leech ever identified."

Stein murmured, "She is also very bitter, and very angry. All the time, she rages, and she sorrows that she rages, but she can't stop. So she is bitter, and her next violence is in revenge for her needing her last violence."

"When Morgan first came here," BJ asked, "was she as bitter as she is now?"

"She was exactly the same." The Griffin curled a talon and touched delicately at an old, long scar on his belly. "She did love King Brandal—I believe that firmly—but it did nothing to soften her bloody mind and heart."

"I thought love changed people."

The Griffin stared into space, his golden eagle eyes looking unfocused for once. "Love changes people," he said finally, "but never enough."

BJ didn't comment. The Griffin was in love, but not with another griffin: He and a woman named Laurie Kleinman, from the vet school's anesthesiology staff, had developed a strong friendship which had clearly become love. There was little they could do about it.

"I'll never understand," BJ said finally, "how someone like Morgan was tolerated here even briefly."

"She was the queen. Morgan married King Brandal." Stein spread his hands. "He was young."

"Was she?"

"Well, you have to wonder. Anyway, it wasn't long before strange things were happening all over: animal mutilations, stock bleedings—there was even a unicorn tortured to death." Stein shook her head. "A mass grave was found. A mass grave, in Crossroads! So you see, someone had to face her down.

"The Inspector General—" Stein gave a sidelong glance to the Griffin, who regarded him stonily. "Whoever he is, since people aren't supposed to know, this Inspector General confronted Morgan. And Morgan acted surprised and said, 'Please, we should find a quiet place where you could tell me what you know.' "

The Griffin winced. "Whereupon, in a brush maze not far from here, Morgan ran a spear through the Inspector General's guts, and he very nearly died like the fool he was."

"Not fair." Stein shook a finger at the Griffin, whose tail was lashing at the memory. "After all, she was the queen at the time."

"True. It's enough to make one distrust authority." The Griffin added to BJ, with apparent sincerity, "Though I'm sure that sort of chicanery in high places never happens in your world."

"But she was discovered before the Inspector General died," BJ said thoughtfully, "Or you—wouldn't know all this." She didn't add, "wouldn't be alive"; B'Cu and Chris did not know that the Griffin was the Inspector General, the just but merciless head of Crossroads' security. "She didn't kill him immediately, did she?"

"Very good. Morgan is extremely fond of blood. Perhaps 'fond' is the wrong word; she can't seem to help herself." He added detachedly, "She disemboweled him and bathed her arms in his blood. She was discovered shortly before he would have died."

BJ shuddered. "And then she was exiled."

"Oh, yes. She was blindfolded and driven down the Strangeways, into a not-quite-dead world. She was also prohibited," he said delicately and obliquely, "from touching *The Book of Strangeways*, though she can coerce others to read it for her."

"Prohibited how?" BJ asked.

"Ah." He nodded wisely. "How indeed." And that was his only response.

Stefan rubbed his forearm unconsciously. Although it was DeeDee Parris who had given him the morphine to which he'd become addicted, Morgan had set the events in motion to try and steal a copy of *The Book of Strangeways*. "And that was all they did to her? Just only sent her away?"

The Griffin blinked owlishly, looking annoyed. "Many wished otherwise, but King Brandal loved her too much to do anything worse to her."

"And," said BJ, "that's why no one killed the most deadly invader Crossroads has ever seen."

"Oh, no," Stein and the Griffin said in unison. Stein went on: "Young lady, Crossroads has seen much worse. Terrible invaders and losses—"

The Griffin held up a single clawed digit. "It's a fine example for our young pupil. Attend to a piece of focused history; and afterward I'll ask you about the lessons of it." Stefan nodded alertly, leaning forward and twitching his ears in a way that always startled BJ.

"It was in the first or second decade Anno Domini, European calendar. Troops had been dispatched by Caesar Augustus to Northern Europe under Varus, and they behaved as troops always will; they looked for conquest without hardship. But all they found in the German woods was hardship.

"So there they were, being shot at with spears from the trees and moving into a land where it was always cold, and the birds and the animals were different, and every once in a while the fog rolled in and spears and swords came out of nowhere and there were fewer troops. What could they do?"

Melina sat down at a nearby table, fascinated by the story but not yet recognizing it. Once in a while, Chris would step over and hold a small chunk of cooked meat between his thumb and forefinger, dangling it in front of the Griffin as though it were a dog treat. The Griffin always looked pained and magnificently disdainful, but BJ noticed that he always ate the snack.

"I'll tell you what they did," Stein said, slapping the counter. "They did what good Romans did everywhere, trying to hold territory. They made a camp, they did drills, and they built roads. Big, ugly stone roads, that cross Europe even today. Only this time, one of their roads crossed one of ours."

Melina clutched the cross with one hand and said fearfully, "*Milites*," as though they might break down the door at any moment.

"*Milites*," Stein agreed. "Roman soldiers, the best trained fighting unit the world has ever produced. Without equipment, they could equip themselves; without supplies, they could supply themselves. They marched into a world with strange animals and even strange people, and a less trained force would have broken apart and run then and there.

"But they didn't, did they? They stayed, and fought, and grew older. And they won, and they won, and no one could stop them. Even the Stepfather God, defeated and killed—"

"Oh no," Melina said flatly, suddenly relieved. "That's not history. You are wrong. The Stepfather God was never killed. He lives now. You, above all, should know that. You should know that," she repeated, suddenly troubled. "The Stepfather God is—"

Stein interposed, "Back to the main story, I think."

"Very well." The Griffin unconsciously struck a pose, lecturing. "The *milites'* commanding officer was Marcus Gaius Scipio. We know this because he inscribed a tablet at every camp. He was ambitious, and knew that military success often precedes political success. One of the tablets he left bears the name Marcus Transitus—their name for Crossroads. Following the tradition of Scipio Africanus, he chose to win battles in the new land for Rome, and for himself."

BJ was unimpressed. She had seen re-creations of Roman warfare in a few movies: phalanxes of men in sandals and what looked like pleated skirts, waving short swords and throwing spears. "Still, they were primitive," she said.

"You don't know what training does."

"It makes people more organized. Does that really make a difference?"

Stein edged closer to her. "They built a camp. They built walled enclosures, and they rounded up and fenced in all the species they could."

"Civilization," the Griffin said dryly, "is largely a matter of discovering, defining, and eliminating weeds, pests, and enemies."

"But he lost."

"Oh, no." Stein was shaking his head as though she were blind to the truth. "He won. Crossroads fell, and the *milites* conquered it."

Stefan, Melina, and BJ stared at each other in confusion.

"By the time they won," Stein said, "there was no one left but themselves. And one day, they marched down a road they thought they knew, and they were gone for good. No one knows where."

BJ said, "I've always assumed that oral history was only as accurate as the oldest living witness."

Stein and the Griffin regarded her silently. She added uncomfortably, "And even then, it's suspect. How old is Crossroads?"

"Geologically?" The Griffin went on quickly. "Just look at the hills you live in. Aging mountains, my dear, like the Appalachians, as opposed to your Rockies or the younger mountains in northern Crossroads—"

"I was speaking historically. Stefan's question concerned history."

Stefan, not aware of any tension, asked in the ensuing silence, "I have only heard early stories of the *milites*, nothing before them. Please, what is the history before that?"

Stein shook his head. "We're not sure."

BJ frowned. "Have you asked Fields?"

"Who do you think I'd ask first?" Clearly, BJ's question had gotten under Stein's skin.

"And he didn't know any earlier history, either."

Stein bit his lip. The Griffin murmured, "*Touché.*"

Stein sagged. "All right, he didn't. The earliest history of Crossroads anybody knows is that it was conquered by the Romans in the first century A.D. Then the Romans were tricked out of Crossroads, and everybody started coming back. That part took centuries."

"But before they came back, they had to leave. Crossroads completely emptied out, didn't it?"

"Yes."

"Down the Strangeways." BJ's mind leapt forward. "And that's why our world had unicorns, and griffins, and rocs—"

"And fauns," the Griffin finished. "And satyrs, and many others who never made it back into Crossroads and died out. It seems to have been extremely disorganized; individuals and small groups fled to each world, rather than one species per world. Perhaps that was for survival. If so, it was a bad decision, fatal for some species, nearly fatal to others."

"But someone had to guide them, either with *The Book of Strangeways*—"

Stein said quietly, "This is a guess, but we don't think there was a book of Strangeways. We think it was all in someone's head."

"And he died."

"Yes." Stein shook his head. "Maybe. Don't assume before asking."

BJ fell silent, thinking. "May I ask you something else?"

Stein smiled, relieved at the change of subject. "Please do, young lady. Not that I can always answer you, but I'll try."

"Thank you. Once, someone said 'The great god Pan is dead'—"

"Where did you hear that?" Stein stared at her in amazement.

Actually, she had heard Stein quote it, affectionately, to the satyr named Fields who was responsible for bringing veterinarians into Crossroads, and who cared for a great many of the people and animals in Crossroads. "I heard someone say it once. When was it said originally?"

Stein said nothing. Finally the Griffin said, "It won't do to underestimate her, will it? You may as well tell her."

Stein said reluctantly, "First century A.D. It was in the Mediterranean. Someone yelled it off an island to a man named Thamos."

BJ nodded. "Was this around the same time that the *milites* came to Crossroads?"

"Well—yes. A little later, perhaps. But that's no proof the two things are related, you know."

The Griffin looked away in disgust.

Stefan broke in politely. "All this is good to know, but I do not think it will help me with my research paper."

Stein sighed. "Right. Thank you for bringing us back to the present. Is your only problem what to write about and how to research?"

Stefan shook his head, exposing his horns with each toss of his curly hair. "She doesn't like how I put things together, either."

The Griffin tapped a talon impatiently. "She will now, whether she knows why or not. Repeat after me: *Narratio*—No, let's stick with English. Introduction, narration, argument, interrogation, and peroration or conclusion."

Stein nodded approvingly. "Aristotle. Stefan, repeat after him like he said."

Stefan echoed the Griffin dubiously.

"Very good. These are the parts of classical rhetoric. Now we'll discuss what each of them do."

The Griffin lectured; Stefan, tongue poking out at the corner as he concentrated, wrote frantically. BJ listened for a while, then, secure in the knowledge that she would never take college English again, drifted off and watched Chris cook.

BJ filched some olives from Chris's supplies and chewed thoughtfully. If Crossroads had to depopulate again, what would happen to the species here?

She choked on an olive pit; Melina tapped over and thumped her back helpfully. BJ coughed the pit out and gasped, "Thanks."

If Crossroads fell to Morgan, BJ would have to leave with the others. BJ had been dying, slowly but inevitably, when she arrived in Crossroads. Until this moment, she hadn't even wondered what would happen to her own health if she had to leave Crossroads forever.

*   *   *

With evening came the rush of customers. Stefan excused himself to do homework. BJ gave up trying to chat with Melina, who was too busy, and sat waiting, sipping a soft cider and looking for Fiona.

Fiona strode in with the door flung wide, attempting an entrance. She was wearing a different denim miniskirt, one with multicolored patches sewn into it, and she had a black cloak draped over her vest. She had changed her stockings to fishnets interwoven with glitter, and she was pretending to be casual.

A green woman fully seven feet tall brushed past her. Fiona took one look at the woman, who had bark where humans have hair, and slunk in quietly; Stein's was not an easy place to make an entrance.

BJ stood up hastily. "Over here."

Fiona looked around the room. In one corner, a man with antlers was chatting with a small brown man who jumped up and down as he chattered back. " 'And the usual crowd was there,' " she said. "I'm going to like this place."

"Everybody does, once they get used to it." BJ used her foot to pull a chair over for Fiona. "Look, I know you're pretty sophisticated, but you should watch yourself in here. It's usually a friendly crowd, but they offer some surprises."

"I'm hard to surprise." Fiona said. Then, glancing to one side, she squeaked inarticulately.

At the next table, two Meat People were happily eating gyros, delicately flicking the tomatoes and onions aside with their clawed fingers. One of them had noticed Fiona staring, and without thinking had smiled politely, full-fanged, at her. He covered his mouth with both hands, embarrassed.

"Relax," BJ whispered, and said aloud, "It's good to see you again. Let me introduce you." She shoved Fiona forward. "This is Fiona Bannon. Fiona, this is Donrr—"

"Dohnrr."

"I'm sorry. Donnnnrr."

Fiona unhesitatingly extended her hand. "I'm very pleased, Dohnrr."

He brightened. BJ was impressed by, and a little jealous of, Fiona's poise and pronunciation.

He insisted on buying them ale. BJ protested that she had already been paid, but he shook his head and passed Melina part of a gold sixpiece. They thanked him, and he turned quickly and quietly back to his own meal.

Fiona sipped her ale thoughtfully. "For a carnivore, he's sure shy."

The outside door creaked. Melina turned toward it and gaped. Others turned. In the end, almost the entire inn was gaping.

BJ turned, swearing she would not look foolish, and realized a few seconds later that she was sitting with her mouth hanging open.

The man at the door, in a cashmere coat and silk scarf, shrugged out of his coat without seeming to move. Underneath, he was wearing a white cotton dinner jacket and impeccably creased trousers. The coat folded neatly over his arm, and the scarf drifted over it to drape exactly in half. He glanced around, showing no fear of the strange company staring at him. "Is there perhaps somewhere I might hang this?" he said carefully, with just a trace of an Hispanic accent.

Melina, her eyes wide, tapped over to him and held her arms out for the coat. The man looked at her in surprise and smiled suddenly, flashing dazzling white teeth. "Please, I didn't mean to stare. You're quite lovely."

Melina's mouth hung open. He handed her the coat and bowed to her, bending close to her face; he was at least six feet tall. He was in his late thirties, with smooth dark hair and light brown skin; he was almost excruciatingly handsome. "Thank you," he said, staring into her eyes, and Melina, who had seen murder and sword fights and the open copulation of animals, scuttled away blushing.

BJ was gazing intently at his shirt. This man is in the middle of Crossroads, she thought blankly, and his white dress shirt is bleached, starched, and ironed.

She realized that the man was staring back, raising one arched eyebrow. She hastily straightened her skirt and shawl. She had made them herself and loved them, but suddenly felt terribly underdressed.

Chris moved past their table, carrying a steaming plate of arni skordostoumbi, wine-braised lamb. He froze in place, eyes fixed on the man, and his wrinkled face spread into a wide smile as he balanced the plate in one hand and held out the other. "Profess'."

The younger man looked absolutely delighted. "Chris!" He pumped his hand. "How are you, sir? Wonderful to see you." He glanced around. "Running another restaurant, I see."

Stein, coming forward to greet the new customer, stopped dead. Chris laughed and shook his head. "Oh, no, Profess'. I cook here."

He shrugged. "Maybe I make suggest."

"If you know Chris," Stein said, "you'll know he does more than that. Good evening, young man. I'm Stein."

"Ah. The owner." The man bowed, then offered his hand. "Estevan Protera."

BJ whispered to Fiona, "That's Professor Estevan Protera?"

Fiona whispered back, "I thought you knew. You're doing work for him."

"Only by mail. He was on leave last spring and summer; I've never met him."

Stein brought him over. "Dr. Protera, I think maybe you should meet Dr. BJ Vaughan. She's a veterinarian, and I believe you've corresponded."

He faded into the background, satisfied with BJ's look of consternation. She had never told Stein about her work for Protera.

The Professor bowed to BJ fully, then took her hand. "I'm very grateful that you would take time from your own work to accommodate mine."

"You're welcome." Even while Protera was working to put her at ease, BJ felt rough-edged and awkward. Her dating experience had been limited primarily to infatuated and slightly gawky young men from Virginia, none of whom had even owned a dinner jacket. "It's no trouble, really."

"It is, though, and thank you for taking it." He leaned forward conspiratorially. "What is the young faun woman's name?"

"Melina."

When BJ spoke, Melina's ears twitched and she hurried over, ignoring an annoyed call from another patron. "What do you want?" she breathed earnestly at Protera, as though BJ had never spoken.

He gestured at the table as though it contained a feast. "This looks wonderful. Did you help with it?" She bobbed her head. "Thank you for cooking it. I'm afraid that I'm a messy eater; could we please have some cloth napkins?"

Melina blinked, tried to say "yes," then turned and fled. She returned with white linen napkins in seconds, nearly vaulting the neighboring table in her haste.

Protera, taking the linen, bowed so low, the napkins might have been a crown she'd given him. He passed BJ a napkin as though she were royalty. She set it in her lap, suddenly embarrassed that she hadn't thought to request them herself.

Ale came to the table, brought by Chris himself. Protera tasted it, smacked his lips, thanked Chris, and touched steins with Fiona and BJ. He leaned forward. "And now, Dr. Vaughan—"

"BJ. And this is Fiona."

"How nice." His smile all but hurt BJ's eyes, and he seemed to mean it every time. "And now let me tell you what I will be doing with your observations. As you guessed, the presence of Earth's moon over Crossroads is highly significant." He said dismissively, "I've written a small piece, barely a start, suggesting that Crossroads is like our own drifting continent, moving across our Earth—"

"Reality tectonics." Fiona was clearly envious, whether of the research or of Protera's ability to be modest about it was unclear.

"You too? I knew that BJ had seen my essay when she wrote agreeing to make observations for me. At any rate, I hope to pin down more closely where Crossroads, or part of Crossroads, lies in relation to the rest of the globe. Sun and moon positions seemed the most obvious data—"

"Dr. Protera—" BJ was almost bouncing up and down in her chair. She had given this a great deal of thought.

"Estevan." He smiled at her again, and oh my God, but he was handsome.

She collected her thoughts. "The sun- and moon-rises are one thing, but have you thought of recording estrous cycles in animals?"

Protera raised one elegant eyebrow and nodded for her to go on, refilling her stein.

She sipped, feeling as she hadn't felt since the first time her father had taken her to a real restaurant by herself. "Some species go into season once a year." Protera looked politely blank, and she realized belatedly that English was his second language. "Do you know that term? Go into heat?"

He raised his own stein and turned it, admiring it against the light. "I have lived with cats. I know that it means they imitate grand opera for a several days, then set about the serious business of generating kittens if you have not prevented them."

"Okay." BJ was stumbling over herself, full of the wonderful idea she had and could share with this brilliant and urbane man. "There are triggers for the estrous cycle, and we think most of them are seasonal—expecially, according to lab tests, the hours of daylight to which a species is exposed. I could compare common species here with data on species in Virginia and elsewhere, to see if animal cycles were running earlier or later. So, do you want me to record information on estrous cycles and species?"

He smiled appreciatively. "It is a brilliant and perceptive idea,

BJ. The data would be most helpful, if there were enough of it. I salute your fine mind." He raised his stein. BJ blushing, ducked her head modestly and sipped from her own stein.

She nearly choked on the ale as he added, "I think twenty or thirty seasons of data could be marginally significant. Tell me: How long did you intend to stay in Crossroads?"

BJ dabbed at her lips with her napkin, hesitated, and finally said, "Actually, I hadn't intended to come to Crossroads. I have no idea how long I'll be staying."

"Ah, well." He shrugged and pursed his lips, dismissing the suggested project. "Still, a wonderful idea, and thank you."

Fiona grinned at her. BJ shot her a withering look.

Stein came back to the table. "Dr. Protera, I hope you're enjoying your stay. We're about to begin a kind of bar game, with what are called catchlets."

BJ put her hand out automatically. Stein spun a wooden catchlet in the air and she caught it, enjoying the display of coordination in a place where, once, she had been clumsy.

BJ had made a great effort to stay current at catchlets. It was more than a game, much as Stein was more than an innkeeper.

To Fiona and Protera, Stein said, "It's a kind of tagging game. Very popular now. I introduced it."

Fiona accepted hers and turned it in her hand interestedly. It was a short, barely pointed stick with a broad crosspiece; the cross bar, at the start of the hilt, had upturned ends to catch the opponent's catchlet.

BJ held her own out. "If you twist it while you're parrying, you can actually pop the other person's stick right out of his hand—"

"Okay, okay. I see that." Fiona twisted it this way and that experimentally. "What are the rules?"

Stein beamed at her. "We appreciate your not actually killing anyone in disarming them—"

"And?"

He scratched his head. "No, that's all." He passed a wooden catchlet to Protera. "I should mention that it's a wagering game. Would you care to try?"

Protera held it in his hand clumsily and made an awkward feint at the table. He fell short by more than two feet. "I'll do my best," he said, embarrassed.

BJ sympathized. On her first foray into Stein's before her body had begun healing, she had dropped her catchlet several times, and had felt clumsy and foolish the entire evening.

"Well." Stein picked up his own catchlet and said dubiously, "Good luck, then."

Protera whipped his catchlet upright in a quick, chest-high salute, then brought the stick higher as an afterthought. BJ turned away, biting her lip and concentrating.

Stein and Melina distributed the rest of the wooden catchlets as the bar divided into two roughly even sides. Fiona dangled her stick between thumb and forefinger, looking from side to side at the chatting, disorderly players, from the Meat People to the giant green woman. "Well, this shouldn't be too bad."

She raised her catchlet into guard position. BJ frowned. "You're holding it way too low."

"I'll be fine," Fiona said confidently, as Stein called, "Begin!" She held her stick fractionally higher.

Melina, usually so gentle, leapt across the inn with a shriek and kicked a chair over in Fiona's path. Fiona, startled, stumbled backwards against the table. Melina shoved the crosspiece of the catchlet into Fiona's stomach, hard enough to knock the wind out of her.

When Fiona crossed her arms over her stomach, Melina knocked Fiona's catchlet away, tapped the startled woman lightly on the throat and said happily, "Dead." Before Fiona could say anything, Melina was halfway across the room.

BJ disarmed Dohnrr, patted him lightly on the head, and spun in time to parry his spouse. "Step back," she panted to Fiona, and rolled across a table, throwing cider into the face of the oncoming green woman.

She glanced back at Estevan Protera. He was standing, not dodging, and he had not yet been "killed." He was unwrinkled, and with each second he looked more sure of himself.

Eventually, BJ fell to the green woman, who immediately fell to a backhanded stab by Stein himself. It was the longest BJ had ever lasted in a freestyle team fight. She looked around to see who was left beside Stein, who never failed to be last. Usually it was one of the green women, because of their long reach.

The floor was clear but for Stein and Protera. Stein was perspiring, panting, moving constantly: an overhand cut, a low lunge, a sidelong swipe. Estevan Protera, moving his right arm so rapidly it blurred, was otherwise motionless, and still immaculate.

They fought for minute after minute, Stein lunging determinedly, Protera parrying almost effortlessly.

Finally Stein, apparently tired, lowered his guard. Protera lunged, extending himself too far. Stein, his catchlet pulled back almost to his chest, beat Protera's thrust sideways and stepped inside his arm. Protera, startled, pulled his arm back much farther than necessary to get the point of his catchlet between himself and Stein.

Stein, with a grunt of relief, struck his catchlet on Protera's shirt-front, leaving a dent. Protera mock-clutched his stomach and palmed a sixpiece of gold from his pocket, passing the coin to Stein. The older man, barely noticing, collapsed into a chair, gasping.

Protera knelt by the chair, concerned. "I'm so sorry. I meant no harm—"

"That was wonderful." Stein wiped his forehead with a towel. "That was absolutely wonderful. You have a gift. Where did you learn to fight like that?"

Protera missed, or ignored, Stein's use of 'fight' instead of 'play.' "I was a champion fencer in college. International competitions. It has been a decade, but I practice." He smiled ruefully. "At first these sticks seemed so short."

"Close work." Stein nodded. "It was the only way I got you, drawing you in too close and getting inside your guard." He gasped, still breathing hard. "Please, come any time."

Fiona, discontent, turned the stick over in her hands. Clearly, she was seldom this bad at anything. "Excuse me a moment," she said firmly, and added, "I'll be back some other evening. Very nice meeting you all." She walked to the door quickly, catchlet in hand.

Melina moved to get the stick back, but Stein grabbed the faun's hand. "Let her take it." He chuckled. "She's dangerous, that one. Off to practice."

To her surprise, BJ disliked his laughing at Fiona. "I know exactly how she feels," she said. "I felt badly the first time I played—"

"Did you?" Stein said in surprise, but spoiled his sympathy by adding, "You should have. You were terrible."

"And now you do well," Protera put in. "Perhaps we can play at swords some other night." He yawned. "Forgive me; I have traveled farther than usual today. Farther than I know, perhaps."

He stood to go, then turned back. "One other thing, Mr. Stein." He did not drop his voice, but somehow sounded as though he were imparting a secret. "If you could visit me at my cottage two nights from now, when I'm settled, I believe we should discuss some aspects of Crossroads. And please ask your erudite winged friend, the, ah—" He glanced queryingly at BJ.

"The Griffin," BJ said. "I know him; don't worry."

He nodded, relieved. "In that case, please attend yourself. It would help to have someone medical in attendance."

"You have another experiment to run in Crossroads?"

"I hope not." He glanced around the room. "In fact, I pray not. Please don't mention this meeting to any other of our acquaintances."

When Melina came back to the table to refill the steins, Estevan Protera was in the middle of a long, fairly funny story about a train ride from Milan to Geneva with two nuns and four punk rockers. It required a great deal of explaining for Stein; BJ obliged gladly and wondered to herself why, when Protera was asking for confidentiality, he had glanced at Chris.

S·I·X

IT WAS SUNRISE. Stefan, arriving at the inn to sleep after having checked on his flock, had insisted on driving BJ back to her cottage, but had also insisted, politely, that he himself would sleep at Stein's. Horvat had barked at him, and BJ had snapped at Horvat more sharply than was necessary and gone directly to bed.

BJ, tired but wide-awake, let Horvat out and back in, made some tea and sat brooding.

When BJ had first met Stefan, she had been terminally ill and planning suicide; she tried to keep her distance from him. Now she was no longer ill, but he had withdrawn from her during the misery of recovering from morphine addiction.

All in all, their life together was like an endless series of unsuccessful first dates.

When she had returned to Crossroads in June, they had not seen each other. BJ had been setting up her practice and renovating one of Crossroads' many abandoned cottages, relics of past farmers and shepherds. She sent word to Stein's several times, even resorting to messages via Stein's disreputable parrot; Stefan never answered.

BJ found an article in the Western Vee library about morphine addiction among the first anesthesiologists, and copied it for Stefan. Stein took it thoughtfully. She never heard whether or not Stefan had received it, and he never spoke of it.

One day, while she was struggling to plaster the inside walls, she heard a noise out the window. She looked out. Stefan, even thinner than she had remembered, was determinedly sorting and gathering stones for repairing her chimney.

She took a double portion of cheese and bread from the spring-house for lunch. He sat with her, said nothing, and left.

The next day, she asked him at lunch, "Who's tending your flock?"

"B'Cu." His voice, light and musical, was hoarse from lack of use. "He had a flock of his own, but—"

"I know." She had only met B'Cu twice at this time. Once was the day his sheep had been massacred. B'Cu was stoic about the entire thing. "Can you talk to him?"

"By signs, now. The Griffin helps me, but he is very tired. He has been hurt so badly."

BJ said gently, "He'll recover. People and animals do."

"Sometimes." He said little more that day.

The following day it rained in the morning, and they painted the cottage interior white. The clouds broke at noon, and they sat outdoors and watched as the sun left the ground steaming. The small brooks were all full, and rippled into cataracts around all of the rocks. More rain and they would erode the hillside, and might cause mud slides, but at this level they were merely loud and musical.

Stefan stared at it all, his eyes full of tears. "This is very beautiful. This is more beautiful than I think it can be, elsewhere. And I almost helped Morgan take it away, and it feels—" He burst out, "I never thought I would feel anything again."

She kissed his cheek, and held him while he cried. Afterward, he stayed away for several days.

In another week they were talking. The week after that, on a trip back to the vet school for supplies, BJ found out from Laurie that Stefan had applied to Western Vee, and she was furious that he had done it through Laurie and not her.

"Look," Laurie said bluntly, "he'd rather die than be dependent on you."

"But why?"

Laurie scowled. "Don't lie to yourself. You have more sense than that."

BJ bit her tongue before snapping that she didn't need criticism of her love life from a woman in love with a griffin. It would be cruel, and besides, in this instance BJ felt that she had remarkably little sense.

She realized she had let her tea get cold; she sipped it hastily. The cottage was quiet; no clients had arrived, and Daphni was already outside, covering herself with the dying underbrush of autumn and lying hopefully in wait for birds. BJ picked up her copy of *Veterinary Economics*, arguably the most useless prose in Crossroads, and smiled wryly as she noticed that the corner was chewed—

She dropped the magazine. The door was ajar, and Horvat had gone.

She dashed out in panic, staring wildly up and down the hill. She couldn't see him, but he could easily hide if he wanted. What would Gredya say if BJ had lost her child?

A bush rustled near the stream from the spring; BJ dove into it, arms spread. A cedar waxwing flew out, and Daphni mewed reproachfully. "Sorry." She stood. "Horvat!"

To her immense relief, she heard a single loud bark from down the hill. She ran partway down, careful of her footing on the incline, and saw that a man was approaching. She frowned worriedly. Horvat wasn't barking at him, and hadn't run. Normally, a Wyr pup would have yipped at an approaching stranger, or raised his hackles, defending his territory even from other Wyr. Horvat was shy for a pup, and would have run back to her if he were frightened. She returned to her cottage and palmed a metal catchlet, draping a shawl over it.

She stepped back out. Horvat was on his hind legs, bouncing eagerly up to kiss the man in front of the house. Fields bent down and caught him, kissing him back with none of the fussiness most people would show.

As the satyr bent, his horns poked from under his dark locks, and his ears twitched when Horvat licked him.

He was dressed in overalls, as always. He had explained to BJ, recently, how much he loved having pockets. "These," he said, plunging his knobbly hands into them, "these are so you can walk and still have things. So wonderful."

It seemed to her like awfully informal clothing for a god.

Fields set Horvat down and smiled as the pup tugged at the break in his overalls over his cloven hooves. "Good morning, BJ." He smiled at her. "You look well."

BJ had prepared herself for Fields's look, and was able to smile back without blushing or checking to see if she were dressed. "Thanks. Can I offer you tea or coffee?"

"Water. Thank you. Bring it, and a pack; we must go this morning."

She didn't move yet. "Where?"

He smiled very wide. "Should not the unicorns see their doctor, miss?"

She dashed inside, leapt into coveralls and picked up her pack, dashed back, pumped spring water into a glass, dashed back outside and picked a sprig of mint, dashed back inside and dropped it in the glass, and dashed back outside, handing the water to the laughing Fields.

"They will wait." He took the water. "There will be no births today." He downed the glass quickly, some of it dribbling on his beard. The impression he gave was that of a happy animal rather than a glutton. He smiled kindly at her. "We chose the good vet, Doctor. You love this work."

BJ took the glass back and set it by the door, then threw a sheet over the Healing Sign. "Let's go."

Horvat ran around them in circles, stopping to walk beside each of them, then scampering off and having to run frantically to catch up. After the first half mile, BJ quit worrying about him.

As they walked east, the hillside grew steeper, changing to cliffs. Below, they could see the roadway that led back to Virginia (and elsewhere, BJ reminded herself uneasily). Fields strode forward easily even as the ground grew rockier; BJ was glad she had brought her walking staff.

"Have you heard about Rudy and Bambi's wedding?" BJ was half expecting Fields to officiate.

"Of course. I will be there. I will even help to bring some of the guests who—" he winked "—live far away."

BJ said immediately, "Annie. She's a missionary in Chad. I'll write her, but I don't know if she can get here. . . ." She trailed off, feeling foolish. If anyone could get to Crossroads, was there a reason that Annie couldn't?

"For her I will walk to the road myself." Fields reached into a pocket of his overalls and handed BJ a carefully drawn map of Africa. "You send this to her, fast as you can, and we will meet her."

BJ looked worried. "I don't know that I can get it to her in time."

Fields chewed at one of his thick thumbnails, then sighed and shrugged. "There is nothing else to do, then. I will send Stein's parrot."

BJ wrinkled her nose. Fields glanced involuntarily at his own neck, where a recent beak nip was still visible.

She pocketed the map. "I'll give him the message. Give him flight directions and ask Stein to send him by." She resolved to do the talking outside, no matter how cold it was.

They came to a wide stream, impressive even though its bed was only half full. The ripples were obscured by a louder sound, barely under a roar. Horvat, hot from all his playing, crossed the trail beside the stream, lay down in a pool, and lapped blissfully at the water.

BJ followed the trail to the cliff's edge and looked down. A giant hazel eye with a blue pupil seemed to gaze back up.

BJ had a single panicstricken thought of the Great and their pitiless milky eyes with dark pupils. This eye was huge even for them.

Then she saw a cloud, reflected in the blue, and she realized what she was seeing: a bowl-shaped valley, cut in the cliff face, with a circular spill pool where the stream had come down the cliff face.

Fields put a hand on her shoulder and pointed to the trail. "You see why I did not want to take the truck?"

"You hate the truck. But I do see." BJ whistled for Horvat.

They descended on the trail, a winding switchback next to the waterfall. Fields navigated the drop easily; BJ followed more cautiously even with a staff. As they came down into the trees, which still had yellow leaves clinging to them, the sound of the falls became muffled. They followed the trail to the flowers— now dark, dry seed pods—and grass by the pool.

As they approached, first one horned head lifted, then the others, as though there were some bond between them all. They stood, horns raised but not threatening, facing Fields and BJ.

She frowned. They were still beautiful, with large dark eyes and tapered faces that were a mix of horse and goat. Their legs were still graceful, muscled and thin, ending in a split hoof as symmetric as any arc drawn with a compass or a French curve. All the same, something had changed—

BJ stopped dead. Horvat, daunted by the unicorns, came back to tug at the bottom of her coveralls; she barely noticed. Half of the unicorns had full, drooping bellies. Almost all of the mares were pregnant.

"Oh." She ran to the first one and touched its back unhesitatingly. Horvat, subdued, lay down and watched her from a distance.

She collected herself. "All right. This is your first exam, isn't it? First we'll check your eyes, your gums—" She talked smoothly and reassuringly, though the unicorn was calmer than BJ.

She said self-consciously, "Excuse me," and lifted the unicorn's tail. The anus and vagina looked normal; there was no swelling and no evidence of any bleeding or fluid. She took the unicorn's temperature and wrote the figure down quickly in the note pad she always carried on call.

Now she dropped to her knees and felt along the belly. She noticed as she did so that the unicorn's teats, nearly a goatlike udder, were already beginning to fill. She tried to imagine unicorn milk.

For a moment, predictably, she thought of her mother, who had loved unicorns and had sun-catchers and pictures of several. She remembered her mother telling her that unicorn horns could cure any disease—

Sometimes, months after a death, the pain comes back sudden and sharp, for reasons you can't control. BJ's mother had committed suicide rather than face the eventual suffering and mental deterioration of Huntington's chorea.

BJ felt several horns stroke gently at her back; unicorns, who knew both innocence and grief when it was nearby, cherished the one and comforted the other.

Fields said softly, "And what are you thinking, Doctor? Do you maybe need some help?"

"I'm okay, thanks." She brushed at her cheeks before Fields could see her tears. "I'm nearly done." She felt the unicorn's belly some more, not really knowing what to look for, and moved to the next mare.

She did the entire herd the same way. The only other interruption was when a male unicorn stood in her way. "Excuse me?" She wasn't sure how much they understood.

He waved his horn once in front of her. He had a gold band on his horn, the first veterinary work BJ had done in Crossroads.

"Hi, fella." She stroked his mane and, on impulse, kissed his nose. "You look great."

He raised his thick upper lip and licked her cheek with a tongue that barely felt rough at all. BJ moved on, feeling somehow blessed.

The herd—the serenity of unicorns—was large enough that the exams took quite a while. By noon, BJ had a fair understanding of unicorn OB/Gyn., and she was imagining a fine addition to Lao's *Guide to the Unbiological Species*. She did the last exam with a fine professional calm, though she certainly didn't need to make the unicorn more at ease. She knelt in the soft grass and moss and felt the unicorn mare's belly on both sides.

Her eyes widened as she felt it again. Fields's ears twitched back and forth as though they were independent of him as he knelt by her. "What is it that you feel?"

"Something amazing. I wish I were more sure."

"What?" He was crowding her now, excited. "What is it?"

BJ smiled and said, as though imparting a great surprise to a child, "Is it common for unicorns to have twins?"

In the silence that followed, she noticed for the first time the bristly skin near his broad nostrils, with just a hint of a goat's nose. His eyes were wide, shocked, and very human. "Are you sure?"

"I could do a rectal exam, but—" She gestured at the size of the animal. "If they're anything like horse mares, I could hurt her just doing the exam. Anyway, I'm pretty sure. Mr. Fields, are you all right?"

"I cannot believe." BJ took one of his big-knuckled hands and guided it along either side of the unicorn's belly, to feel the two distinct bodies. He turned his head away, saying nothing.

"Is it a problem?" BJ swallowed. In horses, twins can be disastrous. "Do they have trouble foaling twins?"

"I do not know." He managed a weak smile. "It has not happened in my lifetime."

"And how long is that?"

He looked away into the valley, and the river below winding through the trees. The trees were in full color: scarlet, golden, and a rich purple that BJ had seen nowhere else but Crossroads. Soon they would lose their leaves. Fields shut his eyes. "Long enough that it is very unusual. This is bad, BJ. This is very, very bad."

"Maybe I'm wrong," she said finally. "Maybe it won't be twins at all."

The unicorn turned her head and regarded BJ mournfully; BJ blushed. She had always been a terrible liar. She stood. "I'm done here."

"For now, yes." Fields was still staring down the river valley. The other unicorns glided up to him and placed their horns against his body, offering comfort. BJ wondered what was troubling him so. He patted them absently and looked away. "You will come back perhaps when the babies are born?"

"Wouldn't miss it," she promised, wishing that Lee Anne would be with her then. She slipped her backpack on and collected Horvat, who had fallen asleep with his paws in the air.

They stood at the lip of the bowl valley, looking down. The stream flowed out of it toward the broad, meandering River Laetyen; a trail followed the stream down. On the way, the stream crossed the road which, BJ knew, led to Stein's one way, and the other—if you knew all the correct turns and didn't become lost forever—into Crossroads.

She bent, staring down. The metal catchlet poked from her pack, the blade shining. Fields slid it back out of sight for her. "You should never need that when you are with me."

"I shouldn't. I have needed it, when I was with you."

He nodded, looking even sadder.

"Mr. Fields?"

He turned.

"You're close to Stein."

He nodded. "He came to me as a small boy." He smiled. "So thin, so little. I have raised him."

Stein looked many years older than Fields did. As BJ had suspected, unicorn twins were very unusual.

"But you were with us at Stein's inn when Morgan invaded, backed by the Wyr and the others. You never fought when Stein's inn was in danger, never even picked up a weapon."

Fields looked ashamed but adamant. "I will not hurt my children. I cannot hurt one over another when they fight."

"Then you can't defend us."

"I can do that." He bobbed his head vigorously, sending his curls waving every which way. "But I can never hurt one of you."

They walked on down to the meadow lands before the cliffs. Fields stopped and stared down the river valley, seeming to look a long way indeed. "Do you think less of me because I will not fight?"

"Oh no." BJ braced herself and put an arm around his waist. "It makes me think more of you than I do of me."

He laughed. "Maybe, but you will outsmart me often. I am needed another place; may I—?"

Fields would always be needed another place.

"I can walk back alone from here. Thank you, Mr. Fields."

He kissed her cheek, seeming as affectionate as he did salacious. Then he pulled back and winked at her. "I think maybe now you know my real name."

BJ said steadily, "I do, but I met you as Fields. I think I'll call you that, if you don't mind."

He nodded respectfully to her. "If you like, if it is easier, please do."

"Thank you, Mr. Fields." She added awkwardly, "Are you sure you wouldn't like to come home for dinner with me?"

He bowed in acknowledgment of the invitation. "Some other

day." He winked. "But I will call first. I would hate to bother you when you are with my Stefan."

Laughing, he strode easily down the trail by the stream. BJ watched him part of the way, then whistled to Horvat and turned to go.

A cultured voice said reprovingly, "You shouldn't walk unarmed."

"I'm armed." BJ pulled out the catchlet. "I shouldn't walk unready."

Horvat dashed back from where he had been investigating a bush and planted himself firmly between the Griffin and BJ, growling, his tail curved up and forward and his teeth showing.

"Here now," the Griffin said, but he was clearly pleased. "I meant her no harm. Don't bark at your betters, young man."

BJ felt a sudden chill; he had emphasized 'man' slightly. The Griffin—the Inspector General—knew all about Horvat.

He caught her eye and nodded. "Oh, yes. It's not the sort of thing that goes unnoticed, Doctor. Have a care with him. Do not be afraid to ask questions, or tell your troubles."

"I'm not afraid to ask," BJ said.

The Griffin nodded, his wickedly sharp beak seeming to smile as he regarded her. "And we will leave the subject of telling your troubles alone for the present. How are you?"

BJ had the pack open. "I should be asking you how you are. Or telling you. I wish I'd had a chance to do this yesterday."

"I'm fairly well, thank you." He settled back on his haunches, exposing his belly. It was crosshatched with scarring.

BJ ran quick fingers over the newest, pinkest scar, which was marked on either side by suture holes. "That's mending beautifully. With luck you won't have much trouble with muscle tissue underneath." She sighed. "I wish all my patients could heal inside Crossroads."

"Just now they do."

"Good thing, too. I'm still learning." She looked at the three-foot, jagged scar, clearly the oldest, running from his stomach up to his rib cage. "You know, outside Crossroads, you never would have survived that cut."

"I very nearly didn't anyway. That, my dear, was my introduction to Morgan."

BJ shivered. Her own introduction to Morgan had been a very brief encounter with a woman who killed her own troops, bathed in blood to the elbow, and was angry all the time. "I hope she stays away."

"I doubt she will. The one virtue in hatred is that it makes one persistent."

A swallow flew out of the rocks in the cliff below them, diving and soaring. The Griffin watched it wistfully. "Unless you have done it, you can have no idea how wonderful it is to do that."

"You will again." BJ continued, against her will, "But I don't want to see you do it just yet. It should be some time. We all want something we can't have." She remembered having said these words somewhere else recently.

The Griffin flexed his eagle's wings, and they extended easily. When they snapped free at the double-fold, one wing sagged suddenly. He opened and shut his beak several times, but gave no other indication of pain.

BJ helped hold the wing up as he tucked it again.

"I think you should get more extensive X-rays than I can do here. The large-animal facilities at the vet school—"

"You know," he said delicately, "I can manufacture my own excuses to see Laurie."

BJ looked at him steadily and felt a certain power in the fact that she wasn't blushing.

"I'm referring you for the superior X-ray facilities," she said levelly, "plus the on-site blood work for your gout." Inspired by her own poise, she added casually, "Is there some reason that you feel you need an anesthesiologist?"

The Griffin blinked. If he could have blushed, BJ felt sure that he would have.

" 'Need' is perhaps too strong a word." He added awkwardly, " 'Want' would be fair."

BJ wondered why two mature adults, of different species, would be unable to find a satisfying love except with each other.

The Griffin changed the subject. "What good is blood work for me?"

"Quite a bit of good." BJ felt awkward; she seldom felt what a great advantage it was having patients who usually couldn't talk back. "When you were being operated on, when you required a transfusion for surgery—"

"As I lay dying. Go ahead; I remember it quite well."

"All right; you were dying, and we had several pints of blood waiting for you from other griffins. From nearly a dozen different griffins, in fact." BJ swallowed, then plunged ahead. "Dr. Dobbs took the time to analyze the samples individually."

"Ah." The Griffin was trying to sound detached, but BJ could tell that he was furious. "Felt I could wait, did he? Well, research does come first."

"Not at all." BJ and Sugar Dobbs had discussed it only briefly, but his answer had been pointed enough to contain the truth she needed. "No one but a fool would pump that many different blood samples from donors of a new species without checking the contents."

"A benchmark." The Griffin breathed it carefully and thoughtfully, analyzing the reasons. "He wanted to have a benchmark."

"You were dying." BJ was leaning forward, earnestly justifying Sugar's from-the-hip decision as though it had been cool and analytical. "He had to know if any of the blood was damaging, if you needed less from one donor and more from another. It wasn't for the records; it was for you."

After a frozen moment, the Griffin nodded. "All right, then. Granting your first premise, what did he find?"

BJ relaxed, that and remembered. "First off, he found that griffins have two kinds of white cells."

"I beg pardon?"

"White blood cells. You have two discrete types, one for the eagle part and one for the cat—excuse me, one for the leonine part. He couldn't tell me why the two types of cells don't treat each other as infections, but he did say that they seem to get along without destroying each other." She paused.

"That's more than most of us do," the Griffin said softly. "I should be pleased."

Horvat suddenly froze in place and sniffed the air above them. He sneezed several times and growled. The Griffin and BJ looked at where he'd pointed.

Dozens of small dots, rapidly growing larger, approached in a ragged formation. They fell and rose irregularly, and as they grew closer, the air smelled lightly of sulphur.

"Oh, no," the Griffin said softly.

They flew in a broken and wavering V, too far apart for the airspill from each other's wings to be of any use. They collided occasionally; as they drew closer, BJ could hear the yawps as they tumbled and clawed after impact.

The Griffin shut his eyes. "Barbarous."

BJ watched the dark figures as they passed entirely over, moving to the south. She detected even at this distance an additional faint odor under the sulphur, a little like mink and a little like the lion's cage at the zoo. "What are they?"

The Griffin still refused to look. "They are the end of civilization as we know it, for the next few months."

BJ gazed upward, wrinkling her nose. "One of them is moving away from the rest of the—"

"The rest of the what?"

"—the flock, the gaggle—what would you call it?" BJ squinted upward. "I've seen a serenity of unicorns. I wouldn't call this a serenity—"

She broke off as the lone flyer plummeted out of the sky, apparently out of control.

"A chaos," the Griffin said bitterly, as they ran toward the projected point of impact. "A chaos of chimerae."

It lay on the grass, apparently unconcerned at falling. It sniffed at the brush around it, some of which was mysteriously burned. The whiskers on its tortoise-shell muzzle were also singed.

Batwings emerged from its feline shoulders. Its hindquarters were a bizarre mix of overlapping scales similar to those of some foreign armadillolike animal (a pangolin, BJ remembered belatedly) and a scorpion. It (no: *he*, BJ thought as she saw the bulging mammalian testicles hanging below the scorpion tail) was bow-legged.

It focused on BJ and wagged its tail; the sting swished through the grass behind it.

"At least it's friendly." She patted it carefully, ready to dart back at the least hostility. "Shall I give it an exam—?"

She broke off, staring. The Griffin's golden eyes were more angrily intent than she could remember. Every feather was ruffled, and his eagle talons were slashing at the mossy dirt in front of him. The lion claws on his rear paws were fully extended, and his lion fur was fluffed.

"Check them for everything," he hissed viciously. "Lice, tapeworms, some godforsaken lung infection—"

"Psittacosis?" BJ was still dazed, watching the ungainly tumbling bodies in case others fell. "Are you telling me they spread parrot fever?"

"They spread misery." The Griffin lowered his face in disgust, snapping his beak shut with an audible click at the end of phrases. "The poor stupid things would promote barbarism, if they were only advanced enough."

"This one is all right." She scratched it behind the ears. It wriggled happily at her touch. Its fur was unclean and its skin dry and scaly, perhaps with heat rash. Otherwise, it was fairly healthy.

Horvat, jealous, tried to come forward. The Griffin seized him effortlessly and gently with a single claw and held him back. "You want no part of that thing," he said gently. "Sit, young man."

Horvat growled and snapped at the claw that held him.

The Griffin turned his curved beak, nearly the size of the pup, down into his face and purred levelly, "I said, 'sit.' "

Horvat sat. BJ was relieved. She went on doing a quick exam of the chimera. Its front fur turned into rear scales in a single sudden line, marked only by a thin band of dry skin which seemed to be giving the chimera some discomfort, from the number of scratches. BJ checked along it and eventually found a palm-size circle of raw, bald skin, where the heat of infection had killed off the hair follicles.

"It seems to have a hot spot—" She pulled her hand back hastily as the beast dug a scaly rear claw in under the first row of scales. She looked under the plate as it exposed veined pink skin with bumps on it. "It has ticks," she announced unhappily. "Large, overfed, neglected ticks."

"Oh yes," the Griffin said angrily. "And bird lice, and fleas, and probably a communicable mange. Stepfather God alone knows where the filthy things have been. Several unfortunate worlds farther down the Strangeways, no doubt. But now they've come here, and in the process, they've brought with them every repugnant and parasitic passenger that any world can foster and sustain. I hope you enjoy skin work," he said with annoyance. "Because you're going to get a lot of it, even from my people."

"What if I worked up some kind of dip for them—"

"Chimera dip?" He raised a feathered eyebrow.

"Well, it's unlikely to kill them."

"It's unlikely to cure them, either, for any length of time. They'll simply blunder out across the world and find something else—a fungus, an insect, a worm—"

BJ was feeling ill. No one loves parasites. "How long will they be here?"

"Several months, perhaps more."

The chimera scratched one of its scales, raising a hind leg until it fell over. The Griffin sniffed loudly. It looked toward the Griffin and made plaintive mewing sounds. Horvat barked at it eagerly, but his tail was in aggressive posture; he wanted BJ to back away.

"You've hurt its feelings," BJ said.

"Good."

The chimera crouched submissively, like a puppy. It mewed

unhappily; a butterfly in front of it withered and died.

"Say something kind to it," BJ said.

"I shall not."

"Please."

"Why don't *you*?"

BJ surveyed the chimera before answering. "Because I can't think of anything," she said frankly. "And because it wants it from you."

The Griffin cocked an indignant eye at the chimera, who rolled over on its belly.

"See?" BJ said.

"This is completely beyond my patience," the Griffin said, but then added irritably, "Oh, all right. There, there. You're a good little nuisance."

The chimera arched its head back and purred. The grass nearest its nostrils began smoldering.

"You've made it happy. There you go, fella. Griffin, what should I name him?"

Frustrated, the Griffin clicked his beak sharply and frustratedly. "Oh, for God's sake, all right. Name him Fran."

"Fran?" BJ patted the chimera on the dark tuft between the ears. "Are you a Fran?" It rolled half on its side with delight.

BJ could not resist saying, more in fun than seriously, "See? All it needed was a little love."

"And still does," the Griffin said pointedly.

BJ followed his gaze. The chimera, rolling from side to side on the flattened grass, was getting an erection.

"This is just a hypothesis," she said carefully, "but do they come here to mate?"

"With everything that moves. With all who don't get out of the way. Eventually, after much needless havoc, for procreation."

The Griffin raised a disdainful claw and pointed at the chimera. "In the meantime, houses and fields burn, the very air smells foul, countless species are hunted for food or hurt accidentally, and every finer sensibility for miles around is irrevocably offended. And what is the point of all this? Merely the production of its own progeny. Hardly worthwhile," he said, lowering his claw.

"As if we wanted them," he added, rustling his feathers.

He finished, with satisfaction but obscurely: "The mountain labored, and brought forth a mouse."

"Do the other griffins feel as you do?"

The Griffin seemed taken aback. "More or less."

"In that case, I'm amazed that you haven't killed them all."

When the Griffin didn't respond, she added hastily, "Not you, I mean, because of your integrity—I mean the rest of your species—not that they don't have integrity—"

"Are you waiting for me to break in and say something to let you off the hook?"

BJ felt strangely like Stacey Robie.

"Because I'm not going to," the Griffin said simply, and strode off before opening his wings and gliding away. The chimera chirped and padded futilely after him before losing interest and rolling on the grass.

BJ dragged Horvat away, not setting him down until she was nearly home. "There. Now go in."

He yipped at her indignantly.

"I'll be in." She added, "You were very brave." On impulse she kissed his nose.

Horvat wagged his tail and bounded inside happily. BJ shut the door and washed up in the stream, not wishing to use the sink until she had cleaned once. She checked her clothes for parasites. While she was checking, she heard another friendly honk in the distance.

She shuddered. "This," she said firmly, "is going to be an unpleasant autumn."

S·E·V·E·N

LEE ANNE HARRISON was waiting on the rear loading dock of the vet school hospital in Kendrick. She was sitting on a couple of boxes, swinging her long legs over the end of the dock. "Hey, Doc." Her western Carolina accent was stronger than ever.

BJ hopped out. "Hey, Doc. Are those going with us?"

"Uh-huh. You're gonna owe me some money. If it turns out that I've overstepped, I'll pay for them."

"Save the receipts." BJ had no idea how she was going to manage her tax return, although Stein and the Griffin seemed to have something cooked up. Stein had mentioned wistfully that she had a rare opportunity to have tax-free income; the Griffin had responded crisply that that sort of attitude led to anarchy. In the meantime, she was making records for every client who came in, and converting payments in gold sixpiece into monetary equivalents as she sold the gold to a craftsman in Kendrick.

Lee Anne and BJ loaded the boxes, plus Lee Anne's backpack and frame, into the van. Lee Anne gave BJ a packing list, which she read while Lee Anne drove—considerably faster than BJ would have.

BJ read the list with interest. "Pen/Strep?"

"For horses or people. Watch out for allergies—nope, not in Crossroads. Okay, maybe you won't need to substitute the epinephrine I threw in." Lee Anne cut expertly around a tractor-trailer as it downshifted on the long upgrade before the Jefferson National Forest. "Where's my turn?"

"Three roads up on the left. How long will tetanus vaccine keep?"

Lee Anne grimaced, cutting onto the dirt road. "I'm not real sure on that one, to be honest. Keep it in cold storage, if you got any, and don't pass it out. I bet they won't be real anxious to use syringes again."

"God, no." Polyta's beloved husband, Nesyos, had died when DeeDee had, under Morgan's guidance, injected him with morphine. "I'll do the injecting. I'll pick a test case first." BJ snatched up the map. "Left here, then right."

Lee Anne kept her foot down. "Good thinking on the test case. This centaur stuff is weird; I don't know which half to treat."

"Another right. Another left—not too close!" The turtle man unfolded his huge arms and reached for the van as they passed him. "Um. Over the stone bridge, and down onto the river road by the middle fork. How does it feel to be back? Are you excited?"

"You think you're talking to some first-year student from Georgetown? Honey, I've been here before, and it takes one heck of a lot to surprise me—" She looked frontwards, squawked, and hit the brakes. BJ stared out with her.

The blue-gray birds wobbled across the road determinedly, gawking at the truck without fearing or avoiding it. One of them actually pecked at the tires with its ridiculously large, parrotlike bill. BJ worried that it would puncture the tires.

Lee Anne hit the horn. BJ jumped a foot, but the bird didn't even look up. After longer than BJ thought possible, it grew bored and walked away, bumping into two other birds.

Lee Anne rolled forward slowly, trying to nudge the birds aside with the truck fenders. She rolled down the window and stared at them. "You know," she said finally, "when I was growing up, I thought that guinea hens were the stupidest, ugliest birds there ever were. I guess I didn't get out much."

BJ leaned over and honked the horn loudly. None of the birds moved. "Don't tell me you can feel stupid around these."

"Not hardly. Where are they from?"

BJ stared dazedly into the rearview mirror; more birds waddled in back of them. "Mauritius, I think. But they've been extinct for centuries—"

"No, I mean around here. Were they always that color?"

"No idea, to both questions." BJ wondered uncomfortably what other extinct animals were in Crossroads. Then she heard Lee Anne snicker. "What is it?"

"Oh, nothing much. It's just that I'm thinking of every stupid person I've ever called a dodo."

"And?"

Lee Anne stared after the wobbly, gawky birds. "After all these years, it's nice to know just how insulting I've been."

They pulled up late at the cottage. BJ ran up, let Daphni and Horvat out, and quickly helped Lee Anne unload. "They could be here any minute."

"What time does class start?" Lee Anne looked at her watch.

BJ smiled in spite of her growing panic. "A little past midday."

Lee Anne looked at her watch again, then grinned. "Right." She took the watch off and stuffed it in her pack. "Never liked the foolish things anyway."

"They're still good for pulse rates. Let me settle you in—I'll take the bedroll, and you can have the bed—" BJ was frantic to finish.

"Sure." Horvat was growling at Lee Anne as she tried to pet him. "Oh, now. Don't you get tough with me, you cute little thing . . ." Eventually he gave in, sullen as a small boy, and let himself be petted. Lee Anne jumped up and brought her bedroll. "Smart idea, getting a dog. That ought to protect you enough."

BJ let it go for the moment. "The tour doesn't take long here. This is where I cook, and this is where I eat, and this is the bed." She pointed, trying not to seem too proud. "And this side is my clinic." She stepped over and rested her hands lightly on the steel table.

Lee Anne looked around, impressed. "This is a nice setup. Companion animal?"

"Small animal." BJ smiled slightly. "I wouldn't call some of them companions."

"That's for sure true." She frowned. "I don't want to step on toes, but can I make a few suggestions? If you truly need our class for Hippoi, you may need a larger surgery, too."

BJ shook her head. "The big cases I refer."

"When you can. Look, sooner or later you'll have a big case you can't send out. I grew up on a farm—"

"A Clydesdale ranch."

"A farm," Lee Anne corrected firmly. "Ranches have less fencing. Don't rile my daddy. Anyway, let me show you what you need, just for first aid—"

The few suggestions took over an hour. "A hoist outside—it can be a block and tackle off the cottage, and you keep a sling for it inside—a water tank with some pressure on the roof, for hosing down—a side tank for large-animal enemas; yeah, nobody likes it, but when they need it, they need it bad. Maybe I'm too kindhearted, but I'd add some low heat to that tank, at least in the winter.

"Set up a stone table and gutter it, then hammer stainless steel to fit the gutters and overlap the edges. Can you get help with that?"

"I think so." BJ scribbled frantically, sketching alongside her notes. "Polyta's people would drag the stone for free, and the Road Crews have stonemasons—they worked on rebuilding Stein's; I bet they'll help me—"

"How 'bout that. Don't tell the union you're getting all this for free."

BJ's father had been in a union. "I won't," she retorted sharply, "if you won't tell the Confederacy."

Lee Anne grinned at her. "Nice shootin', Tex, but you missed. I'm Southern, not Confederate." She put an arm across BJ's shoulders amiably; Lee Anne was tall enough to do it without stretching. "Don't let me get on your nerves, okay? Friends are rare."

"Got it." They moved around the house. "Now, what about a hospital area?"

Lee Anne shook her head. "You do that, Polyta will cut us right off. No invalids. Let's tackle other problems. Do these folks have hoof picks? Do they get wedged stones, splits, soft spots?"

"No, and probably."

"They have quite the diet, I'll bet. Do they get colic?"

"No idea." BJ was feeling uncomfortably as if she were presenting in large-animal class, without having studied the materials. Since she had come to Crossroads, she had occasionally had nightmares like that.

"What about spavin, glanders, and bots? Sounds like a Washington law firm, doesn't it?"

"I haven't seen any . . . Let me think." BJ was not as good with equine medicine as Lee Anne was.

"Okay, so we'll explore that later." Lee Anne chewed her lip as they both stepped outside. "Terrific. We've got a class that can't read, that doesn't believe in hospital care or surgery, and we don't know what their diseases are. You got anything else you want to tell me to brighten my day?"

"Yes," BJ said with exaggerated calm. "They're here."

Lee Anne stared for five seconds at the small group cantering down the hill behind Polyta; then she dashed into the cottage and ripped open the boxes. She tossed utensils, gauze, and bottles of disinfectant at BJ, shouting the entire time. They tore back outside, panting, in time to pull up in front of the door as the Hippoi trotted to a stop. BJ, with great presence of mind, slammed the door behind her before Horvat could get out.

Sugarly was not with them. BJ bowed, as before. "I greet you, Carron." Polyta nodded formally, her dark eyes impassive.

"I greet you, too," Lee Anne said.

Polyta's mouth quirked, but she only said, "And I greet you, and am glad to see you. Let me introduce my people."

One by one they came forward: Hemera, a seemingly teenaged woman with a bay horse-body and curly red hair; Amalthea, a tall woman with straight brown hair and a sorrel body (BJ wondered how often horse hair matched human hair in Hippoi); Selena, a striking centaur with shiny black hair that fell straight down on either side of her black horse-body, and Chryseia, another brown-hair/sorrel centaur as young as Hemera.

Last came Kassandra, a gray mare with flowing silver hair that trailed down to her horse-back like a mane. BJ nodded to her, but wondered why a Hippoi so old would attend a class about birthing.

Introductions were over. Lee Anne clapped her hands twice. "Okay, class is gonna start. Line up." She gestured. They didn't move. "C'mon, line up side by side in front of me." She slapped her leg impatiently, mostly for the sharp noise it made.

They started, turning to Polyta for guidance. She looked amused and quietly ambled over to the line.

BJ, beside Lee Anne, hissed, "They are *not horses*."

Lee Anne flinched. "Ladies, I'm as sorry as can be if I'm being too rude here. Fact is, I'm not used to—" She stopped. "By the way, where are your men?"

Polyta frowned. "The men chose not to come. They understood that this was a class for birthing, and felt they were not involved."

Lee Anne muttered to BJ, "I'd like to have those guys in a paddock for just twenty minutes. All it'd take."

Chryseis objected. "Your man Nesyos, the old Carron, helped in Sugarly's birth. He insisted."

Polyta smiled. "He was very headstrong. The others accept the old ways, even when they wish otherwise."

"Perhaps they'll come another time," BJ said diplomatically. "Since they're not here, for the introductory class, we're going to talk a bit about other kinds of medicine, detecting sickness and healing it, so that you will have some background before we talk about prenatal care."

Polyta raised an eyebrow. BJ, who had rehearsed that speech for hours to make it work, pretended not to notice. "And now, Dr. Harrison will begin Introductory Healing Arts."

Lee Anne put her fists on her hips. "Let me ask a couple questions, just to get a feel for what you do now." The Hippoi, like students everywhere, tensed in expectation of the questions. "If you had a friend who had a persistent, unexplained hoof lameness, what would you do for her?"

Selena smiled with relief at the easy question. "Speak to the Carron, and leave her to die."

Lee Anne looked at her blankly and finally nodded. "Okay. We'll talk more about that. Now, what if you see a friend rolling on the grass, in pain, what would you do—"

Hemera scratched her red hair in confusion. "I would ask him what was wrong. Wouldn't you?"

"Right, right. You can ask what's bothering him." Lee Anne added, from her heart, "Lucky for you. Takes a lot of guesswork out. So, you ask, and he says, 'My belly hurts. It hurts a lot, and I can't' "—she fumbled for a tactful word—" ' I can't move my bowels,' and then he goes back to rolling. What do you do?"

Hemera said simply, "I would speak to the Carron and leave him to die." The others nodded approval.

Lee Anne muttered to BJ, "I can see the first-aid quiz ain't gonna be multiple choice." To the class she said, "Okay, but there's more you could find out before you leave him to die. Some of it might save his life."

"How?" Hemera asked blankly. She swished her tail to the left, scratching her head on the left at the same time.

"If you find out what's wrong with him, maybe you could make it better instead of leaving him to die. He might not have to die at all." Lee Anne looked at their blank, stunned faces. "Lemme show y'all—let me show you what I mean. Chryseis, we'll do a hoof exam on you; c'mon forward. Raise your left rear hoof." Lee Anne caught it expertly and locked it with her knees, crouching to examine it. "I'm not sure how you do this part without human knees, but you'll find a way. Check the bottom surface of the hoof—"

BJ passed out hoof picks as they watched in disapproving silence. They took the hoof picks and watched as Lee Anne tapped the surface, dislodged a wedged stone, and moved to the front hooves. Chryseis seemed terribly tense about something; BJ did not think it was just the alienness of the class.

On the last hoof, Chryseis flinched suddenly and Lee Anne gave a grunt of satisfaction. "Here's one. Okay, everybody gather round and look."

There was the sound of hooves, and suddenly BJ and Lee Anne were hemmed in by horse bodies. The human torsos towered above them, bent over and staring at Chryseis's hoof.

Lee Anne pointed to the spot she had tapped on the hoof. "This here is an abscess, a pocket of infection that walled itself off from the rest of the hoof. In a couple days, it'll get real hard to walk on, maybe bad enough that you're lame." She grinned up at Chryseis, who was straining to see over her own shoulder. "You want me to talk to the Carron and leave you to die?"

BJ winced. Chryseis twisted still further to look at the hoof, her eyes wide with horror. Her horse body shifted nervously.

Lee Anne quickly put a hand on her back, stroking her reassuringly. "Easy, girl . . . sorry; I mean, relax, ma'am, I can fix this." She got the eyes of the others. "This is gonna hurt Chryseis. Afterward, she'll be sore for a couple days, but she'll be able to walk. If you can let her live through that, she'll be fine."

Lee Anne said to BJ, "Hoof knife." BJ passed forward a knife with a thin, slightly curved blade and a curled-up end. Before Lee Anne could take it, she was being offered several short, sharp knives.

She took one and smiled back at BJ. "I guess I should've figured that you people would have something to trim hooves with. Okay, I'll use one of yours." She took one, testing the edge carefully, and sterilized it. "First you pare down on the abscessed hoof till you find a black spot, if you're lucky. That's where the abscess is." She was lucky; a tiny spot appeared almost immediately.

"You can smell it if you want to be sure. Me, I've never wanted to be that sure. Now you pare a hole over the black spot, about the size of a dime—excuse me, of the end of your biggest finger." She tucked the knife under her arm, sterilized blade away from her. "Now here's the tricky part. Chryseis, this is the part that hurts."

Lee Anne took the pincers holding the hoof upside-down between her knees. "Don't straighten that leg, ma'am, or I'll be hurt myself."

She took the ends of the pincers in both hands and squeezed the hoof, hard. Black and yellow pus spurted out; Chriseis tightened her face, but wouldn't cry out, and she didn't kick her leg.

Lee Anne looked at the size of the abscess and said gently, "This has been hurting for days, hasn't it, honey?"

Polyta frowned. "Chryseis, you could have told me."

"I could have, before you were Carron."

BJ saw the ache in Polyta's face, and realized the distance that separated Polyta now from her friends.

Lee Anne went on, pretending not to notice, "Now, what you do when you feel sore from now on, you tell your best friend, and get her to do what I've just done." She was cleaning out the abscess with a square of sterile cloth. "Get a sterile solution, Betadine or peroxide or some such, from Dr. Vaughan here"— BJ held up bottles, feeling like a flight attendant showing the oxygen mask—"or use boiling hot water, if you can stand it."

Lee Anne plugged the hole in the hoof with pine tar, then wrapped the bottom of the hoof in a leather pad and tied it with a thong, pausing once in a while so they could see what she was doing. "And that's that. She'll limp for a couple days, then get better. Here's some more cloths and sterile solution for the dressing." She held them up. Some of the Hippoi looked anxious, but Hemera snatched at them quickly.

To Polyta, Lee Anne said, "Ma'am, you might consider getting a farrier into Crossroads."

Polyta looked blank. BJ explained. "A blacksmith. The man who does metal work for Stein's can learn to make shoes to protect your hooves."

"Shoes?" Polyta looked at her with polite disbelief. "Like the shoes of men and women?"

"No." BJ drew a crescent in the dirt. "A piece of metal like this, fastened with nails—"

"Hammered and clinched," Lee Anne interrupted, gesturing. "It stays on your foot for good, and prevents wear or splintering. If the smith can learn how, he can even make shoes that help hold split hooves together, and heal them."

Kassandra looked forbidding. Most of the others seemed shocked. Polyta shook her head, rippling her dark hair and dark tail in unison. "Forgive my confusion. This is so much new to think of."

Lee Anne stood back up. "That's about all for the first class, anyway. After you know more, Dr. Vaughan will teach you about different types of abscesses, about a disease called tetanus—"

"Lockjaw," BJ explained, and saw recognition in a few faces.

"Lockjaw, and about diet and avoiding health problems. For instance, there's an illness called laminitis, which can be caused by a high intake of grain—or, I guess, beer—"

"Nephelos will get that." Amalthea giggled. Selena looked highly offended.

Rattled, Lee Anne hurried on. "And, since your hooves are so important to y'all's way of life, BJ—Dr. Vaughan will cover other problems in the foot, from simple white gravel on up to navicular bursitis."

"Excuse me." It was Hemera, holding hands with Chryseis. She was very excited. "Can all these things be healed like Chryseis's hoof?"

Lee Anne frowned. "Most of them. Some of the cures are tougher than others. This abscess, for instance, was the easiest. Always check out the easy stuff first."

"Excuse me. What if it is navicular?"

Lee Anne turned to BJ. "Neurectomy, here?" she whispered from the side of her mouth.

"Possibly. I'd need to review. Lee Anne, how much down-time are we talking?"

"A lot. No travel . . ." She trailed off as she saw Polyta ever so slightly shake her head. They hadn't been talking softly enough.

"What if it is navicular?" Hemera repeated.

Lee Anne took a deep breath. "Tell the Carron and leave your friend to die."

Most of the others looked relieved at getting familiar advice. Kassandra, surprisingly, frowned.

Lee Anne clapped her hands. "That's it, folks," she said, a little feebly. "Sorry if it isn't quite to your taste, but—"

Kassandra said, "I will speak." She did not look at Polyta for approval, and she stepped in front of the Hippoi, neatly blocking Lee Anne and BJ from them. "I am the oldest of you. I was here before Stein's was built, when there was only the one pond on the hill. I was a woman already when little Stein came to Crossroads, with his arm broken and dangling."

Even at this distance of years, her lips tightened. "I will always remember thinking of one of my own, Misenos, who fell on his own arm, and broke it, and was left to die when he took a fever. That same summer. The summer that Stein wore a bandage and a wrap on his arm, and was healed by autumn. And I knew it was different for his people, but I hated him." Her old, skinny fingers knotted into a fist. "Oh, I hated that little boy."

She pointed a finger at each of the Hippoi in turn. "Selena, I made food for your mother when we left her to die. Amalthea, your grandfather and I mated. We left him to die when he had the coughing sickness, and after that the foal died as it came out of me."

She wheeled toward Polyta. "I was there when your lover, Nesyos, was young and saw his parents each left to die. I was here, we were all here, when Nesyos died.

"We left Medéa to die, not so long ago. My oldest friend. I stayed behind and ate with her, even knowing that The Great were coming. I stayed until the wind of their wings was in the air, and I kissed her goodbye, and she grabbed my hand and said, 'Now there is only you.' And she cried for me, being left behind." Kassandra closed her eyes. "And she was right.

"Polyta has begun a brave thing here. It will change your lives. Don't throw it away because it is new."

In the silence that followed, Lee Anne exhaled. "Thanks for coming, folks. Next class will be Dr. Vaughan's, on prenatal care and birthing assistance. You'll learn to watch diet, avoid prenatal stress, maybe some exercises to help in birthing, and how to pull a stuck foal. And," she added, "you get the men here next time."

Polyta said calmly, before the others could answer, "They will come." She stepped forward formally and nodded in a half bow to BJ and Lee Anne. "Thank you for teaching." Amalthea followed her, head back proudly and hooves lifted high, but bowed as deeply and echoed Polyta.

They each said thank you, one by one. Last, Hemera said her thanks and blurted in admiration to Lee Anne, "You would be a good Carron. You can force people to do what you want."

Polyta put her hand over her mouth, hiding a smile. Lee Anne stammered, "It's just 'cause I've ordered—well, I've worked with horses. I really ought to work on my manners. Thanks, I think."

Hemera galloped after the others, and Lee Anne, BJ, and Polyta were alone. Lee Anne stared after Hemera. "She's wrong, ma'am, I can't stand seeing folks die."

Polyta took Lee Anne's hand. "Nor can I. She is very right; you would be a wonderful Carron, and this class will be a good thing."

BJ said suddenly, "And that's why you asked Kassandra to come, isn't it?"

Lee Anne stared at her. Polyta only smiled. "Perhaps I wanted my older friend with me."

"Maybe, but I think you also knew what she would say, and that the others would think about it afterward."

Lee Anne said, "I guess BJ would be a better Carron than I am, ma'am."

Polyta laughed, a lovely, relaxing sound. "I'm not sure what BJ should be, but it is important, I think. And now, before I go, let me say hello as I should have."

She lifted Lee Anne, who was no small woman, as easily as if she were a child and embraced her. "Thank you so. You and BJ will save many lives with these classes."

Lee Anne, back on the ground, said nothing as Polyta hugged BJ. As Polyta trotted after the other Hippoi, Lee Anne turned to BJ and grinned. "So, how's it feel to change civilization?"

"It feels like we'd better be right."

"You bet. We're gonna have a long two days here," Lee Anne said firmly, " 'cause we're gonna review everything we learned in Large Animal classes, and then I'm gonna teach you everything I learned on my folks' farm, and then we'll set up classes together."

"I wish you could stay a while."

"I've got my job to get back to." She poked BJ's arm. "We're not all our own bosses." She stared thoughtfully downhill to the road. "Dodos . . . You know, I'm gonna take some vacation time this fall. I'll be going to the Gulf Coast, maybe to Louisiana." She pronounced it 'Loosiana.' "When I come for the wedding, could you see I get an up-to-date entry map?"

"You're coming to the wedding?"

She grinned. "Wouldn't miss it."

Inside the cottage, Lee Anne alternately chewed bread and coaxed Horvat into being patted. "This is stone delicious. How do you find time?"

"There's more time here." In her old world of phones, timers, and sweep-second hands, BJ had never in her life felt what it was like to have a completely uninterrupted day. Now she had them frequently. "I did this, too." She brought out her prized homespun wool skirt. Horvat leapt at it; BJ tugged it back. Delighted, he planted his paws on the floor and tugged, snarling.

"Horvat, no!" someone said sharply from the door. Horvat stopped in his tracks. Gredya, in human form, stood in the doorway. The wolf pup cocked his head and stared, sniffed once, and yipped wildly, his feet spinning on the floor.

Gredya laughed and reached, but he spun back and ran to BJ, yipping. BJ pointed back to Gredya; Horvat whirled toward the door, skidding. Gredya laughed, a short, sharp sound with the only happiness BJ had seen her display. "So good," she said to Horvat. "So good."

Lee Anne was staring blankly. BJ said quickly, "I'm sorry. This is Dr. Lee Anne Harrison, from my home. Well, from my world. Lee Anne, this is—"

"I know you," Gredya interrupted. She regarded Lee Anne coolly and indifferently.

Lee Anne was baffled. "I'm sorry, ma'am, but I can't place you just now. The last time I was in Crossroads, I met such a lot of people that I just can't—"

"Not people." She said it with easy contempt. "I am Wyr."

Lee Anne gave her a long, hard stare. "You mean the people that scarred me up, tortured animals in front of me, and tried to rip my throat out the last time I was here?" She added dryly, "Nice to see ya."

Gredya stared back at her, unashamed.

BJ moved between them. "Gredya, I hope you like how I've treated Horvat."

"You do well." She looked at Horvat, who was happily spinning back and forth between BJ and his mother as though they were equal. "I am—glad."

BJ patted Horvat, who nipped at her in play. She swatted him, and saw Lee Anne's reaction rather than Gredya's face. She turned quickly and saw Gredya's curled upper lip, exposing teeth for fighting. "I'm sorry. I need to teach him not to bite me, that's all."

"He must learn." The concession seemed pulled from Gredya. "You do well."

"Thank you." BJ struggled for a topic. "How are Katya and Grigor?"

"Dead," she said calmly. "Throat and stomach. The Wyr." She added, a slight tremor in her voice as she looked at Horvat, "He is my only."

BJ knelt by him. He nipped at her knees, and this time she didn't swat him. "Do you want to take him back?"

"No," Gredya said harshly. "He would die. Keep him." She knelt down and put her face to his. He licked it frantically, his thin tail going like a metronome. She licked him back.

She stood. "I will come back." And she was gone, turning her back on Lee Anne as though it was a challenge, out into the late afternoon sunlight and running up the hill, her long thin shadow running on the grass beside her.

Lee Anne exhaled explosively. "There you have it, ladies and gentlemen, conclusive proof: On two legs or four legs, a bitch is a bitch."

BJ, who prided herself on seldom losing her temper, snapped, "Leave it alone, now."

"No, I'm not gonna let up, BJ. What do you know about wolves?"

"Medically?" BJ was angry; to her surprise, part of it was for the snub to Gredya.

"No, no. I know you're gonna be miles ahead there. What do you know about how they live?"

"Enough," BJ said, stalling while she thought. "They're pack animals—"

"Some are, some aren't. The Carolina red wolf isn't." She patted Horvat. "If this little fella is, where's his pack?"

"He's better off alone." BJ reached automatically to protect Horvat; he bounded into her arms. "The pack is fighting just now."

Lee Anne nodded. "Dominance struggles. They're no joke, you know; some wolves get killed. That's one reason you've got to keep him aggressive, so he can return."

"Of course." BJ refused to show her dismay at the thought of Horvat rejoining the pack. "But he's likely to be stunted; it may take time—"

"Which you don't have." Lee Anne pointed a finger at BJ. "You know why they're really born as wolves? So they can grow up faster. How big is he gonna be in four months, in six? When will he hit puberty, and get as aggressive as a human teenager?" She considered. "Worse. Most of the guys I went out with didn't have fangs, no matter what I thought at the time."

"You're wrong." BJ said it as firmly as she could. "He's going to be manageable for me, and aggressive for the pack. You'll see. By January—"

"Show me your arms." When BJ didn't move, Lee Anne said tiredly, "Okay, let's see."

BJ's arms, from a few days of roughhousing, were cross-hatched with marks from bites and dragged teeth. At least one of the bites would have scarred, in any place but Crossroads.

"That's normal," BJ insisted. "It's how puppies are."

"That's right. *And adult wolves fight like puppy wolves.*"

In the silence, Lee Anne went on. "Puppies fight to learn to be grownups. I bet you've seen dominance fights between Miss Kitty over there"—Daphni was asleep on the bed—"and Horvat, haven't you? And now Horvat guards you like you're his own."

In spite of her worry, BJ smiled. Lee Anne shook her head. "Oh, no. It's not sweet. Not when a full-grown wolf greets me at the door. And not when Gredya decides that you're stealing her son away, and she's already a grown wolf."

Horvat, sensing that something was wrong, whined and licked BJ's feet.

BJ rubbed his ears. "We'll do fine. Listen, I hate to run out on you, but I have a meeting tonight."

Lee Anne raised an eyebrow. "A 'meeting,' or a 'date'? Are you and Stefan finally getting together?"

"He's a freshman at Western Vee," BJ's ears were reddening. "And no, we're not. This is a meeting with Stein and the Griffin, among others."

Lee Anne shook her head. "I swear, it's this place. You've been here three or four months, and already you're as secretive as Stein and the rest. You be careful."

BJ put on her shawl. "You be careful. I'm leaving you with the wolf. I'll be back late tonight, I promise."

"If you aren't, shall I assume one of the 'others' you're among is good-looking?"

BJ considered telling her about Estevan Protera, then gave up. "There's a meat pie in the pantry, and milk in the springhouse. Maybe you can get some rest."

"Maybe." Lee Anne pulled a paperback from her luggage and threw herself full length on BJ's bed. "I'll read before it's too dark. C'mon, boy."

Horvat regarded her dubiously. She scooped him up one-handed before he knew what was happening, and plunked him down on the bed. "C'mon, honey, be like a dog and be friends."

Horvat settled moodily on the bed and Lee Anne opened her book. The last thing BJ saw as she left was Lee Anne, heedless of her own warnings, patting Horvath, whose tail thumped her leg. BJ felt a stab of jealousy, and had a tiny sense, as she left, of what Gredya must feel. Lee Anne might be right.

E·I·G·H·T

BJ AND STEIN walked together to Protera's cottage, enjoying the moonrise. A fervent but muted honking greeted the moon; the chimerae felt about the moon the way that moths do about smaller light sources.

Stein watched them, shaking his head. "I've never seen them before, and I'll tell you, I don't want to again. My parrot is bad enough." BJ laughed, hooking her arm through his. She had seen little enough of her mother's father, who had Huntington's chorea, that being with Stein felt new and special.

As they arrived at the approach lane to Protera's cottage, there was a soft padding of feet and a rustle in the grass by the roadway. "Well met by moonlight," the Griffin said.

It was a move designed to demonstrate the Griffin's resources; in a world with no watches, meetings were casual and fairly haphazard. Arriving early was the rule, but people seldom arrived within minutes of each other.

Stein chuckled and patted the Griffin's side. "Sometimes it's good to feel I'm being watched."

BJ smiled, but was not as sure; the Griffin's front talons were bloody.

He followed her glance. "Pardon me." He delicately, carefully licked the blood off each talon, flexing them forward like cat's claws. "I was in the neighborhood, catching up on my work."

"No rest for the wicked," Stein said.

The Griffin smiled, as much as his beak would permit. "On the contrary, there is now."

BJ said levelly, "I hope you don't mind my mentioning it, but there's blood on your beak."

"Thank you for bringing it to my attention." He took care of it with his tongue. "It wouldn't do any good to frighten the good professor, would it?"

But BJ noticed that he left a little, and wondered what good the Griffin thought it would do.

The cottage was like a great many others scattered in the hills, left over from generations of shepherds and wanderers. It was larger than BJ's, and the roof was slate. From the outside it seemed tremendously well lighted.

Stein frowned. "Making himself a target through the windows like that, that's careless. Look how easily anyone could see him."

"I don't think so," BJ said thoughtfully. "I think he's very careful."

The Griffin peered through a window. "She's quite right. The lights are positioned so that people looking in are dazzled, and it's hard to make out details. I imagine watchers would be quite visible to him, if the panes are non-glare. How like a physicist, even a geophysicist, to fight with light."

The door opened as they approached. Either Protera had heard them, or he had some kind of warning system erected; either way, it was impressive. They were momentarily blinded; while they were all three blinking, Protera leaned out.

"I'm so glad you could come." He was genuinely pleased, and sounded excited, like a small boy at a party. As BJ's sight returned, she gaped.

His hair was immaculate and combed straight back. He had earrings—not the small studs many college males wore, but strands of seed pearls alternating with gold beads. He was wearing an elegantly cut, tailored satin chemise with a textured satin kimono. His legs were shaved, and on his feet he had dark blue, open-toed, backless slippers. Stein grunted in astonishment.

BJ remembered that, back at Western Vee, Protera was the faculty sponsor of Lambda House, the gay fraternity, and that his nickname was Señora Esther.

Stein goggled. The Griffin said unhesitatingly, "You look lovely."

"Thank you." Protera gestured to his guests. "Please, come in. Feel free."

There was space in the nearly bare room even for the Griffin. BJ wasn't surprised that the professor's cottage was spare; no

sane person would bring a moving van into Crossroads. Still, there
was a surprising richness of decoration: a wool rug, dyed indigo;
a shelf of small carved figures in complicated and funny poses;
a series of intricate, meticulous executed pen and ink cityscape
drawings on notebook paper, pulled from a journal and matted
for hanging. BJ recognized Venice, Manhattan, and Paris, but
was hazy on the others.

The final drawing was a view of the rebuilt Stein's from one of
the overlooking hills. In the foreground was the mill wheel with
the three drive belts running off it. One of the belts was for the
main rotating spit and one for Chris's vertical spit for lamb; the
third ran to an outside drive shaft, for running a lumber saw. The
windows to the single upper chamber were open, and an older man
was silhouetted in one of them.

Stein looked at the drawing of his inn for a long time. "That's
beautiful. I wish I had a picture of the old inn to show you.
Now, that one we took our time on. But I don't—" He shrugged.
"I didn't think I should make sketches of something I didn't
want seen."

Protera, unruffled, took the sketch off the wall and passed it to
Stein. "Would you like this one, even though it is the new inn?"

Stein said, relieved, "That would be quite nice of you. Thank
you, young—" He glanced at the dress and finished awkwardly.
"Thank you."

"No, it's my pleasure. I loved my time at your inn. Please, sit."
He gestured toward three chairs in the corner, then whirled to BJ,
the hem of his robe moving with a rhythmic sway. He was still
flawlessly graceful. "Have you seen the carvings before?"

"No; they're wonderful. Where did you get them?"

"The Meat People, they are called. A woman named Janhhr
helped me move in." BJ was impressed that he could pronounce
it as the Meat People themselves did. "Please, take them down
and look at them while I get you each something to drink."
He swept into the rear room, evidently an add-on pantry and
kitchen.

BJ loved the carvings: a fat man leaping after a butterfly; a
fang-faced woman singing with her hands clasped and her eyes
closed to a bird perched on her lower fangs, also singing; a squat
boy and girl holding hands shyly, standing well apart. The figures
wore embroidered clothing, with the stitching elaborately carved.
A parallel-groove motif was common on the figures, sometimes
in stockings or in an animal's fur. Stein and the Griffin stood
watching BJ.

"The teeth," she said wonderingly. "They gnaw these with their teeth, don't they?"

Stein said, "I like how you figure things out."

Protera came back with three balanced mugs of tea and a bowl. "I hope this is appropriate, sir." He set his own tea by the empty chair, then set the bowl down on the floor before the Griffin, not spilling a drop.

"Quite nice." The Griffin looked back up; Protera was gone. "My God, he's quiet when he wants to be."

"And in slippers," BJ murmured. In backless slippers. She had always sounded as though she were on a pogo stick.

Protera returned holding a bottle of cognac, four small cups, and a tablespoon. He set a cup and the spoon in front of the Griffin. "I am sorry I don't have a better table setting; will this do?"

"Excellently." The Griffin poured a generous serving of cognac into the cup, filled the spoon and ladled it down his throat. "Thank you for the extra trouble."

Protera said dismissively, "You are a guest."

Stein and BJ each sipped at the cognac. It seemed strong to BJ, but she found that it went well with the tea. Protera returned from the kitchen with a plate of scones. "May I offer you something more?"

The Griffin turned so that the blood on his beak faced the light.

Without pausing, Protera passed him a scone and added, "I should offer you a napkin."

He turned away. The Griffin silently dabbed the blood off his beak; it wasn't disconcerting Protera in the slightest.

"And now," Protera said, settling into the third chair with as much ease as if it had been a recliner, "Tonight's topic."

"Which is?" Stein said.

Protera rested his beautifully manicured fingertips together. "I have a theory on the nature of Crossroads. If either of you has experience that would contradict this theory, I would be delighted." He picked up and sipped his tea, then the cognac, swirling each exactly once. "If either of you knows a way to test this theory, I would be ecstatic."

"What is your theory?" The Griffin said sharply. BJ was amused to see his discomfort; the Griffin preferred lecturing to listening.

"Ah. Well. You will agree, I think, that Crossroads is not like other worlds?" All three nodded. "Yes. Well, it's obvious, isn't it? Crossroads does not behave like the world which BJ and I, and Mr. Stein, grew up knowing.

"Since, according to the physics we know, all worlds behave the same under the same circumstances, I must conclude that there is a force which allows Crossroads access to all worlds, and which allows some of its more unusual species"—a nod to the Griffin— "to exist."

The Griffin, uncharacteristically, chewed at a talon. "And how much are you able to tell us about this force?"

"What it is? I can't tell you." He smiled, winking at them as though sharing a joke. "But I can show you what it is like." He reached under his chair. "Yes." With a flourish like a conjurer, he withdrew a metal bar, a sheet of white cardboard, and a clear vial with something dark and flowing in it. He laid the bar flat on the floor and placed the cardboard over it. "Now watch."

He unstoppered the vial and poured its contents over the paper. BJ was unsurprised, though as always she enjoyed the display. Stein said, "It's been a long time."

The Griffin stared raptly. "Fascinating. That is a magnetic field, and those shavings are iron filings. Am I correct?"

"Nickel-iron. I certainly hope whoever ground them wore a breathing filter . . . Do you know, I didn't expect you to recognize it."

"I do read," the Griffin replied crisply. He had cocked his head to one side, peering closely at the bands of filings. "However, I've never seen it for myself."

Protera bowed slightly. "I'm honored to be the first to show you. This, then, is a field effect. The particles are realigned by the field. If they were left in it long enough, they would become slightly magnetized themselves." He said to BJ, "I assume you saw this in high school."

"Several times," she said, and added, "It always looked a little like magic."

He grinned at her, arching one eyebrow. "To me, also. And still."

"Why did you bring it with you?"

Stein shook his head. "Young lady, I can tell you're a practitioner, not a researcher."

"Practice is good," Protera said immediately. "It narrows choices as fast as it can. Only research needs to be broad and fuzzy."

"You sound like Fiona."

"Who? Ah. Of course. Fiona Bannon." Protera looked disconcerted. "I hope that I'm not wronging a friend of yours, but does it seem to you that she dresses a little, tiny bit eccentrically?"

Stein choked. The Griffin said calmly, "I'm afraid the niceties of human fashion escape me."

BJ looked at Estevan's kimono and said tactfully, "She lacks your taste and moderation."

He acknowledged the compliment with a nod and a smile. "At her age, so did I." He adjusted his robe delicately.

Stein was peering at the iron filings, tracing the pattern with his finger. "It looks just like the one in textbooks."

"As it should. Magnetism is always the same. It is the location of the field, and the individual iron filings, which change. This is true, we think, on all worlds."

The Griffin nudged a row of filings out of place. They flowed around his talon and returned to outline the field. "Will they always do that?"

"In the presence of a source of magnetism, yes."

"And if you put them in another field?"

"For a time, at least, they would try to orient themselves in the new field as they had in the old: the same poles in the same orientation."

He raised the paper and shook it. The pattern blurred, then disappeared completely. He put the magnet back under it, sideways.

"The same pattern," he murmured, "with the parts in different places. Change it often enough, and very little would be kept of the old field effect."

The Griffin said skeptically, "Are you saying that Crossroads differs from other places because it has different magnetism?"

Protera shook his head violently. One of his earrings tinkled; he stilled it with an immaculately manicured finger. "Point one, I suggest but do not say. Point two, I merely suggest that Crossroads behaves like a field; I do not suggest what field it may be."

"So?" Stein was nonplused. "You've got chunks of metal in patterns, and you think some other pattern is special in Crossroads. What's the point?"

Protera smiled approvingly, as though Stein had intentionally cut to the heart of the matter. "The point would not matter, if only iron filings were influenced by Crossroads' field. But somehow the health of animals is different in here—Dr. Vaughan, is that right?"

BJ felt it overly formal of him to call her Dr. Vaughan when he wanted to be called Estevan. "Extremely different."

He set his tea cup down delicately, but with finality. "Exactly so. In different fields, different conditions for the inhabitants of the field. That is important." He sat in silence, waiting for them to realize why.

The Griffin was the first to understand. "So characteristics of species in Crossroads might be quite rare beyond it."

Protera spread his hands. "The characteristics might not be found at all. The species might not even thrive."

BJ stammered, "But Dr Boudreau—"

"Lucille Boudreau." He looked sharply sideways at her. "You've worked with her?"

"Spoken to her, actually. She told me—" BJ bit her lip remembering when Lucille Boudreau had told her that time spent in Crossroads could alleviate congenital conditions, even terminal ones. "She told me about her work with allergies."

"Working with an injured flora—pardon me, a flowerbinder. Among other things, she probably pointed out that cat dander from a flowerbinder would not make her sneeze."

"Yes." BJ remembered that day quite well. Dr. Boudreau had also, without knowing that it was a revelation, pointed out that Huntington's chorea would not kill BJ. "She explained how certain congenital and viral conditions heal in Crossroads."

"Exactly." Protera raised a finger to his quests making an important point. "But she did not understand, because she is a doctor and not a physicist, that some effects are geographic and not physiological."

There was a quiet silence while they tried to understand the import of Protera's observation.

Stein said suddenly and bleakly, "Chris."

"The truth?" Protera said solemnly. "I suspect that if he were to go back home, he would show the same symptoms as he had before, whether they were Alzheimer's or something else, within a short period of time." He added, "Of course, a thinking being is not an experimental subject. There will be no test."

"Of course not," the Griffin said, and Stein said, "I would fight it."

"Yes. Well. Then, if you have no further information by which I can test field effects, I believe that's all I was planning to talk about."

"It was enough." Stein stood. "I don't mean to be abrupt, young—Professor, but I need to get back to my inn to close out tonight." He stretched a hand toward BJ.

She shook her head. "I'd like to stay and hand over one of my notebooks to Professor Protera."

He laughed. "Estevan."

"I'll try," BJ said dubiously, and to Stein, "Anyway, I'll be fine."

"Maybe we'd better get going, then," Stein said. BJ watched Protera's face; he did not miss the 'we.'"

The Griffin rose. Stein bowed toward Protera. "Thank you for the food and drink, and especially for the sketch. You're an excellent host, and I ought to know."

Protera returned the bow, smiling. "I owe it to the world. I've been a guest so often."

Stein and the Griffin left. Protera watched them from the window, amused. "I've given them something to think about, haven't I?"

"Me too." BJ passed him the notebook. "I just wanted to talk some more."

"By all means." He brought in more tea. "So," he said, eyeing her with curiosity but no caution whatsoever, "what do you think of me?"

She thought for quite a while.

"Is it that rude?" he said finally. "Dr. Vaughan, if I had thought that, I wouldn't have asked."

"Oh, no." His misapprehension had given her the words she needed. "Really, I think well of you. When I look at my own life"—she stumbled a little—"I admire you."

He smiled, then, and handed her a cup of tea. She took it and burst out, "Dr. Protera, why is love such a mess?"

"I should think that it's fairly obvious." He stirred his tea delicately. "Women who think they want only love find men who think they want only sex. Women often want love with sex; men usually want sex with love. Foolish species, really. One day a study of sexual differences will make a great deal clear. In the meantime, we all fight, cry, and write poetry.

"The griffins," he added obscurely, "fight amongst themselves, cry not at all, and merely read the poetry. If I thought I were seeing an entire species in denial, I would be in mourning for them. I believe that I'm seeing a gender in denial, instead."

"How many griffins have you met?"

He frowned, considering. "Only the one at any length. The others I met while installing a seismic station which proved nearly useless; there is a damping effect in Crossroads . . . Tell me, have you seen any obviously female griffins?"

Once asked, the answer was obvious.

"But—" BJ struggled. "I'm sure I have. Yes, I'm sure of it."

He smiled. "People, when they say 'I'm sure' twice, often aren't. What made you believe it was female?"

"It had a smaller body, its voice was higher—" BJ trailed off as Protera casually adjusted his kimono, which, she realized enviously, was more glamorous than any bathrobe she had ever owned. "All right, I was relying on secondary sexual characteristics."

"Then you did not actually sex it."

BJ said, a little stiffly, "No one would attempt sexing a strange griffin without its consent. Certainly not more than once." She added in a small voice, "But if there aren't any females, how do you think they reproduce?"

"Ah." He offered her a scone, which she took. "Secretly—that much I know, from evidence. Shamefully—that much I suspect, from conversations."

He fixed her with a glittering eye, like the Ancient Mariner. "And I suspect, but cannot prove, the exact mechanism. I am quite probably the only person now in Crossroads who could deduce the mechanism, and I take little credit for my ability to ignore physical evidence to reach a conclusion."

BJ chose to change the subject. "How did you become so good with swords?"

"When I was young," he said easily, "I studied in Lima. Although my habits might go without notice in Rio, in parts of Peru I was—exceptional. I had my nose broken twice, my ribs broken by kicking once."

His inflections changed; BJ could tell that the next admission was hard, however lightly he told it. "I had a wonderful uncle, a farmer who had fought with his neighbors all his life. He had told me, *Always know war when you see it.* I knew that this was war. I took fencing at college, martial arts on the side, and boxing from a Cuban friend who had nearly turned professional."

He finished coldly, avoiding BJ's eyes: "When I was attacked again, I left two young men with concussions and broken noses, one of them with a permanently disabled kneecap. A triumph, no?"

BJ merely looked at him. He seemed very young and unhappy.

He added with no pretense at harshness, "I saw them lying on the stones in front of me, one of them clutching his knee and weeping, and I knew I would never fight again. I trained more and more—not simply as a fighter, but as a diplomat, a strategist, a scholar, and a spy. I wouldn't have been half as successful, but for that night. Two years ago, when a woman asked me what drove me to such caution in presenting research, I thought—but did not tell—her of the night I left a drunken young man crawling on paving stones, unable to see for the blood in his eyes."

BJ said, "Maybe they were better for it."

Estevan raised an eyebrow. "Maybe a hint would have done as much as a deviated septum."

BJ said, "Do you know why you get along so well with the Griffin?"

"Because any civilized being would."

"No. Because you each know what you are, and would rather be something you aren't."

After a moment's silence, Estevan said a little coldly, "If you're referring to my clothing, a little perception would—"

"Oh, no." BJ realized that she'd spoken too loud, and dropped her voice. "I mean that each of you is a warrior, and each of you would rather be peaceable. But you'll always need to be warriors, won't you? Because somebody has to be."

He didn't reply. After a moment, he stood and stared out the window, which faced the south. BJ could picture him staring over the Laetyen River, across the grasslands, past the canyon of the griffins or slightly east to Anavalon where Morgan had once gathered armies, and would probably try again. Finally he said unsteadily, "That's the thing about being good at something, isn't it? People need you for it, even when it's unpleasant."

BJ was sorry she had said anything.

Protera himself saved her. "You mentioned love, and implied that it was complicating your life."

BJ regretted her original outburst. "Let's just say that I wish I were in love with someone suitable."

"From which I infer that you may presently be in love with someone unsuitable. In Crossroads, 'unsuitable' covers a marvelous latitude. Try to remember that love is not a matter of reproduction or, in Crossroads, even of species."

The last stunned her. "You mean—"

"I mean that Melina looks like the offspring of a human and a goat. An attractive goat, as well as an attractive human, but now it is said. A griffin is part lion, part eagle; did you never wonder how these things came about?"

"I just accepted it." She considered. "That was probably shallow."

"No, no. It is practical, not research-oriented. What I tell you now is that I think the field of Crossroads, whatever kind of field it is, is very forgiving toward animal life. It lets species interbreed;

it saves them from genetic defects and neurological disorders and viral disease—inside Crossroads, all this is true."

BJ was dazed, trying to imagine the origin of centaurs, fauns, and the stag people like Rudy and Bambi. "But this never happens outside Crossroads—uh."

"You perceive."

"I don't want to. You're saying that all these species can't breed outside Crossroads."

"Eventually, no. It would depend on the world they were in. A generation, a few generations—" He spread his hands. "Their children would be strange, or stillborn, and the species would die."

"Is there a way to find out whether or not you're wrong?"

"I don't know." He looked very young again. "I would like to be. But I have thought about it, and I don't think that I am."

Together they sat in silence listening to distant chimerae honk at the moon. BJ didn't think he was wrong, either.

N·I·N·E

It was three days later. Lee Anne was gone; BJ had spent four hours by candlelight the night before, reviewing Lee Anne's notes for Hippoi classes, and had decided that maybe she would sleep in the following morning.

The light from her windows wouldn't let her. She opened her door and blinked, wiping her eyes as they watered. Horvat peered out curiously, sniffing and wagging his tail hopefully. Daphni yowled and refused to come near the door at all.

Kendrick, Virginia, was at roughly 2700 feet, on a plateau in the Blue Ridge Mountains. When BJ had first come to school there she had been fascinated by the weather forecasts that said "Rain, probably snow in the higher elevations." After a few messy winter surprises, she realized that she was living in the higher elevations, and she bought some snow boots.

All these months of living in the hills of Crossroads had not yet brought home to her that she was once again in the higher elevations.

It was what those living in the Great Lakes region of America would call lake effect snow: a concentration of moist air mixing with cold air and condensing the water into huge flakes that clung to each other, gathering mass as they fell until they hit the ground as fluffy clumps nearly the size of someone's thumb. The clouds, coming in low and fast just above the slopes, were galloping north in a gray and white line.

BJ whooped and slammed the door. Thirty seconds later, she ran back out in jeans, boots, a jacket, and a stocking cap and gloves.

Horvat trotted behind her dubiously, then leapt with excitement, barking at the sky.

Not yet finished falling, the snow was already melting on the ground. In the meantime, the entire river valley was white, broken only by the upright trunks of trees, overladen and bulky with their leaves and limbs covered with moist snow. Most of them were bent low; already there were broken limbs. BJ exhaled a plume of breath and laughed, running with Horvat in the snow and laughing when he sank in to his shoulders in a pocket, leaping to get out.

"Hello!" a voice called from below. A figure in a rainbow cloak and a pink tam, high black boots with silver buckles, and black jeans crosshatched with embroidered patches was slogging determinedly up the hill. "Are you okay?"

BJ fumbled for the catchlet at her belt, then dropped her hand. It had to be Fiona.

It was. She jogged the last few feet, puffing but nowhere near what BJ would have been. "I hope I can beg some breakfast off you."

"Absolutely." BJ waved an arm at the white plains above her, and beyond to the white mountains where the heaviest snow clouds were crashing against the slopes to the north and dissipating. "Look at it!" BJ lobbed a badly aimed snowball in Fiona's general direction. "Isn't it amazing?"

Fiona stepped aside, neatly avoiding the snowball. "You're welcome."

It seemed an odd thing to say about ducking a snowball.

BJ tossed another one at Horvat, who leapt at it, staring wildly around to either side when it fell apart as he bit it. "Did you know the snow was coming?"

Fiona rearranged her tam and carefully packed a snowball. "No, but I was pretty sure."

"How? Can you predict the weather from the sky?" She packed and threw two more snowballs, which Fiona once again avoided by stepping aside.

Fiona wrinkled her nose. "That would be tough in Crossroads, wouldn't it? I mean, any current from another world—blowing in over the roads—could change things . . . so I don't think the weather follows normal patterns." She tossed the snowball from hand to hand, weighing it. "No, I didn't predict it."

"Then how could you possibly know . . ." BJ suddenly understood exactly how Fiona could know, and froze in place. "You didn't."

Fiona bowed, straightened, and flung the snowball underhand.

It caught BJ full in the face. "You betcha."

BJ wiped her cheeks, barely caring. "How?"

"I was right." Fiona dropped in the snow, waving her arms and making an angel. "I was right about the edges of Crossroads, where the Strangeways cross. It's all the energy anybody ever wanted, and it's there waiting."

Horvat leapt at BJ's knees. BJ patted him absently. "But—" She struggled to find the right question. "What did you say, do, gesture . . . How did you know what to do?"

"I didn't. I tried a lot of things: chants, charms, ritual blood magic—" Fiona glanced down at the sheath knife in her belt. "Believe me, you don't want to know what all I tried."

"What worked?"

Fiona dimpled, her cold cheeks almost redder than her hair. "You're not gonna like it." She pulled a disreputable, herb-soaked rag from her pocket, then dropped to her knees, patted a mound of snow into shape quickly, and struck it, chanting:

> "I knock this rag upon this stane,
> To raise the wind in the devil's name:
> It shall not lye till I please again."

She tucked the rag back into her pocket and babbled amiably, "Only you have to strike it on a stone. It's from Dalyell's *The Darker Superstitions of Scotland*, which isn't old at all; it's from the 1830's, but I made sure I said 'stane' instead of 'stone' because of the rhyme, even though I'm not Scots. And I don't think the reference to the devil really matters, you know? I think it's a regionalism, what the Christians did to attribute the power of the Strangeways to a force they understood, only I didn't want to take chances changing things too much. I rubbed some celandine into the rag, for success—that's a yellow poppy; some people name it in spells—and I put in a string that I'd tied three knots in and then untied, because that's another way of raising wind, and I mixed in some Thessalian charms . . ."

She looked up, still on her knees, and the moisture on her cheeks wasn't from snow. "It works," she whispered. "I'm going to be a witch."

BJ said nothing as Fiona stood up, still talking. "I started with weather spells because I figured, with all the varied air currents around the Strangeways, weather changes would be easy. That's why they're so common in witchcraft and travel stories, like *The Tempest* or *The Odyssey*."

"You should talk to the Griffin about that," BJ said, to see if
Fiona knew him.

Fiona's self-confidence wavered. "He makes me nervous."

"Good."

A shaft of sunlight struck the snow around them; BJ's eyes
watered with the brightness of it. "How long will it last?"

"Not very long, I hope. There's a way to make spells last
longer, but I don't know if it works." Fiona looked even happier.
"I can try that next time."

BJ looked at the hills above them, then at the river valley
below. "I'm not so sure there should be a next time," she said
slowly.

Fiona was stunned. "But this is important."

BJ gestured at the snow already melting and dripping off her
roof. "How fast will all that end up in the river?"

"Oh, wow!" she said simply and unself-consciously. She collected herself. "Doesn't matter. This storm is too concentrated
to raise a river that big. Now, a smaller stream, in the storm
path—"

BJ's eyes flew open wide, and she grabbed Fiona's arm. "Do
you know where the flowerbinders live?"

"Just yours." She pointed to the doorway, where Daphni was
testing the snow with distaste.

"Can you come with me, quickly? I'm about to need a lot
of help."

Locking Horvat up took no time; driving downhill in eight
inches of snow took a great deal. By the time they reached the
main road, wet boulders were showing through the snow.

BJ lurched onto the road. Fiona, riding shotgun, looked apprehensively ahead. "Should you be doing this without a map?"

"Relax. I know the way." Actually, BJ had glanced furtively
at *The Book of Strangeways* while locking Horvat in. Probably
they wouldn't be near any Strangeways; she hoped fervently that
her memory was good on all turns.

Four miles down the road they saw the roadway was clear in
the sun, and they saw their first ominous trickle of runoff.

Five minutes later, the hills to either side were steeper. They
watched in silence as rivulets off the hillsides cut free chunks of
snow which pooled runoff behind them and gave way suddenly.
On a small scale, it was beautiful.

BJ turned left up a narrow valley road. Her wheels spun several
times; each time she risked leaving the narrow ruts and burying

her wheels to the axle in what seemed to be a new stream in the middle of the road. Finally she shut the engine off and set the parking brake.

Fiona looked uphill to the steeply sloping hills framing a canyonlike valley. "We walk up there?"

BJ grabbed a coil of rope from under the seat. "We run."

The steep cliffs, broken by the occasional trickle, looked much the same as the first time BJ had seen them, sheer and unclimbable. The valley floor was still all white; the same walls that protected flowerbinders from The Great shielded most of the snow from sunlight.

Ribbon Falls was already twice as wide as usual.

Fiona walked between the snowy hummocks left by nearly covered brush. "They must have left already."

"Oh, they're here. They're just good at camouflaging themselves. Flowerbinders are quite smart."

"How smart does a white cat have to be to hide in snow?"

"That's not as important as figuring out how we're going to find them." BJ coughed. A blueback chirped and flew out of one of the nearby bushes, dipping close to the snow in an indigo streak.

A line of paws whipped out of the snow, barely missing the dodging bird. A moment later the paws had disappeared and the snow had shifted, covering the holes in the snow as though they had never been.

Fiona brightened suddenly, whipped off her tam and skimmed it across the snow like a Frisbee.

A paw shot up after it; she pounced, flat on the wet snow. "Help me tie him."

BJ tied a makeshift collar on him, a clumsy bowline that Sugar would have snickered at, and tossed her own cap over the snow. Another paw whipped out of the snow, snagging the cap; BJ looped more rope over the paw.

Twenty minutes later, BJ and Fiona were soaked and panting, and they had caught and tied thirty-two flowerbinders, all tugging at the ropes and mewing.

"How many of them are there?" Fiona said.

"No idea. More than this," BJ said, and realized she was shouting. She tugged at Fiona's sleeve and pointed. Ribbon Falls was four times its normal size, and widening as they watched.

BJ felt a chill at her ankles and looked down. The spill pool below the falls had risen nearly two feet; it was splashing over her boot tops.

Fiona shouted, "We've got to get out of here." BJ could barely read her lips. She nodded and untied the lead end of the rope from the bushes.

At first the flowerbinders resisted, and tugged back and forth. As the roar from the falls behind them grew to a steady thunder, they bunched up almost beneath BJ, nudging her forward. Fiona ran back and forth like a sheep dog, nudging them onto the road that led out.

She ran back, gasping, to BJ. "See?" she said cheerfully. "It's all going to work out. We'll lead them out, and set them free, and they'll be fine."

BJ glanced up. Several human silhouettes, untroubled by vertigo, were leaning over the cliff edge. It seemed to BJ that each of them was unnaturally slender. "Not necessarily."

Normally the way out of the narrow valley was navigable by truck. Half of the path was gone, eaten away by the sudden rush of water. The other half was terribly slippery. BJ, tugging on the rope, skidded off as the edge crumbled under one of her feet; her body swung sideways in the current.

Fiona, kneeling, grabbed the back of her coat and wrapped her other arm in the rope at the same time. BJ kicked frantically until one of her feet hit solid ground, then stood and climbed quickly. She and Fiona charged forward, tugging to urge the flowerbinders out of the deadly canyon.

The sunshine, once they were fully out, felt wonderful. Fiona relaxed. BJ then swung her head around, hearing a mew that didn't come from the line of flowerbinders, then grabbed Fiona's arm and pointed. "We missed one."

Fiona saw it carried by, wailing and struggling in the current. "Can they swim?"

"I don't know." BJ walked to each of the flowerbinders in turn, untying the rope. Each bounded a short distance, grabbed the soggy stems of flowers, and wrapped itself in them, blending into the damp landscape. BJ set the last one free. "That's that."

"And they'll be all right now?" Fiona was nodding determinedly in the manner of people who desperately need an affirmative answer.

"Some will, some won't." BJ pointed to the human figures on the hill. From a defensive circle they'd formed, a gray wolf emerged, sniffing the air and peering from side to side. "And now they're out where the Great can get them, as well." A momentary gust of wind made BJ cringe and check the sky.

She took a deep breath, reminding herself that smacking Fiona back and forth would do no good. "I'm sorry to ruin something you were so proud of—"

Fiona turned back to look at BJ, tears still on her cheeks. "That's what you don't understand," she said in frustration. "That's what you can never understand. It was still worth it."

BJ, coldly furious, drove her home in silence. Fiona, making hasty notes in a pocket pad she carried, didn't seem to notice.

Fiona's cottage, still tumbledown on the outside, was near a fork at the start of a Strangeway. The snowfall here had been particularly heavy; small patches remained.

Fiona leapt out. "Thank God. I've got to change out of these."

BJ followed her inside and stared in amazement at the bookcase.

It dominated the room like a monolith or an altar. It was rich, dark wood, sanded and then oiled to show the grain. It looked heavier than BJ's portable anesthetic machine, which had a metal body with two pressurized cylinders mounted on it. The books on these shelves—

BJ touched the books wonderingly. The bindings were marbled and leather, snake and animal skin. The titles were in Greek, Latin, German, Spanish, and English. She moved closer and read the little that she could.

Every last book was on magic. There were books on Babylonian oil magic, Native American shamanism, Haitian Loa and Voudou, Santería, and Obeah; there was a worn trade paperback about Wiccan, and a history of witchcraft in Ireland. A copy of Albertus Magnus's *The Booke of Secrets* leaned confidingly against his *Egyptian Secrets*; *De Praestigiis Daemonum* consorted with *The Egyptian Book of the Dead*; the writings of Frazer and Campbell took up a shelf by themselves. On the desk beside the bookcase, open with a suede bookmark in it, lay the book by John Dalyell which Fiona had mentioned earlier.

BJ picked up the Dalyell, enjoying the soft feel of old tooled leather. She opened it to the title page, where there was a stamp: PROPERTY OF THE WESTERN VIRGINIA UNIVERSITY LIBRARY.

She checked several more. All had the same stamp; in addition, *De Praestigiis Daemonum* had a raised circular stamp which said RARE BOOK ROOM. "Are these all checked out?" she asked.

Fiona, pulling on a red sweater with a dancing yellow pictograph across it, said lightly, "Oh, they weren't being used. Have you seen my tea set? I wrapped it in towels to bring it in . . ."

BJ pretended to listen, but she was thinking about the stolen books and about Fiona's saying that the risk to the flowerbinders was worth it for the experiment. Was there anything BJ could be so single-minded for?

When she had a chance, she said, "What do you think magic is? Is it like a current, or some sort of field that changes things inside it?"

Fiona pointed to the bookcase as she talked. "Frazer says there are two forces to magic: imitation, like a hunting dance guiding the hunt, and contagion, like the fingernail parings in a voodoo doll giving power to the doll. I guess you could call it a field. Why?"

BJ shrugged. "I like to understand everything I work with."

"Must be nice. I operate at the edge of ignorance all the time." Fiona glanced out the window at the road and smiled. "At the edge of everything."

"Um. Listen, I'd better get going."

Fiona, glancing longingly at her desk, didn't beg her to stay. BJ headed for the door, then turned. "Fiona?"

"Mmm?" She had already picked up a pen.

"Just remember that witches aren't always good role models."

Fiona frowned. "Maybe that's just how they were represented by people who didn't like their finding power. Maybe it's like how the first women in any new field are treated." She smiled. "Anyway, I'll only find out after I know a cross section of witches."

BJ, about to issue a warning about Morgan, dropped the subject. She drove home carefully and thoughtfully.

On her way back she scanned the hills futilely for flowerbinders; inevitably, they were too well hidden. Or gone. BJ chewed her lower lip, wondering what Fiona's next experiment would be.

The stream from the springhouse was still swollen, though a dark track in the grass showed how far it had subsided. BJ parked well back from it and walked the short distance to her house.

The rustle in the brush behind her was not loud. However, it sounded as though it was at least three feet off the ground. BJ checked the distance to her front door, then sighed and slid the catchlet partway from her pack. She faced the brush. "May I help you?"

"Possibly. Is that a scalpel that I see before me?"

The Griffin strode out of the brush, his wings partly extended, his fur ruffled, his tail erect. It was a grand entrance, designed to impress or frighten.

BJ put away the catchlet quickly; it wouldn't stop the Griffin anyway, if he wished to kill her. "I'm glad to see you. Is this a professional visit?"

"For which of us?" But he came all the way forward and bowed his head to her; BJ stroked his feathers lightly, glad that he seemed at ease. "Actually, I just have some questions about my excursion to be irradiated. Do I need to fast, and will I need anesthetic?"

He asked it politely enough, but he was glancing from side to side carefully, scanning up and down the hill.

"Of course you won't need to fast," BJ said slowly. "And you would only need anesthetic as an excuse to see Laurie—which you've already said you don't need me to provide." Horvat, behind the door, barked furiously; she moved forward and unlocked it. "I'm glad to see you, but what are you here about?"

"Oh, idle chat." He peered at the hillside restlessly. "Unseasonable weather, isn't it?"

Ah-*ha*!

She opened her mouth to say something, then glanced at his talons. "You've been getting bloody again."

He snapped his beak once with annoyance and curled the talon under, wiping it on the damp sod. "This time it genuinely was a mistake. I neither want nor need to intimidate you."

Horvat darted forward, sniffed at the Griffin's curled talon, and sat back on his haunches and howled.

BJ froze in place. "Whose blood is that?"

"This is not going at all as I planned," the Griffin said irritably. "All right, it's one of the Wyr. I interrupted a nasty bit of business involving chasing a flowerbinder to death. I have no objection whatsoever to hunting, but torment is inappropriate." He finished wiping his talon and added thoughtfully, "Except as a kind of tit for tat."

BJ swayed as her knees buckled; she caught herself. "And what did you do to her?" She was immediately sorry she had asked; how much could Horvat understand?

"The hunter became the hunted. I was the hunter, and I must say, I was far more considerate about not prolonging things. And I left my usual statement of purpose on the body."

Drawn in the blood of the victim. "In what language?"

"Oh, the Wyr don't read," he said easily. "I simply drew a balance scale. Quite well, I think."

"A bloody scale. Justice."

"You make it sound terrible." He considered. "It is, I suppose.

By the way, I could have dodged your question, since my quarry was male, but that's such a pointless game."

BJ exhaled loudly. "Thank you. For answering, I mean." She added quickly, "Did it tire you?"

"Somewhat. I'm in far better shape than I was, though. Soon I'll be able to fly again." He offered his now-clean claw to Horvat, who sniffed it and then chewed on it happily, his past grief forgotten. He cocked his head at BJ, turning one eye full on her. "And now that I've answered your question, perhaps you'll answer one of mine: Where did this snowfall come from?"

BJ stared at the springhouse beside her cottage before answering. If she didn't turn Fiona over to the Griffin, Fiona might do something even more reckless next time.

If she did turn Fiona over to him, it was possible that the Griffin would kill Fiona.

BJ had a quick vision of the Griffin patiently rolling Fiona in a stream, letting her struggle in a flood, lecturing her about criminal carelessness before holding her head under and dipping a talon in her blood like a steel quill pen in an inkwell. . . . She cleared her throat. "I think that whoever did it was probably experimenting, and is probably remorseful."

"Probably." The Griffin drew closer. "And could this probable miscreant possibly be planning more damage?"

BJ shook her head. "I can't imagine that would be the case."

The Griffin, closer still, peered into her eyes with his great golden eyes, feathered eyebrows drawn low. "Humans are exceedingly kind. Be very sure, if you are being kind to someone, that you're not allowing great cruelty."

BJ said with obvious relief, "I'll be sure. I'll work hard at—" She broke off and sniffed the air disapprovingly. "What is that smell?"

He sighed. "Company, of a sort."

A chimera landed nearby with a loud plop. It picked itself up, shook the dirt off its front paws, and regarded them with imbecilic delight.

Though it was hard to tell on a creature with a muzzle, it appeared to be smiling. It padded clumsily toward BJ.

The Griffin watched dourly. "Don't encourage it."

It sat on its haunches, front legs pulled up against its underbelly. BJ noted distractedly that its whiskers were singed, and that it had similar singeing on its abdomen, where it had cleaned all the hair off itself—feline psychogenic alopecia, a behavioral disorder. It also had at least one gorged tick near the beginning of its posterior scales. For a semi-feline animal, it was singularly unkempt.

BJ recognized the tortoise-shell marking on the head and said unhappily, "Oh, God, it's Fran."

The chimera wagged its hideous scorpion tail and peered interestedly at Horvat, who growled. The Griffin shook his head at the chimera. "Don't try." His voice, though disgusted, was surprisingly gentle.

Suddenly the chimera peered back at the underbrush as it rustled and a dodo emerged. BJ had never seen one in this part of Crossroads; perhaps they had been driven here by the snow or the flood. It looked straight at BJ and the Griffin without reacting in any way, then shuffled unconcernedly toward the chimera, who crouched to play like a puppy.

The dodo finally, at a range of two feet, noticed the chimera and walked, bobbing, straight up to it until they touched, beak to muzzle. BJ was delighted.

The chimera's tail flashed up and over its head and stabbed down into the unreacting bird, pinning it to the mud under the scorpion-sting.

With its forepaws, the chimera pulled the dying bird free, swung its own scorpion tail sideways and out of the way, and belched yellow-blue flame over the dodo.

The air shimmered. BJ's eyes watered from the acrid smell and sudden heat. When she could see again, the chimera was bouncing the scorched featherless carcass from claw to claw, nibbling at the flesh as a finicky cat might do with a piece of barbecued chicken.

Horvat ran forward, yapping, and placed himself between BJ and the chimera. She quickly scooped him up one-handed and tossed him to one side; Horvat looked resentful, but stayed.

The chimera noticed BJ again. He waddled forward on his hind legs, belly jiggling, and dumped the bird in the dust at BJ's feet.

The Griffin said, "Why, how sweet. Go ahead, Doctor; the meat is a bit fatty for me, but some like it."

"No, thank you, Fran," BJ said shakily. The chimera looked at her questioningly. "You go ahead."

The chimera nodded brightly, snatching the dead bird up. He devoured half of it in four bites, then gave an immense and (this time) involuntary belch. It hastily dropped the flaming dodo, clasping its paws to its muzzle to hold the already-escaped flame in and rolling embarrassed eyes. Moments later it poked despondently at the charred remains, gave an almost human shrug, and padded off, slowly gaining momentum and not bothering to spread its wings until the last minute.

They watched it in silence. Finally BJ turned to the Griffin. "Are they all like that?"

"Good heavens, no. Some are filthier and more ill-natured." He watched her face. "What do you find amusing?"

"The poor thing, when it had breathed fire a second time—"

" 'Breathed' is fairly kind."

Kindness again. "And then it was so upset at what happened to its meal."

The Griffin extended a single disdainful talon and flipped the dodo corpse over. Charred flesh flaked off. "Alas, poor meal."

He regarded BJ, and for once his curved beak did not seem to be smiling. "Doctor, it isn't proper for a lay animal to advise a professional, but I do hope you will remember that you could easily have become the same color and disposition as the dodo."

The wind whistled across the hillside, and flecks of ash scattered from the dodo legs, exposing bone. From the distance came several more excited honks from chimerae, and a burst of noise like an explosion. BJ shivered, pulling her thin jacket close and hunching her shoulders. Today she had been kind to Fiona, kind to the chimerae, kind to Horvat.

Horvat nuzzled her, whining. She picked him up and held him so tightly that he struggled as he licked her nose.

T·E·N

BJ WAS BACK in Kendrick. She had laid in supplies for burns, had shamelessly bought an ice cream sundae, and was finishing her errands. She braced herself and opened the door to Gyro's.

The moment that Stan saw her, he hurried around the counter. "Beej." He hesitated long enough that BJ kissed him on the cheek first. "Good to see you. How you doing, Doctor?" he asked, with no real interest at all.

"Fine." She dug in her knapsack. "I have a letter."

"Great, great." He snatched it from her hands almost as she pulled it out for him.

He read quickly, lips moving in a steady whisper, stopping only to laugh. "He says your friends can't cook."

"He's making them learn."

Stan laughed. "That's Papa." He wiped his eyes. "I don't know how you did it, Beej. He sounds like he used to, years ago."

He folded the letter and tucked it carefully in his shirt pocket. "I'll read it again later. You had lunch? You want a gyro?"

"Actually, I'd love a hamburger. I haven't even seen one in months." She added, "And I had a gyro just the other day."

Stan nodded, his smile crinkling at his graying mustache. "When you've had the best, why try the rest, huh? Okay, I'm not too hurt."

He formed a patty quickly, slapping it from hand to hand, and tossed it on the grill behind him without looking. "Something to drink?" he said absently.

"Coke." BJ was determined to get a lot of tasting in.

Stan scooped the ice and filled her glass mechanically. He turned back to the grill, flipping the burger many more times than was necessary, then whirled around. "BJ, I'm sorry, but I gotta ask. I know I said I never would, but I gotta. This place where Papa is, you said you couldn't tell me much about it, I know, but what's it like? Is it okay?"

She said carefully, "It's beautiful."

"But is it safe? I read his letters, and the things he says he's seen, my God! Is it dangerous?"

BJ said slowly, "Chris is in the most protected place he could be."

To her relief, Stan didn't notice her having dodged the question. "And these people he talks about in the letters. Half of them aren't even people, it sounds like. I know he's not having trouble with his mind, because you told me he's not—"

She nodded, wondering uncomfortably what the Griffin as Inspector General would do to her if he found out the contents of Chris's letters.

Stan went on, "So these people, do they like my father? Do they treat him okay?"

BJ thought of B'Cu's sullen glances and Melina's tired patience. "They treat him well. They work with him." She saw from Stan's face that wasn't enough. "They're friends."

Stan nodded, satisfied. BJ ate quickly and left.

The Dart Club, a second-story bar with an outdoor staircase, had been Dave Wilson's favorite haunt. She had been unsurprised when he had suggested meeting there, but was astonished when he met her at the bottom of the stairs. She looked at his spreading waist and receding hairline and thought for one elated moment: He sees it. He's aging and I'm not, because I'm in Crossroads, and he sees it.

Then she caught herself, thinking, it's only been three months. He's probably been putting on weight and losing his hair since he was eighteen; I just didn't notice while we were in school. And, suddenly self-conscious: What will he notice about me?

He gave her a quick, affectionate hug and a kiss. (BJ had long resigned herself, without resentment, to the fact that Dave would never except in moments of extreme desperation be attracted to a woman he worked with.) "Babe, how you doing?"

"It's *Doctor* Babe to you."

"And to you." He looked at her fondly. "Nice clothes. Make them yourself?" She was wearing the wool skirt.

"With help." She noticed that two bulky bags lay on either side of him, and that his hands were reaching for them. "Are you ready to go?"

He grinned. "Let's rock."

BJ had experienced Dave's driving and map reading; she drove and navigated. Dave hung out the window on the passenger side like a dog letting its ears flap. "Man, this is great."

"Watch out for branches and stray monsters," she warned. Dave pulled his head back in quickly. "Did you get my note about Rudy and Bambi's wedding?"

"Sure, but I already knew." BJ had a wild moment of wondering if Dave had a way into Crossroads, when he added, "I went to the AVMA conference, in San Francisco. Rudy was back on campus; we went out drinking."

BJ asked something she had wondered for a long time. "Rudy's mostly human, but he does have antlers. Really, isn't he conspicuous, even in San Francisco?"

"A little," Dave admitted. "But not among his friends. USF has a lot of, uh, foreign students." He laughed, but still sounded wondering. "I wish I'd taken pictures."

BJ wished he had, too. "So, do you miss Crossroads?"

He smiled slyly. "I took some of it with me."

BJ looked apprehensive. "You smuggled an animal out?" She had visions of a unicorn grazing at Cornell.

"Of course not. I'll give you a hint: I have the tidiest lab at Cornell."

"You?" At any given moment, Dave was likely to drop a can, a candy wrapper, or a trash barrel, and walk on pretending not to notice.

"Uh-huh." Dave was enjoying this. "Another hint: If I leave a six-pack and a bag of chips under the table when I go home, it's even cleaner."

"I have no idea what you're talking about."

"That's right; you never saw them do that."

Suddenly, BJ knew what he was talking about. "Oh, my God, the Little Brown Men." They were short, argumentative, rowdy, hard-drinking, and completely mannerless. Dave adored them.

"You got it."

"They came with you?"

Dave's smile faded. "Nearly as many as were left." Morgan's last foray into Crossroads had taken many casualties.

BJ puzzled over Dave's mention of a six-pack and a bag of

chips in exchange for cleaning. Suddenly it dawned on her. "You mean they're really browni—"

"Uh-uh." Dave was serious. "Say 'those guys,' or 'the little guys,' or 'the little brown men.' Never say that name."

But the sudden pinching of her leg warned her more succinctly. Chattering laughter erupted from under the seat. BJ sighed. "No wonder your luggage was so bulky."

Embarrassed, Dave said, "Hey, they were homesick."

They cruised into Crossroads, waving to the heavy, bearded man who was digging at the roadway on the Virginia side. BJ frowned, watching a Road Crew waiting for her to pass. They were sweating freely, and had removed their jackets while they waited, leaning on the double-bladed twybils, ax and hoe both, that they used to tear up and replace roadway. "They look like a summer work crew."

"It's a lot warmer here than it is in Virginia. Or in New York State, believe me."

"You should have been here a few days ago," BJ said. "It was snowing."

They rolled down the windows as they emerged onto the road-way above the Laetyen River. Dave, staring eagerly around him, was too distracted to talk, and BJ had her hands full driving and navigating at the same time. She hoped that Dave would be more impressed with her clinic than Lee Anne had been.

He squinted as her cottage came into sight, and smiled, delighted. "Terrific. That's your practice sign, isn't it?" The Healing Sign swung freely in the warm breeze. "And you have a client."

BJ got out slowly, tucking the catchlet into the waist of her skirt and hiding it under her windbreaker. "I think that may also be the patient."

His hair was dark and sleek, brushed straight back. He was half a foot taller than Dave, and solid, wiry muscle. Other than his scalp, his body looked completely hairless. He watched them with dark, focused eyes that never seemed to leave either of them. "Who is doctor?" he asked.

"We both are," BJ said. "Are you Wyr?" She felt Dave tense.

The figure nodded, folding his arms and standing straighter. "I am sick."

BJ opened her door and motioned the Wyr and Dave inside. Dave muttered unhappily, "Enter freely and of your own will," but came in. The Wyr followed. Horvat growled; BJ raised a warning finger and he shut up.

BJ asked, "Are you sick like this, or in your other form?"

"In the other." He added reluctantly, "Both, now."

BJ pulled an empty file folder and took out a New Patient form. "Your name, please?"

"Roman." He looked down at Horvat with disgust. "He is small."

"He'll get bigger."

"No." This time he grinned, not nicely. "Too small."

"I don't discuss other patients," BJ said brusquely. "Tell me, what are you here for?"

"I do not eat."

"Have you tried?"

He looked at her scornfully. "I vomit."

"Could it be something you ate?"

He shook his head. "Others ate the vomit. They are well."

Dave gulped. BJ was momentarily envious of veterinarians whose patients could not talk. "Do you have any other symptoms? Are you tired, or unusually thirsty, or—"

"I tire," he said hesitantly. "My head spins."

BJ hated having to ask. "Were you ever involved with drug use? Did Morgan or"—she didn't know if the Wyr would know DeeDee's name—"anyone else give you morphine?"

"Yes. I—stopped." He glowered. "You should not know."

"I should, if I'm taking your history," she answered calmly. "Thank you for answering. I have a few more questions."

"No."

"You will answer them or leave without help." Dave stared at her.

Roman answered, not happily. Finally she put down the folder. "That's all. If you would change form, then."

He curled his lip at her. His nostrils flared, then continued flaring as they grew. A trickle of blood came from one of them. Horvat crept forward to watch; BJ pulled him back and held him.

Even braced for the transformation, BJ found it upsetting. At this range, BJ was able to see more detail than before. The veins on the sclera of his eyes began rupturing from the iris out. The human teeth, falling out, had small chunks of bone clinging to them. The muscles to either side of the spine clenched to pull it shorter with a grinding sound. Roman threw his head back and wailed, the wail rapidly turning into a howl.

BJ let go of Horvat so that she could fill a syringe. Horvat came forward curiously as the wolf, by far the largest gray wolf they had seen among the Wyr, raised his head. He snapped casually at Horvat, who barely skidded backwards in time to save his throat.

BJ slammed the table, hard, and her catchlet was in her right hand. She smacked the wolf in the muzzle, hard, with the flat of it. "No. Not now, not ever. He's——" She caught herself before saying 'mine.' "My patient."

Horvat, head cocked to catch every word, wagged his tail furiously. Roman looked up at her and tensed to spring, then pricked his ears forward and sniffed at the catchlet.

"That's right. Silver-plated; I don't know if it needs to be. Want to find out?"

He growled, steadily and low.

"I don't care. It's my place, and my rules, if you want help. Now, get up on that table and lie down."

The wolf glowered at her and rubbed a paw against his muzzle. With a growl of disgust, he leapt onto the table effortlessly. He stood, looking into her eyes, jaws slightly apart. His fangs, freshly grown, were as clean and sharp as a newborn puppy's.

Dave locked the wolf's body under his arm, though he didn't look like he could hold it there. He held off the cephalic vein while BJ injected it with Surital and withdrew before the Wyr could react. Gradually his eyes lost their focus, and his lifted lip lowered over his teeth.

Dave loosened his grip. "Man, you're more reckless than I ever was. This place is changing you."

BJ looked down at the sleeping wolf. "Maybe it's a field effect."

"What?"

"Nothing. Help me roll the X-ray over."

Dave positioned the wolf on his side and measured his abdomen with calipers; Dave was less familiar with the portable machines, but she trusted his skills. She started the generator. Dave opened the window and passed her the switch; he stepped outside with her, and she snapped the picture.

Dave read Lao's *Guide to the Unbiological Species* and BJ reviewed notes on canine GI while they waited for the film. Shortly, BJ pulled a handout and passed it to Dave. "Vis. rad," she intoned. Dr. Truelove had hated typing and issued his students nearly incomprehensible handouts full of abbreviations. "No vis. d.v."

"Bttr vis. lat.," Dave responded ritually. "And lateral it is, not dorso-ventral. Not that it'll show everything we need. I wish I was in my lab; how do you get by, with no blood work?"

"Dave Wilson, I do plenty of blood work. I just don't have an in-house processor, and I probably wouldn't have that even if I were practicing in Richmond."

"Well, you need one."

"I have an automatic developer for X-rays; isn't that enough? Cornell is spoiling you."

The film developed. Dave pulled it and said with relief, "There's nothing," BJ didn't answer. She was staring at the dark spots on the radiograph, running through the intestines in an irregular pattern.

She snapped the corner of the film with her index finger and thumb. "That's weird."

"It's also not worth cutting for. There's nothing radiopaque; where's the blockage?"

"It may not be a complete blockage," she said absently. "And it could be something radiolucent . . . I'm going in."

"BJ, I don't think there's anything there." But he started shaving the wolf; six months ago he would have forced his opinion on her, or on anyone else.

"Bet a pizza on it?"

"Where are we going to find a pizza?"

"Stein's. Greek pizza."

"You're on." Dave rigged a mask on the wolf and opened the isoflurane valve. He picked up the clippers—they weren't electric, but he adjusted to them easily—and shortly, without looking up, he said, "Shaved and ready to roll." Both of them were used to talking without eye contact during surgery.

"Scrubbing time." They scrubbed, Dave glancing around nervously the entire time as though he could watch sources of infection come out of the stone walls.

Dave draped the wolf, and BJ made a quick, straight incision from the zyphoid nearly to the pubis. She pulled the sides open carefully, packing both sides of the incision with saline-moistened lap pads.

"And now," Dave said, without realizing that he'd dropped into lab-instructor mannerisms, "run the GI tract."

BJ smiled but said nothing. Carefully, half a foot at a time, she raised lengths of intestine out of the abdominal cavity and probed them delicately with her fingers, checking for obstructions. Afterward she put each length back in place. After less than a minute, halfway down the jejunum, she stopped. "Hah. I knew it."

Dave reached out carefully. "Wow, there is something."

" 'Something'? The intestine feels like pantyhose with a string running through it."

Stung, he retorted, "Well, maybe I don't know what pantyhose feels like."

"Dr. Wilson, you surprise me. Your reputation with women—"

"Okay, okay. Let's open it." He was blushing; he had done a great deal of bragging in college and vet school. "Jeez, good call."

"Nah. You're too used to watching students." But she was pleased. While Dave held the bowel loop, she incised along the antimesenteric border. She reached in with a forceps and murmured, "What is this?"

She lifted it with the forceps. It came out with minimal force, no problem with knotting or binding.

Dave looked at it with interest. "It's leather. I've taken pieces of dog collar out of dogs; it looks like that after a while." He studied it more closely. "Looks more like a bridle strap. Yep, see where the rings were? If they'd been in, it would've shown up on the film. Definitely a bridle."

"From what? Do you think he ate a horse?"

"I wouldn't be surprised," Dave said grimly. "Let's close— man, I'm sorry; I'm too used to labs. Would you like to run the rest of the bowel and close now?"

"I would love to run the rest of the bowel and close now." She set the strap aside and stitched carefully and quickly, uniform stitches. After checking for bowel leakage, she closed the same way, first the body wall, then subcutes and skin.

She turned around. "Dave, you forgot to tell me to be careful not to touch the pancreas."

"I figured you knew." But he sounded embarrassed; BJ had caught him out. "So now what?"

"Now we clean up, we monitor him, and we watch him come out of anesthetic."

"How long will that take?"

"A dog would take a couple hours; I don't know anything about the Wyr." The only other time she had seen one anesthetized, it came out from under early and went for the vet's throat. "Would you like a weapon?" She offered it the way she might offer surgical gloves.

He swallowed. "Thanks, tea would be better."

They sat together, sipping and watching the patient. "So," BJ said, "how's graduate work?"

"Long hours, low pay. Who can beat it?" But he sounded happy. "I haven't specialized yet. Dr. Mannering acts like I can do anything if I'd only try. He put me in charge of a junior year suture lab." He frowned. "God, I never once thought that they'd be so fumble-fingered. Were we like that?"

BJ had a single dark flash of herself, unable to pick up a pen with confidence at the height of her illness. "I'll bet most of them are like you were. A few of them aren't as sure of themselves."

"Okay. BJ, it's like sitting around waiting for evolution to happen. I swear, if it can walk upright without pissing on its shoes, it takes my classes." He smiled. "I have a couple bright ones. I just wish I could make them less spastic."

BJ admitted something she hadn't even told Lee Anne: "Do you know, I used to buy chicken drumsticks because they were cheap at Kroger's, and I'd cut them with a scalpel and sew them up? Then I'd cook them and eat them."

Other people might have been disgusted. Dave said with surprise, "That's a terrific idea. I'll use that in class." Then he snickered. "I'd be more impressed if the chicken got well."

"I'll bet you're a good teacher," she said, and added, "I don't want to hear that you've been hitting on the good-looking ones."

He laughed. "I try not to think about them that way—Hang on."

The wolf on the table had stirred, its tail and leg moving. It looked up at them with no recognition at all, growling. Then its eyes rolled back in its head and the transformation began.

Dave leapt forward with a gauze pad, holding it against the sutures as the wolf's body stretched out and thrashed. A moment later, BJ was beside him, trying to hold the screaming wolf's muzzle. "Are you crazy?"

"Sure, are you?" He sounded like the old Dave. "This is tricky—"

Roman, half human and half wolf, bucked and sunfished in Dave's arms, leaving the table. Dave dropped to his knees, spreading the Wyr's weight across his shoulders, and lowered him to the floor. He stepped back. "I can't see the sutures any more; I guess that's good."

BJ checked his arm. "You're bleeding."

"Just a scratch." Dave licked his lips. "That business about a werewolf bite producing another werewolf, that's just superstition, right?"

"We've all been bit before," BJ reminded him. It wasn't an answer, but it was what they had.

Roman's tail fell off; he ate it to conserve mass. Finally he stood up and BJ gasped; Roman had a long, angry scar running from his navel down to his pubic hair. It had no sutures, and looked to be several weeks healed.

BJ said, "You should not have changed back."

"I hurt." His hand traced his muscled stomach, searching for the scar. "Now, less."

"I thought that your injuries never transferred from body to body."

He grinned at her. "They must. How would we die?"

"But the other Wyr I've worked on—"

"Small things go. Large things last." His dark eyebrows had a pucker in them, and sweat broke out on his chest. "And hurt."

"I can give you something for the pain—" She stopped; his lips were curled back, and he was exposing his teeth and growling, forgetting that he was human.

He swept a hand out to smash the syringe; she snatched it away. "No drug," he said, and with just a trace of angry shame, "Never again."

"Of course. I'm sorry." She moved to the pantry and returned with an apothecary jar from which she poured herbs onto paper. "This is a blend of spearmint, catnip, and yarrow. Boil it in water and drink the water, or, in your other form, eat the plants. It won't do much, but it may calm your stomach."

He nodded. "Only like this. Not on four." Reflexively, he wrapped his arms protectively around his stomach. "For a long time."

"Just as well." She held up a vial of ampicillin. "Take one of these—it's not a drug—in the morning, one in the afternoon, one at night, until they're done. They will prevent infection." As he took the vial, she went on, "Also, you're going to need healing time. I don't know if you have to change back and spend it as a wolf. If you do, I recommend that you get plenty of rest. Can someone help you find food?"

He scowled, making a low sound in his throat. "No help."

"But won't the pack—" She saw his expression and said hastily, "All right. Just remember, you'll be weak for a while."

"Never weak." He gestured toward Horvat with disgust. Horvat was trying to edge between BJ and Roman, and BJ was nudging him back with her foot. "He is weak. Him I kill."

"No you won't," she said flatly. She held the bridle strap in front of him. "By the way, would you like to tell us how you swallowed this?"

He looked at her silently. She gave up and set it down.

He dressed quickly. With casual scorn he threw a gold coin on the table. She tried to break it to make change, but he waved her away. "My last," he said with disgust. "Keep all. I go now."

"You should rest," BJ said.

He grinned at her again. "I am Wyr. We never stop."

And he was gone, loping painfully but steadily across the hillside.

Dave let out a windy sigh. "Man, those guys are scary. Are they the ones who are responsible for most of your patients?"

"No. I think—" And BJ stopped dead. She had been assuming it was mostly the chimerae. "I think we should go to Stein's; he'll be glad to see you."

"All right." He watched her staring after the Wyr. "What's bothering you?"

"I just want to know what he attacked that was wearing a bridle."

"He won't tell you. Anything else?"

They moved toward the van. "I'd like to know who the rider was."

It was just before sunset when they arrived; the night was still wonderfully warm. Dave shook his head at the new building. "I can't believe Stein rebuilt so fast."

"He had to." BJ held the door open for him. "Remember, it's also a fort." From inside they heard the clink of cups and the murmur of patrons.

Stein's parrot was back on his perch, in the entryway to the inn. He took one look at Dave and chanted in English,

"Welcome to Stein's. Rebuilding is now complete, and for your safety and continued survival, we have a few simple rules concerning manners, gambling, and weapons—"

"I'll fill him in," BJ interrupted. "Come by my cottage tomorrow; I have an errand for you."

The parrot leered and opened its mouth; Dave, with great presence of mind, stuffed a cracker in its beak. It raised one claw and made a gesture neither of them recognized but which was clearly obscene.

Inside, the dinner crowd had arrived, finished with daylight travel and labor. A table in the corner was a forest of antlers, the human faces beneath them intent on something on the table.

Over the muted crowd noise, they heard a familiar voice explain patiently, "So, like, the ones with the eyelashes are women; they're called queens. They beat any of the numbered ones, plus the jack I showed you earlier—"

Dave called out, "Rudy!"

Rudy, faded USF T-shirt on as usual, looked delighted. He bounded across the room on his stag legs, head lowered to charge. Dave snatched Melina's towel and waved it like a matador's cape. At the last minute, he ducked under Rudy's antlers, tucked the towel into them to cover Rudy's face, then spun him around and hugged him around the waist. "You're getting sloppy, man."

Rudy flipped the towel off with a toss of his head and hugged back. "You're getting fat and bald, man."

Melina smiled tolerantly. BJ suddenly missed Stacey's affectionate, unintentional rudeness without being able to imagine why.

"Come sit by me." Rudy waved an arm. "You here for dinner? My treat, man." He waved an arm. Melina ran over with a tray of salads. "You've gotta try this. Talk about terrific. It has some kind of lemon and olive oil dressing—"

"Ladolemona." Chris himself, appearing from behind the grill, poured the dressing over a plate of salad. "You taste." He didn't know Dave, but he smiled at BJ.

Dave, never a salad fan, tasted cautiously. He raised his eyebrows, quickly ate four more forkfuls. Chris laughed and left, shouting orders to B'Cu and to Melina, who waved at Dave from the rotating-spit hearth but who didn't dare leave it to chat.

Stein, stopping at Dave's table, said, "See that? Even salad is good in his hands." He sighed. "Face it, I cooked because I needed an excuse for a fort. He's in a fort because he needs an excuse to cook. I checked on my meat scale; do you know that I've put on twelve pounds since he came here? Twelve pounds!"

Dave said dutifully, "It doesn't show." Rudy snorted.

Stein laughed and patted his shoulder. "You still have to pay for your ale, but thank you, young man."

Behind them, Chris saw someone entering the inn, and called out a short phrase in clicks and glottal stops. B'Cu, his head popping up beside the vertical spit where he was laboriously shaving off slices of lamb, angrily corrected his pronounciation and grabbed another serving dish.

Stein enjoyed Dave's expression. "It's Bantu. Or Swahili, who knows? I know that the first time Chris tried to use it to talk to B'Cu, Chris popped his false teeth out. You should have seen

B'Cu." He chuckled. "I don't think he knew about dentures."

"I could sell him a set," said the man who'd just come in. Stein rose.

BJ and Dave half-rose, then checked themselves and looked around. It was possible that many of the people in the inn only knew the newcomer as Owen, an agreeable peddler with a pushcart, and did not know that he was King Brandal.

He smiled kindly at Dave, and winked at BJ. "I have regular teeth, wooden teeth like your friend George Washington, and windup teeth in case your mouth is lazy. I have Halloween fangs, real fangs, night-gaunt fangs, and fangs from your strangest dreams. Installation is extra, and extras cost." He sat down, pretending not to notice that Stein held a chair for him, but squeezing the older man's arm. "Hello, BJ, and hello to you, sir—Dave, isn't it?"

"Yes sir—sire." Dave sounded terribly awkward.

Brandal looked worried. He was in early middle age, but seemed much younger. "Please, just call me Owen," he said softly. "I'm not King Brandal just now."

"A master of disguise," BJ said.

He smiled, really a charming smile, relaxed and free of the worry he generally had. "Not really. There's no photography here, and drawing isn't that sophisticated. If I say I'm Owen, then I'm Owen."

"Master of acting, then."

"Actually, I like being Owen. I like trading, and bargaining, and offering people new products." He grinned unashamedly. "I thought of bringing in some cameras, but what a disaster it would be for me."

Dave grinned. "Do you still have Glarundel, the Sword that was Useless?"

"Guaranteed to render the user completely vulnerable. Are you in the market?" He added as Dave shook his head, "Nobody is. If I keep it much longer, it'll have sentimental value."

The click of gold pieces at the poker table was audible, and there was a sudden high, happy chattering at the far end of the table. Dave laughed. "I knew those little guys would want to be dealt in." He looked over longingly.

It was the opening BJ wanted. "Why don't you get in the game? I won't be offended."

He didn't wait for another offer. In seconds, Rudy's friends had made room for him, and Dave, taking the deal, was explaining a game called Seven Card No Peek, Killer Queen.

"Killer Queen . . ." Brandal said softly, and for a moment his eyes were full of hurt. He shook his head quickly and smiled at BJ. "That was nicely done. You had something you wanted to talk about with me."

"Yes." BJ said hesitantly. "It may not be important, but could I tell you about someone I know?" She told the story of Fiona and the Stumbling Curse, and continued through Fiona's making it snow and nearly destroying the flowerbinders.

Brandal listened. "And she's doing this at the edges of Crossroads, on the Strangeways? That's completely crazy."

"Not completely, by her standards. After all, it has worked."

"Then it's dangerous." Brandal looked at BJ narrowly. "How has she learned so much so fast?"

"Oh, she hasn't." BJ was quite certain on this point. "She's been researching for ages; she just couldn't find a place where the research mattered."

"It matters here. Have you told the Inspector General?"

"No." In the silence that followed, BJ said, "I didn't want her killed, but I had to tell someone."

Owen stared at the table, considering. Finally he said, "I'll make a trading visit, just myself and the pushcart. I'll take a book she'd find interesting, and we'll talk. I won't tell the Inspector General just yet." He looked at BJ very seriously, for once not appearing boyish. "But I will tell him if I think it needs doing. I've been overly forgiving before, and risked all of Crossroads. I can never do that again."

BJ nodded. "That's why I told you. You'll do what needs doing." She looked away, amazed that she could be so ashamed and embarrassed by her inability to send an acquaintance to her death.

The king put a hand on BJ's. "Hard, isn't it? To judge your own, decide who should be killed . . . I don't know how Polyta stands it."

"Or you. Or Stein." On an impulse she added, "Or Fields."

He looked startled. "Fields never kills anyone. I thought you knew."

"I was fairly sure," she said carefully.

He laughed. "And now you're sure. I wish I were as clever as you are."

"You're good. That's even better. You spend your whole life watching your people, without a castle or a palace. You go from place to place—"

"It sounds worse than it is. I have a wonderful time." He looked at BJ speculatively. "It's no worse than Fields's life. You'd like it, really."

BJ said flatly, "It's hard. I watch some of them die now, and it's hard. What would I feel, if I were you?"

"Or Fields."

"Or Fields," she agreed. "How old is he?"

"Hard to say," he answered easily. "I once heard him tell a story . . ." The story was long and involved, and completely dodged her question. It was pleasant enough that she accepted the dodge.

The poker game was no closer to an end when BJ, exhausted, gave up and said good night. She drove home and stumbled into her cottage, let Horvat out and in, lit candles, put on a nightshirt, and settled in to try and read some more of *Walden*.

The knock at her door was more of a scratch. Half-asleep, she opened the door.

Gredya walked past her to the table. She put her hands on it, palms down, leaned against the corner of it, and rubbed her crotch against it slowly and rhythmically.

Her smile opened into a full grin, her teeth showing and apart. She licked her tongue across her lips. She arched her back, and though Gredya was slender even for the Wyr, she seemed suddenly full-breasted.

Horvat, tail wagging wildly and nostrils flared, came out of the corner to sniff at his mother, and BJ realized what was happening. She pulled Horvat back. "Is this—"

"My season is here."

But she had whelped in the summer. "Didn't you already go into heat for this year?" Wolves only went into heat once a year.

Gredya gave a low chuckle. "With the others. Now, only me."

"You're the only woman of the Wyr in heat right now?"

"Others soon. I come first." She shrugged. "Maybe the drug."

"But why would any of you go into heat? That's more a spring thing."

Gredya tilted her head up, sniffing at the breeze. "The air is strange."

The air was strange: rich and warm, even more so than this afternoon. BJ walked across to close the shutters, and froze in place.

"You think something."

"Nothing much." She closed the window. If this was Fiona's doing, it was a lot more powerful than the snowstorm had been. She was suddenly glad she had told Owen—Brandal. "Do you think the air has made you change?"

"Partly." Gredya rubbed harder against the table, running her tongue out over her lips. "And the drug. It changed me." For a moment, even aroused and wild, she looked immensely sad. "I wish not."

BJ was filled with pity. She had faced the choice of suicide or illness, she had faced the loss of both her parents, and she had faced failure. She had never faced morphine addiction. "You have done well."

Gredya straightened up briefly. "Not for Wyr." Then she was back at the table corner. "They will be wild."

"The pack?" BJ wished that the Wyr were not so laconic.

"The men. They will fight." She grinned again. "Many will mate." The wild light in her eyes dimmed, and she said, "Keep Horvat. Keep him safe. Tonight, tomorrow." She said again, rare for the Wyr, "Please."

"I promise."

"Good." Then Gredya did the only intimate thing she ever did, before or after, to BJ: She turned away from the table and licked BJ's cheek, rubbing her dark-haired head on BJ's shoulder. BJ, unsure what to do, put her hand on Gredya's head. Gredya's hair was fine and new, like a baby's.

She watched Gredya trot into the night, shoulders back and hips swaying sensually. Shortly she heard one howl, then another, then human voices—*not* human voices—shouting in short bursts. BJ shuddered, and thought, Thank God Dave isn't here.

She spent an hour planning the next day's work station. If the male Wyr weren't too proud to come to her, tomorrow would be her busiest day.

E·L·E·V·E·N

BJ SET UP for cases the following morning, laying out gauze, sutures, large quantities of sulfa and amoxil, and putting on a kettle of boiling water to augment her supply of sterile solution. None of the Wyr showed up. Probably they had done all their fighting as wolves, and were healing as humans. Either the wounds were not serious, or the wounded were too proud to come to a vet, and would die.

All she saw was a burn victim—her tenth since the chimerae had appeared. This one, a wide-eyed fox kit, was being carried by a Meat Woman who was shivering; she had taken off her wool shirt to wrap it in.

BJ escorted her inside quickly, gesturing toward the lab table and pulling from her closet a faded Baltimore Orioles sweatshirt many times too big for the little woman. BJ took the frightened bundle from her, passing her the sweatshirt. "Thank you for coming. What is your name?"

She smiled, hurriedly covered her mouth with one hand, and said, "Sahnrr." She turned the sweatshirt over in her hands, trying to understand the design. She pulled it over her head and was delighted when it came to her knees.

BJ was carefully unwrapping the fox, using as little motion and force as possible. She had no way of knowing whether or not the wool might be stuck in an open sore. The fox trembled, and yipped several times; the burns were clearly quite painful.

"When did you find it?" When the woman simply stared shyly, BJ said, "Did you find it last night?"

"Essss."

The last of the wool came away; the kit whimpered. BJ turned him over carefully. Much of his fur was gone, and the singed smell was dreadful, but to BJ's relief, the burns seemed to be largely second-degree only: red, raw patches with blistering. There were no claw, tooth, or sting wounds; evidently the chimera had been curious or playful, not hungry.

What worried BJ a great deal was the sulphurous smell of chimera breath clinging to the burns. She had learned in school that some burns, such as steam burns, hide the extent of their damage. She had no idea whether or not the kit had chemical burns in addition to those caused by the heat. She pumped water into a basin and added Nolvasan, then washed him slowly and gently in it. His ears pricked up, and he looked momentarily happier.

BJ turned to the Meat Woman. "Will you be willing to help him recover? It's going to be a lot of work." Sahnrr nodded vigorously, standing on tiptoe to see over the edge of the basin. "Okay. Watch how I do this.

"You'll need to bathe him this way, three times a day at least. Do it for as much time as it takes bread to bake—Do you make bread?" Sahnrr shook her head apologetically. "Okay, for roughly as much time as it takes a leg of mutton to roast." She gave Sanhrr a squeeze bottle full of Nolvasan. Sanhrr's eyes widened; in Crossroads, the lightweight bottle was as valuable as the contents.

"Every day, check him for necrotic—sorry, for dead flesh, decay, anything like that. And put this ointment on him.

"You'll need to wrap him in fresh cloth every day." BJ snipped a sleeve off of an old turtleneck and poked four holes in it for the kit's legs. Sahnrr looked astonished; cloth, in Crossroads, was valued not in terms of money but by the many hours it took to make. BJ slid the sleeve over him; he looked ridiculous enough that Sahnrr began to laugh. BJ laughed with her, able for once to accept those razor-sharp fangs without worry. BJ cut up the other sleeve and gave it to Sahnrr for a spare. "Be sure you bring him back every three days. I'll be here." The chance of secondary infection was high even with antibiotics; BJ would feel better checking the fox regularly.

Sahnrr reached into her knapsack and held out a small carving to BJ. She took it uncertainly, then laughed with delight; the carving showed a serious-looking, straight-haired woman in a lab coat, striding forward and about to trip over a completely indifferent wolf puppy. "It's wonderful. Did you make it yourself?"

"Esss."

BJ said firmly, "I'll put it in the clinic part of my home, where everyone will see it." She delicately passed the fox kit back to Sahnrr, who took him eagerly and held him, cradled as lightly as possible, to her chest. The kit, not in the least bothered by the fangs, licked her nose. Sahnrr laughed and waved an easy goodbye to BJ.

BJ wrote up the case file, then opened her addendum to Lao's *Guide* and penned an enthusiastic if nonmedical entry on the habits of the Meat People. "Why," it began, "do vegetarians usually seem more innocent than carnivores?"

A tapping at the door interrupted her. She opened it a crack cautiously, then sighed and let in Stein's parrot. He rolled in, leering at Horvat and clicking his beak at Daphni, who gave one look and turned her back. Stein's parrot, with its cocky attitude and ungroomed feathers, looked singularly unappetizing.

BJ let Horvat out and went to the stove. "I have fresh bread, milk-basted crust. Would you like some?" The parrot sidled toward her hopefully.

She gave him a little, then held the rest back. "Half now, half later. Find Annie and give her this message." She recited it. "Say it back."

He stood on one leg, the other held insistently out for bread. BJ gave him a little more, pulling her hand back fast enough to avoid being bitten.

He gnawed the bread, swallowed, cleared his throat, and recited in a singsong voice:

"You are cordially invited to the wedding of Rudy and Bambi; to be held in mid-morning on the day of the second fall full moon. Your local calendar, November second.

To get there, please travel by any means possible to the train station nearest to the place called Jajouka, which I believe is in the Rif Mountains in Morocco. You will be picked up there.

You will be welcome among the bridesmaids, but you must be able to run medium distances rapidly. No gifts expected, no RSVP needed."

BJ nodded, satisfied. "All right. Now go." She gave him more bread at the door. "For the journey."

The parrot took off, wings beating strongly, for the northwest.

BJ wondered how it would find a Strangeway to Africa, and how it would find Annie in Chad once it did, but shrugged and accepted that Fields said it was possible.

A voice boomed, "I waited to see him gone, BJ."

Fields was patting Horvat, who was jumping against him, tail wagging wildly. Only for Fields of all strangers did Horvat act like a dog puppy. Fields was in overalls, with no shirt for once. His chest, back, and shoulders were covered with dark curly hair.

BJ watched the parrot soaring off. "Did you tell him where to go?"

"Of course. He will be there by night."

"There's a Strangeway to Chad?"

"There are many such roads in Africa. It is a large place, BJ. Even to those used to your America, Africa is large."

Which, BJ noted, was not a direct answer. "Would you like some bread?"

"Please. May I have it outside?" He sat with Horvat and watched her run in and out. "Thank you. Why do you wear such a heavy shirt? Are you cold?"

"My summer clothes are packed away." She gestured at the trunk in the corner. "I'll be fine."

He shook his head sadly. "It is a shame, covering so fine a body."

BJ said uncomfortably, "Is there something you wanted besides breakfast?"

On cue, a dodo wandered out of the brush. Horvat stalked it happily, crouching in plain sight. The dodo ignored him, or else it simply didn't know what he was.

Fields snorted. "These fat birds, I am sorry, they are the stupidest things I have ever known." He slapped his knees, raising his hands in disgust. "How can I save them when they are too foolish to live?"

"Find a safe place for them."

"Ah. Safe . . ." Fields said wistfully. "Find a safe place in Crossroads, and maybe I put everybody there. You, too," he added, patting her shoulder.

BJ smiled and poured him more water. "I don't need safe places."

"No. But you might know what one is." He sat on a rock, hands on his overalls. "There is an island to the south and west, off the coast and the salt marshes. Two days' walk from here. I think it would be perfect for them, and safe, but I know little." He leaned forward. "Now you, though, a doctor and a woman of science—"

"I'm not an ecologist or an ornithologist. I'm not even a natu-
ralist. I could miss something important."

Fields spread his knobby, callused hands, palms up. "We have
no one better."

She considered. "How do I get there?"

"There is a possibility. There is a way to drive down, but it is
rough." Fields stared with dislike at the truck. "If you need to
drive your truck later, maybe we can make a better way."

"I don't like to use that much gas," BJ said. "And I definitely
wouldn't want to break down in a strange neighborhood."

"I thought that," Fields said with relief. "One of the Hippoi
will take you. It will be quick."

"When should I plan on going?" BJ chewed her lip, thinking.
She could pack today, if there were no more patients—

BJ froze as Fields said easily, "Oh, she will be here soon."

"I can't go today—that is—" She considered asking Fields to
watch Horvat, but Gredya had specifically asked her. In a society
without contracts, one's word means a great deal. "Do you think
she would mind my taking Horvat with me?"

Fields raised his single, long, bushy eyebrow as high as it would
go. "You know that she would, Dr. BJ. The Wyr eat the Hippoi,
and kill them."

"I know." BJ stood, brushing crumbs off her skirt. "I'd better
change to jeans if I'm going to ride. I'll need to pack, too."

Fields smiled. "Thank you so. You are a good help to this
world." He also stood. "And now I have some others to see. Be
careful on the road, BJ." He surprised her by giving her only a
fairly brief kiss. He winked at her. "Stefan would like me to stay
my distance from you, right?" He laughed and left, shaking his
head; the hair met and parted over his satyr's horns.

BJ hung a sheet over the Healing Sign again, thinking regretfully that she couldn't build a practice, even without competition,
by closing so often. She changed into jeans and hiking boots
quickly. She packed a knapsack with a hatchet, rain gear, a tarp,
matches, enough water, bread and cheese for two, a notebook, and
Walden in case she had time. She looked, perplexed, at Horvat.
How could she keep her promise to Gredya to watch him?

The sound of galloping came from outside, growing closer. She
grabbed her zippered duffel bag, opened it, and half unfolded her
bedroll in the bottom. "Jump in, honey."

He sniffed at it dubiously, but jumped in. BJ zipped all but
the last three inches and said firmly to the nose that poked
out anxiously, "Now you be completely quiet and don't bark

at anything. And don't pretend not to understand me, because I
know better." She kissed the nose, and there was a rustle from
within the bag as a tail wagged.

She walked out, backpack on her back and duffel slung over
her shoulder and against her hip. "All ready."

Hemera, the red-haired bay from the first-aid and prenatal class,
looked down at her with interest. "You need that for two days?
That's more than the Hippoi take for life."

"With luck I won't need it all. May I?" She slung the duffel carefully on Hemera's back, balanced the backpack on the
Hippoi's spine, and hopped up clumsily, accidentally kicking
Hemera, who sighed. "I hope you're not going to do that each
time." Hemera, despite being much taller than a human adult,
was quite young. "Can we go now?"

"Please do." BJ settled her pack on her back and grabbed
frantically at the duffel as they took off.

Hemera trotted alongside the road, chatting happily. "I asked
Polyta if I could take you," she shouted over her shoulder. "You
and your Dr. Harrison have done a wonderful thing for us."

"It was just teaching."

"Chryseis is my best friend," she said simply, and leapt to clear
a small boulder.

BJ clutched tightly with her knees, against Hemera's horse
back. After ten minutes, Hemera said, "Release your legs. I won't
jump high, and you won't fall off."

BJ wasn't much of a horsewoman and found it hard to relax.
After a few jolting bounces, Hemera added practically, "Hold me
around my waist."

BJ, feeling as though she were riding on the back of a Harley,
did so. After a while, it felt natural, and BJ enjoyed the motion
and watching the Laetyen River slide by.

Upstream from Stein's the current grew swifter and the river
shallower. Hemera turned and half-slid down a trail to the river.
To the right, upstream, there were a series of short waterfalls,
above which an entering river doubled the size of the Laetyen.
Downstream was a single falls, seven feet high.

Straight ahead, barely visible under the rushing water, was a
broken ledge extending to a road on the other side. Hemera
unhesitatingly plunged onto it.

BJ hung on as they were swept sideways. Hemera found her
feet and surged forward. The water rose to Hemera's belly—to
BJ's knees—to the top of Hemera's horse back. A whimper came
from the duffel.

BJ pulled it onto her lap. "Isn't there a bridge?"

"I would never use it." Hemera's voice was strained, and she was panting, but she was also excited and proud; this was the place where so many of her people had challenged death and failed. "I will always cross here."

BJ had begun exercising in the mornings as soon as she realized that being in Rudy and Bambi's wedding would involve running. She resolved to push herself much harder.

Hemera pulled free of the water on the other side, gasping. "Not so hard." She tossed her red hair and her bay tail with all the confident vigor of youth. "I'll do that too many times to count."

She galloped up the hill much faster than necessary. BJ, settling the duffel in place, hoped affectionately that Hemera's words would prove true.

They traveled for hours beside the road, which wound south over hills that gradually became wider, lower, and more grass-covered. BJ was thankful that it was cloudy; the sun here would have baked her in between the trees shading the road.

The trees gave way to lines of willow and cottonwood, following the streams. Once, in open land to the right, BJ saw a great blue heron, winging barely a foot above the grass, following a winding stream through the plains and scouting for food.

Hemera paused once by a wide stream, removing her jacket and walking in above her human waist. She scooped water and drank for fully ten minutes. BJ drank for one minute herself, then tiptoed downstream and pulled Horvat from the duffel to drink. She met Hemera with Horvat safely hidden, and she remounted, a trace painfully; this was more riding than she had done in her life.

In the early afternoon, Hemera turned southwest on a barely marked trail. BJ watched the sky and land nervously. Immediately to the south were the craggy mountains where the Great nested and, west of them, the dusty canyon where, BJ knew, the Griffin's people lived. The sky was cloudy and empty, and the dry grasses ahead were broken only by occasional brush and by a field of—

She blinked. They seemed to be huge golden sunflowers, but they were difficult to focus on.

The clouds parted, and the field of huge blossoms was dappled with sunlight. BJ blinked again. The field was moving more than the wind merited. She looked up nervously for the Great, though the wind of their wings would be far stronger than any light breeze.

Hemera pointed and shouted over her shoulder, "Sundancers!"

"What are they?" Clearly, something was twisting the plants every which way.

"Watch." She galloped toward them, her human body leaning forward. BJ leaned forward, too, and clutched Hemera's human body for support. She glanced sideways in the grass, entranced by their shadow; it looked like affectionate sisters, the rear one older, riding a wild young horse together.

As they neared, the flowers split apart on a line in front of them and whirled to either side. Hemera slowed, and the flowers, on thick, knobby stems and muscled, above-ground roots, skipped out of their shadow until the shadow looked like a hole in a garden.

BJ slid down and, incautiously, snatched at a six-foot flower. It struggled in her hand, and its bristly stem scratched at her hand. She dropped it quickly and it scampered off.

"Sundancers," Hemera said, her red hair dropping nearly into her face as she bent to look at them. "They follow the sun, and they are south in the winter. I never see them north like this."

"It's because it's so warm," BJ said, and hoped as she got back on that was all it was.

Twenty minutes later, she felt her duffel bag shift restlessly. She waited until the grasslands were broken by a small stand of brush. "Could we stop? I need to stretch my legs." Hemera obligingly came to a halt.

BJ slid off. "Let me take these off you." She set the knapsack and duffel under a bush, surreptitiously unzipping the duffel and whispering, "Run under the bush." Horvat scampered out with the eagerness of desperation, and squatted.

BJ kneaded her legs; hours of riding had done strange things to the muscles. She put one leg straight back and stretched like a runner, then walked up and down the grasslands. They were near the crest of a high hill. BJ climbed up it and stared ahead. Her breath caught in her throat.

In the distance, sparkling in the patches where the sun shone between the clouds, lay a bay. To the left, sea grass blended with marshes at its border; to the right, a stand of bushes extended to the shore, possibly beyond into the shallow waters. Straight ahead, more than a mile out in the waters, a crescent-shaped island rose over cliffs to a green highland. Even in the fall, even at this distance, huge patches of pink and purple flowers decorated it. BJ had seen a great many natural wonders since she had come to Crossroads, and she had been to the Everglades as a child. The island ahead still struck her as unbelievably wild and beautiful.

Hemera called impatiently, "Can we go again?" BJ ran down the hill, sprinting the last few feet and skidding to a stop, laughing, in front of Hemera.

Horvat, excited by the running, skidded to a stop beside her. He confronted Hemera at close range for the first time, and curled his lip, growling.

Hemera put one hand to her mouth and pointed with the other. Horvat, too late, dashed back into the duffel bag and hid. Hemera stepped across the bag and raised her right front hoof.

BJ dove forward and pulled Horvat safely out of reach. She unzipped the bag and pulled Horvat close.

When she looked up, the hoof was poised over her.

"I wish to crush him," Hemera said simply.

BJ shook her head.

"I know that the Wyr maimed a Hippoi woman recently—"

"Medéa. My grandmother." And she galloped off to the north. Horvat chased after her, then gave up and trotted back, sitting and staring, sad-faced, at BJ.

She sighed. "At least she didn't kill either of us."

One more look from the top of the hill was all it took for BJ to realize that she could never get all the way to the bay and back to her home in two days. She turned around, staring at Hemera's previous track in the grass. She sighted on a mountain to the south as a landmark, cross-sighted for now on a stand of trees near a stream bed on the horizon, and slung her duffel bag over her backpack.

Horvat barked at her, leaping. At first she didn't understand. Finally she put half the contents of her pack into the duffel, strapped the lighter pack onto Horvat, and walked downhill with him. She smiled in spite of herself, watching him pad happily along with the pack on.

"You are never bad," she said fiercely.

He looked back at her in surprise. Clearly, as a Wyr, he had never thought he was.

The walk was long, but not tiring. Hemera's hoofprints in the dry earth were easy to follow. After an hour, BJ reached the spot where they had seen the sundancers. The sundancers were gone; BJ thought she could see them dancing to the north, but she was no longer high enough up to see and be sure. The sky continued to clear. BJ wrapped a kerchief around her bare neck, and fed Horvat water in her palm from the bottle in her pack.

She was nearly back to the road when a shadow darker than any stray cloud passed over them. She saw it circle and come back.

She stripped the pack off Horvat and sealed him in the duffel before checking the sky. She pulled the hatchet from the pack, knowing it would do her no good.

The griffin, a bronze, sailed in with an ease that reminded her of how injured the griffin she knew was. The bronze settled in noiselessly, both golden eyes focused on her over his cruel, sharp raptor's beak. His tail was lashing.

BJ braced herself. "Good afternoon."

"I very much doubt it," the bronze said. His voice was as angry as his tail. "What has that traitor told you about us?"

The duffel moved back and forth agitatedly; BJ ignored it. "Which traitor?"

A blacksnake raced frantically in front of the griffin, desperate to get away; the bronze's claws were a blur as he sliced it into seven writhing pieces without looking. "Don't fence; you know damned well which traitor. You know his real name."

The bronze was speaking of the Griffin, whose name was Asturiel. BJ had learned it by chance, and had only admitted her knowledge to the griffins to gain donated blood to save his life.

She watched as the bronze tossed the snake pieces into his snapping beak. His eyes never left her face. "He's told me about your eating habits," she said. "He's told me about some of your illnesses, and your tendency to develop gout. That was for a textbook I'm writing—well, updating."

"Lao's *Guide to the Unbiological Species*?" He snorted. "Landmark for humans, laughable to other sentients. You would do well to remember that Lao was prolix but discreet."

BJ flushed at being patronized. She had met ten or twelve griffins, an astonishing number to meet and survive. All of them except her friend were annoying.

She said bluntly, "All right, I'll be terse and open. Lao hints at things about you, but says little. Astu—the Griffin tells me mundane things, but refuses even to hint beyond that." She realized, saying it, that it was true.

After a moment the bronze nodded. "For your sake it had best remain so. Why don't you go back to your quaint surgery and putter, ignoring what you cannot appreciate?"

"Because Fields asked me to come this way," BJ snapped. "Why do you ask? What are you ashamed of?"

The bronze reared, flexing the talons which, BJ knew, could tear through solid stone. "I could eat your liver casually for that.

I could do it casually, but I would rather tear it out quickly and eat it in front of you. You are fortunate in some of your friends, or it would happen now."

The duffel zipper pulled back. Horvat leapt out of the bag at the bronze, snarling. BJ dove and tackled him within inches of the griffin's razor talons.

The bronze regarded the wolf pup with contempt. "You are unfortunate in some of your friends. Slumming, I see."

He flew off. BJ drew the hatchet back, but caught herself before throwing it. "Why are they so infuriating?" she said to Horvat as he bounded and leapt futilely through the grass at the griffin's shadow.

As Horvat trotted back, proud at having driven it away, she said thoughtfully, "And what are they hiding?"

They made it to the roadway before sunset; BJ pushed onward for forty minutes until she found a small hill and a stand of trees. She climbed it and found a small clearing, hidden from the road and difficult for anything large to penetrate. "We'll stop here." Horvat, panting, threw himself down and fell asleep immediately.

It took little time to string a tarp over her sleeping bag, still less to gather firewood and light a fire. Supper was bread and cheese—more than enough, since BJ had brought an extra meal for Hemera. Horvat woke to be fed by hand, then turned three times in the grass before lying down.

Quickly, even here in the warmer climate, it was dark. BJ undressed, slid into the sleeping bag, and lay on her side sleepily, staring into the fire. Horvat napped farther away, curled in a ball with his tail over his nose.

Something swooped low over the fire, diving around her. BJ slid down in the bedroll, flipping the top, and her forearm, above her eyes. She wished, for the second time today, that she had brought a weapon besides the hatchet.

The flying thing skimmed across the fire, low enough to scatter the flames for a moment. The silhouette against the light was of a bird the size of a goose, but with a pointed beak and long tail feathers. BJ slid from her bedroll and picked up the hatchet, edging protectively towards the still-sleeping Horvat.

The bird, returning a third time, dove straight into the fire and perched on a burning log.

BJ forgot her caution and leapt forward. Horvat pricked his ears up, but never woke.

BJ squatted in the firelight, watching as the bird began to glow, starting at the feet, clutching a blazing log, and moving slowly upward as its body heated. Slowly and quietly, careful not to move suddenly, BJ gathered more logs and set them on the fire. The flames rose and crackled, and the red-orange color of the bird rose with them.

When the last of the bird turned golden, it opened its beak and sang: heartbreakingly clear, liquid notes with pure joy behind them.

BJ reached a hand toward the fire, pulled it back, and stood listening.

She shivered, suddenly realizing that she was half-naked in the frosty air.

She lay back down, and stared and listened until she fell back asleep.

In the morning, Horvat tugged on her bedroll gently until she woke. He turned toward the east, where the sun was just up, and yipped once, cocking his head at her.

"Thank you." She stretched toward her knapsack to pull fresh clothes into her bedroll and warm them up. Satisfied, he bounded away from the campsite and tried to hunt.

She dressed quickly; the fire was down to hot embers with a fine coat of white ash over them. The bird, a pale pink below and gray-brown above, huddled against the last red embers, then stared unblinkingly at BJ.

"Sorry." She kicked the logs apart, doused them with water, and turned over the ashes and doused them again. The bird, now all gray and brown, flew nearly straight up from the clearing.

A familiar voice called from the road, "BJ?"

"Just a moment." She threw together her backpack and duffel and dragged both to the road. Horvat, proudly carrying a dead pheasant nearly half his size, joined her.

She came free of the trees. Brandal, as Owen, was leaning on his cart. "How did you find me?" she asked.

He pointed behind her. She looked, embarrassed, at the white plume from the dying fire; she couldn't have signaled her location any better. He said, "Fields told me where you might be. I had trade down this way, anyway; the griffins want more books." He gestured at the string-bound stack on his wooden cart; the titles were in English, Greek, Arabic, and some characters BJ couldn't recognize but was fairly sure were not earthly.

Brandal glanced down at Horvat and back at her. BJ said quickly before he could ask anything, "I saw a strange bird last night. It dove right into my campfire—"

Brandal smiled. "A firelover. They're migratory. Usually they stay in the south, but with this crazy weather—"

"Yes, I know." There were a number of topics BJ didn't want to talk about. "Where do they come from?"

"All over, even your world. They started the myth of the phoenix, rising from the ashes. They come back to mate."

The ghost of an idea whispered in BJ's mind. She ignored it for now. "What is the mating like?"

"I saw their courtship flight once." Brandal blinked, as though his eyes were watering. "A male sits in a fire or a heat source until he's bright orange, then he calls until a female sits beside him. They bill"—he stretched his own neck, unself-consciously imitating the motion—"until she's the same color.

"Then they fly straight up, spiraling around each other, and then dive and loop all over the sky in tandem. They only do it at night, and they look like comets. Beautiful. They're considered a sign of approaching passion."

"I'm not surprised."

Brandal raised an eyebrow but said nothing. BJ blushed and avoided yet another topic. "Do they have any natural enemies?"

"The same as any other bird, unless they're around fire." He looked to the north automatically. "And of course the chimerae."

"Why 'of course'?" But she thought she knew.

"The breath. A chimera who sees a firelover tries to catch it. When it can't, and of course it can't, it cries out, and its breath flames. The firelover flies into the flames." Owen tried to sound indifferent.

"Why doesn't the species die out?"

"The nestlings can't fly. I saw a group of chicks once," he said quietly, "running and flopping along the ground, peeping and chasing the chimera who had eaten their parents. They weren't angry; they just couldn't get his attention so they could be swallowed."

"Are their nests safe?"

"I'd bet on it. They nest in volcanoes or geysers, I think. Nobody's ever seen a firelover's egg." He shuffled from foot to foot. "BJ, now that I know you're all right, I have to go. There's quite a lot we should speak of, but I don't think you're ready."

BJ looked at him steadily. "You're right."

He looked back. "Don't wait too long." He picked up the shafts of the cart, but didn't start rolling. "Remember one thing: Horvat is not tame. He's not even an animal, even though he's not human. He's a child, and not your child. Don't lose your life guarding him."

Without waiting for an answer, he rolled away whistling. BJ recognized "How Much Is That Doggy in the Window?" but didn't smile.

The trip back took all day. BJ crossed at the bridge over the Laetyen River, far safer and easier than the ford was. When BJ saw her cottage, she said to Horvat, "If only when we get home, nothing new is wrong." She was exhausted.

Polyta was waiting for them under the Sign of the Wounded Animal. Horvat, with exquisitely bad timing, growled at her. She pretended not to notice and said formally, "I know that Hemera deserted you yesterday—"

BJ interrupted, "Please don't punish her. She only did it because she found out about Horvat—"

"She is one of my people, and that is no excuse." Polyta added, "And she had an opportunity and didn't kill him. For that she will also be punished."

She wheeled and left, this time without returning to say something kind. BJ ached inside.

A dry voice behind her said, "Perhaps you should have named him Ishmael."

BJ, who had gotten through a class on *Moby Dick* only by reading the Monarch Notes, said, "I don't see why. He's not a sailor." But she stepped back and put an arm around the Griffin's shoulder.

The Griffin, catlike, rubbed his shoulder against her body.

"I was thinking of the original Ishmael." They watched as Horvat growled furiously at the door, guarding an imaginary kill from Daphni. "Because his hand will be against every man, and every man's hand against him." The Griffin's fierce golden eyes looked disturbingly gentle. "Not all species get along, Doctor. Believe me, I know."

"I can imagine." BJ made what only seemed like a change of subject: "Can you tell me if chimerae burns leave chemicals in the victims? Please, it's important." She added, "And I think you know."

"Has anyone ever told you that you are annoyingly sagacious?"

"Not in so many words."

He sighed. "The answer is no. For such chronically untidy animals, the chimerae practice relatively complete combustion.

Methane from digestion, carbon from the same, sulphur from God knows where. All gaseous products, along with nitrous oxide. They're like a living Los Angeles."

She broke in desperately, "Could you do me a very large favor?"

"Gladly," he said unhesitatingly, "so long as it neither hurts others unnecessarily, nor invades my privacy."

"Could you pretend to attack me?" The Griffin raised a feathered eyebrow. "I need to train Horvat not to attack, even in my defense."

"It cannot—" He suddenly changed his mind. "Very well. I will try until dark, and then I will go. *En garde*, lupine." He raised a claw toward her, flexing it melodramatically.

BJ shouted, "Horvat, no!" He ignored her, unhesitatingly leaping forward and fastening puppy teeth on the Griffin's other forefoot.

He brushed Horvat off with the back of his other talon. "Well moused. Shall we begin again?" He snapped his beak within inches of BJ's face. Again she shouted, and again Horvat bit him. "This," he said, disengaging Horvat gently, "will be tiresome."

After two hours, BJ gave up. Horvat paid her no attention at all, even when she tried spanking him. He was clearly as frustrated as she was. Finally she gave up, apologizing to the Griffin.

"Oh, don't bother," he said. His taloned foot was barely marked. "Believe me, I understand misplaced affection."

BJ made supper for herself, Daphni, and Horvat. The Griffin politely refused her invitation, and waited for darkness.

Gredya came by, looking ragged and tired rather than sensual. BJ stepped outside to speak with her. There was a deep scratch in her right cheek; BJ moved to touch it. "Are you all right?"

"I hurt." She said it casually, as though it were a fact of life like rain or crop failure. "How is Horvat?"

BJ answered by letting him out. He ran to Gredya, and this time it was BJ who was clearly jealous. "I have to leave for a while," she said to the Wyr woman. "Two days."

Gredya nodded. "Two days. I can watch." She hesitated, and added reluctantly, "Take him back?"

"Of course. Are the Wyr still dangerous?"

Gredya smiled, showing too many teeth. "Some, no. Not ever." Her smile vanished quickly. "Some, even more." She shifted, and BJ noticed for the first time that there was dried blood on the Wyr woman's wool blouse.

"I'll take him back," BJ said firmly.

"For a while." Gredya watched her face.

"Of course for a while." BJ turned away from her abruptly, went back inside, and threw a change of clothes in her knapsack. "Griffin, are you ready to leave?" she asked.

Gredya made a sharp sound to Horvat. He ran back inside to BJ, wagging his tail, and she smiled. "No, you stay with Gredya."

Gredya frowned. BJ noticed with relief that she did not show her teeth. "Come," she said to Horvat. He padded after her up the hill behind the house.

The Griffin, watching her leave, remarked, "She has an appropriate shirt. A wolf in sheep's clothing—"

"Let's go," BJ said shortly. In a few moments, the Griffin was on top of the van, concealed under a tarp, and he and BJ were on their way back to Kendrick, Virginia, in the darkness.

T·W·E·L·V·E

LAURIE KLEINMAN WAS at the loading dock alone, smoking a cigarette. BJ had never seen her for more than half an hour without a cigarette; anesthesiologists were perpetually nervous.

She stubbed out the cigarette against the bricks. "About damn time."

BJ hopped out of the van and began untying ropes. Laurie did the other side in half the time. The Griffin slid easily off the van, a far cry from his last ride in for emergency surgery. He landed in a bow, knees bent.

Laurie ran up to him. She was overweight, and seldom ironed her clothes or had anything but contempt for fashion and glamour. In the presence of the Griffin, she always seemed suddenly beautiful. She panted, "You're all right?"

"Overwhelmed," he said calmly. She knelt and put an arm around his neck, and BJ went for a walk.

When she returned, Laurie was in the hall, pasting a NO ADMITTANCE sign on a storeroom. "I called Sugar. He's on his way. Want to stay and say Hi?"

"I should . . ." BJ considered. "Nah. I'd better get going."

"You'd better do more than that," Laurie said, grinning. BJ ignored her.

Once, going into a dormitory after hours would have made BJ self-conscious; now it was simply a matter of slipping up a staircase and knocking on a door.

A pudgy redhead with a buzz cut opened the door and blinked at her owlishly. "Nnh? Who? Whanh?" He focused. "Oh. He's in the basement. Study pit." He closed the door, muttering incoherently. Probably he was asleep before he finished crossing the room. "Good night, Willy," she murmured.

The basement hall was windowless and lit by fluorescent lights, but it still had that awful one-in-the-morning feel of a place with no sleep and no comfort. BJ found the study pit door and opened it.

A shirtless, slender, curly-haired figure at the end of the room was typing slowly and determinedly on a laptop. Beside him was an empty hot pot and a stained, empty teacup. "Stefan? Have you been here all night?"

He turned around and stared at her emptily. The string of a teabag was hanging from his mouth.

She kissed his forehead. "Stefan, that's terrible. What are you doing?" She pulled the tea bag from his mouth.

He looked at her vaguely. "BJ, how lovely." He was exhausted, and his accent was heavy. "I have a paper due tomorrow."

She stroked his horns. "Let's see."

She moved to the top of the file and read the screen: "CURSE OF THE GODS: religious reaction to inherited illness."

The first paragraph mentioned Herod's illness, *The House of the Seven Gables*, and *Arsenic and Old Lace*, concluding simply:

> *"But little has been written by the families themselves. How did they view their fate, their suffering? Did they live with it arrogantly, like King Herod? Did they intertwine it with the sins thought to cause it, like Hawthorne's Pyncheons? Or did it, as it nearly did the critic in* Arsenic and Old Lace, *move them to deny their own love, for fear of passing on the curse?*

> *"This report will examine the nineteenth-century writings of families with Huntington's chorea, especially those concerning love, marriage, and having children. . . ."*

BJ, shaking, turned to him. "Stefan, that's very good."

He tiredly pointed to the stack of books beside him, Post-its in place with notes and quotes referenced on them. "I know that it should be."

"Who suggested it to you?"

She sounded a little too intent; he focused on her for the first time. "Stein, or the Griffin, or maybe Fields. I don't remember. I said I wanted to write about medicine and history; they said 'Write about it from the viewpoint of the ill.' BJ, my doctor and love, I must work. All night." He took her hand. "I am sorry."

"I'll make some more tea." The cup rattled as she set it down. "Did you talk to Sugar Dobbs about this paper?"

"Dr. Dobbs?" He was punchy enough to find the question difficult. "He asked me about school. I talked to him about Chris, because I wanted to write about Alzheimer's. He told me—" He rubbed his own horns, trying to remember. "He said, 'Alzheimer's is a breaking story,' and there was new evidence about inherited illness. Then he explained about genetic mechanisms and inherited illness—" He looked up defensively. "I knew some of that from biology."

"I'm sure."

"And he told me about Huntington's chorea. I think it was then; I think it was him. He was nice to help me, BJ."

She picked up the empty hot pot. "He likes to be helpful sometimes."

BJ, coldly furious, drove back to the vet school. Sugar's waxed and polished pickup truck was in the faculty lot. She waited beside it for an hour and a half, listening to talk radio and getting steadily angrier and more tired. When he didn't come out, she gave up and drove back to Crossroads.

By now it was nearly dawn. The hollows and valleys on the gravel road were still dark enough that she needed the cabin light to read *The Book of Strangeways*.

At a point where the road crossed the stream and the hills became steeper than any in the Blue Ridge Mountains, BJ saw an immense man with a bushy beard, cutting at the roadbed with a pickaxe. He wore a Red Man cap and a T-shirt from the speedway in Martinsville. She rolled down her window. "Good morning, sir."

The man grunted amiably.

"Is the road being changed again?"

He pointed with the pickaxe, extended at arm's length as easily as if it were a classroom pointer, to a curving line scratched in the gravel and the soil. He had already prepared part of the new roadbed running down it. The line disappeared into the woods.

BJ looked at it uneasily. "Will I be all right driving the old road back in?"

He swallowed, rolled his eyes, made a tremendous effort, and came out with, "F'now, yes'm."

She thanked him and rolled forward carefully. She shook herself to stay awake and alert.

The Book of Strangeways showed the old road, but as the sky grew brighter in the east she could see a faint inked line forming next to the roadway, which looked fainter. She glanced up in time to see the turtle man, hands (were they hands?) on his knees, bending closer to look at her; she swerved. "He used to stand farther away," she said to herself shakily.

She drove slowly and carefully from there, and it was sunrise by the time she reached the steep-walled piece of valley just before the Laetyen River.

A Road Crew was working there; a woman stepped into the road, signaling for her to stop. "Doctor?" she said briskly. "Road changes." She pointed to the divot in the gravel.

"I see that, thanks. Big changes?"

"New forks, new roads." The woman stared down the half-finished new bed into the sloping woods. She licked her lips nervously. "New worlds."

"I don't think I'll try to drive back out till you're done."

She shook her head. "Best not." She wiped her perspiring forehead and added to BJ, "Come help."

It wasn't an order, but it definitely wasn't just a request. Tired as she was, BJ pulled over and shut the motor off.

The woman opened the truck door for her. "Thanks." She gave her a quick hug, which startled BJ; it was as firm and formal as a handshake. "I'm Betts."

"I'm BJ." She gestured to the line sketched in the dirt. "Who laid the new road out for you?"

Betts looked astonished. "Fields."

"Oh, of course," BJ said immediately, and it did make sense. "What do you want me to do?"

Betts gestured at the rest of the crew. Two of the large, green-tinged people were pushing a barrow full of gravel. The rest, fairly normal if short humans, were tearing apart the old road and piling it for moving to the new. "Carry. Dig. Chop." Betts held out a tool. "Use a twybil."

BJ took the twybil awkwardly. It was an ash pole the thickness of a hoe handle, with two steel blades on the end, twisted at right angles to each other. One blade could be used for hoeing or breaking like a pickaxe; the other, curved at the outer edge, for chopping. Both were honed until they gleamed, sharpened to an edge no wider than a human hair.

Behind her, much of the Road Crew bent and swung as twybils spun and rang in their hands. The handles seemed more like axles as the twybil blades blurred and flickered in the early morning sun.

Arms folded, Betts followed as BJ found a work space along the old road and raised the twybil, using the hoeing blade to break up the gravel bed. BJ struck jerkily, knowing that she was missing the essential grace of the process.

"Work in rhythm." Betts moved forward with her own twybil, both blades pointing sideways. "One-and-two-and-three, and ONE-and-two-and-three, and . . ."

On "one," she spun the hoe blade forward and struck simultaneously, pulling back on "and." On "two," she chopped sideways in the empty air, spinning the axe blade frontwards. On "three," she slid her upper hand up the handle, bringing the tool sideways for a moment as though she were bunting. "Better for your back. Helps your balance."

It reminded BJ of a kendo class she had once seen at a county fair—and after her own training in Stein's catchlet games, the application of the memory was not lost on her. She took her own twybil and walked through the motions, accepting corrections patiently as Betts criticized her feet, her posture, and her grip on the twybil.

The motion was easy and natural, and if it wasted energy, it made the work go faster. BJ's muscles held up well. Eventually they moved to a new patch of woods, and BJ practiced bunting first, then chopping, then hacking with the other blade.

BJ had expected blisters; to her surprise and pleasure, her months in Crossroads had toughened her hands for this sort of work. Exhaustion caught up with her, though, and as they came near the finish, she said apologetically to Betts, "I need to go sleep."

"Best sleep, then," Betts said brusquely, and hugged BJ quickly and tightly. "Thanks for your toil." She turned back, shouting to the crew.

BJ kept *The Book of Strangeways* open on the seat beside her, glancing down from time to time as she drove back to her cottage. The old road faded, and the new line became a trail and then a road, until the old was replaced by the new. As always, the page looked ancient, the paper yellowed and the sepia ink lines feathery as though drawn with a sharp quill on parchment. BJ closed the book carefully and drove on.

Daphni, entwined with dried brush but fairly obvious, scampered to the truck as BJ pulled up. BJ was happy to see that the flowerbinder was nearly recovered. She brushed the leaves off the big cat, looking down the river valley where it shone in the morning sun.

In the distance, she could see a field of golden flowers. She thought that the field was moving, but that could have been her own fuzzy vision. She opened the door to her house, and fell into bed.

As she lay down, she drifted from thought to thought: vague worries that the Strangeways were changing and being changed, and that Fiona was out in them alone. Her last thought, as she drifted off, was unarticulated but disturbingly certain: Sooner or later, I have to tell him.

She slept until the following morning, when Horvat, returning with Gredya, bounded through the door she had left wide open and licked her face to wake her.

T·H·I·R·T·E·E·N

SEVERAL WEEKS PASSED; BJ barely noticed. Crossroads, a place where peace had been available at the opening of a window, was becoming monstrously busy.

The number of burn and hunting victims increased. In two days, BJ worked on a hawk, a deer, three sheep, a flowerbinder (she locked Daphni outside while she put it to sleep), a pig, and innumerable dodos. Some of these were burn victims; many had predator wounds from narrow escapes.

Once, exhausted and barely able to move her pen, BJ wrote, "I've never seen a baby chimera. Is this because the entire species is infantile?" She would later reread this passage frequently, with a great deal of regret.

In a second night trip a few days after her first, she brought the Griffin back from Kendrick. Laurie rode in with her, ostensibly to help BJ carry in a long list of supplies. In the end, her coming was fortuitous; a badly wounded chimera dropped near the cottage door, mewing for help.

BJ ran to it immediately. "Stay back," the Griffin said urgently to Laurie, but she shook her head and followed BJ.

Laurie looked it over with disgust. "It's filthier than anything feline has ever been. How's the wound?"

"Eight inches long. No major organs, and no major blood vessels; talk about luck—" The gash, in the side of the abdominal wall, was nearly an inch deep at the point of entry, shallower as the wound approached the groin and the chimera's scales. "The wound is fresh and the edges are clean . . . I can take care of this, if you can anesthetize it."

"Gas something that's part cat, part bird, and part scorpion? Gee, I don't see any problem." Laurie pulled out a cigarette and felt for a match. The unhappy chimera belched a fireball; Laurie bent and lit the cigarette in it. "Thanks."

The Griffin, disgusted with the whole proceeding, went his own way.

In the end it wasn't a problem; Laurie titrated the gas concentration by effect. The surgery was fairly mundane, and Laurie helped BJ brush the steel table free of parasites and scrub it free of blood and fluids afterward. She watched other chimerae in the sky. "Are you gonna work with those often?"

"God forbid."

"Get welder's gloves," Laurie said flatly. "And goggles. Anything that can belch its way out of a nylon muzzle, you'd better handle with protective gear."

She added, with a typical wicked smile, "So, how's Stefan? Doing, I mean."

"He's fine." There was a great deal in her life, BJ reflected, that she should handle with protective gear.

She had driven Laurie back to Kendrick, seen Stefan for a sentimental and highly enjoyable weekend, and worked furiously since then. The air had finally become cold again; whatever Fiona had done, if it was Fiona, had finally worn off. Most of the trees were losing leaves quickly, and mornings found a rime of frost on the grass and shrubs. Daphni picked each paw up hastily, with distaste, after setting it down outside.

Two days before Rudy and Bambi's wedding, the air was crisp and clear, the kind of day on which you can see twenty or thirty miles, or think you can. Rudy had agreed to bring Dave in, through San Francisco; Lee Anne was driving herself, with a map sent by BJ. All that remained was bringing Annie. BJ drove to Stein's, where she met Fields and, to her surprise, Estevan Protera.

Fields, wearing a cotton T-shirt under his overalls and a faded baseball cap over his curly hair, explained. "The doctor has a lot to do, BJ. He has an astro—a sexto—" He waved his arms helplessly.

"I brought a sextant," Protera said smoothly. His denim jeans were ironed, but his hiking boots were scuffed and water-stained. "I want to check our position as we walk." He also had a beautifully polished walking stick, four feet long, with a crosspiece four inches from the end and a grip for his hand on top. As always, he looked happy and excited, like a child headed for a party. "Please, can we start now?"

Fields laughed and hugged his shoulder, almost a caress. "That way."

They followed the road by the Laetyen only as far as the ford and turned north, following the steep banks of the aptly named High River. Fields caught BJ glancing back over her shoulder, to the south. "It is all right," he said quietly. "I will provide a way to check the island for the dodos later. I am sorry for your inconvenience."

BJ said nothing for half a mile, then: "I'm sorry I didn't finish. I couldn't have done anything just then but save Horvat."

He turned and smiled. "Neither could I."

Protera called, "Pardon, am I still going right?" He was nearly out of sight ahead of them. Fields and BJ hurried to catch up.

She had never been in this part of Crossroads. The grass was more spare, the rock outcroppings clearly layered and broken by rushing streams. In a short time, they passed the last of the deciduous trees and walked steadily upwards through a stand of fir trees. The wind sighed constantly in the branches, and High River became a narrow stream of alternating rapids and falls.

The fir trees grew smaller and sparser, then disappeared completely; they were above the tree line.

Fields seemed not to notice as the path grew more rugged. His hooves dealt readily with the rocks and ledges. Protera, staff in hand and sextant at his belt, paused occasionally to shoot the sun, striding effortlessly forward at other times.

BJ, panting, was determined to keep up.

They paused at a high pass. BJ looked behind her and was entranced.

The air was clear and cold. She could see the High River and the forest below them, and the hill with Stein's beyond that, and the snakelike valley of the River Laetyen all the way to the grasslands.

Fields walked forward, dragging the stick behind him. "Please, stay on the line I draw."

Protera, with the easy grace of a gymnast, put one foot in front of the other almost without looking. So did BJ, at first.

The trail became much steeper. BJ took off her jacket and tied it around her waist. Often they used their hands to help them. Once they had to chimney up a ledge to the next part of the trail,

moving up a pass. Fields marked the stones, a barely visible line
of dust and splinters, with his stick.

At the height of the pass, BJ looked over her shoulder for a
last look down the mountain.

The view was gone. Behind her, a sheer basalt cliff, vertical
columns fissured into hexagonal pillars of stone, rose far above
the ravine they traveled now.

For the next half hour, BJ walked down the line almost heel
to toe, like a tightrope walker—and that was how she thought
of herself, as someone desperately balancing so that she didn't
fall from the world she knew into something frightening and
unexpected.

Fields called to her anxiously, and she realized how far back
she was. Being alone here could be as dangerous as wandering
into another world. She gritted her teeth and hurried, carefully
checking the line ahead every third step.

He waited for her. "My BJ, you look troubled."

She said in a small voice, "There isn't any Strangeway from
here to Morocco. I checked."

He laughed. "There will be, I promise. I said I would help you
bring your Annie back for the wedding. Plus I have a need of
my own to go to Africa." For a moment he looked eager, but
finished, more practically, "I also need to find a home for the
sundancers."

"Can't they go back where they came from?"

"No," Fields said, troubled. "Someone closed off the Strangeway."

BJ was stunned. "You mean, without permission?"

Fields smiled. "BJ, this is no thing of asking 'May I' and seal-
ing off a world. The Road Crews take apart the roads, and walking
is more dangerous, but there is still a way if you can find it." His
smile faded. "But someone found a way to close off even that."

"Someone besides you, you mean."

He patted her shoulder. "You are very good. Yes, if I can open
Strangeways, I also can close them. But not the way this person
did," he said worriedly. "I think this was done by magic, or by
some machine."

"And by someone who's looking for a way to open Strangeways," Protera added. He had stopped to shoot the sun again and
was writing down the results, shaking his head. "I can't imagine
being that reckless."

"I barely can," Fields said. "Shall we go on?"

They continued to climb, sometimes down now, often still up.
Once BJ had a chilling thought: *If he dies here, we have nothing*

to get us back but that single line in the dirt. She looked behind
her to see if it were still there. The view in back had shifted
again; now there was nothing but an endless range of craggy
mountains.

She turned around and nearly bumped into Protera, who was
sighting with his sextant and scribbling frantically. He hooked it
on his belt again and watched Fields intently.

Fields was standing to the right of the line, patiently scratching
a fork in the ground. He drew one line to the right, curving
towards a ledge on the mountainside, then stepped back and
scratched the left half towards an opening between two hills.
When he kept on the side track, BJ and Protera followed him
tentatively.

Ahead of Fields, the mountains in the distance blurred and
faded, going blue as though they were on the far horizon. Gradually there was nothing but sky. The land below it was deep green,
fuzzy with layers of jungle vegetation.

They drew closer. The trees, giant trunks with layers of green
at different levels, closed over their heads. Thick vines like lianas
hung from the layers. On the ground, plants with huge cordate
leaves, cupped to catch rain water, trickled water from the point
of the heart down from leaf to leaf. Even the sunlight, filtered
through layers of leaves, was greenish.

Gradually the mountain air gave way to humidity, and the warm
scent of blossoms and pollen, a smell that had given BJ hay fever
in the years before she had come to Crossroads.

Fields gestured. "You are the doctors. What do you think?"

"It looks fertile," Protera said dubiously. His hand rested lightly
on his sword.

BJ peered through the dense undergrowth. "Do you hear anything?"

They listened. There was next to no noise, not even the rustling
of leaves. "Where are the birds?" She gestured at the ground cover
around them. "Where are the animals?"

Protera said, "It does look like a very good world for sessile
plants. Do you think this is a safe world for your sundancers, for
plants that move?"

BJ heard a grating cry, as though a rusty door were opening.
A crimson mouth a foot and a half wide, fringed with fangs
just inside russet hair and dangling from a twenty-foot cord of
muscle and fur, swung toward Fields. BJ didn't see any eyes.
At the nadir of its swing, it slashed sideways with its fangs,
snapping shut.

Fields ducked. A second mouth swung by, lower than the first. Fields backed away. A third mouth, still lower, screamed down and tangled with the first two; they snapped viciously at each other's cords, swinging crazily to and fro.

Fields and the others backed up until the swinging mouths were blurry. Fields stood up shakily and stepped back to the main line. "I don't think so. Not this world."

"Not a place for any species you like," Protera said.

With his left hoof, Fields erased the line in the dirt. They went onward through the mountains, and this time BJ didn't look back at all.

Half an hour later, Fields created a right-hand fork from the main line. He looked it over carefully, and they edged down it. BJ's ears felt the increase in pressure as they walked.

The mountains blurred out, and a high, rolling plain flickered in. The grass was seven feet tall, and yellow with autumn except along the stream beds, where it stayed green. There was a lake in the distance. BJ saw birds circling, and watched as a small quail-like bird with large eyes froze in the grass, spreading its wings to shelter its chicks as a shadow crossed above them.

"This looks better," she said flatly.

Protera frowned. "From ten seconds' observation? I trust your eyes, BJ, but I would like to be sure."

Fields looked at him bleakly. "You can never be sure. All you can do is to try, maybe watch over them, and hope for a good future." He smiled down at the crouching bird. "Still, I think it is good. I should have come here first."

They retreated to the line they knew and walked on, and suddenly BJ had a great many questions in her mind. She reached surreptitiously into her backpack and flipped open *The Book of Strangeways*. The trail out of Crossroads was already marked, and the fork to the grassy world shown, with an odd picture-writing labeling the lake and the hillside. There was no trail ahead of them. She watched the book as the line Fields drew in the land was echoed on the page.

Suddenly there was Arabic lettering beside the trail, labeling a mountain range. She looked up in confusion; the peaks high above them on either side were snow-covered. "Where are we?" she called to Fields.

He laughed happily, like someone nearing home. "The Atlas Mountains of Northern Africa, and soon the Rif Mountains; please, hurry now."

She tucked the book away and hurried to get near him and Protera. "Did the parrot have to come this way?"

"I sent him direct to your Annie." Fields was almost hopping down the slope, digging the dirt in front of him. "I came this way today because I must meet someone."

BJ's ears popped again; Fields' trail descended far more rapidly than any human path.

"How are we going to find her?"

Fields only smiled and kept walking.

BJ was unprepared for how cool the air was; a breeze off the sea helped a great deal. They stopped a moment while Fields masked his hooves with lace-up boots and put on a broad-brimmed hat.

The trail dropped into a canyon; the canyon bent to the right. They turned with it, and suddenly the canyon walls were whitewashed masonry, houses so close together that the streets seemed like tunnels. They were inside a town.

Even Protera stared for a moment before he caught himself. From where they stood, they could see a market square, with stalls overhung with cloth canopies. The noise of trading was loud and incomprehensible. A moment ago they had heard nothing.

BJ repeated as they walked toward the square, "How will we find Annie?"

Fields laughed and pointed to the other side of the square. A tanned blond woman waved frantically from the road, beside a dusty and ancient Mercedes.

It took BJ a second to realize that it was Annie. She was a deep brown, with weathered skin; never plump, she had lost the last of her baby fat and had prominent cheekbones. She was dressed in khaki, with a battered Aussie hat, and Stein's parrot perched on her shoulder.

She paid and thanked the driver, who had stayed with her. The driver, a small dark man with a drooping mustache, smiled and bowed to her. As she turned away, Stein's parrot squawked something in Arabic at the man, who made a furious gesture with his fist and spat over it. The car behind him was spattered with droppings.

The parrot flew to Fields's shoulder and pecked at his neck, making a happy chuckling noise. Fields flinched. "Yes, I am sure you were very good. When we return to Crossroads, I will see that you are rewarded."

The parrot settled back and looked smugly at BJ, who said to Annie, "You traveled with him?"

"He was company on the trip," she said tactfully.

"Dr. Annie." Fields extended a hand politely, even though he was leering at her. "Was your trip hard?"

Annie insisted on hugging him and giving him a kiss on the cheek. "Leaving the mission was hard. Flying from Chad to Marrakech, and taking the Tangiers train, was easy. How are you?"

BJ watched as Fields introduced her to Protera. It amazed her that Annie was at home, here in a land that had prayer calls and men in djellabas. To her, Africa was as wild and great an adventure as Crossroads.

Fields hopped from hoof to hoof impatiently. "And now," he said, "the errand I must run."

BJ had no idea how far they traveled; with Fields's help, it was a short walk. They crossed some rough terrain again, and passed villages that had probably been deserted since the fall of Carthage. BJ noticed that Fields was no longer creating the road with his stick, and didn't have to think to remember the turns.

The people who greeted him said nothing. They crowded up, touching him, looking questioningly into his eyes and half-reaching to touch his hair. An old man, every wrinkle in his face a smile, embraced Fields unreservedly. "*Bou Jeloud*," he said happily. Fields squeezed him back.

BJ was shocked when Fields took his shoes and hat off, but the smiles it provoked relieved her. Thereafter the touching became tugging, and they were half-pulled to a nearby hillside where some musicians were playing, and the audience, rocking back and forth, listened raptly.

The people were all olive-skinned. They looked like Berbers, though it was clear from the ceremony they were performing that there were differences between them and some of their Islamic brothers.

The music was complex and compelling: Percussion and wood-winds called out over the land incessantly, and their song had a pattern too complex for BJ to grasp. She suspected that it was as old as the ruins they had passed.

The drums and the strange double-reed instrument (Fields called it a *rhaita*) stuck in her mind the most; they sang to each other as much as to the audience. When one musician changed a theme, the others changed as well, sometimes improvising, sometimes musically nudging the wayward player back to the original theme. BJ shook her head and realized that she had been listening, stock-still, for quite some time.

"These are the greatest musicians in your world," Fields said. "They play for their entire lives. No one plays more, or thinks more while playing."

A wiry boy leapt off the rocks and watched them. He was hollow-cheeked and dark-eyed, frantic with the energy inside him. His legs were wrapped in goatskins, wool side out, and he wore goat's horns on his head. A series of dark curlicues, done in black ink with a geometric, Hellenic feel, adorned his chin; he was too young to have a beard. He stared at Annie and then at BJ with naked lust, then leapt up the hillside again. From above he turned to watch them; if Fields's glances at women were usually suggestive, the boy's were raw and intent.

"You are privileged," Fields said to their amazed, upturned faces. "You have now seen the god Pan.

"The boy never takes off the goatskins. He never sleeps indoors or tills fields. The village leaves him tribute food; young women will give their bodies to him. They are the last in this world who worship Pan, through the chosen boy. He will be Pan for all of this year." He chuckled. "A god for one year!"

The drums insisted, and the *rhaita* called coaxingly. The boy leapt back down to dance. While Protera and Annie watched him, BJ said quietly to Fields, "And what were you before you were the great god Pan?"

Fields looked back at her, apparently unsure of what to say. He glanced back at the others and stepped away from the dancing; BJ followed.

"I was young," he said slowly. "Hard to think of now, and hard even for you maybe to imagine, but I was young. I was a shepherd, on the island of Propaxos."

BJ glanced involuntarily at his legs. He nodded, smiling. "Oh, yes. No one minded then. I could run the hills, and tend sheep, and dance with women and men, and no one minded. I had fled Crossroads with the rest, to be safe from the *milites* of Augustus. It had been many years, and they never came for us. I cared for sheep, and I made music and fed the sea birds, and that was all."

"And there was another Pan?"

"I had seen him before." His eyes shone. "When I was a boy, I saw him play his pipes and dance in the hills, and many women danced with him. Can you think what it is, to see a god twice in your own life?"

"I'm having difficulty."

He waved an arm. "Do not think me a god, little Beej. I am just someone who loves much more than he should."

"Perhaps that's what it is to be a god."

"To act as a god, maybe. To be one, though . . ." He shrugged. "So, I saw him, and it had made me glad to see him. It made me feel like more of myself, I think." Fields rubbed absently at the ample hair on his arms. "On Propaxos I grew strong, I played with joy, I cared for my flock and for my friends. I even cared for the flocks of strangers, and for the strangers, too. The Romans want tribute; I give it. The Zion rebels, wounded and hiding on our island, need healing; I give it. The children of Crossroads, all the half-things who cast strange shadows and filled our dreams, they flee to our land and need care; I give it. Why not?"

Now he looked at BJ, his dark eyes filled with awe. "That was what made him come to me: the caring. When a faun came to me, one of his legs broken so he could never dance, could I refuse? When a firelover, shivering from the sea spray and half dead, landed on my campfire, could I put it out? And the unicorn—when the first unicorn came to me, broken innocence with an arrow in its side, how could I say no and let it die?"

Annie laughed at something Protera had said; he smiled at her and half-bowed. BJ said, "I can't imagine letting it die."

"So." Fields ran a callused hand through his hair, twisting it around one horn like a trellised vine. "They know me, then, and more and more animals and people come to me when they need me. Some I save. Some I don't. You know."

BJ nodded mutely. Any vet knew that.

"And my sheep are not cared for and unthrifty, so I give them away. And my home is sagging, so I sell it and use the money for medicines. How can I refuse? How can I stop?"

BJ started. She had never considered the consequences, to Crossroads, should she one day close her practice and move back to Virginia.

"And one day," Fields went on, "two brown-skinned men with long horns, like gazelles, they come to me with a stick platform with a blanket over it. They sing the whole time they carry it, and they move their feet like tiny birds, right over stones and thorns with bare man-feet, but they never cut themselves. And their song is the kind that makes you crazy, or it makes you weep.

"And they drop the stretcher and run off, but they never stop singing the whole time, in these tiny voices with the sound of birds. And when they're gone, I go over and lift the cloth on the stretcher and look down.

"And he looked back at me." Fields's voice was rich with grief, as though the shock were fresh. "Looked back with his one remaining eye, and his smile that no one could kill. One of his horns, it was split to the root, and blood flowed from it. And his chest over his heart was—" Fields's voice trembled. "He smiled, then, up at me, and said, 'I hear that you are good to the dying.'

"Oh, BJ, he was broken, and bleeding, and so fat, and ugly like the legend has always said, and to me he was so very beautiful, I could feel my heart swell and throb. I was on my knees—that is not easy for my kind, but it was right of me—and I said, 'If I can save you, I will. If it needs my life, I will give it.' "

Fields's eyes shone. "And he touched me, and his skin felt soft like a deer's on the back of my hand. And he said, 'You cannot save me, but you can give your life.'

"And where his hand touched me, I felt everything in the world flowing into me.

"And he held my arm so tight it hurt, and he was gone. Nothing but a body. His followers called out across the sea to a ship captain, that the great god Pan was dead."

"I've heard the phrase," BJ said slowly. Stein had used it once, with affection, to Fields.

"So." His eyes were full, remembering. He wiped them, snuffling like an animal as he blew his nose. "And I stood up and looked out to sea. And I could see the ship, and the mainland you call Greece, and Italy beyond it, and Europa and Asia and the places no one knew about yet, even the place you were born, little BJ. And I saw the planets, and the stars, and knew all about the stars, even those I couldn't see, *and I knew how to walk to all of them.*"

BJ felt a chill. She had thought about walking to other worlds, but had not thought in terms of Mars or Saturn, or of places even farther away. "And you became a god?"

He shrugged. "I became better at taking care of Crossroads. And later, when all the animals could come back, I walked them home."

"Over the new Strangeways you made. You can create a Strangeway whenever you want. Why don't you do it more often?"

"And leave this world open for the ones who don't need it to walk in? And watch when they kill my children?"

After a moment's thought, BJ nodded. "The more roads, the more contact. It means the land falls apart faster."

Fields smiled ruefully, glancing at Protera in animated conversation with Annie. "Your Dr. Protera, he must teach you fast. Yes, that is right; the more roads, the greater the loss."

He looked back at the Atlas Mountains. "And now there are many roads."

It was dark by the time they arrived at Stein's. BJ had other questions for Fields, but she was too afraid to ask them.

F·O·U·R·T·E·E·N

THE NEXT MORNING, Annie came by the cottage. BJ, feeling guilty but selfish, threw a sheet over the Healing Sign so that they could talk in peace. Unlike Dave and Lee Anne, Annie fell immediately in love with the place; she touched the table, the portable X-ray, and the anesthetic equipment as though it were magical. "I can't believe you've brought in all this equipment. It's perfect."

It was, BJ realized, the difference between university or urban medicine and a practice in the Third World; Annie had lived with inadequate equipment since shortly after graduation.

She also adored Horvat. "Come here. You're so pretty, come here." Horvat backed up, showing his teeth. BJ picked him up and he consented, grudgingly, to having his ears scratched and stomach tickled.

Daphni rubbed frantically against Annie. BJ remembered that Annie had once walked into a circle of Wyr to rescue a flowerbinder; perhaps Daphni could sense something.

BJ made them breakfast (fresh venison from the Meat People, two eggs each, sliced fruit and fresh cream) while Annie read BJ's additions to Lao's *Guide*. Then, at Annie's insistence, BJ sat and read her friend's diary while Annie did the breakfast dishes.

The diary made BJ uncomfortable at first; in addition to being Annie's record of her time in Chad, it was a devotional journal. Annie interspersed the high and low points of her work with prayers for safety, for the health of others, and in praise of Jesus for everything from the arrival of a vaccine shipment to

173

the continued survival of their rusted and dented '74 Chevy truck. BJ murmured polite comments at first, then became absorbed.

Annie had carefully and without exaggeration recorded all the harrowing details of work in a refugee camp: of seventy-two-pound adults who could barely crawl, of children scarred with stray bullets from civil conflict in Sudan, of the constant fight to keep flies away from children too listless to protect their own eyes.

There was a clatter at the pump by the sink. "These are done," Annie said mildly. "Where do they go?"

BJ looked up blankly, completely disoriented. How could Annie come back to dishes and cupboards so easily? "Up there, on the left."

"Thanks." Annie smiled and washed out the sink, while BJ looked wonderingly at her.

BJ had felt noble about meeting the needs of Crossroads, and self-reliant in setting up her practice. She couldn't imagine making the sort of sacrifice that Annie had—not for anyone, let alone strangers.

When the cottage was straightened, Annie picked BJ's notes up, and the two of them read in that amiable, Sunday-morning fashion that happens once in a hundred mornings. After half an hour, BJ looked up, startled. "What's that?"

Annie, enthralled by BJ's notes on firelovers, murmured, "Just a truck." Then she dropped the notes, looking up.

BJ remembered. "Lee Anne." The two of them ran outside as Lee Anne, in a white van with the name of a commercial bakery carelessly painted out, rumbled up the lane at twice the speed either of them would have dared in a truck.

She parked alongside BJ's truck, the walk-in back of the van with its windowed doors dwarfing the vet truck. BJ and Annie walked to the back to unload it.

Lee Anne leapt out and threw herself against the rear doors. "Don't look!" She slipped in the grass, sitting on the rear bumper.

BJ peered through the glass automatically. Two dazed, narrow blinking faces peered back.

Lee Anne said, "I asked you not to do that."

BJ said, "What are those?"

Annie, hands to her mouth, said an uncharacteristic, "Oh my God."

Lee Anne snapped, "Look, it's not like I broke all Ten Commandments; I just took an endangered species for a little ride, that's all."

BJ was weak on birds, but had a sudden horrid suspicion. "Egrets?" she said with little hope.

Lee Anne grinned and opened the doors. "Close. Whooping cranes."

BJ looked at the burlap-wrapped birds, who lay on the truck floor with their legs bound together, sticking straight out. "You could have hurt them."

Lee Anne banged the floor with her hand. "Truck's lined with foam rubber."

"How did you catch them?"

She pointed to the net slung on the van wall, camouflage gear hanging beside it. "That was the tough part. I had to get help from a poacher."

She added pointedly, "Making sure I had a young male and female was even tougher."

"A breeding pair?" Annie stared at the helpless birds. "You stole a breeding pair out of their natural habitat?"

Lee Anne put one boot on the truck bumper. "I stole them, as you say, right out of a bird sanctuary. It's a nice place, but it ain't forever."

"And Crossroads is," BJ murmured.

Lee Anne looked at her in surprise. "Well, sure." She grinned again. "Anyway, I knew I had a good getaway."

"My map, right," BJ murmured. "Does that make me an accomplice?"

"I sure hope so. You'd better know where we're going to take these guys."

Even in Crossroads, they felt furtive. The few people they saw, and the single group of Hippoi, stared at Lee Anne's van as long as it was in sight. Lee Anne said irritably, "Does everybody here have to stare?"

Annie said calmly, "You'd think they'd never seen a van before." Lee Anne glared coldly at her; she smiled back. "Did you bring that little pistol?" Annie sounded disapproving.

Lee Anne grinned and patted her pocket. "Don't leave home without it. Wanna see?" It was a .22 handgun which the others had seen before when they were students.

Annie stared out the window. "I don't like guns."

"Now, why is it always the people who never even see guns that think guns ought to be taken away—?"

BJ, her nose in *The Book of Strangeways*, lifted her head for a moment. "I've read her diary. She's seen plenty of guns." Lee

Anne shut up. "Left at the next fork." Fields had put the road to the island in place.

"But we want to head to the right—" Lee Anne began.

"And we will." BJ closed the book, holding her place with a finger. "By going left." She looked up.

The left fork seemed to head into the mountains where the Great lived. Lee Anne, hanging onto the steering wheel and tugging it back and forth, dodged rocks with the ease of someone who had long practice on country roads. "That's right, folks. We're climbing to the seashore."

For the first time, Annie looked concerned. "Is it possible that all of Crossroads is below sea level?"

BJ said thoughtfully, "Actually, I think it's hard to tell what the real elevation of any given point on a road is. Relative height means less on a Strangeway."

They both stared at her. Lee Anne snorted. "You've been listening to strange people too much."

But shortly thereafter, they drove onto a ridge and stared downhill through gently sloping brush to the salt marshes and the sea. Lee Anne stopped the truck, looked in the mirror, and stuck her head out the window to stare.

They got out and looked. Behind them, rising above the ridge they had just climbed to, were the high plains below the mountains where the Great nested. The range in the north of Crossroads, so close when they had started half an hour ago, was a hazy blue line behind them.

Annie and Lee Anne stared at BJ, who shrugged. They got back in silently and rode through the tall grass to the bay and the great island that BJ needed to learn about.

As they came close, Lee Anne slowed to a crawl, peering at the damp and puddled lane before her. Twice the van tilted as the puddles turned out to be deeper than she expected; once she needed to rock backward and forward to get unstuck. Finally she shut off the engine. "One of these is going to be over the hubs, and we'd either better stop first, or be real fond of where we are when it happens."

She opened the back. Annie, reluctantly, and BJ, still more reluctantly, helped her lift the still-dazed birds out.

Annie checked their eyes. "Are you sure you got the dosage right?"

"Not real sure. I talked to a zoo vet in New Orleans before I tried. C'mon, honey, wake up." She snapped her fingers at one of the whooping cranes. Finally it blinked lazily at her, but gave no other reaction. "There. See that?"

"I saw it." Annie, her face a mask of disapproval, carried the female whooping crane down into the tall grass of the swamp.

They carefully removed the burlap from around the wings. The two birds, side-by side in the reeds, stood blinking, stretching and curving their necks.

"Get on," Lee Anne said. They stared at her. She waved her arms and danced at them, looking like a crane herself. "Fly now." Nothing.

"They don't know what to do," BJ said.

Lee Anne said in exasperation, "No wonder they're nearly extinct." She leapt up in the air with her knees tucked, clapped her hands, and shouted as loudly as she could, "FLY!"

The thunder of wings from the reeds behind her startled her. She landed awkwardly, staggered, and fell into the marsh as the first birds airborne panicked the others into flight. Dead reeds dripping across her, Lee Anne looked up gaping as hundreds of whooping cranes launched into the air from the reed bed.

The two she had brought flapped a few times, testing, then joined the flock. Annie, laughing, shouted something to Lee Anne, but couldn't make herself heard.

Gradually the noise died down. Lee Anne, still sitting in the marsh, stared at the cloud of white wings growing smaller as the cranes headed down the coastline toward the mangrove islands. "Well, at least they won't be lonely."

"And why did you do that?" A voice asked.

They spun around. BJ looked back longingly at the van, where her catchlet lay carefully wrapped in a towel. Lee Anne had her hand partway in her right pocket.

The young man in the water stared at them with liquid brown eyes, larger than human. His face—

It was the cast of his jaw, partly; it made him seem to smile all the time. Partly it was the calm in the eyes, and the fluid grace of his movements. Perhaps it was everything about him; he seemed continually happy and at peace.

His skin was mottled like a harp seal's.

"Are you bringing more birds, then? For it seems to me we already have all of that lot we need."

Lee Anne recovered first. "Okay, those are the last ones we'll bring. Would you rather we brought something else?"

"More like yourselves. We couldn't have too many of those." He smiled even more. "Have you names? Myself is Brendan. After the good monk who showed us the way here."

He wore a piece of hide over his genitals. BJ assumed it was for modesty until he turned around; it was simply a triangle held on with three strings.

BJ made hasty introductions. "Can you tell me about the island in the bay? I need to know as much about it as I can."

He grinned. "Then there you should go, dear." BJ, Annie, and Lee Anne looked at each other.

BJ said slowly, "I could never do it alone."

"I can carry one of you on each arm, I'm that strong. One of you would need to stay." He looked mournfully from one to the other.

"That would be me," Annie said politely.

"And that was easy." He slapped his thighs, which made a smack like a wet towel. "Let's be off, then. But are you for wearing all that in the water?" He gestured at their clothing, his expression coming as close to distaste as his happy face would allow.

Lee Anne fingered her soaked shirt. "Probably not."

"Sorry I am that I have no extra thongs. Mind the sand."

Lee Anne shrugged and disrobed, leaving her underwear on. BJ followed. Annie, watching Brendan narrowly, took off only her jeans. "I'll walk partway out with you," she said. She added, awkwardly because Brendan was watching her, "And I can't help but feel that this is a bad idea."

"Honey, you really ought to be more liberal," Lee Anne said— which amused BJ no end, coming as it did from an NRA and former College Republicans member. She strode into the water. BJ followed.

The bay was warm, nearly bathtub temperature, and shallow for a long ways out. They were a third of the way to the island before they were up to their waists.

Brendan floated on his back in front of them, his chest and knees above the water. He reached behind himself, bobbing occasionally, and dug in the loose sand.

He pulled clam after clam free of the waves, piling them in the hollow between his ribs and his legs. Lastly he felt around for a long time, shifting position, and BJ realized that he was walking through the shallows on his fingertips, looking for something.

He smiled and pulled up two flat rocks. He tossed a clam in the air and smacked it between the rocks, then shook the crushed pieces free and dipped the soft inner meat in the waters of the bay.

He cupped it in his palm, offering it to them.

Lee Anne looked faintly green. "Sir, I do appreciate your kindness, but I'm fairly full just now."

Annie nodded. "Thank you." She said it clearly and carefully, took the clam in hand, and slid it down her throat, showing slightly exaggerated satisfaction. She looked meaningfully at BJ.

Africa, BJ reflected, had taught Annie some far-reaching lessons in courtesy. Aloud she said to Brendan, "May I have one, as well?"

"And why should you have to ask, and me with a stack of them on me?" He passed one over.

It tasted strong and slightly sandy and, BJ thought, better than any clam or oyster she had ever had.

"And now the rest of the journey." Brendan held his arms partway out of the water, bobbing fractionally lower as he did. Annie sighed loudly; all three of the others ignored her as she turned and waded shoreward.

Brendan's arms were soft and warm for all their muscle; they were like sealskin pillows. He kicked gently with his feet, and the two women lay, BJ on one arm and Lee Anne on the other, rocking softly in the sun-warmed water. BJ thought she would go to sleep.

Lee Anne said lazily, "This is nice for November. It's warm here."

"It is that. Warmer far than where we were before, I'm thinking."

"Where were you before?" BJ asked. "How did you come here?"

"We were people from the Cold Sea, not far off a beautiful green island—"

"That would be Ireland," BJ said.

He beamed at her. "You know it? Can you tell me of it?" He was disappointed that she had never been there. "Ah, well. So one day, while we were diving for fish and having a fair party of it, a strange round thing floats among us. And what is it but a hide boat, a coracle, with a brave man in monk's robes sailing it."

"You make it sound like you were there," Lee Anne said.

"I was, dear, since my people were. We tell our tales careful, to last for all time. What he said and did, I know like I was there. Best you let me tell it, or you'll never know."

Lee Anne shut up.

"We welcomed him and offered him fish. And he thanked us, and told us about lands to the east—some of those we knew—and south—and those we'd heard rumors of—and another land he was trying to reach now, a new world. And didn't he make it sound fair wonderful, with the animals, and the trees, and things in between we'd never dreamed of." He continued more mundanely, "He talked to us about Christ, too, but not much. Myself, I think he liked travel better, monk or no."

BJ said, "And he knew a way to Crossroads, by sea?"

"He called it the trackless road. I think he'd read about it somewhere. He was the one for reading, so the story goes."

"Did he have a book with him?"

Brendan turned to BJ in surprise. "Don't you know, that's the next part. He had a book, all maps, and that's how he knew the way. He wouldn't tell us where the book was from."

"A monastery library somewhere." BJ tried to imagine the course of that book: how it got to Ireland, and how a monk found it in an island country and was willing to risk a sea route to Crossroads. "The trackless road," she murmured, and shivered.

Brendan wrapped his arm tighter on her and said angrily, "There, love, and I've been dragging out a story, with you not used to the water. We'll go straight to your island." He kicked hard enough that he puffed.

The island rose up before them in ten minutes' time. The cliffs were sand, gravel, and earth; the topsoil, visible at the cliff's edge, was thick and rich. BJ and Lee Anne scrambled up a gully in the cliff.

They emerged on a green hillside dotted with pastel flowers; the shrubbery had thick, rubbery leaves, and was hung with vines that looked and smelled like passion flower. There were berries on at least half of the bushes, and the taller shrubs were hung with fruit. Song birds flitted back and forth, warbling.

BJ knelt, checking the soil. It was rich and black, built by centuries of nearly undisturbed vegetation. "You're the bird expert, Lee Anne; would this place be a good habitat for dodos?"

"My lord, don't bring them here. It's too good for them."

BJ touched a golden fruit dazedly and sniffed at it. "Is there any fresh water?"

Lee Anne pointed towards the middle of the island. In a depression were two huge ponds. "Got to be fresh. It's forty feet above sea level." She seemed almost angry. "I can't believe the dodos are gonna get this."

BJ sighed and moved back toward the cliffs. "The rest of us have to work for a living."

The trip back across the bay was lazier. Low clouds had moved in, but the air was still warm, the water still perfect. BJ stared at the mangroves to the northwest, and tried futilely to identify the birds perched in them. More of Brendan's people were swimming and walking around them, too. She wondered sleepily if they were all as casually generous as Brendan was.

When they were halfway back, Brendan said, "Wasn't this a grand time you had, then?"

Both of them murmured happy agreement.

"Lovely." He coughed, intended as a subtle noise, but it was a loud bark that echoed across the bay. "It did cross my mind, y'know, that next spring will be coming before you know it, and I'll be needing as many of you as the world can spare."

Lee Anne rolled sideways and cocked an eye at him. "As many what?"

"Cows, of course."

Lee Anne sat bolt upright and sank instantly. BJ, alerted, slid off Brendan's arm and swam. They were still some fifty yards out.

He caught up with them easily, gliding by. "You're lovely both, you know, though you don't move well in water. Still, I'd be glad to have you."

Lee Anne reached the shallows and stood. "Thanks for the offer, sir, but I'm not available."

"Is there another, then? Surely I'd fight him for you." He looked at them earnestly. "A rare fight I'd make, for the right to bend you both over a wet rock some sunny morning."

It took BJ a moment to place the sound; she could not remember ever having heard one like it. Annie, standing up to her waist twenty feet away, was snickering.

"I'm afraid not, Brendan." BJ was doing her best to handle this politely. "Thank you, but we're not interested in joining your harem."

"But they're lovely girls, all of them. You'd have a grand time . . ." Brendan's hopeful voice faded as he tried to read their faces. "You swam with me," he said, at a complete loss. "You ate my clams."

"And that's all you're gonna get," Lee Anne said firmly.

"That's all right, then." He returned to his normal, peaceful expression. "I'll be off now. Maybe I'll write a song about you. I've never had my heart broke by a woman before." He looked dreamy-eyed and inspired. "It's grand."

And off he swam, singing cheery snatches about wicked eyes and bold deceivers.

Lee Anne was seething as they splashed shoreward. She snapped at Annie, "Don't you try to tell me we did something wrong. This here had nothing to do with right or wrong."

"It has nothing to do with right and wrong," Annie agreed. They waded on in silence.

Finally she said, "However, it has everything to do with 'I told you so.' " She added, snickering again, " 'Bend you both over a wet rock!' "

Lee Anne splashed ashore angrily. "That's about the most sickening, uncouth thing any man has said to me since my first dance in junior high."

Annie said, "You really ought to be more liberal."

"Hey, do I trash BJ for fooling around with a faun?"

"Do I?"

BJ was bright red. "You seem to assume," she said carefully, "that I'm sleeping with Stefan."

Lee Anne stared. "That's right. And I figure if you're not, you oughta be."

Annie said, "I wouldn't go that far, but I'll admit I assumed you were. I've assumed you two would marry," she said almost shyly. Annie, a Born-Again Baptist, did not force her morals on others, but she did believe that those morals would be good for them.

"I'm not sleeping with him. I'm not engaged to him. I'm not—" BJ ran out of steam. "I'm not sure what to do from here."

"We can talk in the van on the way back," Lee Anne said, all the edge gone from her voice. "If you need anything—"

"Thanks, but it wouldn't help." How do you explain that you carry a genetic disorder, with a fifty-fifty chance of passing it on to your offspring? How do you explain that Crossroads is the only thing that prevented you from deteriorating balance and declining mental health?

Annie said sadly, "You've always kept your own secrets."

"I still need to. But thanks, both of you." She moved toward the van, out into a bare patch of sand open to the sky.

Overhead they heard a blast like a gas explosion. All three ducked by reflex. A whooping crane, still burning, plummeted into the swamp in front of them. The water hissed as it entered.

Lee Anne splashed over quickly, pulled the struggling bird upright in the water, and ran her hands over it, ducking and blinking as the bird's good wing flapped frantically. "Broken wing. Broken leg. Splintered lower beak. Multiple severe burns." She took a deep breath and moved her hands to the bird's neck, flexing her shoulders once. "Broken neck." The bird was still.

Lee Anne looked back up, wet-eyed, at BJ. "What the hell did that?"

A chimera sailed low overhead, hooting, then turned and goggled at BJ. It sailed lower, finally landing with a soft thump that drove its feet a good three inches into the moist ground. It crouched in front of BJ, seemingly ready to leap.

Lee Anne came forward, reaching into her pocket. "Don't shoot," BJ said quickly, and, to the chimera, "Fran?"

He wagged his tail happily, smacking the scorpion sting against the ground.

"You know this thing?" Annie said dubiously.

"We've met. He probably flew down because he saw me."

She moved forward cautiously. Fran's liking her meant little in terms of safety; Fran liked most of the things he hurt or killed. She edged around Fran, scratching the dirty flea-laden fur between the chimera's cat ears, and stopped when she came to the leather strap.

Lee Anne was eight feet in front of the chimera, sensibly out of range of the tail. She had her .22 pistol out, and was sighting down it at Fran. "Everything all right here?" she said, as calmly as a cop at a fender-bender.

"It's fine." BJ felt around the leather strap until she found a ring and two more straps. "Don't excite him, and don't get closer. They belch fire."

Lee Anne's eyes flickered sideways at the whooping crane corpse. "Never woulda guessed."

BJ lifted the reins dangling from the muzzle. They were broken off; the chimera had been tethered.

Lee Anne said, "My lord, who wants to ride one of those? You'd need to swim in sheep dip afterwards."

BJ, feeling along Fran's back, came to saddle galls; Fran was still unused to being ridden. "You'd see a lot," she said absently. "Chimerae migrate from Crossroads to other worlds." And her heart felt as though it stopped.

Without a moment's hesitation, she swung onto Fran's back. He mewed at her, and she shifted below the sores. "Okay, boy. All right. Calm down."

Lee Anne frowned. "Get down from there, woman; you don't know the first thing about riding."

Annie said, "Where are you going?"

BJ struggled, hands in pocket, then tossed the van keys to her. "I don't know. Take *The Book of Strangeways* to Stein's. Tell him what I've done, and tell him—" She considered. "No, just tell him that. Keep my keys in case I'm gone, and take care of Horvat. And Daphni," she added, feeling guilty. She slapped the reins and said, far more brightly than she felt, "Okay, Franny. Where we going, fella?"

The chimera purred. Smoke rose from his nostrils. He flapped his wings, padded forward for more lift, and rose clumsily into the air. BJ held on desperately.

When she regained her balance, she looked down at the others. They were already too small to see their features. BJ, rapidly gaining altitude on a remarkably stupid animal that could fly in and out of Crossroads, was glad she could see them at all. In a moment, the fog shrouded them and the land, and BJ had no idea where she was.

F·I·F·T·E·E·N

THE AIR SMELLED like salt, then like dust. The texture of the fog below changed. BJ's ears popped, and she knew that she was no longer in Crossroads.

The fog below BJ and Fran thinned gradually, finally becoming wispy streamers over a brown landscape. The last of the gulls and shore birds disappeared behind them.

It was hot and dry even up here. BJ's throat became sore immediately. She blinked, peering through the heat shimmers at a landscape broken by hills and bushes but few streams.

They soared over a row of small hills that would effectively block moisture from the coast. On the other side, BJ saw a road through the hills, an area of bushes (where the last of the cloud moisture dumped, probably), and, in the valley below them, a small square of dust-covered tents and a single stone cottage. Fran purred excitedly and dove lower.

The camp was laid out in neat rows, with elevated piping for running water and a garbage dump well away from the camp. To BJ, after her months in Crossroads, it looked disturbingly urban. In the middle of it was a roofed platform that was clearly the mess hall.

Beside it were two neatly kept racks of swords, axes, and spears.

At the far end of it was a corral. Fran sped up when it came into view.

The chimerae were in it, facing the fence. A few of them took to the air when they saw Fran, and BJ saw that they were tied by their reins to the crossbars of the fence. On one section of fence a pair of reins drooped.

BJ sighed. "Only you, Fran, would fly back to the place you broke out of." He honked satisfiedly.

They came down hard, dropping to the corral fence. Fran landed on the railing and tried, futilely, to lock his feet on it. He overbalanced a moment later, sending BJ sprawling in the dirt.

BJ lay in the dust, staring up at a ring of interested feline faces. She realized that she was in the middle of a herd of animals with scorpion stings, and that they belched fire sporadically. She realized that they were stupid, unpredictable, and quite likely to kill her.

She suspected they were the least of her problems. A young man with shoulder-length blond hair and a scar from his right eye down to his upper lip was staring at her. He had a curved scimitar at his belt, but he was holding a shovel.

She sat up. "I should explain what I'm doing here."

He looked at her blankly and said four husky syllables which made no sense. His hand was on the hilt of the scimitar.

"I followed Fran here." Fran, for once self-aware, hopped to her side. She got back on him in case she needed to leave quickly. "You see, Fran found me—never mind where—and I saw the reins—"

She stopped. He was nodding in that intense, jerky way that people do when they don't understand a word you say and are still wondering whether or not you're dangerous.

She moved her mouth as though talking to a deaf person and said slowly, "English?"

The boy shook his head. "Anavalerse."

BJ thought, At least he shook his head for "no." She said without much hope, "Spanish?" She had two years of it in high school, her only hope just now.

He turned and shouted, "MORGAN!"

BJ froze.

A tall, energetic woman with flowing red hair came out of the stone cottage. She had a book tucked under her left arm, and she had at least four daggers stuck in the dressing-gown she was wearing. Also hanging from the belt of the gown was a polished, curled horn like a shofar, probably a ram's horn. She nodded to BJ. "I was reading," she said almost mildly.

The boy looked at her uncomprehendingly. She repeated herself, probably in Anavalerse, and his eyes went wide. He bowed, held his arms out palms up, and suddenly knelt and poured dirt over his head.

Morgan looked disgusted and said something in a soothing tone. He stood, sighing in relief, and cast a glowering look at BJ for getting him into so much trouble. Morgan held the book for a moment, staring intently at a page, and BJ could read the English title: *Principles of Cavalry Training*.

"I think we've met," she said to BJ. Her English was slightly accented, a little like the English BJ had heard on Roanoke Island in the Carolinas, and a little like the accent BJ remembered from a movie about Cornish fishermen.

BJ nodded. "You tried to kill me at Stein's."

Morgan looked up from the book and laughed politely. "I think if I had tried to kill you, I surely would have."

Her mannerisms bothered BJ; Morgan sounded like a British academic, not like the butcher BJ had seen her be.

Morgan glanced over her shoulder at the row of clouds, visible beyond the hills. "All that water, and it never comes inland."

"Shore fog," BJ said. It felt odd and unreal to talk with Morgan about something as inconsequential as the weather. "It comes inland in flatter, moister countries, like England." She added as off-handedly as possible, "You might know it as Britain."

Morgan's smile was a terrible thing. "I also knew it as Logres."

BJ asked the question which, sooner, or later, everyone who met Morgan asked: "How old are you?"

"Older than I wish." She closed the book and called to the young man: "Renault?"

He came forward with an outstretched hand, clearly eager to be of service after failing her. He tangled his feet in Fran's reins in the dust, and fell against her.

Morgan casually stuck a dagger in his left side, just under the rib cage and tilting up. He fell into her arms as though he had fallen asleep. Morgan's left arm draped around him, palm against the wound.

A moment later she pulled her stained palm away, cupping it, and covered it with her other hand. She worked her hands across each other, staring dreamily down at the boy who now sagged at her feet.

"I saw you do that before." BJ felt as though someone else were doing all this calm talking for her. "In Stein's."

Morgan nodded. "I remember now. What a wonderful day that was."

The wind whipped through the camp. Only the young body at her feet, dust clinging to the blood stains, was still.

"It was a terrible day. Most of your army died."

Morgan eyed her with apparent calm. "I recruited more. There are always more, here."

BJ eyed the barren, unfriendly hills. She had never seen a countryside so indifferent to life, including films of the Mojave desert. "Where am I?"

"It's called Anavalon. A wounded king ruled here once, and until his wound was healed, the land would be barren. He sent everyone he could, man or woman, to find the cup that would heal him.

"They all failed. He died, and his land died with him." Her didactic tone faltered, and she sounded triumphant.

BJ said with certainty, "Because of you."

"Because I deceived him and destroyed him. As I deceived Brandal." Her smile was taut and cruel, with no regret or remorse. "Not long enough to destroy him, but almost. And I destroyed Arthur. And I'll destroy you."

"Is that why you captured the chimerae?"

"Anyone could, if she wanted." Morgan gestured at the animals, who were growing restless as the sun moved west. All except Fran were staring to the east. "Useless animals, except that they fly from world to world."

BJ said with a certainty she didn't really have, "Not reliably."

"Usually you're right," Morgan said. "However, they breed in Crossroads, don't they? They all want to go there now; if I didn't feed them so well, they'd never come back when they break free."

The chimerae shifted back and forth as far as the reins would let them, all still staring east. BJ glanced over her shoulder, but saw nothing but another row of hills.

More than anything, BJ was finding Morgan's apparent politeness upsetting. She sounded like a teacher or a doctor, not like a warlord with blood drying on both her hands.

Aloud she said to Morgan, "That's an interesting horn."

"Oh yes." She barely glanced at it. "It's hollowed and carved for blowing."

"Assemblies, charges, retreats?"

"Exactly." Now she smiled again. "It's from the head of a faun, much like the young faun you know, but with bigger horns. I pulled it from his skull while he lived."

BJ licked her dry lips, watching the chimerae grow increasingly restless. Fran, his head held facing west by the rein ends in her hand, was undisturbed. "You're exactly the same inside, aren't you? The politeness is for show. You're angry, and you need blood."

Morgan unconsciously rubbed her left palm across her right hand; Renault's blood was already flaking in the harsh, dry air. "I'm sorry I can't play the horn for you; it has a beautiful sound. But I would rather kill you without your being seen." She glanced to one side at the nearby camp.

BJ was thinking, Why? Why would she try to hide my murder, but not Renault's? Suddenly, the chimerae all cried out together, all except Fran. BJ turned. The moon, nearly full, had broken over the eastern hills.

The chimerae rose on their tethers, tugging in vain at the fence rail where the reins were tied. The wood creaked. Morgan and BJ were ringed in by the flapping bodies and by the dust cloud they generated in the corral. Morgan stepped forward, a dagger sliding effortlessly into her hands.

BJ twisted Fran's head around so he could see the moon. Fran hooted at it and rose with her into the air again. Behind her, the others strained to follow.

Morgan threw the dagger and flipped something upward from her other hand; BJ kicked Fran forward. A thin stiletto struck but did not penetrate the scales on Fran's hindquarters; the chimera honked plaintively and flapped off toward the distant mist.

Morgan pulled the horn at her waist and blew on it: a single, sad note. Men and women leapt out of the tents, running to the weapons display. Morgan shouted, "Felaris!" and a huge woman, all scars and muscle, mustered the troops, glanced upward, and ordered spear-carriers forward. Another contingent ran to the corral to mount chimerae.

Fran, interested, swooped lower to watch them.

BJ said, "Fran, no." He paid no attention. "Go away." He flew still lower, hovering close to the corral.

She turned his head back toward the moon and they began to fly east, away from the camp, but away from Crossroads.

She said desperately, "Do you want to see my home? Do you want to see Crossroads?" In a sudden inspiration, she added, "Do you want to see the Griffin?"

Fran gave a loud, happy honk and turned back to the northwest, flapping strongly. Soon, but not soon enough for BJ, they were over the eastern mountains. The flying figures behind them turned back, probably on orders.

BJ didn't touch the reins until they were back through the

mist and clearly over Crossroads. With a sigh of relief, she began experimenting, tugging this way and that. Fran uncomplainingly followed her guidance, and without much difficulty, and in surprisingly little time, they arrived at BJ's cottage.

Fran lit not far from BJ's truck, which was still there; evidently the others had gone directly to Stein's. BJ slid off Fran, not entirely happy that chimerae were so easy to master. She tied the reins to a thick-trunked bush and ran inside.

Horvat bounded back and forth excitedly, then ran outside. He barked at the chimera. BJ dove forward and pulled him back, then dragged him to the other side of the cottage to relieve himself undistracted. She dragged him back, got a stout rope to better tie Fran while she thought about what to do with him, and came back outside.

The bush was uprooted. The stub of the reins was tied to it; bitten and clawed pieces of the reins lay nearby. The ground for yards around had deep claw divots. From behind the fallen bush came a low whimpering.

Holding Horvat by the scruff of the neck, BJ came closer.

The chimera was alternately stretching full length and curling into a ball, whimpering. Puffs of smoke were coming from his mouth so frequently that his whiskers were nearly crisped. His scorpion tail, arched over his head, struck continually at nothing; the tip was dry.

She tied Horvat to the bush, out of range of the chimera. "What is it?" she whispered to Fran, trying for a soothing tone. "It's all right, baby. What is it?"

Fran glanced at her once, pleadingly, and turned his face away, staring up at the moon.

Fervently hoping she was not about to die, BJ knelt by the chimera and felt his side. The chimera quivered at her touch, but otherwise made no response. His fur felt strangely oily, like a civet cat's or a ferret's.

The scaled hindquarters seemed normal. BJ checked the legs, noting with approval no recurrence of parasites, and ran her hands gradually around the legs. Cautiously, she lifted one of the chimera's hind legs.

Fran's reptilian genitalia were falling off. The penis, a sheathed organ with its own large belly-scale over it, was hanging by a bare thread of pink flesh. The testicles had extruded themselves between belly plates, and were half fallen out of their tunic.

In her shock, it took BJ a moment to notice that there was no bleeding, nor any other exposed flesh. The only other unusual sign in the hindquarters was a disturbing looseness and separation to the scales under the arched tail.

As she watched, the chimera shuddered and several of the rearmost scales fell off. The flesh beneath, rather than looking raw and injured, seemed to be normal mammalian skin, with feline fur.

Under the tail was a vulva. It was dripping a slight amount of blood: BJ thought it was damaged until the labia, engorged with blood, pulsed in the fashion which, in horses, is called "winking."

BJ smelled a strong mammalian, musky odor, raw and unpleasant. The chimera's whimpers turned to restless yowls, and he—now she—went immediately into heat.

Behind her, the Griffin sighed tiredly. "And I suppose you're going to say that you never took anyone unsuitable home to meet your parents."

BJ whirled. "It's how you reproduce."

"Correct."

"The chimerae turn female and mate with you. That's why nobody sees female griffins, only males and immature males."

"Also correct. Don't be startled by the sex change; other species do it, including frogs."

"Not with another species."

"Think, Doctor. They're not another species; they are the same species with extreme secondary sexual characteristics." He closed his golden eyes for a moment, sighing. "And I am going to mate with this one."

"Can you stop yourself?"

"Why should I?"

"Well," BJ said finally, "what about Laurie?" There was a silence long enough for her to consider the wind all around her, and the liquid cries of the firelovers.

"I have never asked her," the Griffin said finally, quietly, "whom she makes love to, or whether she does. She would never ask me."

When BJ said nothing, the Griffin snapped, "Have you never loved someone absolutely and completely impossible?"

Horvat bounded interestedly around the two of them. "Of course I have," BJ said finally. "Just recently, in fact." She added, "But there wasn't a world at stake when I did."

The Griffin looked away. "How fortunate."

After a short silence, BJ said, "Morgan is using them for cavalry."

"Ah."

"If the other chimerae seek out the griffins when they change, then she'll be able to ride them into Crossroads."

"I can't fight against them, you know."

"Others may have to." BJ said, a little surprised at herself, "I may have to."

"Certainly."

That left no room for more argument. BJ looked at Fran, whose mammalian nipples had developed into dugs. "Are the offspring all griffins?"

"The females are chimerae, the males griffins. Once the young are weaned, the adult chimerae revert to males and migrate. The young females grow external armor and male genitalia, and go off into the wild world. The young griffins stay in this world and begin their education."

"I'll bet they're cute."

"So they are. I find 'cute' overrated." He sighed, flexing his wings. They had improved remarkably over the past few weeks.

"I am now going to mate with this wretched thing to perpetuate my race. I am hoping I can convince her to forego the courtship flight, since I cannot yet fly. Please allow me some shred of dignity, and do not watch."

BJ said, "I would never." She went over and stroked the griffin's fur as though he were a huge pet. "And yes, I still respect and admire you."

He turned to her and gravely offered a talon as he bowed. "As I you. Doctor, whatever happens in the next few weeks, remember how greatly I enjoyed your company, and how grateful I have been for your work. We may never speak so well of each other again."

BJ was near tears. "I can't imagine that."

"Then you know nothing of civil war." He turned back to the frantically stretching and purring Fran. "Please excuse us."

BJ half-dragged Horvat away, walking to the bench in the circle of stones. She made a quick notation of the time and position of the moon. She sat there for some time, trying not to listen to the impassioned squawking of the chimera and the urgent whispers of the wretchedly ashamed Griffin, trying to silence it.

S·I·X·T·E·E·N

THE NEXT MORNING, BJ regretted giving away her truck keys, but was glad that she had made spares. Losing her keys or having a truck breakdown in Crossroads was a longstanding nightmare of hers.

She tried to sleep in, but when she drove up to Stein's she was still up earlier than the others. Stein was in the doorway of the inn, staring at the sky speculatively; it was still the light blue of just after sunrise. "Should be all right. Beautiful day for a wedding." His breath showed in small, rapid puffs; northern Crossroads was reverting to its normal climate. "I imagine, young lady, that you have something to tell me."

In a few brief words, BJ explained what she had learned the day before. Stein listened, pursing his lips. "Bad. Morgan can get back in at any time, then. Does the Inspector General know?"

The full impact of the problem hit BJ. "He may not help us."

"Explain that." Stein dropped his quiet attentiveness and became a commander.

BJ reflected on the Griffin's dignity, then gave up. "Yes, sir. Please, I think he would prefer that this was private. . . ."

When she finished, Stein sighed. "I wondered how griffins breed; this hasn't happened in my life here. The poor creature. Imagine, needing those filthy animals to breed. And him so sophisticated . . . I'm his friend. Unless I must, of course I won't say anything to him."

He shrugged. "For now, we're safe. Morgan won't come to the inn again, and she doesn't know where there's another copy of

193

The Book of Strangeways in Crossroads. She'd have to be crazy to mount a full invasion based on the chimerae; it's like trusting your whole life to idiots." He patted BJ's shoulder. "You did very well, and you're a smart young lady. You relax and enjoy the wedding."

He smiled at BJ. "It makes you think of all the weddings you've ever been to, right? Not that I've been to many. We've had a few at the inn—the old inn, of course—and I remember . . ." He was smiling, but his forehead was puckered as though it hurt. "Now that's been a while. My oldest sister, the one I barely knew before she moved out, she got married when I was very young. This was before all the trouble in Warsaw, or before I knew about it anyway. She bent down and smiled at me, just before the ceremony, and I remember thinking she was the most beautiful girl there could ever be."

He turned suddenly and went inside. BJ remembered that his oldest sister was certainly dead now; possibly in the Warsaw Ghetto uprising, otherwise in Treblinka or Auschwitz or Majdanek. She assumed that Stein wanted to be by himself.

But he came back a moment later; he and Chris were carrying one of the canopies for outdoor eating. "You never know. Help us with the uprights, won't you, Doctor?"

They set it up by the main door to Stein's. "We can serve under it, if it rains. You can't trust weather here; storms blow in from different worlds—" He chatted amiably, his other troubles apparently forgotten.

Chris winked at BJ and passed her some dolmades, grape leaves stuffed with rice and pine nuts. They were salty from the packing brine, inappropriate for breakfast, and absolutely delicious. She went inside briefly and watched, fascinated, as Chris deftly rolled grape leaves like miniature cigars, and B'Cu, frowning and watching intently, rolled clumsier ones.

Chris spoke to her once: "Doctor. You see my Stan? Any letters?"

She shook her head, and he went back to rolling dolmades.

When BJ went back out, the other guests had arrived.

Almost all of them were Rudy and Bambi's people: some with gray mixed into the downy fur over their legs, some young enough to be slightly dappled. A few, darker brown and with spiraling and less branched antlers, were probably distant relatives. They were carrying duffels and knapsacks, chatting amiably in clusters. Not surprisingly, they liked being close together.

Two of the women spread a blanket on the grass, and two men walked over to it immediately and called to a young stag boy.

He bounded over, restless and excited. One of the does, speaking softly in her own fluting language, put her hands on the boy's shoulders and tried to calm him. Then she walked away; apparently, this wedding would be even more rigidly single-sex than the weddings BJ had been to before.

She watched attentively. She had never been part of a wedding where there was no rehearsal; she was afraid she would get her part wrong.

One of the dark stags squatted down awkwardly, applying paint to the young boy, carefully dappling him with white paint until he was marked like a fawn.

Annie, behind her, said interestedly, "I've just seen something like that, in Chad. You know, agricultural societies have more brains than to create tuxedo rental stores."

BJ said only, "It hasn't come up in my life."

They watched the young boy stand, look with disgust at his white spots (clearly an emblem of childishness), rub at them with one hand, and be reprimanded. He bounded off to sulk, only to be surrounded suddenly by his mother and several scolding aunts.

From beside BJ, Rudy said apologetically, "It's a traditional wedding. We wanted something looser, but you know, the parents—"

"I know." She smiled up at him. "It's very nice."

He smiled at her, happy and not nervous at all. "It's okay." He gestured at some of the stag men, who were painting their bodies in some kind of geometric pattern. "It's not my idea, but I can be cool about it—"

BJ reached sideways and hugged him. "You can be cool about anything."

Bambi, standing with Dave Wilson, noticed them and waved frantically. Rudy waved back, his antlers tossing and bobbing. "Almost anything." He said, a sudden tremble in his voice, "Oh, man, I've never wanted anything as much as I want her."

He bounded off. Bambi bounded into him, almost knocking him down, and BJ was left thinking: Do I know how that kind of wanting feels?

Yes, I'm afraid I do.

" 'Behold, he cometh,' " Annie said softly, " 'Leaping upon the mountains, skipping upon the hills. My beloved is like a roe or a young hart.' "

Melina stood by her. " 'But my horn shalt thou exalt like the horn of a unicorn: I shall be anointed with fresh oil.' " BJ stared. "It's from the Psalms." Melina concentrated. "Ninety-two, I think."

Annie put an arm around her. "Now that I'm used to them, I kind of like your horns."

Lee Anne scooted in place beside them. "Did you see Rudy's face? It oughta shame me to think it, but he may consummate this marriage before we see the deed done." She frowned. "Isn't it bad luck to see the bride before the wedding?"

Bambi's ears twitched; she had overheard, and looked confused. She walked over. "We've already seen each other, or we wouldn't be marrying."

"It's some American tradition, babe." Rudy squeezed her. "European, too, I think." He turned back to the humans. "We've got different customs." To BJ's amusement, he sounded faintly like an anthropology professor. "For instance, we always marry in the fall. You marry all year, but mostly in June. I couldn't believe all the June weddings at USF. Why do they do that? Graduation, I guess."

"Gestation period," Annie said. "Spring births. Tell me, how long is the time from conception to birth for you?"

"Seven months," Bambi said. Rudy looked stunned. Apparently, he hadn't been considering a birth.

The crowd was knotting closer together, chatting and kissing. It looked remarkably like nuzzling. BJ thought, a little wistfully, that it looked like a large happy family. Families with Huntington's chorea did not stress reunions.

An older stag man, his beard shot with gray in a pattern that looked eerily like a graying muzzle, raised both arms. The crowd was immediately silent. The stag man did not lower his arms, but left them raised. Gradually BJ became aware of the sounds around her: the wind across the bare rocks, the ripple of Stein's canvas by the door, the plaintive warble of a firelover searching for warmth.

BJ's mind drifted back to other weddings she'd been to: a seemingly interminable Catholic wedding with a Mass, a ten-minute Methodist ceremony that latecomers missed entirely, a Society of Friends wedding that was part meeting and part ceremony.

For one moment, she ached, realizing that she would probably never marry. Offering someone her genes for his children wasn't an enticing dowry.

Suddenly Bambi was in front of them. "Could you come over?" she said shyly. "It's part of the wedding . . . I didn't want to tell you—"

Annie said brightly, "We'd love to." She was the first one to kneel on the grass, though Lee Anne was the first, at the attendant maids' insistent gestures, to take off her clothes.

BJ knelt, shivering in the late autumn air. Bambi's friends, naked around her, didn't notice the cold.

An older woman, probably Bambi's mother, came forward and put a wreath of flowers around Bambi's neck. The two of them laughed, hugged, cried a little, and licked each other's noses.

Bambi's friends painted BJ, Lee Anne, and Annie quickly, laughing to themselves as they smeared ochre over the women's legs.

Lee Anne snorted and said aloud, " 'Dear Mom: I've finally found something more humiliating than buying a rainbow pastel bridesmaid's dress.' " Annie shushed her.

The stag priest came over. He carried a dark wooden staff. He had dark brown stripes painted across his chest, rib marks with wounds slashed across them. "My name is Suuuno. Thank you for coming," he said in English which was relaxed, but far more precise than Rudy's speech. "Did Rudy or Bambi think to tell you what was expected of you?"

Lee Anne cleared her throat. "We know that we're supposed to run, and that we'll be with the womenfolk. Sir, if you don't mind my saying so, you speak English awfully well."

He smiled. "I should. I did five years of study at USF long before Rudy heard of it."

He enjoyed their faces. "I'm the reason he went there. During your World War Two, USF was short of students. They allowed women's colleges to send students over, and they were frantic for others. I wanted a religious education, and they were a good Jesuit school." He smiled, remembering. "With beautiful gardens, then. Rudy tells me the gardens are mostly gone now."

BJ stared above him. He automatically touched his antlers, reassuring himself. "I cut these off for those years. We didn't know San Francisco so well then." He shrugged, dismissing the topic. "I learned a great deal about how to deal with other cultures. As the ceremony progresses, I will explain it to you."

He spoke in a friendly tone, and was clearly quite kind, but BJ shivered. Suuuno had duties to this ceremony, and they took precedence over human frailties like pity and fear.

He raised his fist, and for the first time, BJ noticed the obsidian knife in it. The knife was stained sienna; BJ couldn't tell whether the stain was paint or dried blood.

Suuuno called out a liquid word, then said quietly to them, "Be ready. First, the woman is hunted."

Bambi, with every semblance of real fear, fled around the corner of Stein's. Her maids leapt after her.

BJ had suspected this part, and had been dreading it. For weeks she had been running, building alternately her endurance and her speed; she was now in the best shape she had been in her entire life. She ran at full speed, grateful for the springiness of the grass on her bare feet.

But the bridesmaids bounded past her easily, leaping fifteen feet at a stretch. One of them leapt over BJ's head, landing beyond her and jumping again before BJ even had time to react.

Bambi's parents and her older sister each dropped to one knee in front of her, heads lowered, trying to protect her. The bridesmaids dashed past her, BJ well behind by now.

Polyta, a braided wreath of sundancer flowers waving in her dark hair, galloped by, snatched BJ up easily in her strong arms, and swung her onto her horse back. Annie, already riding, steadied BJ, who gripped Polyta's slightly bristly back with her bare legs and found her balance. Lee Anne, swinging on behind BJ, settled in place immediately.

Polyta, head thrown back and laughing, wove in and out among the bounding does until they were at the front.

BJ called over her shoulder, "Hold me," and, as Lee Anne grabbed her waist, she hung down over Polyta's heaving sides in a manner that would have made Dr. Sugar Dobbs, former rodeo rider, proud.

She gave a sickening slide, which stopped as Annie belatedly turned back to help hold her. "Not much farther," Annie grunted, sounding polite even in strain.

BJ snatched at Bambi's neck; Bambi glanced over her shoulder in a sudden look of panic, stumbled, and gave a small cry as BJ broke the necklace of flowers. BJ lifted it up, waving it in the air as though it were a trophy.

No one noticed; they were all watching solemnly as Bambi, head bowed, was touched in turn by each of the does, who circled her and finally pressed her to her knees. Polyta, her face pitying, bent slightly and touched her.

BJ, Annie, and Lee Anne slid off Polyta's back and each touched Bambi once; Bambi, eyes lowered, did not move. Bambi's parents walked away slowly. The Bride-Hunt was over, and the bride had been killed.

Suuuno met them at their return, holding their clothes. "Well done."

They dressed quickly, feeling the chill even more as they watched Bambi frozen in place.

Lee Anne, voice muffled as she pulled on a sweatshirt, said, "Sir, what happens next?"

He pointed with his staff. "Now the groom is hunted."

Instead of fleeing, Rudy backed against the ring of rock, his head lowered.

The stags leapt toward him, gesturing with powder-smeared sticks and shouting fiercely. Annie cried out and pointed. Dave, stick-antlers lowered, stood with Rudy's parents and tried to defend Rudy against them, but was driven aside finally. Rudy dropped to his knees and received the stick-spears, his chest mottled with the ochre points. He froze in place like Bambi.

Dave scuttled over to BJ and sat panting. "How did I do?"

"Fine. You looked perfect." She touched his horns. "They look good on you."

"I like 'em." He shook his head once, then shivered. "Wow, is it cold."

Annie passed him his trousers, and he fumbled into them standing up, neck bent so he wouldn't miss any of the ceremony. He hugged Annie and, cautiously, Lee Anne, who snorted and gave him a bone-crushing embrace.

The stag priest said quietly, "The survivors mate."

Rudy approached Bambi and suddenly seemed shyer than she, stepping forward timidly. She circled him, bowing her head in rhythm, and finally nuzzled his chest.

Startled, he leapt to one side. She followed, and suddenly they were leaping together, dancing instead of chasing, a mating ritual.

Stefan had been ashamed to come to the wedding; the last time Rudy and Bambi had seen him, he had been going through morphine withdrawal. BJ thought sadly, I wish Stefan could see this; he loves dancing. She was startled at how strongly she wished she could see him now, at a wedding.

For the first part of the dance, Rudy and Bambi kept their arms to their sides. When they embraced, it was again as dancers, Rudy behind her, moving his hips into her in an unmistakable but graceful simulation of mating.

Bambi held her stomach and arched forward as though carrying a child. The does and stags came forward in a ring; BJ, Annie,

Lee Anne, and Dave joined them hastily.

When they backed away, the stag boy appeared between the bride and groom, pretending to totter on a newborn's legs. Rudy and Bambi each licked him carefully and lovingly with their large, ruminant tongues; predictably, he made a face, but stood still. The crowd chuckled softly, a whickering ripple passing among them.

They cleaned his ears, his chest and back, the buds of his antlers. Then they turned to either side of him and faced outward.

Although they had not known them long, the veterinarians felt close to Rudy and Bambi because, together, they had once fought Morgan. They had all nearly died, and had accepted dying together; that changes you. Dave wiped his eyes as a group of older stag men, antlers wrapped and faces painted, approached the couple.

The face paint was geometric, but identifiable: cats, birds of prey, and, BJ noted, a face which was human on the right and wolf on the left. One was simply painted with a human face, but more cruel than his own.

The stag men stalked forward, encircling Rudy and Bambi. They growled, yipped, howled, and closed ranks. For a moment BJ could not understand the dance. The figures moved around the couple, making thrusting and darting motions, pausing while Rudy and Bambi cried out and contorted their limbs.

It was obvious, but it was a few moments until, appalled, she understood: Rudy and Bambi were once again accepting their deaths.

A cry went up from the circling hunters, and they raised a red-smeared pair of antlers. Annie sucked in her breath sharply, and BJ leaned forward anxiously until they saw Rudy's unharmed head where he lay, stretched out on the grass. Bambi lay beside him.

The boy was nowhere to be seen.

The hunters looked wildly left and right, peering under their raised hands, studiously avoiding looking at the hill above them.

BJ heard a giggle and looked up.

One of Bambi's friends nudged her. "Dono lookup," she said in liquid near-English. "Verbad lucky."

"For the bride and groom?"

"Noo. Theydead." She looked fondly, but with tears in her eyes, down at the couple. "For all-us."

BJ saw that Rudy's and Bambi's parents were standing together, tears trickling down their noses, snuffling like animals. For all that, they were smiling proudly.

There was a rustle and a scamper in the grass above them. BJ sneaked a quick peek; the boy was gone, the grass closing behind him.

Bambi's friend sighed. "Safenow," she fluted.

A sigh rippled through the herd, and the wedding was over.

There was time with each family, and then the newlyweds walked over to the humans.

"Thank you so for coming back," Bambi said shyly. She licked Dave's nose and, for good measure, his new bald spot.

He hugged her. "I had to." He licked her nose, then turned and hugged Rudy.

"Do you know what my people call themselves, man?" Rudy half-whispered. "The Ones Who Die. Like we're the only ones. Until I studied about hunting cultures, I didn't get it.

"That's why today's important." He turned to face the others as well as Dave. "We're a hunted culture. From today on, the herd won't protect us any more. From now on, we're the outer circle, the ones who do the protecting. The ones who die, man."

He looked frightened but very proud. BJ hugged him, and one by one the others did as well.

Chris and Stein had carried an entire banquet outdoors during the ceremony. Chris seemed distracted by something, but he smiled at the bride and pointed significantly at the huge, carefully decorated cake at one end of the table. BJ laughed with delight: It was glazed with cream cheese and honey and covered with all manner of fruits and nuts. Chris had done a cake for the wilds.

Suuuno raised a horn—a cow horn, hollowed out—to his lips and blew; BJ was reminded uncomfortably of Morgan. The guests ceased talking and lined up near the table. Chris filled and passed out steins for a toast.

Rudy and Bambi were at the head of the line. Before he began serving, Stein looked quizzically at Rudy. "So, are you married now?"

Rudy nodded vigorously, his antlers swishing.

"Good to hear. Can you do me a favor, young man?" He beckoned.

Rudy, mystified but too happy to question anything, bounded under the canopy. Bambi accompanied him.

"I have a glass to get rid of, that's all. Too breakable. Never liked it anyway," Stein said vaguely. He held a champagne flute up, wrapped it in linen, laid it on the ground, and gestured.

Annie smiled suddenly, almost mischievously. Rudy, oblivious, stamped with one hoof, shattering the glass.

"Thank you." Stein picked up the cloth with the shards inside, and patted Rudy's shoulders in a loose hug. "And now, congratulations."

"Mazeltov," Annie said, raising her stein. Raising an eyebrow, Stein toasted her back.

Predictably, the banquet was vegetarian. Considering that it was autumn, the holdings were surprisingly varied and included cucumbers, tomatoes, and artichokes. BJ, pulling a steamed artichoke leaf, glanced curiously at Stein, who said immediately, "Rudy knows people in California, and he knew what he wanted. What could I do?"

"Practically anything," BJ said.

Stein, pleased, kissed her hand with elaborate show and went back to serving. Chris, frowning at the credit Stein was taking, pointed emphatically to the artichokes. "I cook."

"And well." The artichokes had been steamed over spiced water, and were dressed with mustard, garlic, and vinegar. BJ's mouth watered as she smelled them.

Chris smiled at the compliment, but the smile faded as he stared thoughtfully around the party. Something was troubling him.

It couldn't have been a reaction to the banquet. The artichokes were popular, the dolmades an incredible hit. Rudy's and Bambi's people, after assembling buffet plates, wandered off in small groups and spread out. BJ thought it was rude until she realized they were being good grazing animals, moving to their own patches and not crowding each other while they ate.

BJ finally got her own plate, and took a fair-sized portion of everything. How many times do you get to eat a low-fat wedding feast?

At last, she stopped and stared at the final fruit plate, where the fruit was unsliced. She had never seen it before, in Crossroads or anywhere else.

It had a fine downy fuzz over it, a vertical cleft like a peach, and two soft, rounded nodules at the end of the cleft. BJ smelled it, then picked one up. It felt amazing in her hand, a little like a peach, and a little like a cat. She couldn't put it down. At first she couldn't imagine biting through the fuzz; then, she couldn't imagine anything else.

A voice beside her said, "Tempting fruit."

BJ, frowning at the fruit in her hand, said absently, "I didn't know you were here."

"I try not to miss the real occasions: weddings, funerals, insurrections. . . ." The Griffin sniffed disdainfully at the vegetarian buffet. "A fairly insipid banquet, to my tastes, but a wide-ranging one." He cocked his head toward her, bringing an eagle eye to bear on her plate. "That fruit which you're tearing apart, for instance, is called vulloi. It grows, but only rarely, in parts of Crossroads as well as in one other world." He added dryly, "A world known for its fecundity."

BJ was munching avidly at the fruit. "Imagine that. And it showed up at this banquet."

"Hardly surprising." The Griffin looked back and forth at the guests. "Odd fruits have a way of showing up at fertility rituals, and in your species, if you don't mind my saying so, people get the damndest cravings. For example, a land called Indonesia on your world has a fruit called durian. It has a very strong smell, which foreigners find repulsive. It has been banned from import by several countries, and has been banned on several airlines. Even so," he added thoughtfully, "there are those who crave it so much they will smuggle an otherwise worthless fruit, merely to have it with them. Desire is an odd thing."

"But not always difficult to acquire." BJ bit the vulloi again, running her tongue across her lower lip to catch the stray juice droplets. "The taste, I mean."

"Of course you do." The Griffin regarded her enigmatically, then blinked and looked away—his equivalent of a shrug. "Well, the vulloi is a special case."

BJ tried to understand him, then went back to the table for more vulloi.

She had eaten seven vulloi, and had looked blankly at one of Rudy's friends when he made an odd joke (translated by Rudy) about her capacity.

She kissed the bride, once, and the groom several times. Predictably, Dave wanted to stay at Stein's and party all night; less predictably, Annie and Lee Anne insisted. "There's more room for us here," Annie said, and Lee Anne said only, "I got the feeling it's a good idea."

BJ said good night and drove home. She could have stayed with them, but she was restless.

Poor Horvat was tapping from one paw to the other; she let him out immediately. When Daphni mewed, BJ said irritably, "Shut up, can't you?" She made tea, and sat up in her clothes. She tried lying down on the bed, in her clothes. She tried it for a longer time. Finally she sat up, angry without knowing why.

"I don't want to sleep." She threw the pillow across the cottage.

A moment later she flung *Walden* after it. "I don't want to read."

The cottage was too small, and she was pacing it over and over. She was too warm; she half-unbuttoned her blouse, moving faster and faster around the room. Horvat followed her at first, then lay confused and watching.

There was a knock.

Not bothering to reach for a catchlet, she threw open the door.

It was Stefan.

"Did the wedding go beautifully? I didn't feel that I could face them after I had—after last spring."

"It was wonderful." She leaned against the table, thinking briefly of Gredya. "You look very nice."

"You too." He added dubiously, "Your hair is strange."

It was very strange, curling at the ends and the curls clinging to each other with a light glow of perspiration which seemed to have come from nowhere.

"You came back without the truck. How did you get here?"

"Your Mrs. Sobell showed me how. She is a great teacher, very kind." Unable to contain himself, he threw his knapsack on the floor and grabbed a folded paper from the pocket, waving it at her.

"I got an A. In English, I got an A, and she wrote 'Excellent' on it. The exams don't count for much, and I did well—are you happy for me?"

BJ, standing closer to him than any friend, licked his neck slowly and happily. "I'm happy with you." She unbuttoned his jacket and, as an afterthought, pulled off and set aside his fedora.

She kissed him, suddenly and a little wildly.

"My doctor," he said between kisses, "My only heart's true one." Then something struck him, and he pulled back.

"What's wrong?"

"You have been to a wedding," he said carefully. "There was a lot of food. A lot of drink."

"Good stuff, too." She smiled down at Horvat, who was sulking jealously in the corner. "I wish I'd taken a wolfie bag."

"Ah." He was trying to look wise; he merely looked resigned and sad. "And now you want me. Is it just something you ate or drank?" With a flash of insight, he added, "Is it just seeing two friends love each other?"

It would be lovely, she thought ruefully, *to blame the wedding or the fruit entirely.*

Instead she kissed him, not frenziedly, but thoroughly. "I had a lot to eat and drink, and I did see friends love each other. All that wouldn't disturb me if I didn't love you so much." She touched his nose. "You must know I love you."

He nodded seriously. "I know. I knew before you, I think." He smiled shyly. "And I have always loved you. From the first time I have seen you, caring for my sheep."

"Absolutely." She pecked his nose with kisses. "Curing each. Little. Shoop."

He kissed her back, protesting, "I have not called them that in months. I know English better."

Both their clothes were flapping loose; BJ had no memory of undoing a single button or belt. "I know you better, and I want you. You're my dancer." Kiss. "My scholar." Kiss. "The most magical person I've ever met."

He was on the verge of tears. "How could anyone be so magic as you?"

Their next kiss had all the desire of the first kiss and all the love of the others. BJ's hip hit the table on the way to the bed; she barely noticed until, next morning, she lay watching Stefan breathe in and out, and she noticed the bruise on her side.

S·E·V·E·N·T·E·E·N

STEFAN WAS SOUNDLY asleep. BJ felt no worse than the slight fuzziness people do after a long, successful party; she wasn't up to doing a crossword puzzle and would have hated a tough diagnostic problem, but otherwise felt quite good. She sat watching him sleep, then picked up his essay from the floor and read it thoughtfully.

Stefan had found a great many quotes from a range of people with the gene for Huntington's chorea: married, widowed, divorced, even young and in love. He had done a fine job of pointing out their anxiety at sharing their lives with anyone and their frequent depression and bitterness at being incurably ill. "Although much of the depression may be a symptom," he wrote carefully, "even if it were not, it would certainly be understandable."

She threw together a medical kit, popped it in her knapsack, wrote a quick note in case Stefan woke up, and was out the door—leaving the whining, anxious Horvat behind.

A brisk walk took her to the valley where most of the flowerbinders lived. The stream had returned to normal, and the road in, while gouged with runoff, was passable. A few quick flashes of white in the underbrush assured her that the flowerbinders had returned and were once more happily camouflaged. She trudged on up the valley towards the falls.

Two-thirds of the way upstream on the left was a cave in the cliffs. She pulled a flashlight from her knapsack and hurried in.

King Brandal's shield—bearing a triskelion with a hoof, a claw, and a human foot—hung at one of the landings on the stone stairs down. His crown hung on a peg. Brandal was not one to wear robes except on formal occasions. BJ, descending, suddenly wished that she had worn a lab coat.

Pencil-thin stalactites and huge ribbed columns hung to either side of the stairs; the farther down she got, the more natural cavern and the less stone carving was evident. She shivered, though the cave air was no colder than the autumn air above.

She stepped off the last stair onto the cave floor. Ahead lay a pool with a mirror-perfect reflection of the cave roof in the flashlight beam. Beyond it were two low-hanging stalactites and, hanging from them, two bats.

The thing between them smiled at her without joy. "And how are we this morning? Happy?"

"You know exactly how I am," she said to the seer.

"Of course. Just making small talk." He gestured with his stone hand at the bats, Thought and Memory. "The art of conversation is dying, down here."

"How have you been, Harral?" It always felt disrespectful to use the seer's name, but he had requested it.

He shrugged, insofar as a man with roots instead of feet can move. "About the same. World without end. You know."

"I don't." But she opened the knapsack. "I brought some things for you—"

"First ask what you came for," he said with no patience at all.

BJ had little of her own. "All right; I did come with questions." She was excited, almost on tiptoe, feeling as she hadn't felt since an early teenage party when she had asked a Ouija board about her new boyfriend. "I want to know about my future."

The seer nodded tiredly. "My, what a surprise. Details at eleven. Your future, or the future?"

"I was interested in mine."

He pointed his stone hand at her sternly. "You should be interested in more. It will change yours. You have learned about Morgan, the wounded land, and the dying king. Do you understand yet about sacrifice?"

BJ felt as though she were being quizzed in Sunday School. "It's a surrender of self in order to gain an end. It's like your bargain with the Six Kingdoms, in exchange for knowing all things."

Harral had entered into the Pact of the Six Kingdoms (earth, air, fire, water, animal, and plant) to know everything they knew. In exchange for the knowledge, Harral's legs became roots, his left hand stone, and a breeze blew endlessly around him, sending the smoke from his smoldering hair into his weeping eyes. The reminder of the pact, from each kingdom, was continual and painful.

Harral said irritably, "I knew you'd say that."

"Of course you did."

"Yes, but it's also wrong. I bargained because I wanted to know. I was like Faust, or the Sorcerer's Apprentice, or your awful acquaintance Fiona—willing to do something rash for the sake of knowing. Sacrifice is a gift of oneself, not a bargain. It is painful and permanent, and the loss helps someone else."

"Do I need to know about sacrifice?"

"All of Crossroads does. Any future at all for Crossroads depends on a great sacrifice, and a costly one."

"Oh." BJ had no idea how to respond to that. "I think before I ask, I'd better think. Can I treat you, first?"

"By all means. Think as hard as you dare."

BJ stood on a rock and tied a padded cloth around the seer's head, to hold his hair off his forehead and away from his eyes. She pulled charred remnants of the previous band out of his hair. "This one should last better."

"That's what Rome said to Greece."

She put an ointment around his eyes, to soothe them, and laid an ordinary Band-Aid below the lower end of each lower epicanthus fold, so that the tears would run down the Band-Aid and drip off his cheeks.

Lastly, a touch she was proud of, she produced a small bottle of plant food from the knapsack and emptied it around his roots. "You have an awful lot of minerals down here, but you don't have much soil." She sprinkled the green liquid with water and stepped back. "That's it for this month."

"It is, and thank you." For one moment he seemed like a grateful human in need. "I wish I could give you something back; it's traditional after kindness."

Then he spoiled it by waving his arms and intoning, " 'Because of your great goodness, O maiden, I will grant you questions three.' That's traditional, too, giving the girl three questions instead of just one. Do you remember saying that the Strangeways were a bit like fairy tales?"

BJ was used to Harral's knowing everything she had done or said. "I meant the monsters and the journeys."

"And here I thought you meant that journeys cause growth, and that fairy tales require it of heroes. Sometimes the growth involves courage. Sometimes it's as simple as unselfishness." He was eyeing her strangely.

When she didn't respond, he sighed. "Go ahead, just ask what's on your mind."

BJ cleared her throat and spoke carefully and precisely.

"You know that I was terminally ill outside Crossroads. Can that be changed?"

"Yes."

"If I were to be still so when I leave Crossroads, might I be able to change it by my actions?"

"Yes."

BJ realized suddenly the trap she had fallen into in the second question; she wished that she had asked the Griffin to write out the questions for her. He loved grammar, and just now she found it dangerously tricky. She asked her final question: "And if I am still so when I leave Crossroads, will I have the chance to make that change?"

He closed his eyes. "Your answer is yes."

Thought and Memory covered their faces, chanting, "Yes. Yes. Yes."

Harral sighed. "That's all I can tell you."

BJ, suddenly uncertain, said, "Thank you."

"Oh, don't thank me." His bitter smile was back, cynical and distanced. "It's your journey; I only give vague directions. Try to remember what I said this morning." He watched without speaking as she packed and left; the only sound was the mocking laughter of Thought and Memory.

BJ went back to her cottage, sure that she had missed something important in the seer's words, but unable to find it. She kissed Stefan awake, helped him make breakfast, and made love with him once more before midday.

Stefan had an afternoon class at Western Vee the following day; he had to go back to Virginia. He said, "I'm sorry, BJ." But he had already packed his knapsack a few minutes after he woke up; he loved school and adored being at a real university with computers and teachers and all the things which, for him, were completely magical.

BJ kissed him. "It's all right." She understood completely. Crossroads, for her, was completely magical.

Horvat watched her jealously; Daphni had been ecstatic to find Stefan in her bed, but Horvat, relegated to the foot of the bed, hadn't liked it one bit. At sunrise he had barked once peremptorily and then pulled the bedspread down and urinated on it, a move that BJ suspected was no accident.

BJ made the bed, fed Daphni and Horvat, and stepped outside with a sheet, leaving the door ajar so the animals could come and go.

"Before we leave, I want to stop by Stein's and say goodbye to everybody."

He turned to her hopefully. " 'We?' "

BJ threw the sheet over the Healing Sign. "I should drive you back." Seeing his face, she added, "And everybody needs time off once in a while."

"My roommate, Willy, will not like this," Stefan warned, but looked quite happy himself.

All successful parties leave behind some damage. The ground beside Stein's was trampled, crisscrossed with cloven hooves as though a herd had been through—which, of course, it had. B'Cu was using a stick to poke divots back into place; Melina used one of her hooves to tamp them down. Fields, standing outside with an arm around Stein's shoulders, was surveying the damage, evidently making suggestions about smoothing it over. The Griffin, by the door, was watching alertly, without helping in any way.

Lee Anne's van was pulled up near the door; Dave and Annie were putting their gear into it. Stefan waved to them from the truck and, still self-conscious about seeing them, pulled out one of his textbooks and began reading. He quickly became absorbed in it. BJ hopped out and asked Lee Anne, "Is everybody going back with you?"

"Nah. I'm driving the schoolbus, is all. We figured, since I had one of the two sets of wheels in Crossroads, I could drive these two to their turnoffs."

B'Cu was in earshot. BJ, always cautious about mentioning *The Book of Strangeways* in front of others, said only, "Do you need help?"

Fields said easily, "I will take them." He winked at BJ. "Nice night?"

"The nicest," she said calmly. Annie, Dave, and Lee Anne were studiously not watching her, but Lee Anne was smirking.

BJ hugged them each in turn, warning Lee Anne last, "Don't get any more bright ideas about endangered species."

She grimaced. "To be real honest, I don't recall having one bright idea yet." She hopped into the driver's seat and gestured;

Fields, suddenly less certain of himself, climbed into the passenger side and stared uneasily out the windshield. Lee Anne revved the engine, honked her goodbye (possibly to see Fields jump), and they were gone.

BJ sighed. "And now, if we don't have any more goodbyes, or any passengers of our own—"

"Ready for go."

They turned. Chris was standing in the doorway of Stein's, a battered leather bag in his left hand. His mustache was as full and carefully combed as BJ had seen it; his hair was combed carefully to the side and slicked down. He was wearing a dark, rumpled suit cut from another time.

"I wore this"—he thumped his chest—"when I enter America by myself."

BJ could imagine him, a black-and-white photograph of a curly-haired man at Ellis Island, all alone but unafraid. "It still looks good on you."

He patted it, smiling. "No, no. Is no style now. Too old. Like me."

Stein said blankly, "You thinking of leaving us, Chris?"

"Oh, done thinking." He reached inside the door and picked up a battered felt hat that had been on a peg near the door ever since he came.

BJ shifted from one foot to the other. She looked at the Griffin, who regarded her steadily. When no one else spoke up, she said, "Chris, there may be a problem with your leaving—not our problem, though we'd miss you—there might be a health problem—"

"I know." He smiled at her. "Before, out there, I was sick, yes?"

BJ nodded hesitantly.

He frowned, remembering. "Hard to talk. I remember when all the words, they sound funny to me, and I don't know where I am sometimes." He grinned down at her again. "Here, I still don't know where I am, but that's right, yes? And I get better . . . even my knees get better. I should be happy. It's good, what you did, darling. Thank you." He patted her head, realized how old she was, and pulled his hand back awkwardly. "You mind?"

"I don't mind." BJ was afraid she was going to cry.

"Stan, he told you he is not born in America?"

BJ nodded.

Chris looked into the distance, squinting as though it hurt his eyes. "I had no word from Sophy. All the time, I dream what things might be happening, if she is alive or not. Then I got news, a single letter written by a priest. A short letter: 'There was no way to ask you about a name. Sophia said Constantine was your father's name, and I knew your father.' "

Chris broke off and smiled. "So then I dream for two of them. All the time. They dead, they hungry, they sick . . . When I saw Stan the first time, and then my Sophy, I cried all night."

In the truck, Stefan had pulled out a notebook and was writing as he read, propping the text on the steering wheel to leave his hands free.

"And I was not apart from the two of them again, more than a night. When Sophy died, it was Stan and I. I dream of her again, for a while after she died, but I did not tell Stan."

BJ said suddenly, "And now the dreams are back."

Chris nodded happily. "You a smart girl."

Stein frowned. "You could have waked me. We could have talked."

"What you gonna say? That Stan's okay, he's not hungry, he don't miss me?" Chris's eyes were moist. "I get smart again here, sure. That's good. But I can't stay."

He stared off over the hills to the east, as though he could see America. "I get sick again, out there."

"Maybe," Stein said.

Chris laughed. "Maybe, sure. I was sick there, I get well here, I go back there; what do you think?" He patted Stein's shoulders. Chris had never gotten over treating Stein like a youth. "That's okay. I got to go see Stan, little Constantine, my boy. Family . . ." He looked at Stein in surprise, as though seeing him for the first time. "Family . . . is good, that's all." He looked embarrassed.

"Of course it's good." Stein frowned and gestured towards the Griffin and back at the inn. "Don't you worry about me, Chris; my family is here. Has been for years."

Chris nodded.

Melina, running back to say goodbye to BJ and Stefan, stopped in her tracks when she saw Chris's bag. He turned to her, stooping a little to look her in the eyes, and held his arms out like a grandfather would to a child of five. Melina bounded forward and embraced him; he kissed her on both cheeks, then her forehead. "You visit, maybe? In Virginia, at my Stan's restaurant?"

She nodded, big-eyed. "I go in for church, once a week." She touched the Coptic cross Annie had given her. "Maybe I can get a ride into town to see you."

His eyelids crinkled and he touched one of her woolly knees. "Wear long skirt, okay?"

She nodded quickly, then turned and ran into Stein's, hiding her face. Fauns, BJ remembered, laughed and wept easily and openly.

B'Cu stood looking at Chris unhappily. Chris shook hands with him, then gave him a quick hug. B'Cu still looked unhappy, staring at him with dark, grave eyes.

Chris said something, a series of clicks and an odd vowels sound. B'Cu's entire face smiled as he said nearly the same thing, correcting Chris. Then the shepherd turned around and went back into Stein's, his farewell over.

Stein shook hands with Chris. "You know you can come back here."

Chris shrugged. "I know."

He carried his own bag, and tapped on the window of the truck. Stefan, absorbed in his textbook, jumped guiltily and unlocked the door, leaping out his own side to help Chris in. Chris was already in before Stefan got around the truck. He rolled down the window and waved, then rolled it back up and gestured to Stefan to turn on the heat.

The Griffin murmured, "There goes a man who knows exactly what his life is worth."

BJ shook her head. "How do you find that out?"

"Give it more thought. You've come close yourself, a time or so."

"I've risked my life," she said slowly. "It's not the same thing, is it?"

"Very good."

She hopped in the back seat of the truck, opening *The Book of Strangeways*. Chris leaned back and stared out the window, smiling as the strange landscape rolled past. Except for BJ's directions to Stefan, none of them spoke on the way in.

It was raining in Virginia, the sort of beautiful-but-grim day when heavy clouds slouch over the mountaintops and roll slowly down, tracking the ravines and stream beds until they level off to hang low above the valleys. Chris turned his collar up as they reached Virginia, and pulled his hat down as they rolled into Kendrick.

When the truck stopped in front of Gyros, Chris said "Thank you very much," as formally as he might at the end of a dinner party, pulled his own bag from the truck in the slanting rain, and walked with careful, balance-conscious steps through the puddles on the sidewalk. Stefan and BJ stayed until he opened the restaurant door, when they saw the middle-aged Stan drop his spatula and leap the lunch counter like a twelve-year-old.

Stefan said, "He made a good choice."

"I guess." BJ thought of how Chris had been before: lost, barely articulate, frequently confused. If Estevan Protera were right, all that might happen again soon.

Stefan pulled into a university parking lot and shut off the van. "You are going to stay with me?"

"Tonight. I promise." BJ kissed him, glad he was there.

BJ reached for her own knapsack and tied a surgeon's knot, one-handed. Her fingers felt supple and sure of themselves, far from the frightening, intermittently clumsy things they had become just before she had gone to Crossroads for the first time.

"And maybe you can come out and stay more often now." Stefan looked at her earnestly.

She finished tying the string, and untied it. "Sure," she said lightly. "Why not?"

E·I·G·H·T·E·E·N

FOR THE FIRST time in months BJ became aware of the days of the week again. Her life settled into a pattern: work frantically for five days, return Horvat to Gredya, or beg Melina to check on him, and drive into Kendrick for the weekend, leaving as late as possible Sunday night.

After two weekends in a row, Melina balked. BJ, in a move she was ashamed of later, told Melina a legend she'd heard in an art history class, describing how Saint Francis had miraculously tamed and blessed a marauding wolf. Melina, in tears, promised devoutly to puppy-sit as often as she could.

On the weekends in Kendrick, BJ stayed awake as much as she could and Stefan took as much time away from his work as he dared. They went to movies on campus and watched videos in the library; BJ was determined to show Stefan the best of the best, and share the moment of discovery with him.

He loved *The Wizard of Oz*, and danced the Scarecrow's floppy dance on one of the campus access roads, step-for-step from memory. She teased him about dancing in the middle of the road, and he said seriously, "But of course they danced down a road. How can you see the wizard, except by taking the road?"

BJ opened her mouth and shut it. She was having trouble separating reality from fantasy these days.

After that they watched *Easter Parade* with Fred Astaire, whom Stefan all but worshiped, and BJ rented a videotape of the Motown television concert in which Michael Jackson had moonwalked across the stage. Stefan was entranced, but wistful when he discovered that the backward slide looks less impressive with hooves. "Everything he does requires lifted heels or pointed toes, BJ. It is not fair."

"Well, he can't leap five feet straight up and land balanced on one hoof. I think."

Star Wars was not the hit she thought it would be. After seeing the Great and walking a Strangeway, special effects weren't impressive.

The latest film they had seen together troubled him. They went out for coffee afterward, and he tried to express his concern. "Do you feel that way, BJ? That the problems of people in love don't amount to a hill of beans in this crazy world?"

BJ answered carefully: "Remember that it's a movie. Besides, Casablanca in wartime was in a little more trouble than Kendrick, Virginia during football season."

University classes were doing well by Stefan. "You didn't really answer."

Damn, she thought. "The problems of people in love matter a great deal, but sometimes the world has bigger problems."

When Stefan didn't answer, she said, "Did you like it?"

"I think it is the best movie I have seen, and that is why I am not sure I like it."

On reflection, BJ didn't like it either. That night she had a vet school nightmare, worse than her usual not-prepared-for-exams dream. In the middle of a surgery lab that BJ was butchering, DeeDee Parris strolled in, escorting Morgan while Fiona watched through the glass door. DeeDee had a syringe full of morphine; Morgan had a dagger. They both wanted to assist. Fiona smiled tolerantly.

BJ woke up sweating. It wasn't hard to decode the symbolism in the dream, and she realized how guilty these weekends made her feel.

On Sunday morning she stopped by the lab and administration building of the vet school to check her mail and use the phone. The receptionist, a work contract student, was there doing data entry; lab work fosters odd work hours. BJ waved and went to her mailbox.

There was a packet of notes from Lee Anne, painstakingly entered on her computer; Lee Anne swore that computers were more efficient than handwriting, but she couldn't touch-type. A tissue-thin international letter from Annie announced her safe arrival in Chad, although "safe" might be a loose word in an area of famine and of refugees from civil war. There were seventeen circulars addressed to Dr. Vaughan from pharmaceutical companies, two catalogues for kennel cages and pet supplies, and one *AVMA Journal*.

Laurie Kleinman stubbed her cigarette out in the hallway canister before coming in. "That's right, show off all your mail because you're a doctor and I'm not." But she sounded glad to see her.

BJ looked through the *Journal* to see if anyone from her class had published or perished. A postcard fluttered to the floor; she picked it up.

It was a sepia picture, taken in Northfield, Minnesota, in the 1870s, of a dead robber propped up in his coffin. The man's chest was bare; the bullet holes were large and deep.

BJ turned it over. On the right was her address, care of the vet school, and a Minneapolis postmark. On the left was a simple, block-printed, "I REMEMBER YOU" and two interlocked D's.

"Nice when friends think of you, isn't it?" Laurie didn't miss much. "Unsigned. Would that be someone I remember?"

BJ sighed. "I think so. She's written me before."

Laurie leapt up with remarkable agility for a heavy woman and perched on the counter in front of BJ. The work-study student behind it looked astonished. "Have you talked to anybody?"

"You mean Sugar? Now that she's graduated, I don't think he'd be much help—"

"Of course I don't mean Sugar." Laurie waved an elegantly dismissive hand, then spoiled the gesture by automatically flicking a nonexistent cigarette. "Not that I don't love talking to Sugar"— she rolled her eyes with mock passion; Sugar was muscular and good-looking—"but we have a mutual acquaintance who would be more help. You know exactly of whom I am speaking."

"Someone who would insist on your saying 'whom.' " They both smiled. "I could, but I don't even know where Dee Dee is." BJ considered. "I suppose he'd say my first step is to find out where she is."

"Everybody always said you were smart. Me, I think you need to get ruthless." Laurie slid off the counter. "Watch your back out here, and tell him in—tell him when you get home."

She added as she walked away, "And please say hello for me." Despite her flirtations and often lewd remarks, Laurie lived alone, and had not gone out with anyone in the time BJ was in school. The Griffin was everything to her. BJ watched her striding briskly down the hall, and ached to think of the Griffin's secret.

She said to the work-study student, "Mary Ann, I'm going to

make some calls. Be sure to log them so that I can pay the school back."

She waved without looking up from the computer and BJ realized, amused, that Mary Ann was doing a term paper at work. BJ went into the Assistant Dean's office and dialed, logging the call herself in case Mary Ann forgot.

The call to Lee Anne took twenty minutes and five pages of notes. Most of it concerned prenatal care and nutrition; the Hippoi had simply eaten more to compensate for pregnancy. Lee Anne asked several pointed questions about parasites; BJ promised to get more information from Polyta, as well as a few stool samples.

Lee Anne asked about Stein, Brandal, and, disapprovingly, about Gredya. Her main questions were about Stefan. "I want dirt here, girl. No dodging about moonlight and violins." BJ dodged dedicatedly, but yielded up a surprising amount of detail. Lee Anne grunted. "Doesn't surprise me. I grew up around two sisters and four cousins; no romance was secret or sacred."

Her last question was an amused, "How's that redheaded girl, filly, whatever? The friend of the one whose hoof I worked on? I figured her to talk up a storm."

"Not really," BJ said lightly. Hemera had skipped the class following BJ's trip on her back. Polyta had forced Hemera to attend the rest of the classes, and made a point of asking her if she had questions. Hemera answered in monosyllables, and always looked in BJ's windows to see if Horvat were there. She never spoke to BJ away from class. "Listen, I've got to go," BJ told Lee Anne.

"I wouldn't doubt that." Lee Anne was a shadow away from snickering. "You have a good Sunday afternoon." She hung up.

BJ checked her watch; it was eleven-thirty, ten-thirty central time. She smiled to herself and dialed a number in Chicago. The phone was answered on the eighth ring. A male voice said hoarsely, "I knew I should have turned that damn answering machine on."

"I hate those things," BJ said frankly.

Her brother yelled delightedly, "BeeGee!" She winced at the pet name. "It's like you to wake me up on a Sunday."

"Hi, Peter." As always, once she started talking to him it was hard to find things to say. "Just checking in."

"How's work? Where are you now? Are you getting any rest?"

Clearly he didn't care about the answers, and had something more exciting to tell her. BJ answered him briefly. "Is anything new with you?"

"You might say that." He paused for suspense. "I've met someone."

He spoke softly, which meant that he wasn't alone in bed. BJ braced herself. "And you're in love."

Peter went on. "She's not like anybody else I've ever met. She's a little younger than I am—listen, BeeGee, I'm dying to tell you, but she wants to keep it quiet and not tell anyone till she's got her own personal life straightened out."

BJ frowned. "That's not so good."

"How's your health?"

"Fine." It wasn't idle chatter for either of them.

"What are your chances of coming out to Chicago? I know it's a long way."

BJ was about to put him off, when a thought struck her. "Actually, I may try. I'll call you back in a week or two. I might be able to make it."

"How? Fly? Drive that awful Chevette of yours?"

"I sold that and got a used truck." Actually, Fields had paid for it, though the registration was in her name.

"A truck? BeeGee, you've lost it. Do you know how long it will take you to drive a truck to Chicago from there?"

"I know a shortcut." She said goodbye and hung up before he could ask about that.

She had walked to the school; her truck was parked in the visitors' lot at Stefan's dorm, and she didn't want to lose the parking space. Freshmen were on the upper campus, and it was easy to swing onto Main Street and look around.

As she walked past a dress shop with angular and distorted mannequins, her mind drifted. She thought about Peter's taste in women. When he was in high school he had gone through a steady succession of the One Woman Who Matters, each with a glaring personality defect: one with a nasty temper, one with a God-given talent for breaking other people's things, one who insisted on helping to cook and set fire to everything.

Sandra, a particularly memorable one, borrowed his car and used it to ram the brand-new Trans Am of an ex-boyfriend. Peter referred to all of them, afterward, as "flawed." BJ and her mother had called them "the trolls." BJ couldn't even imagine what he'd managed to find, out on his own now, in Chicago.

A hand touched her elbow. "Watch where you walk," someone said sternly. "God knows where you could end up."

BJ blinked and looked up. Fiona was standing beside her. She looked normal—perhaps not "normal," but much like she always had. Her sweater was emblazoned with a salamander wearing wraparound shades, and she had matching sunglasses pushed up on her head. Her pleated orange skirt clashed with her green fishnets, and neither of them went with the Frye boots.

Her eyes looked different. Fiona had always looked confident and intelligent; now she looked obsessed, the look that absolutely brilliant people have in old photographs of test sites at Los Alamos and in Nevada.

"When did you come back?" BJ said.

"A while ago." Fiona was enjoying BJ's surprise. "I'm getting used to coming and going. I haven't been back for a couple weeks, before this."

"Where have you been hiding? Do you realize how many people in Crossroads are looking for you?"

Fiona looked suddenly cautious. "Are they people?"

"Most of them. Listen, can we get some coffee somewhere?"

Fiona chose Fairweather's, on Main Street. It was painted black and white, the servers were called "waitroids," and the owners had spent a lot more on neon than they had on blends of coffee.

Fiona sipped, looking around for friends. "Thanks for thinking of this," she sighed, stirring her coffee with a neon-colored swizzle. "Now this is homey."

To BJ it was more like hallucinating in a lab. "Fiona, I have to ask some things about your work. It's important."

"You have no idea how important," Fiona agreed. "It's gone better than I ever dreamed." Her eyes shone. "It's just so nice to have someone I can tell—"

"Fiona, when there was a warm spell in Crossroads, was that you?"

Fiona nodded. "How long did it last?"

"Long enough to screw up migration and breeding cycles. The sundancers moved north and the Wyr went into heat, if you know what they both are."

Fiona clapped her hands like a small child. "Terrific. Can you believe I managed that?"

"That one I can almost believe. The one I can't imagine is that you closed off a Strangeway. Did you?"

Fiona, glowing, nodded. "I can't be sure—I'd have to see *The Book of Strangeways* to know for sure—but I used a Spell of Binding, only I directed it at the road instead of at a loved one, and I'll bet that it can't be reopened exactly the same way." The waitroid brought a plate of geometrically cut crackers with pimento cheese spread on them; Fiona munched happily.

BJ felt helpless. "Listen, you closed off an entire world. The sundancers might have died—"

"But they didn't, did they?"

"No." BJ hesitated, then said, "Someone was able to help them."

"Exactly." She thumped the table; the Euclidean crackers bounced. "There's always going to be someone like that when you need them. BJ, you really ought to trust people more."

Right. "Look," BJ said flatly, "You've heard of the Inspector General by now, right?"

"Oh, yes," Fiona said calmly, and shattered BJ by adding, "The Griffin."

"How did you know that?" The Inspector General's identity wasn't as well-kept a secret as it had been before Morgan's first raid on Crossroads, but it was still known only to a very few.

"Research," Fiona said smugly. "And let him come for me. We'll talk, and I'm sure he'll see the value of what I'm doing."

BJ shook her head, trying to find the words. "He won't talk. I love him, and trust him, but I've known him to disembowel those who deserved it. And they were just attacking sheep—and Sugar Dobbs, and a few vet students." She shivered, only half from remembering. "I have no idea what he'd do to someone who threatened an entire species."

Fiona was jarred for a moment, then rallied. "You know, it's not like I did any permanent damage. This is the kind of accusation that's always leveled against a woman who seeks alternative power." She looked as though she would say more, but stopped and left it vague.

"No," BJ said firmly. "I'm teaching a class in alternative power to the Hippoi. The woman who set it up will never be accused by anyone of being thoughtless. And even so, she has second thoughts all the time, for the sake of others."

Fiona frowned. "You're saying I'm selfish. You can't imagine what I'll be able to do with my work; I'm recovering skills lost for centuries, from all over the world. Let's ignore what weather control could do for agriculture; what if I could open Strangeways myself?"

"What?"

"I've closed one; why couldn't I learn to open one? What would that do for underdeveloped countries, trade agreements? Maybe even space exploration?" Fiona stopped suddenly and picked at the crackers. "Of course, I didn't learn anything from *The Book of Strangeways* at the Western Vee library, and I can't take it out, so I'll never know."

"How would it help?"

Fiona looked at her in exasperation. "It's a book of maps that automatically correct themselves; it's linked to the Strangeways. I'm sure it would help."

"I doubt it. The Book shows, but it doesn't tell how." BJ was thinking again about her brother. "Otherwise, I'd be sure how I could get to Chicago."

"From here? Twenty hours by bus, four by plane because you have to fly to the hub in Charlotte first—Wow! You're thinking of using the Strangeways, aren't you?"

"If I can." BJ was lost in her own thoughts. She wouldn't consider asking Fields to make a road for something this frivolous. Was there a road that ended near Chicago? "I don't remember . . . Well, I can look it up tonight," BJ said vaguely.

Fiona opened her mouth, then suddenly changed her mind. "I'd better get going. I need to get back."

BJ, absorbed with curiosity about her brother in Chicago, let her go and paid the tab even though she hadn't eaten any crackers.

Just before the campus drive, BJ stopped in front of the hardware store and stared in the window. For a moment she thought that the moon was up; she turned and stared at the gray sky.

Then she looked back at the window and laughed. A moment later, she came out of the store rolling a glossy white circular patio table with no legs. The owner, watching her, scratched his head. She hadn't purchased the legs, the umbrella that fit in the center hole, or the chairs, but she seemed inordinately pleased with herself. The owner called out, "I close early Sunday afternoons, ma'am; you're sure you don't want me to deliver that?"

"Thanks, I'd better take it with me."

Sunday afternoons were contests between passion and guilt. BJ's goodbye, which she tried to deliver in good faith at one P.M., took until two o'clock, when Stefan sighed and said, "I love you, but I must work or fail Biology."

"Don't exaggerate." She lay still, ruffling his hair. "You know the book cold; you just love it too much not to read it."

He smiled shamefacedly. "I have had bad dreams about homework this weekend, BJ."

Nothing else he could have said would have made her go quickly. They kissed, long enough that Willy, checking on the status of the room from the stairwell, coughed discreetly and finally said loudly, "Jeez." BJ laughed and left.

The ride in was uneventful. She opened the book at her side and watched it, patting it fondly when she arrived in Crossroads. She thought of what Fiona had said, and was suddenly troubled. Somewhere in their conversation, she knew, she had missed something important.

Half an hour later she heard the sound of hooves. She dropped her book and ran out, thinking happily that Polyta or Hemera had come to make up.

It was Sugar Dobbs.

He was on Skywalker, a magnificent brown Thoroughbred which a student's father, unable to pay for treatment and unable to sell an ailing horse, had donated to the school for the tax credit. Sugar had cured it, followed up, and frequently ridden it, affectionately dubbing it Walker.

He leapt off, clearing the saddle and horse easily. He was on his knees undoing the saddle girth almost as he landed. His hair was plastered to his forehead with sweat. "Take the saddlebags," he told BJ. "Gently."

She took the saddlebags, on one of which was hand-tooled, NEVADA ROPERS AND RIDERS, off the horse. The bags were disproportionately heavy for their size, as though they were full of water. She patted the mare. "Hey, Walker." She felt the horse's heaving, soaked sides in wonder. "Did you come down 481?"

Sugar didn't answer. "A towel," he said, panting nearly as hard as Walker. "And a blanket. Will she be all right out here?"

BJ considered, uneasily, whether or not Gredya would attack a horse. "I think so." She ran in for the towel and blanket.

She dashed out immediately, carrying a towel, a blanket, and an Orioles T-shirt. "It's a large," she said, not mentioning that she slept in it. Sugar grabbed the towel and scrubbed at Walker's sides; BJ put the shirt to one side. "Did you come the usual way?" she asked again, with visions of Sugar galloping up 481. The visions weren't without romance, but seemed unlikely.

He shook his head. He had an ear cocked, listening for something. "Fields knew a path. He went somewhere else, left me to ride in. He traced it in the dirt." Sugar led Walker to the stream from the spring; she drank deep.

BJ blinked. "You galloped down a line in the dirt to get here?"

"Had to." He smiled wanly. "Ain't like I was real happy about it." He shook himself. "Let's pack the van. Sheets for bandages, as much antiseptic as you've got . . ."

The list went on. BJ had a horrified image of a war somewhere, particularly since Sugar kept listening for something. She carried out her spare sheets, badly folded and flapping in the light breeze. She threw sulfa, Betadine, alcohol, cotton balls, almost her entire supply, into cabinets on the truck. Sugar helped pack, looking almost like a small boy as his hair ruffled in the breeze.

"Good enough," he said suddenly. "Hop in."

BJ, falling back into school habits, obediently trotted to the passenger side of her own truck. She caught herself. "Do you want to drive?"

"Doesn't really matter." He hopped in the passenger side. BJ got in the driver's seat, put the key in the ignition, and felt Sugar's hand on her arm. "Just wait."

The wind picked up, and the van began rocking. Sugar said, "Fasten your seat belt."

The wind roared around them, and the sky was suddenly blotted out on BJ's right. She could barely make out shiny straight lines in the blackness: the quills of immense wing feathers, shifting as the enormous wings beat up and down.

BJ shouted, "It's going to land on us!" just as Sugar bawled, "Hang on."

The van suddenly righted itself, not quite fully upright. BJ sighed with relief, closing her eyes for a moment. The wing noise was still there, but if she and Sugar weren't already dead, perhaps the Great had other plans.

She opened her eyes and stared out the window, confused by what seemed to be a shrinking rectangle with dead grass on it. She couldn't imagine what was on the ground in front of the van that would look like that or shrink so quickly.

Then she saw the Healing Sign on the front of it, and the landscape snapped into focus. They were already eighty feet up. The cottage vanished quickly under them.

Sugar had one arm up, hanging onto the handhold over the door. "I didn't know if you'd get in if I told you."

"Next time, tell me." She looked in the side mirror and saw what looked like a magnification of a chicken claw: a yellowed, knobbly knuckle bone the size of a tree stump, with the separate talons disappearing below the truck. The truck shifted once, and the claws flexed. The cabin body creaked and groaned.

"Fields said it'd be all right." Sugar clearly felt badly about not having told her. "He said they can grip things pretty lightly."

"When they want to." BJ felt even more helpless than she did on airplanes. "Let's hope it keeps wanting to."

BJ remembered a lecture on raptors and talons: how an eagle can hold a man's arm as long as it wants to, and how the clutch of some raptors may suffocate their prey. She looked away from the mirror and tried hard not to look back.

They followed the course of the River Laetyen for a while, winding rapidly along it. Soon they found themselves over the southern grasslands.

Sugar said, "Have you read more in Lao about these jokers?" His attempt at lightness was feeble.

"I brought it with me." BJ found the entry. "You remember the passage about the roc being like the behemoth and the leviathan? And the passage about their nests . . . here's more: 'Like the condor, the roc is vulnerable at birth—' "

"We both know." They had worked on a roc chick together, back when BJ was a student. "The things are altricial—can't walk, see, or stand; can't do much. Skip that; we'll be working on a grownup."

BJ read on. " 'The chick is father to the adult. Difficult as it is to think of something as mighty as the Great being vulnerable, they are. In flight they are strong but slow; at rest they are powerful but unable to hide or shelter themselves. An enemy foolish enough to attack the Great might well win.' "

"Why foolish?" Sugar said.

BJ read on mechanically. " 'It is for this reason that the Great exercise the effort necessary to exterminate any species which challenges them. The sins of the father, mother, cub, or littermate fall on the entire race.' "

By now they were over the southern mountains cradling a bowl valley they had driven into once before. Several of the mountains were capped with immense piles of tree limbs, tucked and woven together to form nests the size of an aircraft carrier.

The waving, half-flattened trees in the valley below were darkened with immense shadows, bird silhouettes the size of cargo planes. The Great were all gathering at the nest ahead.

One by one, they lit on the spine of rock overlooking one of the nests. In front of them, just off the nest on a mesalike platform, one of the Great lay with its head against the logs. As the truck came closer, BJ could see how unnatural the angle of the body was.

The landing was smoother than some potholes BJ had hit. The bird carrying them glided to the far end of the nest, settling noiselessly.

She rolled down her window and listened to a pulsing hiss like water hitting fire. She looked around uneasily for the volcano.

The injured bird lay sprawled across the mountains, one wing bent back. Its beak open and shut regularly, in rhythm with its rasping breathing.

Sugar and BJ slid out quietly and began grabbing supplies. He stared over his shoulder at the bird. "It's like treating a 747."

"She is in pain," someone said. They turned and saw Fields, stepping through a pass at the lip of the mountain. "You treated her nestling last spring; now she needs you."

Sugar gestured, not too wildly, at the surrounding birds. Their beaks hung above the rocks, and their bodies blocked more than a third of the sky. "And they all turned out to watch? Spectator sport?"

"I'm afraid not." Brandal, still dressed as Owen but showing a great deal of dignity, came up the pass behind Fields. "They have a decision to make, after you're done."

The gigantic beaks swung toward him, then back. Sugar licked his dry lips and nodded. "All right, then. Dr. Vaughan, you hit her high and I'll hit her low."

BJ began climbing the spine of rock parallel to the bird. Sugar walked half-under the bird and shone his flashlight upward, commenting as he walked.

"Loss of blood isn't too bad." He stepped over a clotting, three-foot pool and stood under the wing. "That's ugly." He tried to stand on tiptoe in his boots, pointing to the unnatural angle in the humerus. "I could pin it, but chances are it'd never fly again; I can't see how it holds its weight aloft as is. Mr. Fields, what are the odds the others would feed her and take care of her?"

"They are good. She could still nest." Fields pursed his full lips, thinking. "The food for the young ones would be the hardest, since they eat more than their own weight every day until they are grown, but—yes, they would do it. They are good to each other. It is how they have survived."

"Okay." Sugar felt along the sides, looking for other damage. "Gonna lose a lot of plumes on the wings; the vanes are torn and the barbs are all tangled. Maybe regular molting takes care of that—do these fellas molt, Mr. Fields?"

"I think so."

"Anyway, she'll lose a pair of feathers on each wing for balance, whether she flies or not. She's gonna be pretty naked." Sugar checked the legs and said with sudden relief, "And no damage at all to the legs. She could perch, and feed, even if she couldn't fly. Okay, Dr. Vaughan, your turn."

BJ climbed the narrow ridge of rock beside the fallen bird. She scrambled toward it, careful not to look down on the left as she moved along the beak and approached the head.

The pale iris of the eye, from this close, was the size of a set of double doors. The head shifted toward her only slightly to focus. "The muscles around the left eye are gouged. It looks like it happened in landing."

"How's the eye itself?"

"There's too much blood in it for me to tell." She shone a flashlight in the eye, bracing for a reaction. The head didn't move, and the pupil shrank immediately. "Normal PLR." BJ stretched up as high as she could, reaching for the top of the head.

She moved opposite the neck and stopped.

Sugar said sharply, "Keep talking." He was rattled by their enormous, silent audience.

BJ took a deep breath and said in a steady voice, "The neck has been slashed perpendicular to the spine. The wound is two feet deep at its deepest point, which comes between"—she counted quickly—"the fifth and sixth vertebra. The spine is exposed, though not severed. The main artery to the head is visible at the upper end of the wound." She slid down on the rocks until she was almost under the neck. "Shine your flashlight down here, Dr. Dobbs." When he did, she said in a small voice, "Oh."

Sugar didn't push her this time. She said dully, "The slash continues in a downward spiral around the neck, culminating in a deep slash that opens the thorax, and has probably damaged either the syrinx or one of the anterior air sacs. Breathing is labored, and the respiratory system is filling with blood."

There was a long silence, then: "I ain't arguing, BJ. I still gotta come up and look."

Sugar scrambled up in half the time BJ took. He stared down at the ruined neck, and pointed out the bubbles coming from the thorax. He gestured to BJ. They scrambled down together.

Sugar dusted off his hands and said, "We can't save it." He looked pleadingly at Fields, trying not to stare at the curved beaks over his head.

"They will understand," Fields said quietly. "Finish quickly, and put her out of pain." He stood by the giant bird, touching her beak as tenderly as someone might pet a canary.

The veterinarians walked quickly to the truck. BJ opened the rear cabinet. "I hope you brought something; I don't have anything powerful enough to put her to sleep."

"Check the saddlebags." She opened them, and shivered. Sugar had brought two horse syringes and bottle after bottle of T-61, nearly an entire case of it.

Their work fell into a simple, ghastly rhythm: Sugar would pop a syringe through the rubber bottle top and drain the bottle, then finish filling with another, handing the half-empty bottle to BJ. While BJ drained the remains of that, Sugar injected the first syringe into the bird. BJ would finish filling her syringe with an entire new bottle, and would inject the bird as Sugar began filling his syringe again. At first, BJ strained to think of something they might rig up to catheterize a wing vein; eventually, she gave up.

All the while, Fields stroked the bird's beak, speaking softly. He said heavily, "They will need to know who did this." Brandal, beside him, looked grim.

Sugar scratched his head. "I can't even imagine the animals that could do this." He pointed to the length of the claw wound. "Something sailed right across her neck and ripped it open with one slash." Fields just looked at him, and he added unwillingly, "Griffin, maybe?"

"No," BJ said quickly. "They wouldn't." She smelled the feathers near the wound; there was a swamp-gas rotten-egg odor, even though there were no burn marks. She said immediately, "This was done by the chimerae."

"By what?" Sugar said sharply. "What are they, and why didn't you tell me?"

"They're migratory. Part lion, part eagle, and part scorpion. And I didn't tell you because they don't come here often." BJ added, to Fields, "Is there anything else I should say about them?"

Fields said only, "That is more than I would like to say about them."

"And do you think they did this?"

"I would not wish to—" But he looked up at the huge eyes of the waiting birds, and he sagged. "Yes. They did it. Poor stupid things, they break other people's hearts so easily."

"That was pretty accurate cutting," Sugar said. "If the chimerae are as stupid as you say they are, then somebody guided it." When Fields did not respond, he said, "So now what will happen?"

"The Great will exterminate them all."

BJ said blankly, "The species?"

"And by doing so, the griffins, who will fight to stop them."

Sugar said slowly, "I can't imagine that these birds would be able to . . ." He stopped. Of course they could.

When they began the cycle of injections, BJ could hear the tortured breathing out the larynx. As that faded, she put her ear close to the exposed artery, and caught the muffled echo of the bird's giant heart. Now she was listening with a stethoscope as the beat got slower and farther away.

At last Sugar stepped back. "That's all of it. Sure hope it was enough."

BJ looked up and took her stethoscope off. "She's gone." She felt dull and tired, though the entire process had taken less than an hour.

"Okay." Sugar glanced upward. "What happens now?"

The great beaks above them rose up, and the pitiless blue eyes regarded each other.

Sugar turned to Fields. "How smart are they? How much can you explain to them?"

Fields said, "They understand that she is dead. Explanations do not matter, Sugar. Now they will decide whether or not to kill some of us."

"Who is 'us'?"

Fields arched a shaggy eyebrow. "Chimerae, humans. Don't you want everyone to live?"

Sugar, abashed, muttered, "Well, some more than others, mostly."

Brandal came forward. "I will find the ones who did this; I promise. I will punish them myself."

One of the great beaks came very low indeed, almost scraping the ground.

"I must ask you not to punish the chimerae," Brandal said. "For the sake of a friend"—he glanced at Fields—"whom I love and respect, I must ask this."

BJ whispered to Fields, "You told him."

Fields whispered back, "Who told you?"

Sugar said disgustedly, "Shoot, nobody tells me anything."

Brandal went on. "I will see to it that the guilty are punished when I am sure who they are. All I ask in return is that you keep things as they are." He paused. "Including your bargain to defend Crossroads. Eat any of us you wish, fly by night as you choose, but defend Crossroads."

There was a long, long silence. BJ looked in wonder as Brandal stood waiting, unafraid, the image of a king.

All but the bird that had brought the truck turned away. BJ clutched Fields and Sugar clutched a rock as the mighty wings raised dust and even small stones. In a moment, they were alone in the afternoon sun, on a vast plain with an empty nest and two birds, one living and one dead.

Brandal sagged. Fields caught him, holding him as easily as he might carry a small boy. BJ and Sugar ran forward.

"You okay, Highness?"

BJ said, "That was wonderful."

"A background in sales sometimes helps." Brandal's forehead was covered in sweat.

"Will they defend Crossroads again?"

"One more time. In spite of their having been betrayed twice: once when the Wyr savaged a chick this spring"—he grinned feebly—"as you may remember. The other time, this attack. This they regard as their final obligation, unless they destroy one or the other of their attackers."

"But Morgan probably directed this attack, testing the chimerae. The Great could kill Morgan and—Oh." Now BJ understood why Fields had not responded when Sugar asked who guided the chimerae.

Brandal barely needed to say it. "The Great don't make nice distinctions. If a species attacks, kill the species." He looked worried. "We have always had an understanding with the Great. I don't think it will survive another wrong done them."

The single bird, grim and black, waited at the far end of the plateau for them to finish talking. Sugar walked back toward the truck and, as the giant bird shifted preparatory to taking off, turned to Fields and Brandal. "Need a ride?"

Fields paled, which was not easy for him to do. "Sugar, I would rather leap off the edge of this cliff." He put a hairy hand on the vet's shoulder. "You take the regular way home now, Sugar. That quick way, I don't know how long that one is good for."

"Meaning," BJ said, "that you closed it already."

Sugar looked at her in astonishment. Fields, despite his exhaustion, chuckled. "That one thinks a lot," he said.

The ride back was quick, a single long glide. BJ remembered a griffin quoting something to her about the danger of a swift and easy descent. She shivered. Sugar said, "Do you need this shirt back?"

"I'm fine."

"How's your health these days?"

It was the opening she'd been waiting for. "My health is my
business. You shouldn't have suggested that Stefan do a paper
on Huntington's chorea." She searched for something strong to
say, and settled for "It was arrogant, and rude, and it wasn't your
place."

Undeterred, he said, "You told him yet?"

"No."

"You going to?"

"That's my business."

"Okay, it's your business." Sugar settled back. "I figured it
might be his."

That was the last they spoke until the bird was on the ground.

They emptied the van together and stood awkwardly, not sure
what to say. Sugar took off the Orioles shirt and put on his own
still-damp shirt. Walker ambled over to Sugar and nuzzled him;
he patted the mare absently.

Finally BJ glanced toward her door. "You can stay over. I have
a bedroll."

"Thanks, but Elaine's too close to delivering. I better get home."
He saddled up easily and quickly, double-checking the girth cinch,
threw the saddlebags across, and was in the saddle before BJ had
seen him step up.

He flipped the reins once, then pulled back and turned to look
over his shoulder. "BJ?" She said nothing. "If things are falling
apart here again, you get out and stay out."

He kicked Skywalker twice and slowly rode off. BJ waited
until he was out of earshot to say quietly, "If I can."

N·I·N·E·T·E·E·N

THE SKY WAS gray and forbidding; BJ drove to Stein's hoping that breakfast was ready.

Stein was up stoking the fire; Melina was still asleep. BJ looked around. "Where's B'Cu?"

"Checking Stefan's herd. I don't know why I think he works for me; he likes sheep better." He put the kettle on and sat, staring out the window at the winter mist over Laetyen River.

Melina, wearing a long wool nightdress and the Coptic cross Annie had given her, trotted in sleepily, her hooves clicking against the floor. She kissed Stein on the cheek and went to the pantry to begin breakfast.

Stein sighed loudly. "You see what I put up with, eh? Complete informality."

"I see. Could I have some breakfast?"

"Talk to Melina; she runs this place now that Chris is gone."

BJ lingered over breakfast, enjoying the eggs and the thick pancakes with butter and honey. She explained about the patio table to Stein, who was intrigued. "It could work. It should work. Young lady, if that works, you've done a very good thing, you know that?"

There was a noise at the door. BJ shifted; before she could reach her catchlet, Stein was armed and beside the entryway.

Stein's parrot walked in, tail dragging. His crest was missing, his wings were bedraggled, and the feathers on his belly were singed.

Stein looked down unsympathetically. "So, you tried to *shtup* a firelover again." The parrot clucked mournfully. "You could at least have waited until she cooled down."

BJ shook her head. "I'll take him back with me and treat him. I owe him anyway. C'mon, fella."

The parrot, too tired to fly, walked up her jeans leg and climbed her jacket up to her shoulder. Too exhausted even to peck her or soil her jacket, he locked his feet in the fabric and put his head under his wing.

Stein shook his head. "Someone shows up one day, needs the work, you give him a job. See what you get? Next time I want help, I'll advertise."

The burns were slight and superficial. BJ suspected that the damage to the parrot's ego was worse, and unfortunately not serious. "Do you think you can fly?"

He flapped his wings, blinking at the pain, and hovered above the table. He dropped back in place.

"Do you think you can keep away from firelovers from now on?"

He screeched, "Ooooooooh!" and flapped frantically, a light in his eyes.

BJ gave up. "Stein's right. Wait until they cool down." She finished applying ointment to his underbelly.

Horvat was barking. BJ set down the ointment and went outside to quiet him.

He was staring up at the southern sky, his tail curved upward, his lip curled, growling. A large flock of chimerae, with a single leader, was headed toward the cottage.

The chimerae had riders.

BJ spun back to the parrot. "I need you, now. I'll pay you later. Find Stein or Brandal. Say this: Morgan has come with"— she squinted, counting—"thirty soldiers to BJ's cottage."

She moved the parrot to the window. "Tell Fields if you see him. And tell them to get the white tabletop out of my cottage, to use it if I haven't." She wanted to explain more, but time was essential. "Go. Go away, now."

The parrot dropped into the grass outside her window and rolled quickly out of sight. A few minutes later she saw a flash of color, thirty yards away, as the parrot flew off.

She opened the door to her house. "Daphni. Out, now."

Daphni bounded into the brush and camouflaged herself. Horvat whined and cocked his head to one side, watching her.

She threw a clod of dirt at him, hating herself. "Go away. Go find Gredya." He looked hurt and ran off.

She ran back in and tossed *The Book of Strangeways* into the rafters; it was the only hiding place she could think of that might escape a search for long enough to matter. She took a syringe, filled it with T-61, capped it again and tucked it in her jacket pocket. It wasn't much of a weapon—it certainly wouldn't kill a human—but she might be able to bluff with it, and at least no one would be ready for it.

She picked up her catchlet and walked calmly outside, feeling faintly ridiculous for going to battle in a lab coat. Self-consciously she brushed the parrot feathers off it.

Her door had an iron lock with an old-fashioned keyhole. She had never had to use it. She turned the key in the lock, threw the key as far as she could, and waited, catchlet in hand.

One chimera led the group. The lead man was riding Fran.

BJ shook her head sadly. "Oh, Fran. You led them back here?" The chimera wagged its stingered tail proudly.

Morgan, riding straight and tall on the second chimera, halted in place. This time, she carried only two daggers, but she also wore a naked, well-polished and sharpened sword. The curled horn was at her waist. "It's good to see you again," she said smiling.

Her fingers held the reins loosely; while she stared at BJ, her hands washed, one over the other, restlessly. "I understand you have a book I want." She was using an understated, almost academic tone.

"That's a misunderstanding. I know a library that has a copy; I don't."

"The library copy is—unavailable. Believe me, I've tried." Morgan was still smiling, but her hands never stopped rubbing each other. "Strange, how libraries try to prevent readers."

"Libraries try to prevent theft." BJ spoke too loudly.

Morgan's smile twitched. "Oh, please don't be nervous. I've simply come for the book."

"I don't have a copy."

Fiona slid off from behind Morgan. "Yes, you do."

BJ felt sick.

"You said you'd check the book at night. You were going back to Crossroads at night." Fiona added, trying to play off their friendship, "You know that I only want it for good reasons."

BJ said steadily, "You do know that she'll kill me."

"That's a misconception. She only has troops because she's been threatened and exiled, and needs them for survival . . ."

Fiona faltered, looking for the first time at the faces of the men and women around her. Their expressions were far more dangerous than the axes, swords, and daggers they carried.

Morgan slid off the chimera, holding its reins. "We know you have the Book."

BJ said only, "It's not available."

Fiona said plaintively to Morgan, "The troops are to protect you in exile, right?"

Morgan ignored her. "We'll find it. It's easiest to pass it over."

BJ wondered what she could possibly say to keep Morgan talking. "The book won't help you if all the roads are closed."

Morgan smiled. "Your fat horned friend would weep if all the roads were closed. He needs them."

"No. He knows others need them."

Morgan shrugged. "For my purposes, isn't that the same thing?" Fiona looked at her as if she had torn off a mask.

Suddenly impatient, Morgan snapped her fingers. "Felaris." The large, scarred woman leapt off her mount (who looked considerably relieved) and stood beside her. "Find the book." Felaris walked toward BJ's front door.

A huge, gaunt she-wolf appeared around the corner of the building, lip curled. Felaris hesitated.

Morgan laughed. "I know you. You have served me."

Gredya curled her lip even higher, mouth all needle-sharp fangs, and snarled savagely. BJ said, "I wouldn't have reminded her."

Felaris stepped between her and Morgan, who frowned and said in her old, angry voice, "Kill her and get the book." Fiona seemed to shrink into herself.

Gredya moved in front of BJ, nudging her aside as though she were a pup. Every last fang in her mouth was showing.

"No," BJ said. "Go away. Take Horvat with you."

She had even less success than she had with Horvat. Gredya, crouching, growled and snapped. Felaris, sword ready, swung it to and fro looking for an opening.

The wind picked up. BJ stiffened, than tried to act as though she hadn't noticed; she wondered if Morgan would recognize it.

Horvat appeared behind Gredya, yipping furiously.

BJ ran to him and screamed, "Go away!" He ignored her. Morgan looked at the wolf pup with interest, then snapped her head sideways as one of her soldiers, a gaunt man with an eyepatch, shouted in a strange language and pointed at the sky.

The clouds were boiling in the sky to the west as the Great suddenly plunged down near Stein's. They rose again almost immediately, flying towards BJ's cottage.

Morgan gave three sharp blasts on her horn. Her soldiers slapped the reins, kicking the chimerae and shouting. The chimerae rose into the air.

Three of the Great pursued them. A fourth dropped down towards BJ, gliding on the grass.

Gredya, looking up, barked to Horvat, who made a whining noise but followed her in a dash for the underbrush. BJ, unable to sprint as fast, stood waiting for the talons.

The bird passed over her and her cottage, and landed, with surprising grace, twenty feet on the other side of the small stream.

BJ blinked as Estevan Protera stood up, just below the bird's neck. He was wearing a white linen suit and white gloves; he was carrying a full-size rapier with a filigreed basket hilt. "I hope you'll be willing to join me," he said as politely as though he were asking her to dance. "I'm not quite sure what to do."

BJ ran forward, catchlet in hand, then spun back around and ran to the truck, opening the front door and grabbing the fire extinguisher. She passed it up to Estevan, who took it without comment and helped her up. All this time, the roc was waiting, one cold eye cocked toward the sky and tracking the chimerae as they rolled, dodged, and attacked in the sky.

"How did the Great get here?"

Protera, holding her in place one-handed as they took off, shouted into the wind, "Owen spoke to them and told them to watch for an invasion. He was with them alone just a day or so ago."

BJ remembered Brandal's presence in the nest as Protera shouted, "He's more than a peddler, isn't he?"

"He's the king. His name is Brandal." They were rising into the air rapidly, the great bird gliding down the hill to get aloft and rising as it flapped its wings.

"And Stein is a war commander. Very good."

"But how did they know to get you?"

"They knew to get Stein. I was there for lunch." He flashed a brilliant smile at BJ. "Lucky me, no?"

"Depends." The roc they were on wheeled and ducked as they came into the chaos of chimerae; BJ and Protera clung tightly to the bird.

Ahead of them, the man with the eye patch was goading his chimera into position in front of them, trying to make it belch fire.

One of the Great dove above him, talons tucked back. The point of the curved beak sliced across one chimera, cutting it nearly in half. The chimera screeched and spiraled down; probably it was dead of blood loss before it hit the ground. Its rider, the man with the eye patch, pinwheeled his arms and fell for what seemed like a long time.

Around them, the Great dove at the chimerae; Morgan's soldiers struggled desperately to keep control of the frightened beasts. BJ and Protera's mount, beak forward, headed towards a chimera; BJ recognized it as Fran. Protera said happily, "I may not need this sword, if this keeps up."

Suddenly a flash of white and gold plunged across them. The roc flinched; BJ and Protera grabbed frantically for a purchase in the giant feathers. "Leave her alone," a sad, angry voice shouted almost in the face of the roc.

BJ cried out inarticulately. The Griffin, talons extended, was doing his best to stay between the bird and Fran.

Protera said, "Sir, please leave." He was pleading, not ordering.

With a great effort, the Griffin hovered. "I will not leave," he said, panting, "and I must fight you." He dove toward the face of the roc, out of reach of the giant bird's talons.

BJ stood, one hand on Protera's shoulder for balance as she lunged forward. She whipped the fire extinguisher up and fired it straight into the Griffin's face.

He shut his eyes, crying out in anger and pain at the sudden cold. He wiped at his beak and eyes furiously with the back of his talons, and tumbled beyond the roc's head, within range of BJ and Protera.

Protera, pushing BJ to her knees, stepped forward quickly, flipping his sword over in his gloved hand; he struck the hilt against the Griffin's skull with a smack audible even in the rush of air. The Griffin drifted down rapidly, then plummeted.

BJ screamed to the roc, "Catch him!"

It glanced downward, but flew on. The Griffin, half conscious, flapped his wings clumsily to break his fall. BJ shut her eyes with the thud of impact.

Protera, still standing, stared over the side at the Griffin. "I hope," he said seriously, "that our friend is not—"

And Protera was gone, sliding off the side. BJ grabbed futilely at him, ducking as a chimera claw passed barely over her head.

This time the big bird dove and reacted, stooping with folded wings. BJ clutched the feathers, squinting over the side as one of the roc's claws plucked Protera from the sky. It was too fast to be gentle. Protera cried out, his leg bent backwards. The roc let go of him as they landed.

The sun came from under the clouds as BJ jumped off to check Protera. He lay with one leg bent under him, but he was pointing at the hillside above.

Melina was crawling in the window of BJ's house; the shutter lay to one side. She struggled, kicking clumsily with her hooves in the air, and disappeared.

The door opened a moment later. She emerged, rolling the white tabletop at an angle to the sun. It flashed like a semaphore, the white disk suddenly brilliant.

The chimerae hooted excitedly and dove, ignoring the shouting and tugging from their riders, ignoring the Great above them.

BJ ran uphill to Melina. She heard four short blasts on Morgan's horn, but didn't even look up. When she reached Melina she panted, "Give me that," and shouted into the sky at the approaching disorderly ranks, "FRAN!"

A riderless chimera waggled its wings, speeding quickly ahead of the others. As Fran skidded to a stop, nuzzling the disk plaintively, BJ recklessly slashed Fran's reins with her catchlet, then dragged the disk behind Fran before the chimera's fiery breath could annihilate it. Dodging the deadly stinger, BJ lashed the disk under Fran's tail, then slapped the chimera with the flat of her catchlet and shrieked, "Get on! Get out! Go!"

Poor Fran, startled and confused, rose into the sky. The disk behind her flashed in the sun.

The other chimerae hooted and called, flipping over to dislodge their riders. They sped after Fran, who panicked and flew even faster.

Morgan, already flying low, jumped off her chimera as it struggled to be rid of her. Fiona, draped over the chimera's back, dropped like a discarded doll into the nearby shrubbery. Morgan grabbed her arm immediately and pulled her upright.

Melina ran up to BJ, swatting at the vet's head frantically; only then did BJ realize that her hair was on fire. She bent forward while Melina patted it out. "It's over. We've won, if the Great will catch Morgan—"

A sudden, vicious wind knocked them both over. All across the hills the Great were landing, the few being ridden bending their necks almost double to force the riders off. One of the riders was Stein, who ran, limping, to BJ and Melina. "Are you all right?"

"What's going on?" BJ pointed to Morgan, who was blowing her horn and regrouping her forces on the ground. "If we hurry, we can—"

Stein shook his head tiredly. "No, we can't." His next words were nearly lost in the rising wind. "They're leaving. They won't help anymore, not now that the Inspector General attacked them."

The Great rose in a single flock; all the combatants on the ground crouched, covering their heads to duck debris and trying futilely to keep out the freight-train roar of the wind. The bushes and trees rocked sideways, and suddenly the hills and the valley were very quiet as the huge, dark figures flew south, ignoring the chimerae and the battle.

Stein dusted himself off. "If Morgan turns around, we're dead. I'll check Dr. Protera; you two check the Griffin." He sped down the hill, hand on his catchlet.

BJ and Melina ran to the untidy mound of broken wings in the grass. The Griffin turned his head in their direction, dazedly focusing a golden eye on BJ. His head was still covered with drying CO_2 foam. "You still don't understand combat, do you?" he said mildly. "You really should have killed me."

"I didn't want to." BJ knelt. "Are you all right?"

"I'm wounded. I'm devastated. I'm bereft. I'm well on the way to becoming extinct." He sighed and stroked her hair awkwardly. "I'm fairly well."

BJ looked around anxiously for Morgan, but didn't see her. Behind her she heard a plaintive honk; she spun. A lone chimera, struggling to fly but tied by its reins, was near the cottage door Melina had left open.

"Oh, God." BJ said quickly to Melina, "Stay with him," and dashed uphill, not sure what she could do.

She was nearly even with the chimera before it noticed her. It thumped its tail on the ground futilely, trying to reach her, and made a terrible, desperate noise as it begged for release. BJ fell back as a fireball belched from the chimera's mouth.

A small, furry streak leapt from the brush nearby and dashed between BJ and the chimera. Horvat, fierce and unafraid, leapt immediately to her defense.

Without blinking or flinching, the chimera ripped a claw upward, tearing holes in Horvat's chest and throat and flinging the tiny body backwards.

BJ instantly stabbed forward with her catchlet, lashing at the hapless chimera. It whimpered, burning BJ's arms; she didn't care. She slashed the reins and battered viciously at the chimera;

it bleated plaintively and fled, slashed wings flapping in the breeze.

Gredya dashed forward, howling as she came. To BJ, the she-wolf seemed to melt, rising from wolf to human with an audible popping and grinding of bones, fangs exploding from her mouth, ears bleeding with the sudden change of skull. She stumbled past BJ and dropped to her knees, wailing inarticulately. BJ spun around and saw Horvat, tossing and thrashing in pain between them.

Suddenly the battle seemed far away and unimportant.

BJ dove for Horvat, but was too late; Gredya was already holding him, licking his wounds with a bloody human tongue and nuzzling his mouth as he whimpered. Tears flowed freely, unstoppable, down the Wyr woman's cheeks.

She held Horvat up to BJ, in the midst of the fire and cries of war with the chimerae, but it was clear: Horvat's neck was terribly torn, a line of ribs sprung back and his lightly bubbling lung exposed. BJ knelt, wanting to touch him, but pulling back in the face of Gredya's bared teeth as she clutched Horvat's body and rocked back and forth.

"Go." Gredya's voice, commanding Horvat, was broken and terrible. "Go to man. Go now. Go or die."

"Change, honey." BJ was pleading, not sure how to say it. "Make yourself human. Come on, please, baby, change for me."

Horvat melted, more rapidly and seemingly more easily than Gredya ever had. The pain was loud and agonizing; the pup howled at first, then wept, and pulled free when Gredya and BJ tried to grab him.

Fur sloughed off. Teeth dropped out, and claws dropped in the dust as fingernails grew. BJ, who had seen the entire process in adult Wyr, for once disregarded the pain and the contractions. She sat, fists clenched, waiting for it to end—

For barely a moment, a torn and bleeding human infant sat in the dirt, wailing with incomprehensible pain. Its mangled throat and chest bubbled as it cried, and one lung threatened to spring free of the body.

Then the change came back, as swiftly as it had been. Lighter, feebler from the loss of mass, in more pain, Horvat lay in the grass and dirt. He would have rolled in the dust, but BJ grabbed him, drawing him into her lap.

Gredya said tightly, "Now you know. Only death helps."

"Then he needs us, doesn't he?" she said, and pulled the syringe, still whole, from her shirt pocket.

The process was as easy as though she were back in Virginia, putting someone's much loved dog to sleep.

In the middle of a battlefield, without the aid of a technician, she hooked her left arm around Horvat. Fortunately, his foreleg was unbroken; he had landed on his other side. She reached forward with her left arm, pulling his forepaw straight, and used her thumb to pinch his vein off as she twisted her arm outward, pulling the leg taut and exposing the vein.

She tapped the leg, checking the condition of the vein. She put her head down against Horvat's muzzle, saying almost into his ear, "You know that this isn't going to hurt, don't you? You can be good, can't you?"—and, automatically, because veterinarians said it so often, "Are you a good boy? Are you a good boy?"

Horvat, straining, licked her cheek with his bloody tongue. Yes, he was a good boy.

Sometimes it's hard to find a vein, as though at the last minute the entire body resists what is coming. The good veins collapse; the others never rise even under pressure or tourniquets. BJ prayed silently for an easy stick.

The needle slid in as gracefully as ballet. BJ slid the plunger home smoothly. Horvat barely shuddered once as the liquid sped through his blood stream; then he was still.

Then he was gone, snatched away. Gredya rocked Horvat's body in her arms, howling as the dead wolf pup was transformed with cruel ease into a dead human baby. BJ's arms were empty.

"They die so young, don't they?" The voice was harsh and brittle, full of the edge and anger of successful battle. "You shouldn't have bothered. They make terrible pets. I know; I've tried."

Without hesitation, BJ threw her catchlet straight into Morgan's chest, where it stuck.

Morgan fell back—but stood up, biting her lip so hard it bled, and tugged the catchlet free with a jerk that made her hair shake and jump as though she had touched a high-voltage wire. Morgan looked down at the open wound in her chest and repeated, "You shouldn't have bothered."

Gredya, rocking the dead pup ceaselessly and crooning, never looked up. But she shifted her arms tighter, and Horvat's body shifted to expose his wounds.

Morgan's eyes widened, her nostrils flared ever so slightly, and she reached out to touch the blood.

BJ, weaponless, knocked Morgan's arm aside. Morgan gaped.

BJ, neither cold nor angry, looked up at Morgan and said evenly, "I will kill you. I'm very smart, and I'm very patient, and I will kill you."

Morgan stopped smiling.

Felaris walked up behind her. Her face was crossed with scars: knife, sword, one that must have been an axe. Her nose was broken, her ears notched. Only her smile looked normal and human, and even that seemed cruel.

Without turning, Morgan said, "Felaris?"

The scarred woman said, "Got it." She held up BJ's copy of *The Book of Strangeways*.

BJ snatched her bloody catchlet from the grass where it lay and threw it at Felaris. It struck the woman a glancing blow in the arm; she swore, jerking her arm back. The book slipped from her fingers and spun crazily in the air, in an arc toward Morgan.

Morgan gave a sudden cry and threw her arm up, palm out, then shrieked as the book struck her hand and fell.

Felaris caught the book and held it up curiously, upside down; clearly Felaris couldn't read.

On the cover of *The Book of Strangeways* was a brown, smoking palm print. Behind Felaris, Morgan stood clutching her smoldering hand and weeping involuntary tears of fury and pain. "Bring it," she snapped at Felaris. "I'm sounding retreat."

Felaris hesitated, looking down at BJ, who was standing unarmed again. Morgan saw. "Forget her. We have the book; retreat, before we lose it."

Felaris stepped forward and shoved BJ backward and sprawling. BJ lay helpless; Felaris looked at her in disgust but did not bother killing her; Morgan blew the ram's horn, and her surviving troops ran south, disappearing quickly into the tall grass by the river. Probably they would head for a rendezvous point later, marching out of Crossroads as easily as they had flown in.

It took a long time for Gredya to let BJ hold Horvat. They wept together, and after that, it took a long time for either of them to let go.

A few moments later, BJ was lying alone among the wounded and dying. Stein stood over her and offered a hand. "Are you all right?"

"All right," BJ said bitterly, "is a loose term."

Horvat was dead.

The Great were leaving.

And Morgan had a copy of *The Book of Strangeways*.

PART

·2·

T·W·E·N·T·Y

COINCIDENCE IS OFTEN noticed when it is delightful, best noticed when it is embarrassing. Almost exactly four months after they had met there the last time, Stacey Robie bumped into BJ at Kroger's in Kendrick, Virginia, and BJ was once again preoccupied with her own thoughts.

"Daydreaming in class, Ms. Vaughan?" Stacey intoned. She was the kind of person who thought that any joke was funnier twice. "Hey, girl," she added, and, as BJ turned around, "Jesus!"

"Stacey," BJ said vaguely. "Why, how nice."

"What the hell happened to you? You look like hell."

"I'm a little tired, that's all." She leaned on the cart, not quite hard enough to make it roll out from under her.

"Well, get some rest. You're dead on your feet."

"I'm having a busy winter."

Stacey looked at her strangely; veterinary work is usually seasonal, like farming. "Well, anyway, late Happy New Year. I stopped by the school to say Hi. Say, did you know that Laurie Kleinman took a leave of absence from anesthesiology?"

"Yes. I think it was to nurse a sick family member." At the end of the aisle, BJ picked up two cartons of menthol cigarettes.

Stacey made a face. "Did you start smoking?"

"Nope. These are for a friend."

"Oh." Stacey collected her thoughts. "The vet school, right. Did you know they made a video of you surgerizing a goat? Taking a pair of pantyhose out of his guts?"

Sugar had requested the tape "as a benchmark for what a first-year graduate can do." Given Sugar's ego about surgery— he frequently criticized the other surgical faculty harshly—BJ had been tremendously flattered, though she also knew that Sugar was obliquely apologizing for invading her privacy when Stefan wrote his term paper.

"Of course I know about it," BJ said gently. "I was there."

"Right, right. I watched a little of it." Stacey hesitated, then burst out uncharacteristically, "My God, you were good. I mean, not a wasted motion, every cut just perfect, and stitches evener than a sewing machine." She sounded more like the old Stacey as she finished: "How the hell did you ever get so good at cutting and stitching? I mean, you were such a klutz."

BJ looked back at her with no resentment, just weariness. "You want to know how to get good at surgery? Just do it. Every day. All the time."

"I do as much as I can," Stacey muttered.

BJ loaded ten bottles of vitamins into the cart. "I do all I have to."

"Good thing you're buying those. Do you really need all of them?"

"Oh, they're for patients. And for friends. I said I'd buy them while I was in town."

"Maybe you're trying to do too much, honey." Stacey shuffled from one foot to the other uncertainly. "So how's everything else? Still got the fella?"

"I didn't say I had one."

"You didn't have to." She winked exaggeratedly. "How's it going?"

"It's wonderful," she said with little enthusiasm, "but the commute is a problem."

"Tell me about it." Stacey's engagement ring was back. "Can't you find a job closer to him?"

BJ smiled thinly. "I may have to, but that has its own problems."

"Mmm." Stacey was already looking at her watch. "Gotta go meet Ken. So long, honey. Take better care of yourself."

"I'll try."

"Remember, your health is all you've got."

"That's good to know."

Stefan met her in the parking lot and helped her load the cart. "Time to go," he said quickly.

"Did you fill the list for me at the vet school?"

"Love my own, can't you tell?" The truck cabinets were jammed with gauze, splints, antibiotics, three gauges of suture material, autoclaved surgical packs, new scalpel blades, and an appalling amount of T-61 for putting animals to sleep. "Can you go now, drop me off at the dorm?"

She shook her head. "I promised Melina I'd stop at Gyros and say hello."

Stefan hesitated. "I don't think that's so good, BJ."

BJ looked at him narrowly. "Is something wrong?" When Stefan didn't answer, she felt a sudden chill. "Let's go."

The sign on the restaurant door said CLOSED. BJ, seeing Chris, knocked on the glass. At first he waved an arm without looking up. Finally he sidled to the door and opened it, looking worriedly at them.

"I have tried," he said. "Everything, I have tried. They won't go away."

They followed him to the booth. He had laid out eight table settings. At each place he had set an individual-serving potato chip bag, a spatula, a pencil, and an uncooked hot dog.

BJ said quietly, "Where are they, Chris?" After her time in Crossroads, she half hoped that the Little Brown Men were somehow involved.

He looked at her vaguely, waved an arm and wandered back behind the counter and began throwing hamburger patty after patty on the grill, which was shut off, the power locked out with a padlock.

They heard a thumping at the rear door and Stan stumbled in, carrying grocery boxes piled higher than he could see above. "Papa, I got supplies!" He was using the bright, singsong voice parents use to coax children.

BJ and Stefan each took a box from him and set it on the counter. He looked at them with surprise, but no pleasure. "Thanks." He dashed behind the counter. "No, Pop. No more burgers. We'll put those in the fridge until somebody orders one, OK?"

Chris gestured back at the corner booth. Stan barely glanced at it. "I'll take care of them." Chris ran over, swept the potato chip bags up in one arm and gathered the hot dogs, pencils, and spatulas with the other. "See? They're done."

Stan shrugged helplessly at BJ and Stefan. "I hate to leave him for a minute."

"How long has he been like this?"

"Like this, only a few days. Going downhill, almost since he came back, faster than the first time." He grabbed a mop and went behind the counter, and they noticed the puddles of spilled soda, condiments, vegetable oil. "Beej, this can't go on. I can't handle it forever."

They watched, unsure what to say. Finally BJ said, "We'd better go." She gave Stan a peck on the cheek, then leaned over the counter and kissed Chris, who didn't seem to notice.

Behind them, Stan flipped the door sign to OPEN.

Stefan put an arm around her. "I did not want you to see."

"I needed to. Does Dr. Protera know about this?"

"I told him." Stefan, who normally walked as though he were dancing, was nearly shuffling his feet. "He said that it was predictable. He said"—Stefan concentrated—"a field change to an organism would be rapid, because the environment field overwhelms the individual. But a field reversion in the original environment, that would be even faster. The organism's original field reasserts itself."

BJ nodded. She looked very calm as she asked, "Did he say what happened after the reversion?"

"He only guessed. He said he thought changes in progress before the first field change, they would be very much faster." Stefan opened the driver's door to the van for her. She slipped getting in, possibly because she was tired.

Stefan said conversationally, "Did you know that now they think that Alzheimer's sickness is also partly genetic? Like the sickness in my paper."

"Like Huntington's chorea. Yes, I know." She drove very carefully to the visitors' parking lot outside his dorm.

Stefan slid out easily, then came to her window and stretched on tiptoe as she rolled it down. He kissed her on the mouth, thoroughly, several times; she kissed back. "I wish you could stay here with me," he said. "I wish you could come back to Virginia while I go to school, and be with me forever."

He dropped back down and half-ran, half-danced up the dorm steps. BJ, watching him, said aloud, "Well, we can't always get what we want."

She took out a photocopy from the university library's *Book of Strangeways* and drove alone back to Crossroads, noticing the beginnings of buds on the trees. Spring would come to Virginia soon, the northernmost reaches of Crossroads a little after that.

By that time, Crossroads would be all but empty, devoid of species, done with its need for a vet.

When Morgan attacked, even BJ would have to leave.

The moment she left for good, she would become terminally ill again, a victim of Huntington's chorea. If she returned to Virginia—to any part of her world—she would deteriorate quickly and die, physically helpless and mentally ill.

T·W·E·N·T·Y-O·N·E

BJ BARELY HAD time to stop at her cottage and unload the truck; Stein had asked her to come to the inn on the full moon after Midwinter Night. She went gladly, though she was terribly tired; for weeks she hadn't even had time for a nice dinner out.

Stein greeted her at the door with a mug of hot cider. "It's been a long time. Let me take your parka."

BJ stamped the snow off her boots and barely opened her arms in time as Melina kissed her and gave her a quick hug. BJ hugged back firmly; Melina, emotional to begin with and attached to Horvat from all the sitting she'd done, had found the wolf-pup's death painful.

BJ looked around the inn, surprised; it was nearly empty. At a table near the fire sat Fields and Brandal; a relaxed-looking Estevan Protera, in a walking cast, lounged beside them. The Griffin lay nearby, a small pitcher of cider steaming before him. He was heavily bandaged and splinted, but still looked dignified. Seeing him at Stein's was a rarity, these days.

B'Cu, chopping mutton for a stew, regarded them dubiously from across the room, but did not participate. Melina tapped quickly back across the floor and chatted, distracting him.

Protera stood easily and quickly as she walked over. "Happy New Year, Doctor." He tapped his mug against hers.

"Many happy returns," the Griffin said dryly. "You have a package for Laurie, don't you? I'll be seeing her shortly."

BJ opened her knapsack and took out the two cartons of menthol cigarettes. "I hope you don't mind?"

He shrugged. "We put up with each other's vices. She smokes, I eviscerate. I'm trying to quit."

"I wish you weren't," Stein said frankly. "I'm telling you, the more people realize there's no threat of an Inspector General, the more chaos there's going to be." He nodded towards BJ. "Ask the sleepy surgeon, here."

Protera said easily, "You do realize that I'm missing some parts of this."

Brandal smiled. "Don't worry; we haven't gotten to the important part." He folded his hands on the table. "We've admitted that there's going to be more chaos. We're adjusting to the fact that we've already lost a war that hasn't been fought yet, and we're trying to save lives."

Protera scratched his head and somehow made it look graceful. "How?"

"By moving species out of Crossroads," BJ said.

Protera stared; Brandal was stunned. Stein beamed. "So smart. Once, tutoring, we talk about it, and she knows all about it from there."

BJ blushed. "I also saw Fields make a road for the sundancers."

"So did I," Protera said. He smiled at her, delighted and unembarrassed. "But I didn't think about the possibilities that presented."

"I understand your wanting Professor Protera along," BJ said. She desperately wanted to avoid another commitment. "He's studying the ways in which worlds meet, and he would love to come." Protera nodded vigorously. "But what can I do? Why do you want me?"

Brandal ticked them off on his fingers. "Because you know animals' needs better than we do, and can judge whether or not species will survive where they're going. Because we will be risking injury, and it's good to have a veterinarian along. Finally, because we're going to do this many times, and quite a few of us will need to learn how to send a species to another world."

BJ said, "Then I'd better go home and get my business wrapped up, so that I can go when you're ready."

Stein said, "No. Stay here tonight; we'll leave in the morning."

"We're starting so soon?" BJ was already overworked; now she was overworked and rushed.

Brandal said, "We started two days ago. Tomorrow morning we leave Crossroads." He changed his tone. "Will your cottage be all right without you, BJ? I'm sorry for the lack of notice. You still have a flowerbinder—"

"Daphni will be fine." BJ had litter-box trained her for the winter. "Melina, if I get into trouble, will you—"

"You won't get into trouble, but I will care for her if you need it, yes."

"Thank you so much." With forced casualness, BJ asked the question she had been dreading: "Who leaves first?"

"The sundancers," Fields said.

BJ nodded. "Of course. You'd planned on showing them a new road to make up for the road Fiona closed."

Brandal said, "And it's easiest to start with them; they're migratory, and they needed the road to another world."

"And after all," Protera broke in, "a migratory species stands a better chance of finding its way back if the new world isn't suitable."

The others wouldn't look him in the eye. The Griffin said gently, "Professor, I'm afraid your own innocence does you a disservice here. If we leave a world open to the Strangeways, then Morgan can follow the roads to the new world."

Protera was momentarily silent. He looked away, staring into the darkest corner of the room, then said unsteadily, "Well, we'll just have to cut off entire worlds, won't we?"

"No, sir." Fields was correcting, not scolding; his face was troubled. "Not 'we.' I will, sir."

The meeting broke up, the participants moving off to various corners to get their bedrolls. BJ slept on the floor, wrapped in a down quilt so thick that she could barely sense the boards beneath her. Stein had brought it down from his quarters upstairs, saying, "This ought to give you some sleep. You need some; you look terrible."

"Thanks," she had said, without sarcasm. She knew she looked terrible.

She watched the fire drowsily. Shortly before her eyes closed, she realized that the fire was watching back; a firelover had flown down the chimney. Glowing orange, it perched on a blazing log and regarded her solemnly.

"Don't worry," she said sleepily. "We'll take care of you." She shut her eyes.

In the morning she was wakened by the sound of hooves. She looked cautiously out the southern window. Rudy and Bambi were bounding up the hill, kicking back huge plumes of powdery snow.

"Are you up yet, Doctor?" Stein was packing bread, meat, and cheese for the trip; clearly, he had been up for hours. The others, dressed and jacketed, were eating breakfast.

BJ leapt up, pulling on her jeans and her sweater. She was done in time to look relaxed as the front door opened. She heard Stein's parrot make a leering chuckle and say something in the deer people's flutelike tongue. Bambi laughed in shock; Rudy said, "Back off, man."

He ran around the corner. "BJ! All right!"

"What are you doing here?" She hugged them both. They wore wool jackets and breeches, dyed in earthtone colors that reminded BJ of camouflage. In a winter forest, the two of them would be invisible.

Rudy spread his arms. "I graduated. I had all the requirements done; I was just hanging out. What a city."

BJ asked Bambi, "Did you like San Francisco?"

Bambi, arm around Rudy, laughed in embarrassment and shook her head. Rudy kissed her. "The crowds got to her, Beej. She's an animal, but not a party animal."

"I like family," she protested. "It's just—strangers. . . ." She shuddered.

Rudy turned to BJ. "Besides, we gotta set up house somewhere. We're having a fawn, can you believe that?"

"And we can discuss it on the road." Stein had his coat on, and held BJ's parka out to her. "Believe that."

The Griffin, too injured to hike, stayed behind with Melina and B'Cu. The rest set out, walking toward the bridge on the Laetyen River. Fields held a pole with a circular cosmetic mirror attached to it on a gimbal. He wore inexpensive wraparound sunglasses, and looked incongruous even for a satyr.

Estevan Protera, too, wore sunglasses, but his were streamlined and black-framed, slightly more glamourous than Wayfarers. He, too, had a mirror tied to the top of a staff—but he also had his cane, with a scabbard tied to it, holding the rapier with the basket hilt.

Protera followed BJ's gaze. "Toledo steel," he said fondly. "Modeled after a seventeenth-century dueling weapon for grandees. You should hear it whistle through the air."

"She should not," Fields rumbled.

"I have," she reminded them. "I just didn't get a chance to inspect it that day."

Brandal said sadly to BJ, "I couldn't talk him into trading for Glarundel, the Sword that was Useless."

"I assume you provided the mirrors."

"And one pair of sunglasses." BJ didn't have to ask which pair.

She squinted at the bridge ahead, wishing she had sunglasses. The mass of bodies on the bridge didn't make sense to her; it seemed like a large, moving carpet. "Someone's crossing."

"Someone and something." Fields laughed, waving and shouting, "Io!"

Every head turned; half the heads had antlers. One in front, with a walking staff with a branch in leaf at the end of it, held the staff up in greeting.

"Time to tell the folks," Rudy said, grinning. He poked Fields softly in the belly. "We're gonna have a fawn, can you imagine?"

"Oh?" He leered fondly at Bambi. "And how did that happen?"

For once, Bambi laughed out loud and Rudy was embarrassed. Fields's laughter echoed off the snowy hills rising ahead.

Suuuno, the stag man who had conducted Rudy and Bambi's wedding ceremony, called orders out in his own soft language to his people, each of whom had sticks. They poked, cajoled, and waved their arms, slowly moving forward.

Among them, the sundancers turned frantically this way and that, trying to turn back to the warmer weather. "It is my mistake," Fields rumbled, watching. "I had not thought of moving them during cold weather."

Protera said to Bambi, "Your people have done marvelously." He stood the mirror in front of him. "And their work is about to get easier."

Fields and he sighted off the sun and adjusted the swinging mirrors until Suuuno waved again and called, "I see the flashes." The sundancers suddenly turned toward them, a single burst of golden blooms. The pace at the end of the bridge quickened as the mobile plants struggled uphill towards the light.

The walk up the northern mountains went quickly; Fields's and Protera's mirrors were augmented by the glare of the barren, snow-covered mountainsides above the tree line. At one point, when the sun reflected off a patch of glare ice on a cliff face, the party actually had to jog to keep pace with the sundancers.

Stein and BJ walked to either side of Protera, but he had little difficulty, always balanced despite his walking cast. "If you look at the sole," he confided to BJ, "you will find that I have strapped on the bottom of a golf shoe. I'm leaving hideous tracks."

"But so much more sensible than heels," BJ said solemnly.

"Absolutely," Protera said, enjoying Stein's discomfort. "But style should afford feeling, not make sense. For instance, pumps are always sensible, but with an evening gown—"

Stein said, "Could we move a little faster here?" and moved so rapidly that Protera was unable to keep talking and could only wink at BJ as he glided forward. After she slipped twice in the snow, BJ gave up other thoughts and concentrated on keeping her footing.

It was nearly noon when they stopped, panting, in a mountain pass. They had covered more ground than BJ had ever walked in snow; she was glad that the return trip would be downhill, and was sorry they didn't have a bobsled.

Fields, twin spumes of steam coming from his nostrils, was using the end of the mirror pole to etch the line in the snow for the others to follow. He stopped briefly, walked in a circle with furrowed brow like a man who has forgotten what he came to the store to buy, and poked a turnoff line slowly and carefully into the snow.

"Are you having trouble finding your way?" Protera asked—admirably, BJ thought; he didn't even sound nervous at the thought of being lost between worlds.

Fields smiled at him, the kind of smile parents wear at graduation ceremonies for their children. "I am only having trouble finishing."

They followed him down the line. The sundancers were harder to herd now; the snow made them sluggish and tractable, but the glare from it surrounded them. The noonday sun provided no direction at all.

As they moved down the line, the ground became slush-covered, then barren and muddy, and finally sprinkled with green shoots. Fields stopped and stood to one side. BJ looked ahead to where the divot Fields had in the damp ground merged with a previous path, half-obscured by waving grass as it weaved down a sloping hillside toward a lake.

"We'll take it from here, man." Rudy took Fields's staff; Bambi gently disengaged Protera from his.

The sundancers milled aimlessly in place under the noon sun, directionless. The deer people moved forward, stopping only because Suuuno, in the lead, blocked their way.

He knelt to Fields, bowed to Brandal, and shook hands with Stein. He took BJ's hand. "Thank you for your kindness to our children. I wish we would see your world again some day."

"I wish you would, too." BJ held onto his hand. "Suuuno? You're a shaman—"

He shook his head, his antlers casting shadows across her. "Don't think of magic or prophets." He looked in her eyes. "If you've ever known a prophet, you'd know that they are very little help."

"I believe you," BJ said evasively. "But—" She looked at Rudy and Bambi unself-consciously holding hands. "I think advice is better than prophecy."

"From me?" He smiled with the quiet amusement BJ associated with paintings of mystics. "You might not like it, Doctor. Remember, I counsel The Ones Who Die."

"And what's your advice?"

"Die well." He put his hand on her forehead, as though it were a blessing. "After all, you have to anyway. Die well: for something, and not alone."

He turned and was gone. The rest of The Ones Who Die followed him unquestioningly.

Rudy and Bambi, the last to go, laid the mirror staves against a rock and walked toward the others. Fields put a hand on each of them. "You know that when I once close this road, you will maybe not find it easy to return. Maybe never."

Rudy nodded, and BJ was astonished at how mature he suddenly seemed. "We talked about that. Both of us wanted a new world. I'll miss San Francisco, and we'll all miss Crossroads—" He gestured at the path behind them, where Crossroads was no longer visible. "But it all changes. Some of what we missed is already gone, you know? And the rest is going soon." He embraced Fields, who ran his hands over his antlers and then held Bambi briefly. She didn't seem at all shy towards Fields.

Rudy shook hands with Protera. "Later." Bambi smiled shyly at him, and nodded goodbye.

They licked BJ's face; she felt for a last time how rough their ruminants' tongues were, no matter how gentle they tried to be. "Say goodbye to Dave for us," Bambi said, and snuffled.

"C'mon, babe, don't cry. She's so emotional now. We're gonna have a fawn, did you know?"

"I know."

They danced forward, each holding a mirror and flashing it toward the sundancers, which focused on them and followed, falling neatly into two rows like a well-planned commercial planting.

The others went in behind them.

BJ watched them go until Fields tapped her arm. "BJ, I must close this path now." He put a warm hand on her shoulder and caressed it. "Little BJ. Always you will feel loss hard now, won't you?"

She stepped back slowly, watching the grassy world shimmer and fade. "Yes."

The walk back was rapid, and the entire party felt relief when the valleys and mountains of Crossroads were visible below them again. Yet none of them spoke. BJ, stumbling and exhausted, wondered if, like her, the others were feeling that Crossroads was a little less rich and strange, a fraction emptier and more barren.

T·W·E·N·T·Y-T·W·O

BJ WAS UNABLE to go see Stefan for the next three weeks. The winter was magical and bleak. BJ had no time to think, or she would have remembered it as the strangest and most wonderful winter of her life, and the most horrific.

The weather was alternately pleasant and wild. BJ saw more snow than she had seen in her life. The heavy "lake effect snow" was the hallmark of moisture traveling into Crossroads. Either it was dry cold air producing nights with the most stars BJ had even seen, or it was a mass of snow that dropped almost instantly onto the landscape, transforming and isolating it at almost the same time.

In spite of the snow, BJ had all the cases she could handle, and more. Some time in January, partly in response to a letter from Lee Anne read at midnight when BJ should have been in bed, BJ wrote dazedly, "I should be doing more diagnostic work."

Instead she was spending her days in surgery. Before dawn she would throw back the covers, put tea on the wood stove, let Daphni out of doors, and lay down blankets in the snow for the cases to come. Generally she would take in at least one case waiting at the door. Often as not it was a worker from the Road Crews, a Meat Person or a human, cradling a damaged animal and saying nothing.

Usually the animals brought in were the young: calves, kids, pups—the helpless and hurt, the traditional victims of politics. BJ went through the motions of discussing price with the Road

Crews, but both sides knew that she would heal the animals, no matter what.

Only BJ knew that her drive to treat and heal all the clients who were victims of violence stemmed from her hatred of Morgan, and her frustration at being unable to stem the increasing violence and pain in Crossroads.

Always she started with a bleached white lab coat which she would attempt to keep clean. Always she finished with a blood-stained, excrement-smeared jacket that no one could make glamourous, no matter what mythical species had fouled it last.

The Meat People were the oddest of all: pointy-toothed, salivating carnivores who cherished the species they preyed upon, and could not accept death and injury to others. BJ vividly remembered L'razz, a Meat Woman who single-handedly carried in a mangled buck deer and insisted on holding it while it was stitched, watched in disbelief while its blood pressure dropped, then wailed, fangs to the sky, and held the dead deer to its breast as though nursing while BJ had said over and over, "It's dead. You did your best. It's not your fault. Look, it happens."

On this morning, BJ stumbled out, tea in hand, ready to write off the dead, assess the wounded, and assist the survivors.

The first case was pathetically easy: a disemboweled sheep, probable victim of famine and infighting among the Wyr. Following B'Cu's training, BJ cut its throat; there was a glut of mutton just now, but meat should be saved for future use.

The next two cases were quick, easy stitches: a capybara-like rodent, brought forward by a human member of the Road Crew, and another sheep, half-carried by B'Cu. Both had facial slash wounds characteristic of Wyr attacks. BJ would have butchered the sheep, but B'Cu shook his head violently; if the sheep could be saved, it should be. BJ talked through the entire surgery, bitterly, about what had happened among the Wyr. B'Cu listened, and BJ thought that he understood a great deal. He stayed for lunch, insisting on cooking; he had to wake BJ up when it was ready.

The next knock at her door was Laurie Kleinman, in mid-afternoon. "I'm here to raid your supplies." She moved quickly through the exam side of the cottage, putting together a small package of splints and bandages.

"How's he doing?" BJ said mechanically.

She glanced at BJ. "Badly, but better than you. Can't you take a break?"

"I want to, but who's going to spell me?" She gestured toward the steel table. "That thing's full every day. And my batting average is going down—What is it?"

Laurie was staring out the window. "Let's hope your batting average picks up." She fumbled for a cigarette. "I'll wait here and set up for surgery, just in case." She gave a sickly smile. "Isn't it great that I just happened to be here?"

BJ ran out. A procession of Hippoi was coming uphill in the snow; one of their number lay on a travois. The travois was towed by Chryseis, who was tearful, and Kassandra, who looked grim. Polyta, holding Sugarly's hand, walked behind them both. Several of the other women from the first-aid class followed respectfully, but anxiously; something was worrying them a great deal.

BJ ran directly to the travois. Hemera stared up. "It was a Wyr." She put a hand over the bloody bandages on her torn and ragged chest; it hurt to talk. "He leapt from rocks, above me—" She blinked rapidly and turned her face away from BJ. "I should have killed him, too."

"You could not help it," Polyta said kindly. "No one blames you." She said with great formality to BJ, "Doctor, Hemera's wound has already been treated."

The Hippoi looked at each other. This was why they were nervous. Hemera's chest was wrapped tightly in wool, a white cotton pad under the bandages. Her human body was wrapped in a blanket, in treatment for shock. "Good job," BJ said, removing the wrappings and bandage carefully. "Who—?"

"I did." Chryseis shot a frightened look at Polyta. Kassandra folded her arms defiantly.

"And then you came to me, and we brought Hemera to Dr. Vaughan to see what her"—Polyta hesitated over the unfamiliar word from the first-aid classes—"her prognosis is."

"All right." BJ went into the house and put on surgical gloves and also a white lab coat, mostly as a symbol of her authority in front of Polyta. She carried a cold tray back out with her. One of her eyelids was twitching.

BJ knelt down next to the travois and listened to Hemera's lungs with a stethoscope. There were no crackles or wheezes. She removed the bandage and pad, then pulled a curved hemostat from the cold tray, probing delicately at the wound. Hemera flinched, trying hard not to. "It hasn't penetrated the chest wall," BJ said.

"What does that mean?" Polyta, arms folded, was concerned but unyielding.

"It means that she's less liable to dangerous infection, and could be cured by surgery. I could suture the gash while she was under anesthesia. In a few days, she'd be able to walk; in ten days, she could probably bear heavy loads."

Polyta said noncommittally, "And in the next seven days?"

BJ stiffened. "Five days from now, she would be able to walk long distances if it wasn't strenuous—no mountain climbing. Three days from now, she would be able to walk and feed herself; two days, she'd be aware." BJ continued unwillingly, "For one day, she'd be semiconscious. For a day after that, she'd need special care."

Polyta nodded, eyes solemn and compassionate. "I thought that would be true." Between them, Hemera gasped at a stab of pain. Polyta bent low, stroking Hemera's hair; a curl twined around her fingers. Hemera, trembling and trying not to cry out, laid her cheek against Polyta's hand.

Polyta pulled her hand back. "You have a chemical solution in your office, Doctor. Kill her now."

In the frozen instant that followed, BJ said, "I won't."

"Dr. Vaughan, there is no other choice. We go south tomorrow."

"Hemera will be well in five days."

"We can't wait five days. Our food is to the south; we need to go. You must kill her, BJ, or I must, or I must be more cruel and leave her to die." Polyta was reasonable, sensible. "This is hard, BJ, but part of our tradition. We go south together—"

"I don't care."

Polyta raised her eyebrows. BJ's voice was much too loud. "It is not your choice, Doctor. Hemera is one of my people—"

"Well, she's one of my patients."

"Do veterinarians never kill patients at the request of clients? Have you not done it?"

BJ shook her head violently. "Not to a thinking being. Never to a thinking being." She thought of Horvat, and realized it was a lie.

Polyta said calmly, "I have left thinking beings to die. I have chosen the ones that must die. That is what the Carron does, BJ. It is important to our lives that I do it—"

"You want to kill someone?" BJ stepped in front of Hemera's body. "Kill me. Now, right now. Kick me in the face with a hoof; leave me to die of brain hemorrhage. Kill me, then Hemera."

All the centaurs, including Chryseis, were staring at her. BJ broke. "I can save her, Polyta. Please; I know I can. Just sign her off, the way humans do to their pets—"

"She is not a pet, BJ, and I could never 'sign her off.' I don't make this decision out of lack of funds or love; you know that."

"All right, I know that. Give her up for dead here. Leave her here to die." BJ was breathing hard. "If she doesn't heal completely, I'll kill her myself."

"You promise that?"

"Yes, I promise that."

"And it will be painless?"

"It will. Look, it won't come to that." BJ knew that she was talking too loud; she couldn't seem to help herself. "I'll do the surgery, she'll heal, and she'll catch up with you. I'll kill her if I'm wrong. I promise." She took a deep breath. "If I break the promise, come back and trample me to death. Whatever."

Polyta stared at her for a frozen moment, then whipped her head around and said to the others, "We'll go south, without Hemera. If she doesn't meet us, I will return briefly. Thank you all for the good you tried to do Hemera." She trotted off slowly. The others followed, Chryseis last and looking over her shoulder. Only Kassandra stayed a moment, standing by Hemera.

BJ said, "Why do we have to fight all the time?"

Kassandra said, "Because change is hard for us, and she is learning to change."

"Not fast enough. She wanted to let Hemera die."

Kassandra put a hand on BJ's shoulder, and pressed down; BJ found that she couldn't move. "You listen. I speak my mind"—she glanced back at the retreating Polyta and smiled wryly—"which is not always liked. Polyta mourns her Nesyos, and that's good, because she should. He loved her better than any of our people have been loved—and that's good, because he should have. She thinks that Nesyos was the best leader the Hippoi have ever had— and that is bad, because he was not. She is.

"Under her, and with your help, we have learned to heal ourselves and care for ourselves. We kill each other less readily, and we gain in wisdom by having older Hippoi." She scowled at the retreating Chryseis, who was still staring back at them. "Some of us don't always know it, but it's so. Polyta will be remembered always."

BJ wrenched her shoulder free. "So when she is angry, I should accept it?"

"No." Kassandra leaned down, her face close to BJ's. "When she gives an order and relents after your argument, you should acknowledge greatness."

BJ spun around and trudged into her cottage, slamming the door. Laurie, cigarette in hand, looked up from her texts. "Are you all right?"

"Now I know why they shoot horses."

"You're crying, BJ—"

"Prop that door open and scrub."

Laurie shut up and scrubbed.

The surgery would probably have been simple for a human. The horse surgery would have been simple for a vet.

Hemera lay on her side on a Mylar blanket, the largest thing BJ had for outdoor surgery on top of the snow. BJ lay on her side beside Hemera, reaching up the way a mechanic would to undo an oil plug, and scrubbed around the wound, alternating Betadine with alcohol.

Laurie brought out an IV setup, stabbing the support pole into the ground. "Nothing like jury-rigging. Ain't it grand, doing campfire surgery? What's next, cutting with thrown knives from across the lawn?"

Hemera stared up, the whites of her eyes showing on all sides of the iris. She was showing symptoms of shock, but she clearly hadn't missed a word. Laurie patted her arm. "Don't sweat it. We know exactly what we're doing, and BJ's a hell of a fine surgeon. You'll be fine." She slid the catheter into Hemera's vein and stood back, muttering, "Jesus, I hate patients who can talk."

Draping was difficult but not impossible; BJ slung the drape over Hemera's side and warned her not to move. Hemera nodded slightly, and stayed rock-still from then on.

BJ was cleaning the wound itself now, checking the edges. She waited until Hemera went to sleep to ask, "What did you use?"

Laurie adjusted the flow. "Surital. What the hell, it's a barbiturate; if it works on horses and people it ought to work on horse people."

"How'd you figure out a dosage?"

"Human plus horse, by effect, right? Don't ask." BJ glanced up, saw the steady stream dripping into the tube, and decided not to ask.

Not much later, BJ pinched Hemera's arm, got no response. Laurie said, "She out?"

"I think so. Anyway, I'm starting; I don't want to keep her under long."

From here it was fairly routine surgery, BJ told herself. Except for the ugliness of the wound, except for the surgery being on a human body, and except for the surgeon having to lie on her side, it was fairly routine.

She began at the deepest layer of the wound. Laurie, kneeling behind her by the tray she had laid out, squinted in. "Look at the muscles on this babe."

"The Hippoi are all very strong. Look at how big her body is, to fit in proportion on top of a horse. I'll need Aught-Vicryl or Number Two Vicryl."

Laurie passed over the suture and needle. "God, it's like sewing with string."

"It has to hold. She's going to be lifting things again in ten days." BJ placed large, boxlike mattress sutures in the muscles. When she got to the end of the wound, which curved over Hemera's heart, she sighed. "Another inch deeper would have killed her."

She started again at the subcutaneous layer, this time with lighter-gauge suture. Laurie said, "So that's human fascia? It looks just like it does in animals."

"I guess tissue is tissue." BJ used a quick continuous pattern, suturing from one end of the wound to the other rapidly.

Laurie blinked when BJ reached the end. "That was fast. How did you get so good?"

"Too much practice." BJ's arms were tired from the awkward angle, but she didn't dare stop. "Okay, now the skin."

Laurie frowned, watching. "She is gonna scar like mad."

BJ snapped over her shoulder, "That's too bad, isn't it? I can't afford any tension on the wound, so I'm placing cruciates. That's how it is."

"Okay, okay." Laurie looked at BJ curiously, but shut up.

Laurie was right; the suture would leave a dotted-line scar. But the wound would heal. BJ tied off the last X, removed the drape, and stumbled inside to clean up.

Laurie leaned in a few minutes later. "She's waking up partway already. Guess I cut it a little close." She grinned. "Physician, heal thy centaur. Nice job." She lit up a cigarette. "Does this mean I can work on humans? That's where the big bucks are."

BJ sat shaking. She couldn't stop. "Why not?"

"Good." Laurie gave a quick look over her shoulder at Hemera, then strode in and threw BJ's knapsack on the bed. "Pack. You're my patient; I'm prescribing a vacation."

"I can't." BJ was trembling now. "Look around; this place is falling apart, and nobody can step in when I'm gone—" She started to cry.

Laurie shook her head. "I've seen you like this before, just after your mother died."

BJ's mother, who also had Huntington's chorea, had committed suicide, leaving a note that explained BJ's chances of having it. It was the first time BJ had known that her mother was ill.

"You weren't sleeping well then," Laurie said. "How have you been lately?"

BJ, stressed and exhausted, didn't answer.

At the door, the Griffin said mildly, "May I say a word?"

He slumped on the snow, exhausted by the trip up. Laurie said, "You shouldn't have come."

"I was worried about you." He turned back to BJ. "I know that you take your responsibilities seriously, and I find it laudable. However, you have already lost control of your emotions, and you will soon be working with impaired judgment and be of no use to anyone."

He studied his talons for a moment before continuing. "Therefore, although I am a lay person, I strongly recommend that you take seven days' vacation, in the American university setting of your choice so that you can rest among friends"—he coughed discreetly—"and we can get in touch with you in emergencies. I will tend your patient, with Laurie's guidance after she returns from taking you to Virginia. I am prepared to offer you some small incentive to agree to this."

BJ raised her tear-stained face. "Which is?"

"Go, or I'll kill you."

Laurie helped her pack, and Laurie drove the truck. BJ stared blankly out at the landscape lit by the bouncing headlights as though it were the surface of the moon.

Later she woke to find Stefan lifting her from the truck, carrying her in his arms. She laid her head against his chest and went back to sleep.

T·W·E·N·T·Y·T·H·R·E·E

LATER, BJ WOULD be sorry she remembered so little of that vacation.

She woke up in Laurie's apartment. It was terribly comfortable, although, not surprisingly, it smelled heavily of cigarettes. She spent the first two days asleep, and the third wandering around vacantly, more than a little empty. Stefan came to her before classes, between classes, every chance he got. He cooked her simple meals, brought her videos, sat and talked. He didn't ask about making love until she had enough energy to bring it up herself.

Laurie's apartment would have kept BJ occupied without company; the range and scope of the books fascinated her. There were paperbacks on mythography, coffee-table books of Ansel Adams photographs, books on chaos theory and on robotics. There was an impressive desktop computer with CD-ROM, a scanner, a modem, and a synthesizer; BJ was afraid to touch it. She walked around the apartment, staring at the details of the carved jade mountain on the coffee table and enjoying the unexpected richness of Laurie's life.

The next few days were a fast frenzy of moving around the town, sampling ice cream, eating pizza, relishing things she hadn't thought she was missing. She and Stefan avoided Gyro's, avoided even talking about it; for BJ, brought up in a family where people studiously avoided discussing the illness of relatives, that part was easy.

She checked her savings account, which was phenomenally

high since she was often paid in gold and had few opportunities to spend money. She bought Stefan a plant for his dorm room, and three music cassettes for his roommate, Willy, for being so patient. She wrote Annie and Lee Anne and Dave, bringing them up to date on Rudy and Bambi, and saying nothing disturbing about Crossroads. She called Peter in Chicago, listened to him patiently about his wonderful new woman, and promised to visit.

By Friday, she was restless and strangely depressed. She paced the apartment aimlessly, bumping into furniture, and sat down to make a quick list of things to do before she went back.

She went out, stopped at the hardware store where she had purchased the table, and picked up insulated gloves for handling hot objects. Stefan, meeting her for lunch, was amused. "BJ my love, what will you need them for? The chimerae are gone."

"They could come back. A firelover may get hurt. I think they'll be handy." And that was all she said.

Finally, she went to the Western Vee University Library, to the reference desk. A gray-haired woman in her sixties was seated behind it, her head barely a foot above the surface of the desk. BJ smiled, listening to her calmly answer an irate sophomore who wanted to know why "there weren't ever any books on *his* courses."

When the student retreated, chagrined, BJ moved into his place. The woman, calmly filling out a question log, said without looking up, "Thank you for waiting. I'll answer your question in a minute." In her own way, she sounded as sure of herself as the Griffin.

"Mrs. Sobell?"

She looked up quickly, unsurprised but delighted. Mrs. Sobell was very proud of the fact that nothing surprised her. "How very nice to see you again, BJ. How is your practice doing?"

"Busier than I'd like. Otherwise it's fine."

Mrs. Sobell nodded. "Well, perhaps in a few years you can take on an assistant. How is your friend Stefan? I've seen him in the library quite a bit."

"He's doing well in school." BJ felt as though she were conducting a romance in a downtown shop window; did everyone know about her private life? "Mrs. Sobell, I need to ask a favor of you. It's fairly unusual."

The librarian smiled. "Do you remember your first question to me? You wanted practical medical research about unicorns. BJ, all your favors are unusual."

"This one is a little more than most."

"We'll see. What can I do for you?" She waited calmly.

"I want you to help me steal some library books."

After the slightest of hesitations, Mrs. Sobell said, "Well, I'm sure you have your reasons, dear. Would that be a circulating, reference, or special collections book?"

BJ explained what she wanted. Mrs. Sobell considered for a long time. "You're asking me to do something I have always considered immoral, you know. Not simply a bad habit or a vice: a sin, in the same category as murder or treason."

"I'm only doing it because it may save a country."

"That's the problem, isn't it? 'May.' Not 'will.' " But finally she sighed loudly and smiled at BJ. "Well, every life needs a few good sins, just for contrast."

She led BJ into a room with a special computer terminal. "I don't imagine you know what this is. Most students graduate without using it. This connects Western Virginia's library catalog to the catalog of nearly every major university in the world. And now—"

Four computer screens later, she had an answer; it was that simple. Mrs. Sobell looked up. "There are copies in London, Peking, San Francisco, and Chicago. Which is easiest for you?"

"Peter," BJ said quietly.

"Excuse me?"

"Chicago. I'd like to run an errand there anyway."

"Certainly." Mrs. Sobell pressed a function key and waited. "Perhaps you could see Wrigley Field while you're there; it's one of the nicer old-fashioned parks . . . here you are. University of Chicago, Harper Memorial Library. Does not circulate." She coughed. "I'm afraid it will now."

"Thank you so much, Mrs. Sobell. That's really all I needed."

The older woman looked up at her with sharp eyes. "Don't you want to steal our own copy, here?"

"People here are going to need it a little while longer." BJ smiled. "Besides, I just couldn't ask you to steal from your own library."

Stefan and BJ were eating supper, in the midst of a heated but highly enjoyable argument about what the ten best movies of all time were, when someone knocked at the door.

BJ opened it. Melina stood outside, eyes wide, numb with grief.

"Melina." She pulled her in. "Are you all right? What happened?" She had a horrible thought. "My God, is Stein all right?"

Stefan leapt forward and held her. As Melina had said once, they were lambs together; she was the closest thing he had to a sister. He said something soft in Greek and finished, "Fields?"

Melina shook her head angrily, her lips tight. "Chris." She started to cry.

It was raining, the kind of cold, gray day that would normally have found BJ writing close by her fireside in Crossroads, Daphni cuddled at her feet.

Instead, she stood with Stein, where Melina normally would have been. Stein wore a greatcoat, and he insisted on keeping his hat on during prayers. He looked weary and extremely old. Stefan, in a dark coat and scarf, held his fedora in one hand and kept the other on BJ's arm.

On the opposite side of the grave, Melina stood crying almost continually. A slender, serious young man of twenty-five, with dark hair and steel-rimmed spectacles and a threadbare coat, stood by her, sheltering her with an umbrella. He was the preacher at the church in the hills, where Melina hiked out of Crossroads to worship. From time to time he put an arm around her.

The graveside service seemed long because it was in a foreign language and because the weather was terrible; actually, it lasted less than half an hour.

There was no family present besides Stan. A Greek Orthodox priest from Roanoke led the graveside service, in Greek.

The sound of the rain on the surrounding stones and the trees left the priest's words muted and hard to hear. The gospel, read in Greek by the priest and then in English by Melina's preacher, was one BJ remembered, dimly, from her early years, going to church with a loving but grimly determined mother: "Today you will be with me in Paradise." BJ daydreamed about Crossroads, with the birds coming back and the new foliage coming in.

B'Cu, in a borrowed trench coat and broad-brimmed hat several sizes too big for him, looked childish and immensely sad. He stood slightly apart from the mourners; he was never comfortable in crowds.

Even if the service had been all in English, BJ would have understood nothing. She stared at the open grave, remembering standing at her mother's grave less than six months ago. She remembered her brother, Peter, his fists clenching and unclenching as he watched three of their mother's friends and three of their own act as pallbearers. Uncle Roger from Williamsburg, defensive about not carrying the coffin, was an honorary pallbearer. Looking back, BJ should have noticed how few living relatives over fifty she had on her mother's side.

Before that, her father's funeral was vague to her. Most of all she remembered the moment, at the end of her mother's funeral, when she realized that she was an orphan.

She looked across pityingly at Stan, whose mother was long dead and whose sister had died when he was a child. At least BJ still had Peter.

A large wreath at graveside caught her eye; for a funeral decoration, it had more greenery than blooms. She looked at it absently, then more carefully, then smiled involuntarily. It was woven of rosemary, sage, parsley, garlic stems with the bulbs intact, oregano, and a knot of purple flowers that it took BJ some time to identify as chive blossom. She bent and read the card, which said simply, "For remembrance. A. Griffin."

The service broke up into an informal receiving line. Melina came forward to shake hands with Stan. "I am sorry for your grief—" she began, and started to sob again. Stan opened his arms, and she fell into them, holding her face against his coat. He patted her hair, sharing the grief but hardly looking at her. If he felt her horns, he gave no notice.

Eventually Melina straightened up, kissed him, and walked away under the umbrella of the waiting preacher. BJ walked up to Stan. "I'm sorry."

He opened and shut his hands, as though wringing out a towel. "You know, I always thought tradition didn't mean much. But I came out here, to the family tomb, and I pulled out the bones of my mother, and of my kid sister, and I rubbed them with rosemary, just like I'd been taught years ago by Papa. I don't even know if other families do that, or just us, but it felt right, you know? It felt like I was telling them, 'Here comes Papa,' and they'd be ready for him—"

His voice broke. He looked at BJ bleakly, without pride, and didn't bother wiping the tears on his cheeks. "Now I'm a grownup."

BJ had often wondered when she would feel like a grownup. She didn't tell the truth to Stan: Hardly anyone feels like a grownup. They bounce checks, they lose their tempers, they face deadlines with fear and crises with panic, and they wonder if they'll ever grow up.

B'Cu walked up unself-consciously and dropped a number of gold pieces into Stan's palm. Stan stared at him, astonished. "*Mafundu*," B'Cu said simply.

"Funeral receipts, in the old Congo," Stein said to Stan. "It's a way of paying respect and showing how close he was to your father. Please, take it; he'll feel terrible otherwise."

Stan pocketed the gold uncertainly. "Thank you very much," he said loudly. "My father thanks you."

B'Cu nodded. "T'ank." He clicked his tongue loudly in the middle of the word. He looked inexpressibly sad, pressed Stan's hand, and said with quiet grief, "K'ris."

He turned and was gone, waving Stein's hand away to walk in the graveyard all alone.

Stan turned to BJ, beside him, and said almost conversationally, "I remember when I was way little, Ma would tell me, 'Some day you will see your papa, if Hitler doesn't get him.' "

Stan laughed, his eyes filling again. "I was a kid; what did I know about Hitler? I figured a Hitler was some kind of monster. I had nightmares about a huge, scaly Hitler grabbing a man everybody said was my father, and I couldn't stop him. After I met Papa, the man looked like Papa in the dreams. I had the dream again last night."

Stein grabbed one of Stan's hands in both of his. "The monster didn't get him. He loved you enough to come back; life itself wasn't that important to him. Believe me, he's the bravest and luckiest man I know."

Stan nodded and turned away, wiping his eyes. Stein, watching him go, murmured thoughtfully, "We worry about Morgan; he still dreams about Hitler."

BJ took his arm as they left the grave. "Don't you?"

"All the time." Stein walked very carefully and sternly; BJ realized how determined he was not to look weak. "That is why I try very hard to dream only about Morgan." He pulled his arm free, gently. "I'd better go find B'Cu."

The truck was parked away from the cemetery, at the edge of the curbless road. BJ, stepping over the gully at the pavement's edge, stumbled. Stefan caught her. "My only love, you do that too much."

"I do."

"Are you going to tell me what is wrong?"

"All right. I will." Stefan edged back as though she had tried to hit him. She smiled and held onto his arm. "Do you remember how hard it was for me to talk about love to you, or fear, or even anger? I never talked about my feelings," BJ said quietly. "The one thing you never did, in a family where half the people had a terminal illness and it might be you or your children, was talk about your feelings. But I'll try."

"I will listen." Stefan sounded frightened but determined. He held onto her shoulder as though she were drowning. "Someone in your family, he had a sickness." He stressed the 'he' as though it could never be a 'she.'

"I have a disease," BJ said, "called Huntington's chorea. It's relatively rare, in the United States, but it's common enough among my relatives. It's hereditary. Half of my mother's family has it. I know you know what it is."

Stefan nodded mutely.

"But do you know what that means? It means some of your grandparents are missing, for a start. It means, if you have it, that someday you'll get clumsier and clumsier, and maybe moodier and moodier, and you won't know why. Or if you have a genetic test, maybe you'll know it's coming."

"Not you." Stefan trembled, holding her. "Never you, my only love."

"Not me," she agreed, "if I stay in Crossroads. But I took a genetic test, and yes, me. And now that I've been out a full week, I'm dropping things, and my hands shake sometimes, and I lose my balance. I didn't know my body could change back so quickly, but I don't really know why it changed in the first place. The longer I stay out of Crossroads, the worse I'll get."

Stefan stood very still. Finally he said in a small voice, "BJ, without I come to the University, I will never have a dream of my own."

BJ closed her eyes. She had been sure that was what he would feel, and had been afraid that was what he would say. "I know."

"And I want you more than anything in my life, BJ." He glanced over his shoulder. The cemetery was on a hill overlooking the university. "Except—"

"Except," she agreed. "And I stayed out for a week, and I'm clumsy and stumbling. Would you like to see me stick out my tongue and try to hold it out? Would you like me to ask Dr. Boudreau for a second genetic test? She'd love to oblige; she's been doing a study—" BJ stopped. Tears were coursing down Stefan's cheeks; she felt a brief rush of grateful love, then remembered that fauns cry more easily and oftener than other species. "I'm sorry. But it was time that I tell you."

"It was past time." Stefan held her as though he would never let go. "BJ, doctor, only love, I want you well."

"Yes." She said it carefully, as though her tongue might at any moment flutter out of control. "But you know and I know that Morgan is invading Crossroads, and that soon it will be empty."

"I want you well," he repeated, sounding almost like a small child demanding a better answer of a parent.

"Yes." BJ looked through the rain at the campus and at the wooded hills beyond. "Well, we don't always get what we want."

T·W·E·N·T·Y-F·O·U·R

FIELDS MET BJ in front of the cottage. She came out with tea for him, and they stood in the chilly air, sipping in silence.

Shadows passed over them quietly. After a momentary flash of fear, BJ realized that this couldn't be the Great; they would have made a sound of powerful wings and, anyway, they were long gone.

She squinted into the sun, then turned questioningly to Fields.

"Yes, BJ, it is the griffins, all but our friend. They go to find their mates. I gave them three roads to try." He sighed. "In a week, even if they have not returned, I will close all three."

"The sundancers, Rudy and Bambi's people, the griffins—it's strange, watching them all leave. Will anyone stay?"

"Stein. He says he has left one home in war, and will not again. I will stay also." Fields stared into BJ's eyes. "And you?"

BJ shrugged. "I have nowhere else I can go."

For some reason, the answer seemed to please him a great deal.

Gredya came out of the house, wearing a blouse of BJ's, which was tight on her, and khaki pants which no longer fit BJ and were loose on the Wyr woman. She walked awkwardly in the tennis shoes, which were padded with two socks each.

Fields looked at her. "Gredya is going with you?"

"The Wyr can smell their way along Strangeways. If you need to, close this road, and make another; she'll help me find my way back if I don't have the Book by then." BJ added, "And I think she could help me."

"Well, all right." Fields turned to Gredya, his automatic leer mixed with concern. "You must be careful. Have you ever seen a city? Thousands of people in one place?"

Gredya looked defiantly back at him. "No."

"Ah. Then I ask a hard thing, for a Wyr: Do everything that my BJ tells you to do. For your safety." When Gredya curled her lip, he added quickly, "For hers."

"I will do it." She turned to BJ. "We go."

The road was long but easy, soft earth over foothills which, as they left Crossroads, gave way to miles of virgin prairie. There was snow to either side for some of the journey, but the road was clearly marked.

Toward the end of the road the snow was gone and the prairie looked more and more like dead grass in a public park. BJ had been on a trip to Chicago before, just after high school, and was able to tell Fields where to put the end of the road.

The sudden rush of wind off Lake Michigan startled them both; the air was warmer than a land wind, but damp cold. She and Gredya emerged on a turnoff from a service drive at the Shedd Aquarium, off Lake Shore Drive downtown.

Gredya turned back toward the city, and her eyes went wide as she stared up at the buildings. "So big." The wind died for a moment, and she shivered as the barrage of downtown city noises hit her.

"Gredya," BJ said calmly, "I picked this path because it was the only place I knew in Chicago where you'd have time to adjust. We'll stay here until you're ready." She realized that she was using the soothing tone she adopted when examining spooked animals. Gredya didn't seem offended. "After that, we're going to ride in a car, that's like my truck, and go to the University of Chicago Library, a building with more books than you can imagine. More than I can, either," she added frankly.

Gredya didn't smile. "The books. They kill Morgan?"

"I'm not sure we can kill her. One of them will help us fight her."

Gredya, on the edge of trembling, nodded. "Then I am ready."

As BJ had expected, it was easy to get a cab near the aquarium. She said carefully and clearly, like an American in a foreign country, "University of Chicago, William Rainey Harper Memorial Library." She helped Gredya in and sat near her. At first Gredya was afraid, then she rolled the window down and sat with her head nearly out of it.

"That air smells," the driver complained.

Gredya turned toward him. "Yes," she said coldly. The driver shut up.

BJ had brought sixty dollars U.S. with her; she was surprised by how little the cab cost. They stared up at the campus buildings. BJ, who was used to the inexpensive and fairly recent fake-Gothic buildings of Western Vee University, was amazed and a bit daunted by the elaborately neo-Gothic buildings on the Chicago campus.

At Harper Library, BJ was momentarily afraid that they would need student or faculty ID's to get in, but they entered without being checked. BJ sighed. For her, that part was tougher than the cab ride.

Gredya stared at the alien-looking arched windows and at the shelves of books, all unreadable to her. "What do I do?" she asked simply.

"It's my turn." BJ walked to an online terminal and punched the subject heading: CROSSROADS.

After a long wait, long enough to discourage a casual searcher, seven titles flashed on the screen. BJ noted, with some pride, that Western Vee University had more publications on Crossroads than the University of Chicago did. The second entry was "Book of Strangeways, The." She pressed "2" and waited for five minutes. Gredya, beside her, grew restless.

Finally the screen renewed itself slowly and deliberately, line by line from the top down:

Author	Title	No. of Copies	Location
Unknown	The Book of Strangeways.	1	Main Library

LISTING BY AUTHOR: None
LISTING BY SUBJECT: Crossroads
LIBRARY OF CONGRESS NUMBER: PYZ 1993.7 STR Ref.
                          This is a completely unreal
                          number.

** DOES NOT CIRCULATE **

"Now we go?" Gredya said hopefully.

"Now we find the book."

The map section was well-lighted and well-marked, with the flat steel drawers for U.S. Geodetic Survey photographs and maps, the mounted star charts, and the usual bookshelves for octavos, quartos, and odd-size volumes. BJ found it confusing, as she did all libraries; she had never spent much time in them. She walked from shelf to shelf, checking the labels.

When she got to the section of books on legendary places— Eden, Hell, Avalon—she checked more carefully. She found Utopia, Atlantis, and King Solomon's Mines, but no *Book of Strangeways*. She checked the call number again, but it was, after all, not a standard number, and she wondered uneasily if other librarians might hide the book more thoroughly than Mrs. Sobell had at Western Vee.

After fifteen minutes, she shook her head. "I can't find it." She turned to Gredya, about to ask for help.

Gredya, head tilted back and nostrils flaring, ignored her. "Home."

"The smell of home? Find it, Gredya." In her excitement, BJ spoke as she would to a retriever.

Gredya walked from aisle to aisle, head tilted as though she were reading titles. A student worker with a reshelving cart rolled past and stared; Gredya's eyes were shut.

Gredya spun around and put her nose nearly against a row of books. "Behind." BJ reached behind the books and pulled out a copy of *The Book of Strangeways*, marbled end pages and all. She flipped through the parchment-thick pages and found the road to Chicago, no newer or older-looking than the other maps. She slid the book into her knapsack.

Gredya said again, "Now we go?"

"Now we find a fire door. Then we go one more place before returning. I'm sorry, Gredya; it's my last chance to see my brother."

The fire alarm at the door didn't upset Gredya; the elevated train to Chicago's north side terrified her. BJ sat with a hand on her arm, something Gredya would never submit to at other times, and told her that it was normal for the car to rumble back and forth. A man in his twenties, long hair pulled back and books on his lap, smiled across at them. He gestured at Gredya. "Foreign student?" he said to BJ.

"Very."

He put his arms behind his head and sat back. "I can always tell."

Gredya sighed loudly as they left the train. "We walk from here."

"We'll have to take the train back—"

"We walk," she said firmly. "I lead."

BJ thought of trying to force Gredya's obedience, but relented. "We walk. If we can." She checked the street signs and her handwritten directions to Peter's apartment.

The building was indistinguishable from twenty other concrete-and-brick apartments. BJ pressed the outside button opposite a card reading "P. Vaughan" and was unsurprised when the door lock buzzed open without anyone asking her name. Peter had always left doors unlocked and windows half-open. They climbed the stairs together, Gredya pausing at each landing to check the view from the windows as they went higher.

"I'll do most of the talking," BJ said outside her brother's door.

Gredya smirked. "More than I? Always." She stood back as BJ knocked.

The woman answering the door had short, straight black hair, mirror sunglasses, and garish lipstick; she looked like a fairly morbid art student.

She looked out at BJ without speaking, and BJ was suddenly convinced that she knew this woman and something was terribly wrong.

"Excuse me," BJ said, "My name is BJ Vaughan; I'm Peter's sister—"

BJ was thrown aside as Gredya, with a full-throated snarl, threw herself against the door.

The woman on the other side tried to slam it. BJ joined Gredya and rocketed into the door, springing it open.

They fell in as the dark-haired woman ran, not toward the phone, but into the kitchen, reaching for one of the drawers. BJ leapt up, but not as fast as Gredya, who dove forward snapping her teeth and growling. In her fury, she had completely forgotten she was in human form. The woman collapsed on the floor.

BJ opened the drawer and pulled the carving knife out. "Gredya, move back. It's all right."

Unwillingly, Gredya moved back. The woman with the dark hair, breathing hard, sat up on the kitchen floor and glared at BJ with pure hatred.

BJ said, "Hello, DeeDee."

At six-thirty, Peter Vaughan came in. He needed a haircut and his shirt needed ironing; it probably had in the morning when he'd left for work. He looked happy to be home, happier still when he saw BJ. "BeeGee!" He grabbed her and hugged her.

"This is great. When did you get in?" He nodded to Gredya, who ignored him. Then, following Gredya's baleful stare, he saw DeeDee in a chair, her wrists tied with an extension cord. "Dale. What happened? Are you okay? BJ, thank God you're here; you know medicine. This is Dale—"

"We've met," BJ said tiredly. "Clean your apartment, top to bottom. She'll have stashed morphine in it. Later she was going to turn you in to the police; possibly she was going to shoot you up with drugs first."

Peter protested, trailing off when he saw DeeDee's face. "Why?"

"Because that's what I did to her." Peter's foolish face infuriated BJ. "Look, she committed a crime in a place where she couldn't be tried for it. Among other things, she addicted this woman"—BJ pointed to Gredya—"to morphine."

Peter stared pointedly at Gredya's arms, which showed no needle tracks. Gredya shook her head. "No more." She turned back to DeeDee.

BJ continued. "I took her morphine back and planted it in her apartment—"

"And shot me up," DeeDee said bitterly.

"I wasn't the one who did that, but I would have."

"That's why I wanted to break your heart."

Peter was watching as though it were a tennis match with his heart being smashed back and forth over the net. Finally he said pleadingly, "Dale—"

"My real name is DeeDee."

"Did you do the things BJ says?"

She shrugged indifferently. "I didn't do anything wrong."

BJ's anger snapped. "Look, you killed several people—"

"People!" she spat.

"I said people, not humans."

Peter's eyebrows disappeared under his hair. BJ went on. "And you seriously addicted a number of others. You can't be punished here for that, and you know it."

Love makes people remarkably stupid, and Peter was remarkably stupid about love. "I can't believe that someone you think is such a terrible criminal would fall in love with me."

"Was he always this dumb?" DeeDee asked. Peter looked stricken.

BJ ignored her and spoke to Peter. "She wasn't in love with you, not ever. She didn't hate you, either. She was doing this to get back at me." She added mechanically, "I'm sorry."

Peter slumped in one of the chairs, rubbing his face. "What are you going to do now?"

"I'm taking her back to stand trial."

"To have me killed," DeeDee said.

"Probably."

"BeeGee, you work for the Government?" Peter said blankly.

"Sort of. But I didn't come here for that; I came to see you." And now the hard part. "Peter, I'm going to be out of touch for a while. A long while. I just wanted to say goodbye before I—left."

He nodded. It was easier than it should have been for them both. Their shared family history, with half of their mother's relatives having Huntington's chorea, meant that they had often seen family members fall out of touch, usually permanently. "You'll write?"

"Not for a while." She hugged him. "And when I come back, I hope you'll have found somebody better, okay?" To Gredya she said, "You'd better change."

Gredya, tactfully moving off the carpeting and onto the kitchen linoleum, stepped out of her clothes.

Peter rubbed his eyes tiredly, trying to adjust to all this. He said, still with his face in his hands, "By the way, your other friend there is very good-looking. What's her name?"

Gredya laughed, a sharp bark. BJ said tiredly, "Peter, give it up."

Gredya howled and dropped to all fours as her teeth fell out and her fingers dropped off. DeeDee watched indifferently. Peter swallowed, trying not to be sick.

They made a makeshift leash and collar for Gredya, who agreed only when BJ pointed out that there was no other way to walk DeeDee safely out of Chicago. BJ kissed Peter as she left. Gredya walked less than a foot behind DeeDee, growling softly and continually.

The walk from Chicago's north side back to Shedd Aquarium was the longest, most stressful hike of BJ's life; they passed four policemen and an animal control van. DeeDee, with the dual reminders of BJ's knife and Gredya's low growl, didn't try to speak to them. In fact, she didn't say a word to BJ, who was glad.

They arrived in the neighborhood of Shedd Aquarium in the dark; BJ had worried about being locked away from the road back until Gredya nudged her leg, herding her towards a path behind some shrubbery. BJ turned onto it unquestioningly, keeping a hand on DeeDee. They stopped in the brush and BJ, holding

The Book of Strangeways up to catch the glow from the city lights, checked the Chicago map and sighed with relief. Fields, accustomed to creating Strangeways, had laid down a second access to the road out.

Moments later, the glow of city lights in the sky faded and disappeared, and the long walk back to Crossroads began.

They arrived exhausted, in mid-morning the following day, to the field near Stein's. BJ wanted nothing more than to turn DeeDee over to Stein and Brandal and get some sleep; even Gredya looked weary, her tail sagging and her tongue hanging out.

They weren't far from the bridge over the Laetyen River. BJ turned, hearing the thunder of hooves from the road above it. She wondered what she would say to Polyta when she saw her.

The galloping grew louder, and suddenly Stein was running towards them, carrying weapons. BJ cried out in panic, and DeeDee laughed with delight; the galloping was not the Hippoi, but an orderly charge of riders on ponies. To the rear, each on larger horses, were Felaris and Morgan.

T·W·E·N·T·Y-F·I·V·E

DEEDEE'S END WAS simple and ironic; she snatched a sword away from the astonished Stein and charged into battle on Morgan's side, shouting incoherently. One of Morgan's mounted soldiers attacked her; DeeDee, who had never practiced with weapons to BJ's knowledge, leapt up and decapitated the soldier with her first stroke. She ran on into the ranks and spun around, pointing to Stein and to the ragged force now emerging from their noon meal at the inn.

Gredya, still in wolf form, attacked the cavalry, dodging swords and hooves. BJ lost sight of her quickly.

For an assault on a sophisticated culture, a midday attack was insulting; it should have been either a pre-dawn raid or a night ambush. Instead the attack was arrogantly simple and devastating.

A small party of Morgan's warriors led the first raiding party. Perched on mustang ponies of the type found wild up and down America after the arrival of the conquistadors, the raiders made no attempt to steal, conquer, or establish territory. They simply slashed at one and all with short swords, established a secure territory by drawing the ponies in a line to either side, and gave a blood-drenched salute and the loud, relieved victory cry of the winners.

The Meat People, twybils shakily in hand, cowered in their path. A rider slashed a sheep; a Meat Man dove desperately after it, cradling the blood-stained body in his hands until the invader slashed the Meat Man's short, squat neck in half.

Felaris, perched on a full-size horse, watched attentively from the rear of the raiding party. Fiona sat behind her, bound upright on the horse with *The Book of Strangeways* tied to her body. She looked numb and haggard.

The second wave, entering battle from between the line of ponies, was mixed: swordsmen, lamiae—snake people with a mock human body for bait—and horse-drawn supply wagons. The raiders clearly didn't need the extra supplies; BJ was unsure what the wagons were doing there at all. Morgan rode beside them, blowing commands on her horn. She pulled up to stand beside Felaris, but she was clearly impatient.

DeeDee, bloody sword before her, ran through the troops toward Morgan, who looked surprised and delighted. DeeDee cut one of the Meat People, then one of Morgan's own, only to get to Morgan.

DeeDee leapt at her, sword poised to kill. Morgan beat it aside with a single stroke that roused sparks, then reopened her arms. DeeDee leapt into Morgan's embrace. They stayed together for a moment, sisters or lovers.

DeeDee slid slowly to the ground. Morgan's sword, and her clothing from her chest to her knees, were drenched in arterial blood.

The lamiae, with their passively stupid simulacra of human torsos mounted on serpent bodies, coiled and uncoiled across the battlefield. BJ watched as one of them opened her mouth and kept on opening it, dislocating her jaw until her mouth was two feet wide. She ate the dead Meat Man end to end, ignoring the rest of the fight. Two of the other lamiae, observing her, slithered quickly over to the nearest corpses, ignoring the battle. Felaris was angry, Morgan appalled and strangely restless.

Morgan blew two rising calls. A detachment of swordsmen encircled the supply wagons, and a man and a woman dropped their swords and went to the backs of the wagons, pantomiming the unloading of supplies while they counted loudly with each load. Morgan looked more pleased after they were done, but she still seemed restless.

There was a sudden movement in the brush near Felaris. Stein, staring at the motion, said softly and fervently, "Don't do this."

Brandal leaped forward from the brush, swinging a battered, wretched sword. Felaris, startled, fell back, and Brandal swung the bound Fiona off the back of Felaris's horse. Felaris rushed forward again and cut *The Book of Strangeways* free, leaving Fiona in the dirt.

Brandal stepped forward again, standing between Fiona and Felaris.

Morgan stepped toward him unhesitatingly, swinging her blade forward in a terrible arc. It passed easily through Brandal's sword, snapping it in half without slowing down, and plunged on into his side and halfway across his abdomen before stopping. He stood staring at her, his hands down and face blank with surprise and hurt as she tugged her sword free.

BJ grabbed the twybil dropped by the devoured Meat Man and leapt at Morgan, holding the double-bladed tool like a Louisville Slugger she was choking up on to bunt. Morgan, spinning to face her, swept her sword down to parry the axe blade of the twybil.

BJ spun the blades perpendicular to her body, letting Morgan's sword fall past them. She swung the pole sideways quickly, blocking Morgan from raising her sword hand, turned the axe blade forward, and swung it into Morgan's chest with all her might. The axe blade thudded and stuck.

Morgan shuddered, but reached down with one hand to pull the blade free. "You don't listen," she said to BJ exasperatedly, as though coaching a pupil. "You don't learn." She rubbed her arms in her own blood, caressing her own wounded chest.

Then she was gone, sounding retreat. Felaris and the troops swept her up, and it was as though Morgan had never been in Crossroads, except for the wounded and the dead.

Stein, pacing back and forth with his sword, was more furious than BJ had ever seen him. "Easy," he said to himself bitterly. "She made it look easy."

"It was easy." BJ slumped on a rock and checked her watch. Ten minutes had passed. "But she didn't take anything this time. She already had the Book—What did she gain from this?"

"Experience." Stein gestured at the horses. "She trained a small cadre of cavalry, they made a test run deep into enemy territory, supply wagons and all. They proved that Morgan's army could come in unopposed and do what they wanted." He added bitterly, "Do you think it was a success?"

"Do you need to ask?" BJ gestured at the battlefield. "Hardly any excess blood, hardly any dead of theirs. This wasn't war; it was practically surgery."

Stein grunted. "Well, at least it may not satisfy her, then." He moved from place to place restlessly, checking the dead and directing the binding of wounds. "So, it was coincidence that Morgan came back just after you brought in DeeDee?"

BJ shook her head. "I can't believe that. I think she saw the new road in the book, where Fields let Gredya and me in, and she thought enough people would be distracted that it would be a good time to fight."

"A good time to fight . . ." Stein shook his head. "Bad for us, when she thinks ahead." He stopped in the field and said tightly, "Dr. Vaughan, come here, will you?"

He had been hidden by the body of one of Morgan's ponies. Brandal lay propped up against it, his shirt pulled up. Stein was washing the king's wound, but it was no use; blood welled from it in a pulse that grew fainter as they watched.

Brandal glanced at the shattered sword beside him and smiled up at BJ. "Glarundel, the Sword that was Useless. Now cheaper than ever."

BJ knelt silently to check his wound. Brandal waved her away. "Don't worry . . . Your red-haired friend—I saved her, didn't I?"

"You did, Highness." Stein was snapping his fingers for hemostats, bandages, more gauze, anything that would stop the life flowing out on the ground. BJ had no supplies with her at all. "She'll survive."

"Ah." Brandal leaned back further. "That's good, then." He was speaking in a whisper. "The only . . . real . . . bargain . . ."

Stein stood up, his face working like a small child's at a disappointment. "All that, and I couldn't even close his eyes."

BJ felt a nose in her hand, and looked down to see Gredya. The Wyr woman was scratched, but not seriously; a quick transformation would heal her.

"She won," BJ said. "Again. DeeDee is dead, but Morgan will be back." Gredya closed her eyes and padded tiredly away.

Fields said, "I need help here." He was cradling Fiona.

BJ knelt by her, amazed; hardship made people old immediately. Fiona was holding her wrists together; BJ gently lifted them from each other and stared at the narrow, blood-soaked line around them.

"Wire." Fiona was hoarse. "A running noose of silver wire on each wrist. If I fought back too much, I'd sever an artery." Her eyes were wide open, as if the aftermath of a battle had nothing to show her.

Stein was there, washing her wounds and offering bandages, trying with every move to do for her what he could not do for his king. "How bad is she?"

"Beaten severely," BJ said, looking at the welts on Fiona's legs. "Get me some blankets; she's in shock. Fiona?" She tapped Fiona's cheek softly.

Fiona shifted and focused on BJ. "She taught me a great deal," she said clearly and distinctly. "Not the charms themselves, but where to use them and how. She showed me where the foci of power were. She made suggestions about which spells I should try."

"That explains all the damage you caused." BJ felt along Fiona's leg for broken bones. Fiona cried out from time to time, but it seemed always to be from bruising. "Why did she keep you alive once she captured you?"

"Teaching." Fiona clenched her teeth and hissed through them as BJ rotated a damaged knee cap. "Map reading, battle history— she—asked for—classes all the time—couldn't lie—"

"You wouldn't have survived a lie," Stein said crisply. He hadn't spoken a word of forgiveness to Fiona, but seemed ready to treat her as a victim rather than as a guilty party. "Doctor, is there any permanent damage there?"

"Broken rib—" BJ pulled up Fiona's blood encrusted shirt. "Multiple bruises in the kidney region—this looks like a brand mark, with secondary infections in the burn sites—Fiona, what else did she do? What else did she do to you?"

"Oh, things," Fiona said vaguely, and turned her head to cry.

In the end it was Stein who wrapped Fiona and carried her off for treatment. BJ and Fields were left to carry the body of the dead king back to the inn.

Fields smiled fondly down at Brandal. "He was the best of them all, the greatest king Crossroads ever had."

BJ said, "I can't imagine another as good after him, either."

Fields looked at her in surprise, his ears twitching forward. "Don't you understand? There will never be another. Crossroads is ending."

BJ looked around a long time to find any evidence for denial. In the end she gave up and helped carry Brandal to the inn to prepare for burial.

T·W·E·N·T·Y·S·I·X

STEIN SAT WITH his hands on the table. "We need to move faster."

He, Fields, and BJ had taken Brandal's body to the cave of Harral the seer. Harral had watched in silence as they buried him next to the pool, and had then said two things, both chilling.

The first, to Stein, was, " 'King' is the wrong word. He was Crossroads' protector, and now he's gone."

The second, to BJ, was, "Brandal is not the sacrifice I mentioned earlier."

Now, Stein, BJ, and Fields were seated at a table in the inn.

Fields frowned. "I can only do so much, you know."

"I know," Stein said, "and I'm sorry." Determined though he was, Stein did look sorry. "But we have to get everyone out of Crossroads, and as fast as possible."

"All right." Fields sighed and sipped from the ale stein in front of him. "I can do the flowerbinders. I know a place for them."

"Is it safe?" BJ asked.

"What is safe? It's good country. I don't know who lives there. How do we get them there?"

"We lured the sundancers with mirrors. Maybe we can lure the flowerbinders with food, or—"

Fields and Stein said at once, "Fish."

Stein smiled, satisfied to have things moving fast. "I think I'll set out some nets tonight. BJ, have that pet of Stefan's ready to go in the morning; we'll test it with her. If it works, I think we can do this fast."

BJ bit her lip and agreed. She hadn't thought about giving up Daphni, even for the cat's own good. "One more thing," she said to Stein. "Can we take your copy of *The Book of Strangeways*? In case we need it, I mean."

"We're not going to need it," Stein protested. "Not while we have—"

He looked at Fields, struck by a new and unpleasant idea. Fields nodded. "Maybe something will happen to me. This was smart, BJ."

Stein stood up and pushed on a corner chimney stone; it rotated with a grating noise, and he reached behind it. "I hardly ever use it anyway. Keep it overnight, if you want." He passed BJ *The Book of Strangeways*, warm to the touch from the stones.

The warm feeling reminded BJ of something. "Why can't Morgan touch these books?"

Stein looked astonished. "Because she can't, that's all. It was part of exiling her. Look, don't ask me how it works; I'm just glad it worked. Some curse, I think."

Fields said, "A curse. That is why she needed your friend Fiona—"

"My friend," BJ said bitterly. "Well, she only needed Fiona until she could teach Felaris to read maps. How is Fiona?"

"Resting, in the Griffin's quarters. His Laurie is nursing them both." Fields shook his head. "I wish they both would leave."

"You wish we all would leave," Stein said.

Fields smiled ruefully. "Yes, I do."

BJ spent the night hugging Daphni too hard; the big cat, disgruntled, finally slept on the floor. In the morning BJ groomed her, hugged her again, and took her outdoors.

Stein was waiting with a basket of rosy fish, the size and shape of trout. "Try one." He passed it over. Fields watched anxiously.

BJ held the fish out, leaping backwards as Daphni lunged eagerly for it. "It'll work." BJ lifted her knapsack one-handed, holding the fish up.

Gredya came around the corner of the house. "You go? Where?"

"I'm coming back, Gredya." BJ held the fish out of the reach of Daphni, who mewed desperately and pawed at it. "We're going to move the flowerbinders to a safe world—"

Gredya said, "I will go."

BJ glanced nervously at the others. "Thanks, but I think we can manage."

"I will go," Gredya said firmly, and that was that.

"Don't argue with her," Fields said. "She knows what she wants. The Wyr are powerful when they want something. Have you seen one in heat?" He winked at BJ.

They walked back into the valley where the flowerbinders stayed, where the seer's cave was. BJ was glad that there was no need to go any farther than the lower edge of the pool.

Getting the flowerbinders to come along wasn't a problem; hiding the fish was. They held it on poles, and the big cats rubbed against them and purred like thunder, desperate for the fresh fish. BJ and Stein, struggling to keep the poles upright, staggered along the path out of the valley.

Fields, with Gredya, gestured quickly. "Up this way."

"The path doesn't go that way," BJ said, and could have kicked herself. She turned up the new path, which started by going uphill and quickly descended into a ravine which BJ had never seen in Crossroads. At the bottom of the ravine was a cobblestone road. Fields sighed as Stein and BJ lured the flowerbinders onto the road. "From now it is easy."

It was surprisingly easy from there; the mountains ahead of them seemed to get farther away, fainter and hazier. Finally they were no more than rugged hills, much like the ones they found themselves walking between. The rocks were interspersed with what an art history teacher of BJ's had called "broccoli trees," twisted bare trunks alternating with planes of foliage. A warm wind blew continually, under a deep blue sky.

The sun came out, and, as they progressed, beat down. Fields panted, sweat beading on his bare arms and shoulders under the overalls. Stein wiped his forehead frequently with a pocket handkerchief. BJ's jacket grew slick and her shirt developed dark stains under her arms; finally she took the jacket and shirt off, hiking the rest of the way in a T-shirt. Gredya, in a blouse and breeches, didn't acknowledge any change, nor did she offer to help with the poles.

BJ stopped twice and checked the flowerbinders for dehydration and exhaustion. They were doing fine, though they were uncomfortable on the road. BJ fed them each a few tidbits of fish.

Stein, panting, said, "This is good enough."

"No," BJ said. Stein looked at her coldly. "We have to find a water source. What if it's too dry for them here?"

"We're headed downhill," Fields said reasonably. "We'll find water at the bottom, I think."

Gredya sniffed the air. "There is water." She sniffed again and looked distrustful. "And people."

Stein, glancing at the cobblestones under his feet, looked unhappy and surreptitiously palmed his catchlet.

The water was visible at the bend in the road: a deep blue-green pond, fed by hillside springs in three directions. At the top of one of the hills, the source of the people was visible. The building was worn gray stone, in a style that had not been used for centuries. At one end was a campanile, with corroded bells. A high stone wall surrounded it.

To either side of the stone roadway leading up to it were vineyards, with muslin strung over ancient trellises. The vine trunks were as thick as human legs.

The campanile bells rang, and doves exploded from the tower in all directions, settling in the trellises on the slopes. The flowerbinders bounded happily into the vineyard, which rustled as they dove under the bunches of grapes. As more doves nestled on the trellises, the vines chirped invitingly at them.

Stein looked gloomily at the stone building. "We'd better check with the landlord before we leave them here."

BJ looked at the building curiously. "It looks like something from the Middle Ages. Maybe we can ask about it when Fields talks to them—"

Fields looked upset. "Oh no, BJ, you do the talking. When I am excited, I lose the sentencing, the words, all of it." He looked down at his hooves sadly. "I would have wanted my king Brandal to talk for us."

They walked carefully up the stone road, which seemed more like a long, flattened flight of stairs; every eight feet or so, the cobblestones were walled by a four-inch rounded curb.

"It's for walkers and carts," Stein grunted. "An old style for hill villages. Very old."

"But there's no village." BJ, at the gate of the building, touched the huge double doors in the stone wall. She pushed on the doors, but they didn't move. A rope hung from a bell, suspended in a niche high in the wall. She took it in hand and looked anxiously at the others before tugging it.

The bell rang five times before nodding to a standstill. By then they heard the bars of the door being lifted. Stein drew his catchlet, holding it hidden in his sleeve; BJ put her knapsack in her arms and held her catchlet under it.

The door swung inward, and a gaunt man looked out. His hair was cut in a tonsure, and he wore a homespun brown robe with a rope belt, and sandals with straps that wound up the legs. He looked at the three of them, at Fields the longest, and bowed slightly to BJ. "*Buon giorno, signorina*—"

BJ said tentatively, "English?"

The monk turned and called, "*Inglese!*"

The word was echoed, in various accents up the hill. A fat man with a bald head and a flowing white beard scurried out of the monastery, still tugging at his sandal straps. "*Aspett'*, Dominic!" he shouted.

While the gaunt man's head was turned, BJ hastily slid the catchlet in her backpack. She felt as though she had brought a grenade to church.

The fat man stumbled once over his sandals, and came forward rapidly. An ordinary house cat, a striped tabby, crossed his path; even in his haste, he paused to pet it.

BJ said to herself, "He looks like Father Christmas."

Dominic laughed and pointed. "Si! Si! Ecco, Babbo Natale!"

The fat monk smiled without embarrassment. "That's right, I'm Father Christmas. What do you want?"

For one wild moment, BJ considered all the worlds she had seen, and thought, *Well, why not*? She felt seven again, happy and innocent and eager to blurt out the one thing she wanted, more than anything.

Instead she took a slow breath and extended her hand. "I'm BJ Vaughan. I'm a veterinarian—an animal doctor."

He started to bow, corrected himself and shook her hand. "Doctor. This man is Dominic, and I am sorry not to be the real Father Christmas; I'm only Ranolf." He didn't ask the other's names, and they didn't volunteer them. Gredya, arrogantly aloof, hung back from the others.

"That's an old medieval English name."

"I am English."

A thought struck BJ. She tried to hide it.

Ranolf said, smiling, "What is troubling you?"

"Nothing." But something clearly was. "It's a personal question."

"Ask. I can always not answer."

BJ struggled, lost, and blurted out, "How old are you?"

"Sixty-two this next summer." His vanity won out. "How old did you think I was?"

She muttered, embarrassed, "Oh, seven or eight hundred years. Never mind."

His laughter, rolling and rich, made several heads pop up in the refectory. He blew his nose. "No, BJ, I'm just a normally old man with a funny name."

"I'm sorry. I saw the monastery, and the robes—"

"The monastery is the original building," he said quietly, with a certain pride, "and the robes are those of our order. We were established while Saint Francis still walked the earth."

Fields, BJ, and Stein looked at each other, and even Gredya looked startled. Stein said, "Excuse me for asking an odd question, but what exactly do you mean by 'walked the earth'? Which earth?"

"Come in," Ranolf said. Fields, entering, took off his cap. His horns showed plainly. Neither Dominic nor Ranolf showed any surprise. Fields hitched up his overalls to negotiate the steps; his hooves didn't bother them, either.

Ranolf took them past the refectory. "It's early for meals. I'll show you around, and in a few minutes you're welcome to eat."

"Is there enough for us?" Stein asked.

"There is always enough for guests first. Besides, we don't eat much; there are fewer than twenty of us here just now. I'm sorry that most of the other monks here can't speak to you."

"Ah." Stein smiled patronizingly. "Some kind of vow of silence?"

"No, but most of them don't speak English." He took them past the chapel. The walls had no murals, the corners no statuary. The chapel held benches and a simple crucifix.

In the corner was a font, and beside it lay a rudely carved bowl of olive wood, dark with age. Stein looked at it curiously. "Pardon my asking, but is that bowl somehow part of services?"

"It shouldn't be," Ranolf admitted guiltily, "but sometimes we touch it when we pray. We all do. That was Francis's bowl, that he ate from when he came here."

Stein looked cynical, Fields unreadable, Gredya disturbed. BJ asked, "How did he come here?"

Ranolf folded his arms over his belly as he took them back to the refectory. "There's a legend about that. You know, there's an old story that one of Saint Francis's miracles involved a pact with a wolf—"

Gredya gaped at him. "The promise," she said simply. "And the walk."

"Exactly," he said as though her demeanor were normal. "The wolf, who had been terrorizing a small town in Italy, agreed to go away when Francis asked it to. In addition, our legend says that Francis walked with the wolf when it left, to see that it was all right—"

"No wolf," Gredya said. "Wyr."

Ranolf stopped in his tracks. "You know that part of the story? Not many people do."

"It is old." She looked around the walls, as though she expected them to confirm it. "But the man? Just Francis. Not Saint Francis."

During the silence that followed, Ranolf opened the refectory door. "Well, he wasn't a saint then. The wolf took him here, and somehow Saint Francis—somehow Francis was able to find his way back to Italy. Perhaps the wolf showed him. But he saw this land, and thought it was beautiful—it looks like Italy, doesn't it?"

"I wouldn't know," Stein said, but Fields nodded vigorously.

"And he built part of the chapel with his own hands—before he founded the Franciscans, he spent part of his youth rebuilding chapels—and he brought some of his order here." Ranolf spread his hands as Dominic brought out trays of bread and soup. "And here we are. Please, eat."

After a polite interval of eating, Ranolf asked, "And what brought you here?"

The others turned to BJ. She choked on a bit of roll and drank from her wineglass. The wine was red and quite good, a little like Chianti. "We're looking for homes for a type of animal—"

"The large cats in the vineyard," he said calmly. "Brother Kurt saw them from the wall; he's very excited. He loves cats. Not that I hate them, you know." He paused. "When you say, 'looking for homes,' you don't mean as pets, do you? Because we're not supposed to have pets. We let Marthe and a few other cats live here, but they're not really pets. Not exactly."

He sounded uncomfortable; BJ was reminded of Stefan when, as a shepherd, he always found excuses to feed Daphni.

"All we want," BJ said carefully, "is for them to live in a safe place, where they can hide and hunt. They wouldn't need to be fed, or looked after in any other way." She added, not looking at the others, "Except in emergencies."

"That goes without saying. Of course we'll let them stay." He had a second thought. "They don't eat grapes, do they?"

Stein said, "No. And I don't think they'll eat your cats, either."

They listened to the flapping from the campanile as the bells tolled one of the devotional hours. "They will eat doves, though. Sorry."

Ranolf chuckled and scooped the striped tabby from under the table. "Marthe eats them, when she can catch them. Don't you, Marthe? That's all right. That's blameless nature."

" 'Blameless nature—' " Fields smiled. "I like you."

Stein put up the palms of his hands. "That's it, then. They'll be safe here."

Stein and Fields asked to see the wine cellar; Stein, at least, had a professional interest. Gredya and BJ walked outdoors with Ranolf, who showed them the vineyard. While they walked the dusty paths, BJ said, "I have another question."

"Personal, or odd?"

BJ said, "Odd, I assume." It had been bothering her since Ranolf had said he was only sixty-two. "Where do new monks come from?"

Ranolf sat on a stone bench and made room for her. At the moment, he reminded her a great deal of Fields. "That is something I've always wondered, even after I became a monk. Where do all the new monks come from? Why do they come?"

BJ shifted uncomfortably. It wasn't the question she had wanted to ask, but it seemed important to him.

"BJ, I was a teacher in my other life, and I was unhappy. I joined a religious order simply because it made me less unhappy. After several years, I had to decide whether or not I had a vocation to become a Franciscan."

His eyes were focused very far away, somewhere in the puffy clouds overhead, or across the rugged hills with their wind-blown trees. "Do you know why it's called a vocation? Because it is so vocal, inside you. It is a calling, a voice that never lets you rest until you become what you should be." He gestured at the quiet hills, their trees blowing in the seemingly endless wind. "Otherwise, who would come here?"

From behind the bench, Gredya said suddenly, "I would."

BJ, startled, looked at her. "Here?"

"I will stay."

Ranolf was troubled. "There is no sisterhood here. You know that you can't join our order."

Gredya curled her lip. "I would not. I am Wyr."

"Really?" Ranolf was delighted. "Then the Wyr exist. I had thought that part of the story of Francis was a legend."

BJ said faintly, "You'd be amazed how few things are legends." She had never much believed in Saint Francis, and she preferred not to think about miracles.

He beamed at them both. "I've always loved that story. It was a Wyr, of course; we have a very early manuscript showing the transformation. The church never approved of the Wyr, and by the early Renaissance the official version of Francis's taming a wolf was about a real wolf." He extended a hand to Gredya. "Of course you can stay by the monastery. We would never quarrel."

Gredya stood without taking his hand; he dropped it without taking offense. BJ turned to her. "Can we go for a walk?"

"Yes." She walked downhill almost at a trot; BJ followed.

BJ panted, "Gredya, I know that you're looking for a place safe from everyone, even from your own kind—"

Gredya stopped. "You know why?"

"I know exactly why. You're pregnant again."

Gredya said nothing.

"And you think this world is safer than Crossroads will be."

"Morgan will come. You will die," Gredya said matter-of-factly.

"Possibly," BJ said. "But what about your delivering alone? What if there's a problem?"

"No," Gredya said flatly. "Not before. I am always alone." She said it easily and without self-pity.

"But—all right. Will you be able to hunt here, and eat enough to have a healthy litter?"

"Yes," she said hesitantly. "There is game." Then she said, "BJ?"

BJ could not remember Gredya's sounding so uncertain before. "Ask me anything."

"Yes. The birth. Will I have—" She licked her lips, suddenly afraid. "Will they be—"

"They should be perfectly normal," BJ said firmly. "You were clean the entire gestation period, and I assume you've been eating well."

"Then I stay," Gredya said firmly.

"Let me show you something." BJ held Stein's copy of *The Book of Strangeways* out, showing the maps. Few of them had more than one road now; some pages were blank. She turned to the country they were in. It showed steep hills, swift streams, a major lake between two steep hills—and one road. "Once this road is sealed off, there's no way to go back, even for the Wyr."

Gredya looked into the wind, her eyes full of grief. "I would not go. Never back."

"What if there's nothing to hunt? What if the game is seasonal?"

Gredya glanced back toward the thick stone walls of the monastery. "They would feed me."

"They would. And the pups especially, or the babies." BJ stood. "If you're sure, then. I wanted to ask."

Gredya nodded. "You should. We are friends."

"We are." BJ wanted to kiss her goodbye, but knew she shouldn't.

At last Gredya said, "Goodbye." She turned and trotted down the slope alone, into the hills.

The others caught up with BJ. "We may as well go." Stein was jubilant. "That wasn't so hard, was it?"

BJ looked up the slope to where Daphni was hiding with the others; she looked at the pool below, where Gredya was headed. "Oh, I don't know about that."

The walk back to the inn was silent. The inn itself, when they arrived, was not; Stein flung the door open and flinched back as the music and the stomping feet struck his ears like a blow. He said, "Wait here," and plunged in grimly.

Moments later he plunged back out, stein in hand. "Get in here." They followed him.

All manner of people were dancing, waving steins of ale and cider, kissing and singing. BJ had to shout to be heard. "What's the occasion?"

Stein, grinning, shouted back. "It's B'Cu's party. He calls it *Matannga*. It's to celebrate getting out of jail or surviving witchcraft."

"Did we survive witchcraft?" But BJ felt the same way. This might be the last good party in Crossroads.

When she got a stein of ale, she raised it toward the fireplace and shouted, "B'Cu!" He nodded back, sharp-eyed and smiling.

BJ turned back to Stein. "If this crowd breaks out catchlets, they'll destroy the inn again."

"No catchlets tonight," Stein said. He rubbed his hands. "Let's see how much fun we can have."

The buffet took up one end of the inn; B'Cu must have been working on it from the moment they left. He had prepared a phenomenal amount of fresh meat. Even considering the present glut of dead sheep, this was a fantastic banquet. There were skewers of souvlakia, steaks with mint, stews, even Chris's *arni skordostoumbi.*

The Meat People were in heaven. Stein, on the other hand, was looking apprehensively toward the rear of the inn. "I hate to think what the cleanup from slaughtering all this was like." He stepped in to check. He returned from the kitchen delighted and mystified. "Nothing. He got rid of the entrails, the bones, everything."

Fields, listening, smiled. BJ thought that he looked sad about something.

The Meat People had assembled a band: carved wooden flutes, skin and wood drums, even a bladder-and-reed instrument like a primitive bagpipe. Dohnrr called it a fahnss.

Even Fiona came in and sat up for a while, having cider and listening to the music.

Stein took the fahnss in his lap and blew on it, his face turning bright red. He played it, or tried to, for five minutes, while the Meat People applauded and BJ laughed so hard it hurt.

After a hasty conference with the band, Stein taught Melina to tango. When he saw Fiona looking wistful, he bowed to her and they danced briefly, but she excused herself after a few minutes to lie down. BJ, grateful for a long-ago course in square dancing, did a reel with Stein, who also insisted on trying to polka—which started the entire place spinning and stamping again.

And for the first half of the evening it seemed as if B'Cu was everywhere—filling glasses, shouting to the band and waving his arms, giving out third and fourth helpings. There wasn't a soul in the inn that he didn't touch or shake hands with.

By late evening, BJ was exhausted. The Meat People had been teaching line dances for over an hour. She excused herself and sat down, noticing how much quieter people were getting; the party was dying down, like the fire in the hearth. BJ said to Stein, "Thank you. This was just what we all needed."

"Don't tell me, tell the host. B'Cu?" No one answered. "B'Cu!"

BJ opened the outside door. She heard, in the distance, a terrible growling and snarling, a pack fight. She ran back in, grabbed a catchlet and her coat, and ran out.

Stein followed, catchlet in one hand, torch in the other. "What? What is it?" He turned toward the noise. "Oh, no. Not B'Cu."

The two of them ran toward the noise. BJ stopped short as they found themselves standing at the end of a long bloody line of half-chewed sheep entrails, skin, bones.

The ground was torn up with hoofprints and with wolf tracks. Stein's face was grim. "Now we know where the scrap went."

He followed the bloody trail quickly. BJ came right behind him. The sound of the frenzied, fighting pack ahead grew louder as they got closer.

BJ grabbed Stein's arm. "Look behind you."

Stein glanced quickly back and stopped dead. The lights of the inn were no longer visible, and the landscape had changed.

Ahead, the sound died suddenly, as though the volume had been turned down. Fields came toward them, wiping the bloody line away. "Do not follow him."

BJ said, "He told us the truth, didn't he? It was a party to celebrate escaping witchcraft. Now he'll never see Morgan."

Stein looked at Fields as though he had been betrayed. "You knew. And he held a party so we'd be out of his way."

"Not entirely," BJ said. "I think he had the party so he wouldn't waste the meat." Stein looked at her in confusion. She went on, "The missing entrails, hides, and bones. He laid a trail for the Wyr to follow, and he used his sheep as bait."

Fields, looking subdued, said, "It was not a trick. He hopes you enjoyed the party."

Stein bent over, checking the tracks in the earth. "He took half his flock with him." He considered. "Stefan's flock—no, that's not fair; B'Cu earned half of it by watching the flock for Stefan." Stein looked up at Fields. "He took his sheep, alone, into a world with the Wyr? Why did he do it?"

"He knew from your talk that he would have to leave. He knew from the deaths that the Wyr needed food, and they should leave, too. He understands them," Fields said simply. "Nobody knows sheep-killers like a shepherd. He thinks he can live in a world with them."

BJ looked at the the blood in the dirt. "Will they kill him?"

Fields smiled. "A man who has herded animals in a land with lions is not afraid of wolves. And he said to say your world is safer without them."

"I wouldn't have wanted him to do this." Stein was edging slowly back into Crossroads as Fields moved them back, erasing the last signs of the bloody path. "And anyway, I should thank him."

"This was his thanks. He was restless, after Chris's death. He wanted to do something for you." Fields smiled, spreading his hands. "I think he did."

The lights of the inn appeared; Melina, wide-eyed, ran out the door. Stein caught her before she ran past them onto the remains of the trail; she leaned against Stein, who put an arm around her.

He stared into the darkness where B'Cu, the Wyr, and the world had disappeared.

Finally he shrugged and said vaguely, "Well, anyway, he throws a good party."

They went back to the inn to clean up.

T·W·E·N·T·Y-S·E·V·E·N

THE SUN WAS up but not high. Fields, BJ, and Melina were standing on the road by the Laetyen River, scanning the hillside. BJ peered into the underbrush, which already had small leaves again. "Are you sure this is where they'll be?"

"It's where they were yesterday." Fields looked around in disgust. "I fell over one, BJ, and it didn't run away. They will still be near."

They heard a rustle and spun around. The noise of voices brought a few dodos out from behind bushes, cocking their heads and staring around their ungainly beaks. The others, probably assuming the first few knew something they didn't, followed them, more or less, onto the roadway. Ambling unconcernedly, they walked to within inches of Fields, Melina, and BJ.

Melina had brought stale bread from Stein's. She crumbled it on the roadway, making hopeful clucking noises.

A few of the dodos came to the road, nudging the crusts rather than pecking at them. The others followed slowly, haphazardly. Some lost interest in the bread and nudged small rocks.

A voice down the road said dryly, "Breakfast before the big drive?"

Sugar, once again on Skywalker, flicked the reins; the horse ambled forward. There was a coil of rope on the saddle horn and a bedroll and saddlebags slung over the back of the saddle blanket. Sugar was wearing plain leather boots, instead of black rubber Tingleys, and a Stetson. BJ had the odd feeling that she was seeing the real Sugar for the first time.

"You ready to start?" he said to Fields.

Fields said, "I think so. BJ, are we ready?"

"I guess." She hadn't expected to be asked.

"Let's roll, then." Sugar swung Skywalker around until she was facing the northern end of the dodo flock. He raised his hat and waved it. "Yahh!"

Some of the birds watched him with interest. Most did not.

He shouted again, pulling back on the reins. Walker reared, pawed the air, and nearly came down on a dodo. It blinked, looking at the hoof marks in the dirt.

Sugar swung down in the saddle and smacked one of the birds with the coiled rope. It fell on its side, got up slowly and clumsily, and didn't bother moving away from him.

BJ knew it was going to be a problem for her, but didn't care. It was delightful to watch the great Dr. Sugar Dobbs being completely ineffectual.

Finally he said, "I guess I'm the wrong man for the job." He tipped his hat to BJ and Melina. "I'll just give Walker a run. Maybe I'll meet you down south."

He galloped off, slapping Walker with the coiled rope more for show than speed, and disappeared quickly to the south. Fields waited until Sugar was nearly out of sight, then laughed, long and loud.

When he finished, he wiped his eyes. "So, BJ, what do we do now?"

BJ looked at the unimpressed dodos, and at Melina and Fields. She picked up a stick from the side of the road, swatting the nearest dodo on the rump. It shuffled forward three feet.

She handed sticks to Fields and Melina, smiling. "Hit 'em up, move 'em out."

By the end of the first mile, she completely understood the sort of frustration that would cause a seventeenth-century sailor to whack a dodo up the side of the head with a stick. At some point, her entire body screamed for action, any action, that would provoke a response from the birds.

She went back to Melina. "How are we doing?"

"We lost three." She tried to look sad, but couldn't manage it. "They lay down, and other dodos, they just came along and sat down on their heads. And the ones lying down didn't struggle enough to move the sitting ones! BJ, I'm telling you, we will not make it this way."

BJ slumped beside her. "I know." Melina put an arm around

her. BJ laid her head on her shoulder, surprised that the faun's slender body was so strong.

They felt as much as heard the hooves, muted by soft earth just off the roadway. BJ looked to the south.

She had seen most of the female Hippoi together, and once before, briefly, she had seen many of them galloping to Stein's. She had never seen the entire tribe wheeling behind Polyta in a flying wedge, their few belongings in multicolored duffel bags slung over their backs.

Polyta leapt easily and gracefully into the roadway, her dark hair and tail flying in tandem. The milling dodos took no notice.

BJ stood hastily. "I greet you, Carron."

"I greet you, Doctor." But her bow was short, and she was trying hard not to laugh as she looked around at the birds. "Oh, BJ, why is it you always seem to find more difficulties than other people?"

All BJ said was, "How did you find us?"

"Sugar spoke to me." Polyta frowned, watching the birds waddle unconcernedly under the Hippoi hooves; the dodos were bright enough to seek shade but unaware they could be crushed. "He said you might need a little help."

"Perhaps a lot," Melina said. "Please—I know you should make arrangements with BJ, since she is in charge—" BJ, startled, realized that it was true despite Fields's presence—"but I have seen you carry loads, in poles across your backs, balanced to each side, and could you please do it now, if we tress the birds for you?"

"Truss," BJ corrected. "And that's what Sugar suggested too, isn't it?"

"He did, even though he hadn't seen us carry goods that way. BJ?" Polyta lowered her voice. "Can you tell me why Dr. Dobbs stares at the lower half of my body? Your friend David stared at my breasts; that I understand."

BJ smirked. "He loves horses." And I, she thought, will have fun with that if I ever see Sugar again.

She was distracted by a head of red hair, craning from within the tightly packed wedge of Hippoi. "Hemera." BJ ran between the centaurs. "Are you all right? Show me the incision."

Hemera, unembarrassed, opened her wool jacket, exposing her chest. The sutures were fine, and the two sides of the wound had healed together well. There was no sign of infection, no tearing, no pus or redness.

"She's well, BJ," Polyta said. "I am very glad you argued with me."

"I am very glad you consented," BJ said. She reached in her knapsack and pulled out a first-aid kit with a small sharp scissors. "Hemera, if you can bend down or one of your friends can hold me up, I would like to take those sutures out now."

"Bend down to her, Hemera." Polyta clapped her hands twice. "The rest of you, we need poles and we need to load these foolish birds on our backs." The Hippoi obediently ran onto the slopes. Hemera, bending down, smiled radiantly at BJ, who suddenly felt fairly radiant herself.

Cutting and trimming poles from a nearby tree stand took the Hippoi barely five minutes. Melina, BJ, and Fields spent the time knocking over the birds and trussing their kicking feet together, leaving six inches of rope free to tie to the pole.

The Hippoi, using small hatchets with blades on the back of the heads, cut notches in the poles at intervals, and slung the birds on. They took turns balancing each other's loads, ran a single girth with a hitch to the pole, and were ready.

Polyta said politely to Fields, "Will you ride?"

He bowed. "I would love to ride." He looked at her human torso hungrily.

Her smile twitched at one end. "Thank you. Cheiros, please carry him." A grinning, dark centaur man with a dappled appaloosa body came forward. Fields grinned unashamedly as the others laughed; he stepped from a high stone onto Cheiros's back.

Polyta turned to BJ. "You will ride me." It was not a request. BJ struggled onto her back, doing only slightly better than she had when she rode Hemera. The Hippoi watched silently and, BJ felt, disapprovingly.

Hemera offered a ride to Melina, eyeing the faun's hooves dubiously. "Be careful getting on." Melina put a hand on Hemera's back, sprang up, and vaulted astride her, the faun's hooves clearing Hemera's sides by half a foot. She clutched Hemera's sides with her knees, waved an imaginary hat in the air, and shouted in an outrageously bad imitation of Sugar's Western drawl, "Yippie-ki-yo!"

The Hippoi laughed. Polyta, smiling, tilted her head back and gave a loud, ululating cry that was part whinny and part like the calls BJ had heard Arab warlords make in movies. The others echoed it. Suddenly all of them were galloping down the road.

BJ said towards Polyta's ear, "You really won't let Fields ride you?"

She laughed. "It is an old joke between us. When Nesyos was

young, and more jealous, he made me promise never to let Fields ride me." She went on, laughing. "I argued and he foolishly cried, 'I forbid it!' We fought for three days until he apologized to me, and I promised anyway." She shook her dark hair in the wind.

A splash of water fell on BJ's lips and she tasted salt. "Oh, gods," Polyta said unsteadily, "when will I stop missing him?"

BJ held Polyta's waist tighter. "I don't want you to," she said frankly.

Polyta laughed softly, wiping her eyes. "Well, I don't either, but Sugarly's half-brother or sister will not understand, so I'd better stop soon."

BJ said blankly, "You're pregnant?" She felt Polyta's muscles stiffen.

"I did what I told all the Hippoi to do: foal and keep our people alive. I took a mate, named Laios. He is handsome, and dedicated, and very kind."

BJ felt like Lee Anne as she muttered, "And I bet you can tell him just what to do."

Polyta laughed out loud. "Yes. And Nesyos never would do a single thing anyone else suggested, would he?"

They galloped on together, recalling memories. When the present is difficult, the past makes it go by faster.

Shortly they were at the bay. Sunlight flashed through the clouds, making the sea water sparkle.

The Hippoi pulled up short in the swamp; they sank in the soft sand above their hooves. BJ and Melina ran from centaur to centaur, removing the poles without undoing the birds.

A familiar voice called to BJ, "Are these the birds you planned to give a new home?"

She turned to Brendan. He was still untroubled, still clear-eyed and innocent. BJ tried to imagine looking that way after the events of the past few months. "I'd like to put them on the island."

"You won't be needing them, then?"

BJ looked at Brendan carefully to be sure he wasn't joking. "Its not so much need as care for. I want to make sure that they're safe."

"Safe." Brendan looked sad. "That's a dream out of time."

"Probably," BJ said steadily. "But it's our dream, and we'd like you to help us."

Brendan laughed softly and kissed her on the forehead. His arms, as always, were damp. "Help you want is help you'll get."

Then he stuck two fingers in his mouth and whistled. The sea in front of BJ boiled. Calm, clear-eyed men and women who bore an astonishing resemblance to Brendan came out and walked toward the rapidly dissipating flock of dodos.

All of them had red or brown hair. All of them could smile and look sad at the same time. All of them looked balanced but awkward standing upright out of the water.

All of them had six-foot staffs, with five to ten leather thongs hanging from them. They held the staffs parallel to their bodies, like spears. "I got your message, darlin'," Brendan said. "From your parrot. Ugly bird, that."

"He needs the work," BJ said. She looked at the military force—for that was what it was—assembled in front of her. "And can you transport the dodos?"

"Anyone with patience could." He whistled again sharply. The selkies ran from the water with surprising speed and even more surprising balance, headed for the dodos. The fat birds squawked uneasily but did not run as the selkies tied their feet to the poles.

Brendan said heavily, "And now, although you won't consent to be my cow, glad I'd be for the honor of you riding my shoulder to the island."

Polyta looked absolutely appalled. BJ said, "Certainly," and stepped into the water.

Halfway to the island, Brendan said disgustedly, "Will you look at them." Around Brendan and BJ, a number of Brendan's people looked frustrated. The dodos, unattended, dragged their heads in the water, barely struggling as they drowned. The selkies held them higher out of the water, compensating for the birds' stupidity.

Brendan said, "Doctor, love?"

"Yes." BJ had originally resolved to do this evacuation with dignity, but had realized quickly that it was unlikely.

"Shouldn't we just let all these die, and see which ones make it? That way, only the best ones have children." Brendan looked at her hopefully. "Meaning to say, isn't it better to kill as many as you can, so that only the smart survive?"

BJ patted his shoulder. "My God, you really are Irish."

The first selkie struggled to the beach and, with a series of swift strokes, undid the leather thongs. The dodos thumped to the sand. After several minutes, they discovered they were untied and wandered around the shores of the island.

Brendan rubbed his head dubiously. "Are they really supposed to live, d'you think?"

"In my world they've been extinct for nearly three hundred years," BJ said. "They need the help."

"Ah. Well, there you've got what you might call a problem, Doctor. As you might guess, things here have been strange of late."

"Strange?" But BJ saw, as Brendan turned, a vivid pink-white line on his thigh, an entrance wound for something sharp. "Raiders."

"You might say. And we might say, we'll be glad to miss it. We've been everywhere and seen everything, and we miss it all."

"And you're leaving?"

"Taking Brendan's road, and that soon. Not my road, but the good monk's way through the open sea. Some roads never change, love." Brendan looked sad and glad at the same time. "Miss me when I'm gone, will you?"

"I'll try to." She put her arm around him as he lay down in the water to return to the shore. "Anyway, I'm glad I met you."

"Ah. And that must do." He tucked his arm around her.

BJ lay dozing in the waters as Brendan swam back to shore, singing of faithless women, cruel love, and broken hearts. He sounded happy. She kissed his cheek when she stood up, and waved to the selkies as they swam away.

Polyta looked at her strangely. "I spoke to a few of those people as they took the birds from us. Tell me, BJ, can you really understand people like this?"

"Not really." She thought, painfully and fleetingly, of Stefan. "But the more people I know, the more I want to understand them."

"That is good." Polyta was smiling at her, eyes moist. "And sometimes that is hard. BJ, my people are leaving now."

They were re-balancing their belongings, looking from one to the other and checking their loads. The men were doing their best to sound angry and purposeful, the women sensible and efficient.

Polyta led them back to the road they had just taken. A quarter mile back was a fork that BJ didn't remember.

"Kassandra," Polyta called out. The old woman's head snapped up. "If I don't arrive, you are Carron until Sugarly grows up. Can you do that?"

Kassandra nodded grimly. "Even if I don't want to."

"No one wants to," Polyta said gently. "Even my Nesyos never liked it, and he was very strong . . . Go, then, before we waste more time. Hemera, you take Sugarly's hand. Kassandra, be rude to all of them to make them behave; you're very good at that." She laughed, not convincingly. "Sugarly, are you going to say goodbye to me?"

Sugarly began to cry. It had been a long walk, and he was tired.

"Sugarly, that is no way to behave. Someday you will be Carron; you must learn some control." Polyta was doing her best to sound severe. "Take Hemera's hand, and go where she says. I will be with you later, perhaps," she said lightly. "Do you have a kiss for me, Sugarly? Can you give me a kiss?"

Sugarly turned his face away angrily, and wouldn't wave to her. The Hippoi galloped forward, flickering out of sight.

"Like his father," Polyta said, trying to keep her voice steady. "Do you know, when Nesyos lost his parents he sulked and wouldn't say goodbye?"

BJ stroked Polyta's horse back. "I've lost my parents." Polyta nodded, unable to speak.

BJ climbed on silently. Melina leapt on behind her. Fields, staying behind to close the Strangeway the Hippoi had taken, nodded to them and vanished down the road.

As Polyta galloped north, BJ leaned forward, holding Polyta's waist and pretending she didn't feel the centaur's sides shudder with sobs. The ride back, short though it was, seemed very long and lonely.

T·W·E·N·T·Y·-E·I·G·H·T

BJ ROSE EARLY the next morning, feeling better than she had in ages. She watched the sunrise and noted its position, straightened her cottage for half an hour, ate a quick breakfast, and walked out the door to the east. The Healing Sign was still covered from the other night; with so few species left in Crossroads, she no longer felt guilty about leaving it covered.

Fields was already in the bowl-shaped valley where the unicorns lived. He was examining the females, poking at them with a herdsman's fingers. "I should have left this to you," he said as BJ came down the path by the waterfall, "but I could not wait."

"Do they seem all right?"

"All of them." He looked troubled. "You are right, I am afraid; this one will have twins."

"When?" BJ dropped to her knees, checking the unicorn's abdomen. Her sides were bulging, but her teats had not yet swelled the way they do in so many mammals just before birthing.

"This spring, this summer. Maybe longer." He shook his head. "I had hoped you would birth them. They must do it themselves."

"Nonsense." She grinned at him. "There are plenty of vets where they're going." BJ was working at being cheerful; today would be hard for everyone.

Fields's ears twitched as a noise came from down the hill. BJ, who no longer went anywhere without her catchlet, reached for it as they walked to the lip of the valley and stared out of the tiny bowl downhill.

308

Sugar, on Skywalker, galloped up the trail by the stream. The unicorns' heads turned toward him, and he pulled back on the reins, pausing at the lip of the unicorn glade. "Were Polyta and her folks able to help?" He picked up the coil of rope hung over Walker's saddle horn and quickly tied a running noose in it.

BJ said, "They were perfect. Thanks for getting them." She added slyly, "Do you think it will go better today?"

"It had better," Stein said, emerging from the underbrush. "I heard about yesterday."

Fields was surprised and delighted. "How long have you been there?"

"Since a little after you came, a little before BJ. I wanted to see if I were rusty." He called uphill, "We're ready, Melina."

This time they all heard the rustle in the brush as Melina, hand-stitched pack on her back and a homemade duffel in hand, stepped into the clearing. She was wearing sweatpants and a sweatshirt from Western Vee, and she looked terribly uncomfortable.

"I'm ready," she said simply. She passed the duffel up to Sugar, who bound its strap on a cinch behind Walker's saddle horn. Sugar looked inquiringly at Fields and, to her surprise, BJ.

Fields said, "I think so." He pointed at a single unicorn, standing unostentatiously between Sugar and the herd. "BJ?"

She nodded. "We're ready."

Sugar let out an unexpected, loud, and completely happy whoop, spinning the lariat. Walker reared, pawing at the air with her front hooves. The rope settled over the unicorn's horn and slid easily down to his neck; the Nevada Ropers and Riders would have been proud.

Startled, the unicorn planted his hooves just before the rope went taut. He spun his head around, ducking and moving his horn in a circular motion. Sugar was careful to twitch the rope from side to side, always out of reach of the unicorn's horn. BJ and Sugar had seen that apparently round horn slice through a leather bridle effortlessly.

Sugar, never taking his eyes off the rope and the unicorn, looped the rope over the saddle horn and murmured to Fields, "You're sure this is the one?"

"I am sure."

"I'd hate to put an animal through this if it weren't the right one—"

"Sugar, I am sure." Fields was smiling, but he looked immensely sad. "Do what we must."

"Sure." Sugar took a deep breath, then settled back easily in the saddle as though nothing were bothering him. "Hey-ooooh!" He kicked his heels once, then relaxed his legs. Amateur riders stay tense all the time. Skywalker leapt forward; Sugar leaned easily to his right and snapped the rope as it came taut, dragging the unicorn forward.

It resisted momentarily, then trotted easily behind the horse, moving only as much as it required to keep the tautness off the rope. Sugar guided the rope carefully in one hand, keeping it away from the horn. Neither he nor the unicorn seemed especially anxious.

The other unicorns fell in line behind Sugar and the lead unicorn. The procession moved calmly along: Fields in front, with Melina beside him, Stein and BJ following, and Sugar leading a long, sedate line. Looking back over her shoulder, BJ could understand why the correct term, like flock for geese and pod for whales, was a serenity of unicorns.

They came to a stand of trees in the rolling hills to the north. Melina pointed. "This way," she said, and glanced at Fields for confirmation. They moved to the left; between two bushes, barely visible, was a narrow path.

Sugar clucked softly, guiding Skywalker onto it. The rope behind him went taut. He tugged on it, then turned in surprise as his horse stood stock-still, tugging vainly at the tension on it and struggling to go forward.

"They have always feared paths and roads," Fields said. "None of us knows why." He walked back and touched the unicorn, speaking softly to it.

Finally the unicorn surrendered and stepped forward. The rope went slack; Skywalker, relieved, paced onward. The other unicorns stepped onto the path unquestioningly. Fields walked beside them, keeping up seemingly without effort. The woods gave way to a winding path around a cliff, the cliff to brush, brush to grasslands. The grass twisted and became dry, and the dry grass interspersed with rock shelves.

Sugar halted as a man stepped from behind one of the rock ledges. He was wearing a Skoal T-shirt and an Indy 500 baseball cap, and his dark beard was nearly six inches long. He looked impassively at Sugar, but nodded respectfully to Fields. "Yessir."

Fields, puffing, came to a halt beside Sugar. It seemed to BJ that he was remembering to puff. He caught his breath quickly and said, "Mr. Grover, good day to you! You remember what we said?"

"Sure do, or I wouldn't be here." His speech was dry and gruff, but respectful. "I've got a place up the hill."

He gestured up the gravel road behind him.

"Is there room?" Fields said anxiously.

Grover waved an arm around the hills. "More than plenty."

Fields's next question was laced with worry. "And will they be happy?"

Grover's reply was surprisingly gentle. "I can't say as I'm sure, but we'll do all we can. I promise. Can you give us any help on that?"

Melina stepped from behind BJ. Grover's face split with a broad smile, and his eyes crinkled almost shut. "Hello there, little lady."

She nodded shyly. Grover took her duffel from Sugar.

Fields watched as the last of the unicorns moved onto the gravel roads of rural Virginia. "Take the rope off, Sugar."

"You sure?"

"I ask it, please."

Sugar quickly took the rope off the lead unicorn, who looked down at the rope, then slashed his horn sideways three times quickly. The rope fell into three pieces.

The unicorn came forward then and laid his horn across Skywalker's neck. He pulled back the horn, leaving the horse's neck unhurt, and regarded Sugar solemnly, then turned and walked up the empty road.

Sugar carefully felt the horse's neck, then said, "What was that about?"

Fields watched moodily as the unicorns gathered around their leader. "Who can tell? They are very spiritual animals. I think it is a parable, and they want us to know what we don't understand about them."

Melina took her duffel from Grover and stepped up beside the lead unicorn; they began walking together. Melina sang, in her soft clear voice, the song for Greece that Chris had taught her: "Ah, sweet *patrida*, when shall I see you again?"

The unicorns followed her. BJ noted that, where one had come and touched BJ when she was grieving, all of them came and touched Melina in turn, horns moving across her tenderly.

Fields watched them. "That is why they say those horns can heal."

Sugar said, "I wish they could. Stories say they could heal anything."

BJ said, "Anything? I don't think so."

Sugar looked at her sharply, and suddenly looked a little sick himself. BJ didn't meet his eye again before he rode back downhill to Kendrick.

Fields, Stein, and BJ walked back alone, Fields directing the others in erasing the last of the path. The unicorns had made little noise walking through the woods, but this time the walk seemed even quieter.

At the borders of Crossroads, Fields said goodbye to the others and trotted briskly into the hills. Stein turned to BJ. "Would you like some lunch?"

"That would be nice." They walked together, passing BJ's empty cottage, and went back to the quiet inn.

They didn't have lunch immediately; Stein's parrot was hopping back and forth on his perch, screeching. Stein asked, "What? What is it? Are you stir-crazy? What?"

The bird flew outside. They followed.

The firelovers were swirling under the midday sun, gathering from all parts of Crossroads in an elaborate spiral. Some were still glowing with the heat of distant fires; some were light pink, or the pale color of ashes. Stein shrugged and said to the parrot, who was squawking wildly, "It's spring. They leave. You've seen it before."

But the parrot was inconsolable. BJ watched the spiral tighten and coalesce like a hurricane with a well-formed eye, and speed its motion up as the last of the stragglers flew up.

Suddenly the tight circle of birds sang joyously, unstoppably, with a volume that echoed off the northern hills. It was like a choir of birds. BJ stood transfixed.

Then the circle broke into a smooth cone of birds, the point headed west.

Stein's parrot, squawking, rose and flew after them. Stein nodded. "Good luck." The parrot never wavered, beating its wings frantically to catch up with the flock.

They watched until the birds were an indistinguishable mass, the mass a dot on the horizon, then nothing.

A single dirty feather drifted down. Stein watched it. "Rude to the end. He could have said goodbye."

"What was his name?" BJ asked.

"I never gave him one. He showed up one day; I figured if I named him, I'd never be rid of him." They went in.

BJ stopped at the empty perch. "Welcome to Stein's," she said, in a soft imitation of the parrot. Her voice echoed off the walls and floors of the inn.

She sat at a table near the tiny fire left in the hearth. Stein went to the pantry and returned with cold chicken and fresh bread; he carefully and deliberately made her a sandwich, cutting it in half diagonally. BJ felt as though she were at her grandfather's, long ago when she was a child and before he got sick. She and Stein ate silently.

Over tea at the meal's end, Stein set his cup down. "Melina's room is empty now. You want to move in, it's there."

BJ said nothing.

"I just think it would be a good idea, that's all. There's no telling when Morgan's coming back. I don't think she'd attack here."

BJ said, "But what about my patients?"

"What patients? Who's left? Just in case, though, I'd help you move what you need down here. You could set up in—well, in one of the other rooms that isn't occupied. It's no trouble."

BJ thought of staying in her own cottage, with no Horvat and no Daphni. She also thought, with a chill, that she had threatened to kill Morgan, who knew her cottage quite well now. "All right," she told Stein.

He glanced at her empty cup and picked up the teapot, checking the leaves studiously. "That's that, then. More tea?" He stood, looking happier, and BJ realized that she was happier, too.

He hung the cast-iron kettle on its hook over the fire and walked to the door for a moment. BJ joined him.

The air was cold and dry; you could see a great distance in any direction. No life moved. Stein put a hand on BJ's shoulder. "Beautiful. When I was little, you know what my Fehter—my Uncle Isaac used to call America? *Goldeneh Medina*. The Golden Land."

He sighed as a spring breeze rippled the lightly greening hills. "In the south it's warm already. The rivers are high from melting snow runoff, but that will be done in a few weeks. Then there's seven months of mild weather; most of it you can sleep outdoors if you want."

He turned to BJ. "If I were invading, I would do it soon."

T·W·E·N·T·Y·N·I·N·E

THE GRIFFIN LAY beside the inn table. Stein sat on a low bench, so they could maintain some sort of eye contact. Fields sat on the floor, stroking the Griffin as if he were a large kitten. Laurie, frankly bored but unwilling to leave the Griffin alone, sat reading at a neighboring table. Fiona, ambulatory already but easily tired, lay sleeping in Chris's old room.

BJ sat beside Stein, feeling remarkably useless. Except for the Griffin, she had not seen an animal she could take on as a patient in days.

Polyta felt even worse, a leader with no people. She was staying within sight of Stein's, in case there was trouble, but she was withdrawn, avoiding all contact with the others.

Meanwhile the Griffin, a flying animal with broken wings, argued strategy with Stein, a commander with no army. Tempers were fraying.

Stein thumped the table. "It's hard, yes, but not impossible. A smaller force can defeat a larger through planning—"

"A larger, exceedingly well-trained force?" the Griffin drawled. "Morgan's been drilling some of her officers for two years. She has cavalry, swordsmen, lamiae, not that lamiae can be trained—"

"What about terrorism, and an underground?" Stein argued. "Granted, Crossroads isn't urban, and it's not a jungle either, but we could hide, reduce their numbers little by little—"

"Oh, brilliant. Fraught with all the hard-edged realism of dog stories for children."

Laurie, who hadn't appeared to be listening, snickered. Stein shot her a look and she subsided.

BJ broke in. "I know there's something wrong with this suggestion, since it's so obvious, but is there a reason I couldn't bring guns or grenades in? Assuming I could get them, of course."

"Why stop there?" the Griffin said dourly. "Some plastics, as you know, are charmingly explosive."

Fields said gently, "Once you bring guns in, you will not get guns out. I was very sorry when Dr. Dobbs and Lee Anne brought guns in, and grateful that they left. No, BJ; I don't want any more weapons than are here now."

Stein, chin in hand, said, "That is why Road Crews train with twybils as construction tools only. That is why training with catchlets is done only as a game."

The Griffin added, "We are fortunate that Morgan desires direct contact with blood too much to condone any long-range weapons at all. Otherwise, I'm sure we'd have been turned to weeping fragments long before now."

Laurie said, "That's it, look on the bright side."

He retorted, "With her, that is the bright side."

Fields chuckled and stroked the Griffin's fur. "I am sorry, but we have done everything Crossroads did before, to save itself from the *milites*. That is all we can do."

"But the *milites* didn't have a copy of *The Book of Strangeways*," Stein pointed out. "Sooner or later, they were bound to march down the wrong road and disappear; Morgan won't. Not ever."

"Did anyone ever defeat the *milites* back when they were the Romans?" BJ asked.

Stein frowned. "Eventually, of course. The army declined, they were fighting among themselves—"

"I mean at their best, in Germany. Did a smaller force ever beat them?"

Fields and Stein looked at each other and said in one breath, "Hermann."

"Hermann?" BJ said blankly. "Hermann the German?"

Fields sat down, his face showing hope for the first time in a long while. "Arminius, we called him. The Latin name for Hermann. The whole world knew how he killed an entire Roman legion. Rome sent an incredible force to capture him, and they did, but his defeat of Varus, that shook the world."

Stein was pacing, unable to sit down. "It's a classic example of ambush overpowering field tactics. Hermann knew which road the Romans had to take, to get into Teutoburg Forest. He waited at the narrowest point, where their marching line was strung out for miles, and fought them one-on-one, his way." He shook his head, sagging. "Wouldn't work for us, though. Nature gave him the perfect ambush point, and he knew in advance that his enemy, Varus, would take the road. It was the best way to go."

"But what if we know the best way to go?" BJ didn't know much about strategy, but she was sure of her idea. "What if there were a road Morgan couldn't resist?"

The two men looked at her.

"We know that Felaris watches *The Book of Strangeways* for her, or she wouldn't have caught DeeDee and me at the end of the road Fields had just made for us."

Stein said, "You've given this a lot of thought."

"I've been thinking about it all the time." BJ thought again of Horvat's death and Morgan's easy cruelty. "I wish I didn't."

Fields looked at her, troubled. "Think of saving lives, BJ."

Stein said crisply, "This will. BJ, you're suggesting that we create an invasion route so irresistible that Morgan will take it, and so treacherously designed that her army can be defeated on it."

Fields scratched his curly head. "Such a road, is that possible, both things at once?"

"Possible." The Griffin considered. "Tricky to design, but possible. A canyon, some bends, a clear ending to the road in the heart of Crossroads—tell me, sir, if we sketch it, could you find us those things?"

Fields chuckled, sounding almost happy. "Easily."

"I can help." They turned toward the voice. Fiona, pale but determined, was supporting herself with the back of a chair. "I know a way to string Morgan's army out even farther than the landscape will."

BJ nodded suddenly. "That's right. She does. The Stumbling Curse."

"And a way to make it slow down an army, if you'll cooperate." Fiona's voice was soft and husky; her throat had sustained damage in Morgan's camp. "I want this to work."

"Wait," Stein said. "Even if we were to defeat her, even if we take away her copy of *The Book of Strangeways*, there is still the problem of what to do with her. I know of nothing that can kill her. . . ." He trailed off, looking at Fields's face.

He was looking sadly at BJ. "Oh, little BJ. You have been thinking of that, too, haven't you?"

She flushed. "If I were Polyta, you would say I was right to."

"I did not say you were wrong to," he responded mildly. "But I wish you did not have to."

"I wish you'd tell me *how* to," the Griffin said, absently scratching one of the old scars on his belly. "I've failed spectacularly at it myself, and am open to suggestions."

BJ told them. It was simple, and easy of execution, and completely untestable.

Stein nodded when she finished. "Of course, if you're wrong, we still have a problem. Do you have everything we need?"

"I need to go back to Western Vee for their copy of *The Book of Strangeways*. Can you open a road briefly?"

Stein shook his head. "A path, not a road. And it can't stay open long enough for you to go in and out; if Morgan is watching the book, that's too dangerous."

"All right." BJ was thinking as fast as she could. "Fields makes a path for me to go in on. He erases it. Half an hour later, he makes a different path back, and goes in, waiting at the end to erase it when I go in."

Fields frowned. "How will you find your way alone?"

"I'll have a copy of the Book."

"Or you'll be trapped outside," the Griffin murmured. "If I were you, I might find it tempting to go and live happily ever after in my own country."

Laurie said delicately, "I don't believe that's an option for BJ." BJ looked at her sharply. She hadn't realized that Laurie knew about the Huntington's chorea.

Laurie added, "By the way, she won't be going out alone. I'm leaving." The Griffin looked up at her. "Don't be shocked; I'm taking you with me."

"Unacceptable. Completely, absolutely unacceptable."

Stein burst out, "And what will you do if you stay here? Mangled, torn, broken like you are—you're useless. You need to heal, and you need the best medical treatment available for that."

Laurie said, "Let's hear a little school spirit, BJ."

The Griffin opened his beak stubbornly to object. Fields tapped it with one finger. "There is more. If Morgan takes Crossroads, she will go elsewhere. I think she knows BJ's world quite well."

"I know she does," BJ said.

"I do not think she could get there without my help, but I do not wish other worlds destroyed, too, if we fail here." Fields stared solemnly into the Griffin's eyes. "Go, my friend, and heal. Guard those you love, and a world that gave birth to so many of us still left here. If needful and if I can, after the battle I will come for you, and you will have your own war with Morgan."

The Griffin dropped his eyes. "I have failed my king and my world," he said huskily.

"You were our first, best defense," Stein said. "If we fail here, you may be our last." He stood, looking like a commander and not an innkeeper; he saluted the Griffin. "Go."

The Griffin stood shakily. "Dr. Vaughan, is there a chance you could drive me to the edge of the path? This is going to be a fairly demanding trip."

Stein shook his head, smiling fondly. "And you wanted to stay for the battle."

Two hours later, shortly after dark, BJ was staring at the lights of the campus from the Western Vee University agricultural station, where Sugar kept Skywalker. She turned to Fields. "How long do I have?"

"This path is leaving now, BJ. Take less than an hour. I'll walk these two closer to the vet school—"

"You'll do no such thing," the Griffin said faintly but firmly. "I will go into an outbuilding on this farm, and Laurie will call Sugar Dobbs to come with a truck. Go, and do what you have to."

Fields smiled at him as affectionately as if he were a kitten and turned back into the underbrush, disappearing quickly. The Griffin turned to BJ. "You go too, my dear." He raised a talon, with a great effort, and held it out to her. "You have been a pleasure and honor to know. Go, and Godspeed."

He shuffled into a corrugated shed. BJ ran towards the campus.

The library was open but nearly empty; it was a Sunday in the very first week of a new term. BJ stared out a window at the campus, trying to remember how important all these classes and calendars had been to her seven years ago.

She stood at the reference desk. "I'm sorry, Mrs. Sobell. I'll need your copy of that book after all."

The librarian smiled blandly up at her. "I thought you might, dear. Could you excuse me for a moment?" BJ waited impatiently for her to return.

When Mrs. Sobell came back, BJ said apologetically, "I'm on a fairly tight schedule, I'm afraid."

"In that case, we'll take the elevator."

They went, not to the map department, but to a display case on the fifth floor. The subject of the display was bookbinding through the ages, and it looked remarkably unexciting.

Mrs. Sobell unlocked the case and lifted *The Book of Strangeways* from between an ornately tooled dictionary and a steel-jacketed copy of the New Testament from World War I. "Everyone thought I was terribly eccentric, insisting on that exhibit. Actually, it was fun, designing a display so boring you could hide a book in the middle of it."

They took the elevator back down. Before the door opened on the first floor, Mrs. Sobell put a hand on BJ's arm. "You'll have to forgive me, BJ."

"For what?" In the past year, BJ had seen a remarkable amount of deception and betrayal; her nerves were on edge.

Mrs. Sobell said calmly, "I made two other calls when you told me what you wanted, BJ. I owed it to a library patron who frequently used the book."

The elevator door opened. BJ stepped forward, directly into Stefan's arms.

When he released her, he said simply, "I thought I would never see you again."

She nodded, longing to say more but not sure it would do either of them any good. She held up the book. "I have to take this back now."

"You will take one more thing besides the book, BJ." He smiled, but he was regretful. "I have taken a leave of absence for spring term. There was a death in my family. I will go back with you."

"What about college? What about being a vet?"

"Those things must wait." Stefan tilted his fedora at an angle, studying his reflection in the library windows. "When I come back, I will be a better student maybe."

"Stefan, you have straight A's so far."

He burst out, "Yes, but such work! I am up reading in the middle of the night, I take longer than any of my friends in the dormitory—I need to work on my English and my reading skills." He finished seriously. "Perhaps between battles, Stein can help me, if he's not too busy." He looked at her. "You're laughing?"

BJ was trying not to. She hugged him. "I'm just happy I'll be with you."

Mrs. Sobell beamed.

There was one more surprise in store for BJ, though she should have guessed; Estevan Protera was waiting in the library lobby. He was out of breath, but leaned on his cane as easily as if he had been relaxing there for hours. "Mrs. Sobell called me. I did want to see you off," he said to Stefan. "You are certain you wish to go?"

"Of course." Stefan looked with frank envy at the cane. "I will be back in the fall if things go well."

"As I'm sure they will." Protera reached behind the chairs in the lobby and passed Stefan a beautiful dark wooden cane with a brass ring encircling it just below the handle. "You said you wanted one."

Stefan's eyes shone. "It is so very beautiful." He took it by the handle, spun it on his arm, sighted down it like a pool cue, and bounced it off the floor, spinning and catching it like Fred Astaire. "It is perfect. Thank you." He fumbled in his pockets.

Protera waved his hand. "A parting gift, for luck. I enjoyed tutoring you." He looked worried. "Please be safe, and remember all that I taught you."

Stefan smiled, his white teeth flashing. "You will see, Doctor, when I come back. I promise."

Protera and Stefan bowed to each other. BJ reflected that they both had a certain style in common.

As Stefan strolled down the front steps, fedora tilted and cane on his arm, a passing freshman girl stared at him as though her soul were coming awake in front of him. BJ was suddenly glad, for a secondary reason, that Stefan was leaving for Crossroads during the spring.

BJ checked the book quickly. Fields had made a new path to Western Vee, directly from the grove of trees at the edge of campus. She and Stefan sprinted there, hand in hand like dancing lovers in one of the musicals Stefan loved so much. They ran onto the path as fast as they could while BJ read the twists and turns in the dark, and they fell down, breathless and laughing, in the hills above Stein's. Fields embraced Stefan and, nearly as lovingly, BJ. He turned away from them and closed the path, moving rapidly, and left them.

BJ and Stefan were still walking down to Stein's when BJ checked the book again, turning to the page that showed Anavalon. She felt a chill. Slowly and faintly, a tortuous, narrow road was snaking from the desert country directly into the heart of Crossroads. Morgan's route of attack was nearly ready. It had been prepared by Fields, designed by Stein and the Griffin—and suggested by BJ herself.

She hoped fervently that she was right.

T·H·I·R·T·Y

THEY SET OUT before dawn, taking the road Fields had created the night before. Before his departure, the Griffin had argued for making it just before they needed it, but Stein pointed out that Morgan would need time to organize an attack after finding the road. "Besides," he said, wincing, "she already knows she doesn't need to attack at night. Why give us somewhere to hide?"

They made an odd and small procession, the last inhabitants of Crossroads. Fields walked first, marking the path in the dirt. The few remaining Meat People followed him, brushing rock and debris aside and making a clear pathway.

Stein, as commander, led the armed contingent. Behind him came Polyta, the exhausted and barely mobile Fiona on her back, a small contingent of the Meat People, and BJ and Stefan side-by-side.

That was it. Everyone else was injured, dead, or gone from Crossroads.

"I wish we could see the grasslands," BJ said. "It must look nice now."

"It is beautiful in the spring," Stefan said. He had insisted on wearing the fedora and bringing his new cane. He pointed with the cane, its circlet of brass shining in the morning sun. "I used to graze my sheep there, in the winters when it was warmer here than in the north. I would sit and read while they slept in the sun. I wanted to be a veterinarian even then," he said without regret.

BJ took his arm; they walked like a couple returning down the aisle from their wedding. BJ surreptitiously checked her knapsack half a dozen times before he caught her and smiled.

BJ looked nervously at the catchlet Stefan wore at his belt. H
had seldom been to Stein's for practice; only his dancer's balanc
and agility qualified him for the fight ahead. "Remember," sh
said, "you're supposed to make her angry. Don't let her mak
you angry."

He looked away. "Love my own, she already has."

It grew warmer and dryer; the sides of the canyon they walke
through rose higher, and the road grew narrower until it was
trail. As they rounded a corner, the air barely rippled in the dust
but BJ looked behind her and licked her lips; Crossroads wa
gone, and a world of desert lay around them.

"Are you sure she'll come?" she whispered when Stein cam
back to check on them.

"Of course," Stein said easily. He was still the man who ra
Stein's, but something new had been added; he was terribly sur
of himself, calm and obsessed at the same time. "Anyone wh
studied any strategy would take this road. A short supply route
easy travel, no obvious defenses once they're inside Crossroads—
let me tell you, it's an invitation to victory."

"What if we don't win?"

"Then it's an open invitation." He turned to the others. "Thi
is the place. Fields is checking the rest of the road; he'll be back
Climb the left slope and meet at the top of this gooseneck; we'l
pile rocks and wait."

Stefan climbed up easily, offering as much help to BJ as she
would let him. The Meat People turned out to be terrible climbers
they skidded down, caught themselves by hooking twybils in rock
fissures, and laughed self-consciously about their own failings.
Polyta trotted steadily up, Fiona clinging weakly to her.

Fields met them at the top. "You are all here," he said, looking
fondly at them. "Good. I thought it might be hard"—he glanced a
the Meat People quickly—"but you did well. Whatever happens,
I thank you for the brave things you have done—"

"And are going to do, right?" Stein put a hand on Fields's
shoulder and said apologetically, "There isn't much time." He
pointed to the south; a cloud of dust was rising from one of the
pretzel bends in the canyon.

Fields sighed and stepped back as Stein said, "All right. You
know what we do: Cut Morgan off from most of her army, kill
the ones with her, and then Stefan does his part." He frowned.
"You'll remember, won't you, that if she drops her guard, it's
for the same reason that we opened a road, that she's making

you attack where she wants you to?"

Stefan nodded absently; Stein looked suspicious, but went on. "After this young man has made her angry enough to be careless, then we come in again, and then BJ does her part—which we all hope works." He smiled meaninglessly. "Questions? Good. And now, Fiona is going to teach us something, we hope."

Fiona slid off Polyta, who reached an arm back and steadied her. "Please listen carefully," she said huskily. Hearing Fiona's voice now made BJ's throat hurt. "I can't shout, and you need to get every word right. I will tell you the last word first, and want you to say it now: Çélëä!" She pointed down at an imaginary enemy.

They all said it, even the Meat People. Fiona limped over to them and made them say it hundreds of times until, fangs or no, they did well. "All right," she said finally. "Now, repeat after me, moving your arms as I move mine. Don't worry about the sense of the words, and do *not* say 'Çélëä again until I do. Is that clear?"

Fiona, BJ realized, would make a good teacher. She walked them through all ten minutes of the Stumbling Curse carefully and clearly, all but the last word.

She held up a hand for silence. They waited mutely to say the last word.

Silently the Meat People levered boulders in place, dug out rock with the twybils, and prepared a large, barely balanced cairn at the top of the gooseneck. They lay down, peering over the edge without showing silhouettes against the sky.

The road was as barren and dry as though Morgan had already won; the dust kept Morgan's troops from seeing very far. She'd had the foresight to put the ponies in the back for the march, since they kicked up the most dust.

The twists and turns through the canyon had separated her troops into small blocks; the narrow passage forced them into single file. Morgan, glancing back, shouted curtly, "Felaris!"

Felaris, looking even more threatening with a fist-axe in hand, strode back and forth among the company, shouting orders, then hurried back as Morgan rounded the narrowest part of the trail, moving to the north side of the gooseneck. Felaris checked *The Book of Strangeways*, scanning ahead for landmarks.

Fiona, pale but determined, pointed to the portion of the army still on the southern side of the gooseneck, and she said sharply, "Çélëä!"

The soldiers stumbled and, well-disciplined, rose again.

BJ pointed and cried, "Çélëå!" half afraid that it wouldn't work. The rising soldiers fell into the dust again and rose, fallen farther back from the front force.

Stein shouted, "Çélëå!" Stefan shouted it. Each of the others in turn shouted. The rear three-quarters of Morgan's army fell thirty yards behind the front column.

"The rocks," Stein said calmly. The Meat People tugged on the twybils, sending rocks and boulders cascading down in front of the lagging army. Their column officer called for a halt, and they froze in place until the rock-slide ended.

Stein turned to Fields. "Now."

Fields smiled, threw a mock salute, and hugged Stein quickly. Then he was gone, his nimble goat-feet dropping him down the slope to the near side of the dust-cloud over the rocks. The Meat People leapt to either side of him, prying up the road bed with frenzied digging.

Stein said, "The rest of you—" There was no point. Polyta, eyes grim, had already charged onto the northern slope, her horse body angled and skidding down, bearing down on the rear of Morgan's troops. "Let's back her up."

A barrel-chested man raised an axe to point at her and shouted. Felaris turned and barked an order; the nearest six soldiers raised their weapons and formed a semicircle at the point where Polyta would reach the canyon floor.

Six feet from the slope's end, Polyta leapt, passing just over their heads. She kicked down with a rear leg, crushing a man's skull. She landed, kicking again; another soldier fell back, his chest punched in over his heart. She turned and reared, lashing out with first one hoof and then another. One man flew backward, a red dent in his forehead; the other dropped to his knees, clutching in both hands the ruins of his face.

Polyta, uncut, disarmed one of the remaining men with a kick that looked like an uppercut. She picked the struggling man up with her powerful arms, raised him over her head, and threw him on the last man's sword, hard enough to knock the last man down. She trampled them both, shouting something in her own language.

BJ, descending as quickly as she could, watched with a chill, knowing that for the first time she was truly seeing the Carron.

A scrawny, angry-looking young man turned and fled back down the road. BJ saw him and turned to follow; Stein caught her eye and shook his head. There was no way to warn Fields, no way to help but to win the battle. She gritted her teeth and leapt into the road. Felaris opened her mouth again, but BJ attacked her before she could move.

Felaris used the fist-axe to block BJ's thrust, and swung the axe in a wide arc, striking sparks on the canyon wall behind BJ's head. BJ rolled to one side and, with no pretense at form, chopped at Felaris's knee. Felaris drew her leg back and poised the axe to split BJ's skull, then paused, looking confusedly at her other knee. BJ's first chop had been a feint, to make the big woman shift her weight.

The Griffin would have been proud, BJ thought regretfully, as Felaris toppled. BJ stabbed her on the way down, and grabbed *The Book of Strangeways*, stuffing it quickly in her knapsack. As Felaris fell, Morgan blew three quick blasts on her horn. When there was no response, she glanced back over her shoulder, startled, at the road behind her.

All her troops were dead. Polyta was trampling back and forth over them; Stein, watching her, was cleaning his blade as though the battle were over.

Stefan, apparently a latecomer, slid down the canyon wall near her; she swiped murderously at him. Agile though he was, he barely leapt out of reach in time, his cane knocking against the rocks. He held the catchlet clumsily. BJ bit her lips, watching.

Morgan smiled narrowly at him and raised her sword point to eye level. "Blades can only hurt, not kill. Fight me."

Stefan stood in front of Morgan, catchlet in his right hand, cane in his left. He took off his hat, bowed mockingly, and, to BJ's horror, threw the catchlet aside.

Morgan looked at him, then at BJ's expression. She laughed aloud and pulled her hair back from her face as though she were about to give a kiss. "Oh, this will be wonderful." She moved forward, sword ready.

Stefan grabbed the top of the cane in his right hand and cross-drew the sword inside. He offered her the briefest of salutes, tipped his hat, and said, with edgy bitterness, "Would you like to dance?"

BJ realized, belatedly, what he had been studying with Protera. Morgan swung; he leapt, completely over her arm, and swung his own sword downward, cutting her cheek. Morgan lifted her blade, but he was on one hoof, spinning out of reach and coming around each time with a successful parry.

He did a swift clockwise disengage and scratched her other cheek, then dropped to the dirt and did a backward somersault out of range, landing on his feet with his weapon forward as she charged. He was doing a magnificent job of making her angry. Only BJ saw the problem: He was angry, too, taking revenge for the humiliation of having been an addict and an easy slave.

Suddenly Stefan went on the offensive, slashing at her without ever leaving his guard down, making a riposte after a parry, spinning his blade clockwise in a disengage and stabbing at Morgan, cutting at Morgan, twice slicing inches off her hair. Even Stein stared in admiration. Stefan pushed forward relentlessly, forcing her backwards until she was in an open space well away from the canyon walls.

Morgan's guard dropped, exactly as Stein had predicted it would. Stefan saw it, too; BJ gasped, her chest tight, as Stefan lunged into the hole created by the drop, lunging too far and too slowly. He was stretched out full length, off balance with the effort to reach Morgan. If she parried and stepped forward, his entire chest would be open and undefended.

With a triumphant cry, Morgan smashed her sword down on the cane sword—

Which was no longer there. Stefan spun it down, then up in a double-disengage which finished with his blade holding hers down. He stepped forward, his face cold and set, and put all his strength into one left-handed, swinging, backhand slap of her face.

Stein said sharply, "This is not a duel." Stefan moved back and adjusted his fedora; during the entire fight he had never lost it. Morgan, startled, turned to Stein, then nodded. Her cheek was bright red, and she was furious.

They circled her warily. Completely unafraid, she waited, guarding each of them in turn. She turned to BJ and said again, "Fight me!" BJ locked eyes with her, giving Stein time to leap in with his upraised sword.

At the moment of stabbing her, he apparently stumbled. The short sword plunged harmlessly through her cloak, pinning it to the earth but missing her body completely.

Weaponless, he rolled desperately out of range of her arms as she slashed at him on the ground. He rolled quickly sideways, scrabbling desperately at the rock but somehow staying ahead of her as she turned. Again and again she swung at him, only to strike the bare rock of the roadway.

Suddenly she was striking in shadow. She looked up quickly; BJ was facing her, holding nothing but a knapsack.

Morgan tried to lunge forward, and discovered that her right arm was tangled; Stein, by rolling, had teased her half inside her own pinned cloak. Stein leapt to his feet and drew another catchlet; he stabbed at Morgan's side, again catching only the cloak. He sped around her, dragging the cloak with him, and lunged again.

This time he pinned one edge of her cloak over another, trapping her arms inside it. He thrust the end of the sword into her ribs, twisting under and up in what would have been a death stroke on anyone else.

Blood pooled at her feet. She snarled at him and thrashed back and forth, trying to free her arms.

In his final move, he took his last catchlet and stabbed the other end of her cloak firmly to the ground. She was bound upright, bleeding but unable to die, glaring defiantly at them.

"When I heal," she said venomously, "I'll take my time with all of you."

But BJ shook her head. "Not this time." She opened the knapsack as she came forward. "Not anymore."

She handed Stein his own copy of *The Book of Strangeways*. She handed Stefan the University of Chicago copy. She kept the Western Vee copy and Felaris's copy for herself, and handed each of the others a pair of padded gloves.

Morgan stared. "Armor?" she said dazedly, and for the first time in many ages, she seemed afraid.

"Insulated gloves," BJ said. "Useful for treating firelovers and chimerae." She held Felaris's copy of the book up in one hand. "Goodbye."

She pressed it deliberately into Morgan's chest, which seemed to press back as flames exploded from under the book cover against Morgan's body. She pressed the Western Vee copy beside it with her other hand.

Stein, at Morgan's back, pressed his copy into her.

Stefan, head tilted far back to keep his hat out of the flames, pressed his copy into Morgan's left side.

Her cloak exploded into flame as the books charred their way through it. They sank quickly into her flesh, which flamed and ran like superheated paraffin.

BJ's sleeves caught fire, but she held on. Stefan, tears running out of both eyes from the smoke, never wavered. Stein, for all the discomfort he must have felt as flames flickered across his arms, might as well have been made of metal.

BJ couldn't tell how long it took. Eventually, they were standing over a mound of ashes; which were from the books and which from Morgan was impossible to say.

Stein's arms were hairless and reddened. The wool of Stefan's right leg was on fire: he patted it out absently. After a moment, BJ dropped to the dirt and rolled, arms extended. The flames on her sleeves went out. She stood and looked back down at the ashes, drained of emotion.

Stein shook himself. "Fields."

They ran. As they passed around the gooseneck, they saw the angry young man fleeing, sword strapped to his back, leaping over the rocks into the desert above. They ignored him.

On the road below, the few surviving Meat People bound each other's wounds. Stein, looking around him, wiped his eyes angrily. "They learned the games all right. They're just not fighters."

He knelt by Fields. They all knelt.

He looked up at them from the dirt. "Crossroads is safe?"

"Yes. Morgan is dead." Stein traced the huge cut in Fields's hairy belly; it was a grotesque parody of a smile, all red lips and sagging middle. He looked at his fingers, then questioningly at BJ; one look at her face was enough. "Crossroads is empty, but safe."

Stefan stroked his arm. Fields, who had closed his eyes, opened them. "Then you have no copies of *The Book of Strangeways*." He swallowed, gathering energy. "And you will not have me."

"Please don't worry about us," BJ said. She was crying. "We'll be fine."

Fields shook his head almost angrily. "But you will not be." He clutched at her hand, pulling her closer. He was amazingly strong. "There should have been—I needed to make, to choose—" He loosened his grip and stared at her sadly.

"You were going to choose someone, as you were chosen." BJ held his hand up for him, taking over where his muscles had failed. "Who was it?"

He gasped and struggled. "Once—Stefan. He did not want. So—school for him. So later—I choose B'Cu. He did not want. Always a shepherd."

"Why always a shepherd?"

"Someone who cares for animals." His eyes fluttered twice.

BJ said, "I care for animals."

—And so many events in her recent life fell into place as Fields said, "You know, then."

"I didn't." She was stunned with her own certainty. "But asking me to walk Strangeways as you opened and closed them, leaving me in charge of the dodos—"

"Asking you to stay as vet," he said. "Seeing if you would give your life. Watching you lose your health to care for the others. Watching you risk death, here today."

He found strength for a moment. "You know all that I ask?"

She shook her head. "Not completely, but it doesn't matter."

"And you will do?" He looked up at her pleadingly, and the plea had two parts: Take this if you can, but never if it is too much for you.

She took a deep, shaky breath. "I'm ready."

Fields held her hand tightly. She assumed that he would chant, or make signs with his fingers or draw symbols in the dirt. He only stared at her, intently.

BJ felt suddenly dizzy, as though her whole world had moved over a few feet to the right. She was disoriented, unable to feel her hands or feet, afraid even for her heart to beat.

Someone put a hand on her shoulder and spoke to her. She heard the voice twice, once by her ear and once farther away. The distance between the two seemed to be shrinking.

And then there was no distance at all. She looked a few feet away at Fields, who closed his eyes tiredly, and she knew where she was. She knew exactly where she was.

Stein said, "So what do we do now?" He was still acting as commander, but he was asking her.

She stood. "Bring his body."

"Bring it where?"

"Home with us, of course."

The others muttered. Stein said, "BJ, some of us are tired, most of us wounded. It's a long way back—"

He stopped. She was smiling, with tears in her eyes.

She pointed up a small canyon, with a narrow path off the road they had made. "We can go this way. I know a shortcut."

E·P·I·L·O·G·U·E

BJ WOKE AT Stein's, late in the morning. They had arrived with Fields's body at sunset, and at Stein's suggestion had taken turns sitting up with it, in vigil. At the end of her shift, BJ went outside. She stared up at a constellation, named to herself the planets of the closest stars, figured out the easiest walking routes to each of the planets, and went back to bed.

When she went outside, Stein was having a cup of black coffee, looking over the hills. "Polyta's leaving," he said.

"I know. She asked me for a road that would take her to Sugarly. I sketched one out, and I'll walk her to it after the funeral." She looked at Stein, troubled. "It feels so easy."

He sipped his coffee. "If you really know how to do it, I guess it shouldn't be hard."

"Roads between worlds? Not hard?"

He set down the cup. "Listen," he said patiently, "it's not like you signed up for it on a bulletin board in a bar. You loved animals, you sacrificed for others, you risked your life, and"— he tapped her forehead—"more important, you were willing to sacrifice long-term to help others. Not just a blaze of glory, but a life of serving. That's why he picked you."

BJ asked the question she'd been dreading. "Are you jealous that he didn't pick you? After all, he raised you."

Stein grinned. "Not at all, sweetheart. I serve others, too." He picked a gold coin from his pocket and spun it in the air. "But I charge."

He squinted out over the empty green slopes. "Looks like an

330

off-season this year. Well, I'll get some reading done." He was terribly happy.

Stefan stumbled out, scratching his woolly legs. "Am I late?"

"Naked," Stein said, "but not late. Still, it's time to move." He grabbed his cup and went indoors, turning a last time to look at the newly green landscape. "Beautiful."

They took Fields's body to the cave of the seer. BJ had wanted to bury him on a hill overlooking the Laetyen River, but Stein said he should lie near Brandal.

For an empty country, a large crowd accompanied the body to the cave mouth. The remaining Meat People limped behind, playing mournfuly on hastily carved Pan pipes. Polyta, using a rope sling to compensate for her height, carried a corner of the bier.

BJ had thought that carrying him down would be hard; for all his weight, Stein and BJ bore him easily. "I can't believe we can do this," she said on the first landing.

Stein grunted. "Love makes things light."

When they arrived by the pool, they set down the body. Stein wiped his sweating face and sat on a rock.

Harral bowed to BJ. "I understand you've made a career move."

"I'm told it's vocation, not career," BJ said. "I wish I knew that was right."

She looked down at Fields and blurted, "Was he happy?"

"At first he was lonely," Harral said. "Later, he was very happy."

BJ stood. "Thank you. I hope you'll be all right until I see you again."

Harral, unsurprised, said, "Don't you want to ask two more questions?"

"No," she said firmly. "Because even if I ask you, knowing the answer won't help me change the future, will it?"

"No. That's why prophecy is vague."

"And Fields, who grew up in an age of sibyls and oracles, he never consulted you, did he?"

"No. Sound reasoning on both points; you'd have made a fine Jesuit." He added, "By the way, those were your two other questions."

"So they were." She offered her hand to Stein and they went up the stone stairs, leaving Harral to contemplate the future in cynical amusement alone.

*   *   *

Back on the surface, she took her walking staff from Sahnrr, kissing the Meat Woman on the forehead. Sahnrr blushed and all but curtseyed. BJ slung her backpack on and hesitated. Fiona was sitting on a rock near the cave entrance. "You're staying?"

"Yes." Fiona spread her hands, exposing her scarred wrists. "I can't go back like this. How would I explain it?"

"You may not get another chance to go back."

"I have nothing to go back with," she said dully. "What I found, I wouldn't publish, and I wasn't interested in much else . . . Stein said I could stay. I'll rest, work in the inn, try to heal."

"Even in Crossroads, healing isn't always easy." BJ passed Fiona the keys to her truck. "You can use it until there's a full-size road back to Virginia. Don't let it run out of gas. Take anything you need from my cottage."

Stefan broke in, unbelieving, "Fiona, you have spent your whole life with books. How can you give that up?"

"Oh, I won't," she said quickly. "Stein's library will keep me, and as part of my pay he's going to direct a series of readings. It's like an independent study," she said, and her eyes gleamed with some of their former fire. "Do you think he can keep me busy?"

Stein said, stung, "Keep you busy? Young lady, you are completely unprepared for the next year—"

They left, talking. BJ adjusted her pack and walked with Stefan out of the valley and to the east.

Polyta accompanied them as far as the turnoff BJ made in the dirt with her staff. BJ walked the turnoff with Stefan only as far as necessary, but they heard Sugarly's glad cry and Polyta's joyful gallop as she saw him.

BJ and Stefan walked east in amiable silence, above the road but not on it, listening to the rapids on the river and enjoying the few bird songs left in Crossroads, mostly from the bluebacks.

At the valley through the cliffs they turned left, moving upstream. The road ended after twenty feet. BJ drew in the dirt with the staff, following the point. It took only a little concentration to ignore the shifts in the landscape.

She paused once and drew a fork in the dirt. Carefully, one foot in front of the other, she drew a second line and traced it downhill and, suddenly, uphill. At the end of the line, sunlight, filtered through dust motes, shone on strange trees all but covered in vertically oriented bracket fungi.

The turtle man, waiting at the opening to the road, stepped in front of her and knelt, head bowed. She smiled, reaching up to pat his head. "It's all you were waiting for, wasn't it? Go back to your home."

He stood and stepped back, obediently waiting for her next passage in front of the road. Stefan, looking dubiously over his shoulder at the turtle man, followed BJ on up the ravine.

The stone-slab bridge across the stream was still in place. BJ drew her road across it, and they moved uphill into Virginia.

After all they had seen and done together, they said their farewells in Kroger's parking lot, across from the campus. BJ looked around it. "Do you realize how much of our lives together were spent in this parking lot?"

"To me, the parking lot was romantic. Before that, most of my life was spent herding sheep."

She laughed. "I do love you."

"And I love you." He looked at her sadly with his large, dark eyes, "When we met, I began to love you. I thought I was too ignorant and illiterate for you, not smart enough. BJ, my love, I was too young. Maybe I still am, but I know that I want you more than anything."

BJ ached, knowing that what followed was inevitable.

He turned involuntarily toward the university. "But I want to be whole, the way you wanted it. You were sick, but I am ignorant. You found a place that cured you. I have found a place that will cure me."

He put his slender, strong arms around her. "And I want to marry you. I know I will always want that. I ask you now."

BJ heard herself say, "We'll have trouble agreeing on a ceremony."

"In this world it is the bride's choice, and her family's." He added apprehensively, "Does this mean I will need your brother Peter's approval?"

BJ said grimly, "He has no room for disapproval." They laughed together, and looked at each other awkwardly during the silence that followed.

The bells on campus, prerecorded and played on speakers, chimed five. Stefan sighed. "You must go. I will stay here for now, but I will finish my studies and come back to Crossroads." He looked at her with love, but with an edge. "You will not be the only vet there."

"Maybe not even the best." But she looked back at him, and for once, her smile looked wicked. "But I'll fight to be."

He laughed and held her, and they kissed as long as they could.

*   *   *

At Kroger's, BJ looked for light preserved foods. She turned and nearly laughed because it was so fitting. "Hi, Stacey."

"Hey, BJ. God, we've gotta quit meeting in grocery stores. How much do you eat, anyway?" She glanced in the basket. "Whoa. Health food I understand." She poked at the trail mix and the shrink-wrapped meals. "What is this shit for?"

"I'm going to be doing some hiking."

"No wonder you stay in shape. How's the vet work going?"

"It slowed down a little." She thought of the road she had made to get here. "I'm branching out."

Stacey nodded sadly. "Some careers just don't pan out, BJ. It's okay. What are you trying from here, pharmaceutical work?"

BJ considered, glancing at her backpack. "Still vet work, but more of an ambulatory practice." She smiled, thinking of Stefan. "Possibly some animal husbandry."

Stacey, confused, changed the subject. "How's your long-distance romance?"

"The distances are getting longer," she said, "But the romance is getting better."

Stacey laughed. "Mine, too." She held up her finger with the tiny diamond chip in the ring. "I've been scared I'd wear this out taking it on and off. So, are you staying in the boonies another year?"

BJ pointed to her backpack and staff, stowed by one of the cash registers. "You might say I'm getting even boonier."

"Good for you. Take some time off, hike the Appalachian Trail." The old Stacey reasserted herself as she finished, "You never did have much endurance for hard work."

"Oh, you'd be astonished." BJ pushed her cart toward the express lane. "I need to get going."

"Enjoy the hiking, mountain woman." Stacey added wistfully, "A real adventure . . . I wish I could go with you."

"Maybe you can do some hiking on your own." BJ, struggling to measure up to her new goddess-hood, failed in the face of temptation. "I really think you should, Stacey. It would be good for your thighs."

BJ emerged from Kroger's with the glow of someone who has satisfied a selfish dream. As she walked toward the blacktop, a calm voice drawled, "Keep your eyes open. You never know what you're missing in the world around you."

BJ turned. "You can't have been waiting for me."

"Nope." Sugar was grinning; he had always liked startling

students. "But Laurie and I both know a good guesser, and he said if you showed up anywhere you'd show up here, probably late in the day if you'd walked. One or the other of us has been here every night for a while. You want a ride anywhere?"

Laurie, standing beside Sugar, said flatly, "You're coming to my place."

BJ said, "I'd love to."

She sat back and enjoyed the feeling as Sugar drove them up a gravel road into the Blue Ridge Mountains; the ride felt remarkably like her first trip into Crossroads as Sugar's student, barely a year ago. She recognized the road; it led past a small Baptist church in the hills, where Melina went every Sunday.

The farmhouse was barely post-Civil War. It had a wide porch and, more needed just now, a wide front door, elaborately carved. Laurie walked in eagerly. "Company!"

"Formal or informal?" a dry voice answered. "Informal would be better; I could eat them here."

BJ stepped into the living room, which was decorated entirely with nineteenth-century antiques. Predictably, the inner walls had floor-to-ceiling bookcases. On one shelf was a stereo system and, below it, hundreds of compact discs.

The Griffin was on an old-fashioned horsehair sofa, rear legs dangling over one end of it and forelegs over the other. He was tapping at a computer keyboard, peering, intrigued, at the screen.

"I saw more of him in Crossroads," Laurie said. "And our phone bill, Jesus, you don't want to know."

But she wasn't smoking.

BJ looked at the computer with distrust. "Are you hooked up to something?"

"I'm conversing with a gentleman named Chandri, who works at a place called the Jet Propulsion Laboratory. He has been admitting his pessimism concerning cold fusion. Will wonders never cease?"

"Not until I cut the wires," Laurie said. Sugar chuckled.

BJ lifted the lace curtains at the side window and looked uphill. "Have you seen Melina?"

"Every Saturday night," the Griffin said with satisfaction. "As my health gets better, I do more of the cooking. I must say, she never expected that I would pay her back for waiting on me."

"Bet she tips," Sugar said.

"Is she all right?" BJ asked. "Is she lonely?"

"I don't think so," Laurie said slowly. "That Baptist church she goes to has helped her settle in; I know she has Sunday dinners with different families every week. She spends her days up in the hills. She's come down to see Stefan some, but it's hard to get him away from the books to come here. You know."

"It's not a fault," the Griffin rumbled.

"Is too."

BJ said, "She can use the road I walked in on if she wants to visit. Tell her not to take the unicorns back yet; it won't be stable there for a long time." She tore a piece of paper off the Griffin's printer and sketched rapidly. "This is what the new road looks like."

"Do you want to go say goodbye to her?" The Griffin asked.

BJ shook her head. "Why make her restless, if she's happy? We've all had too many goodbyes lately."

Shortly, Laurie and the Griffin were in a spirited argument about capital punishment, Amnesty International, and the need for civil order. BJ and Sugar tiptoed out onto the porch.

Sugar leaned on the railing. "The Griffin bets you're taking Fields's place."

"Good guess. In a way."

Sugar shook his head. "Too bad. Being a goddess is okay, but you'd have made one hell of a vet."

"I still will. Want to see my office?" She opened her backpack. "I'll guess at temperature by feeling animals' ears. I can listen for heartbeats. For infections, I've got a bottle of five-hundred milligram scored capsules of Ampi. And I still have these." She showed her pocketsize black books from vet school and practice, and she held up the treasured copy of Lao's *Guide to the Unbiological Species*—more valuable now because it was a gift from Fields.

He nodded. "Good choices. Don't lose your surgerizing skills."

"Never." She had already been practicing one-handed knots on the string of the backpack.

Sugar said carefully, "Protera was betting that if you took Fields's place, it might do your health some good."

She nodded. "I think it has." Actually, she knew it had. She shook her head, smiling at a stray thought. "Tell him I think of it as a Fields effect."

Sugar nodded, nonplused. "How's everything else?"

"Fine." She was running out of things to say; they had been colleagues, not friends. "How's Elaine?"

"She's fine. Lost eight pounds already. Shane's doing fine, too."

She laughed. "Sugar-Elaine. Shane. Perfect."

He grinned at her. "Born to be a cowboy."

BJ remembered. "My God, I'm sorry. I haven't gotten a baby gift yet."

"You've been busy."

"That's for sure." She stepped off the porch. "While I'm traveling, I'll try to pick up something really unusual."

She walked down the road, pleased to have an exit line that, for once, left Sugar guessing.

BJ walked down the road a quarter of a mile, stopping when she came to a worn path in the woods. It was probably made by cows, coming down to the ditch to check for running water. She nodded, satisfied; she had known it would be there, and it was a good place to start a road-to-road path.

She laid her staff down, frowning at the blisters on her hands. She would have to toughen up. She opened her backpack and lifted out two identical notebooks.

One was her additions to Lao's *Guide*. She put it back carefully. The other was her journal, which she had kept for a few months but had not written in since the early fall.

On the first page was a map of the path she had made for Polyta. On the second page was the trail/road from Crossroads to Virginia. On the third page was the road she was on now, with a tiny stub of a path extending out from the road but going nowhere, as yet. All of the other pages were blank.

She looked uphill, at the clearing in the forest. She saw a slim dark-haired figure, walking with what looked like horses. She thought, faint and far away, she heard someone singing.

Then she shouldered her pack and walked away, making her road as she went.

ACKNOWLEDGMENTS

I would like to thank Drs. Jenny Clark, Jill O'Brien, and Lynn Anne Evans for their skill in treating even imaginary animals. I would like to thank Laura Grant, Chris Doyle, and Lee Ann Lloyd, all of the Barrington Veterinary Clinic, for their patience in taking eccentric phone calls.

June Roberts loaned me one Greek cookbook, and I found another on my own: *The Food of Greece*, by Vilma Liacouras Chantiles. (In both cookbooks, I strongly recommend the lentil soup.) Thanks to Ron Martini of the Roger Williams Park Zoo in Providence, Rhode Island—both for his time and because he has helped raise a wolf cub in a world that needs more of them. The knowledge is theirs; the mistakes are mine.

A large thanks to Don Maass for helping engender the book and Ginjer Buchanan for delivering it alive and well. Thanks also to Bob Salvatore for hospitality and encouragement.

Also, thanks and respect to Mr. Joseph Moretta, the only shepherd I have known personally.

Crossroads is fictional. There are, however, real places to go for information on Huntington's chorea, most notably the Huntington's Disease Society of America, Inc., 140 West 22nd Street, 6th floor, New York, NY 10011-2420. The Huntington's Disease Society of America was not consulted in the research for this book and is in no way responsible for its contents. I am.

This book is dedicated to many related and much-loved children: Jenny and Emily O'Donohoe, Lisa and Valerie Damon, Eric and Katie Evans, Kimberly, Michaela, and Robert DelGallo, and Jessica and Christopher Lussier.

This novel is also in memory of Moth (August 31, 1982–September 21, 1993), the original Daphni, a cure for insomnia, and the most peace-full cat I've every known. That's for remembrance, Mothie.